The Wade Justus Book Series

Absolute Justus

Justus for All

Border Justus

All of the characters in this book are fictional. Several of the locations described in this book are accurate, while others are fictional. The investigative techniques, border surveillance technology, military aircraft, armaments, weaponry and combative techniques are accurate to the best of the author's knowledge and experience and are in use today.

The news stories depicted in this book, including information and stories about transnational cartels, drugs and drug smuggling, border incursions, and international criminal cartel activities are accurate and taken from actual news accounts including statistics at the time this book was written. The Tres Paises drug cartel is a fictional representation of common transnational drug and human smuggling cartels currently operating in Mexico and the United States.

While this is a work of fiction, many of the circumstances depicted and described in this book could happen today.

"We are in a state of war with known and unseen enemies who are systematically destroying America and killing our people. You cannot win a war unless you know and admit you're in one."

Ron Martinelli

Texas Ranger motto, *"One riot, one Ranger."*

Anonymous Texas Ranger circa 1800's.

Table of Contents

ACKNOWLEDGEMENTS

I AM BLESSED to associate with a team of wonderfully talented people who assist me in bringing the character of Wade Justus to life each time he is involved in a new adventure. I now wish to acknowledge them for their exceptional efforts on my behalf.

First, I'd like to thank my wife and life partner Linda who accompanied me on border site visits for background research. She devoted countless hours editing the manuscript making sure that Wade's actions and the book's characters flowed and had continuity.

Long-time colleague, homicide supervisor and retired Northern California HIDTA Intelligence Center Director, Lt. Bob Prevot (Ret.) has been on Wade's adventures from the beginning. Bob provided background on how the DEA and U.S. Marshal's Office function.

Russell "Russ" Jones, a decorated Vietnam Army Air Calvary helicopter pilot, veteran and retired undercover narcotics agent provided the technical aspects of flying the helicopters depicted in this book. Russ's descriptions literally put you into the cockpit.

Travis Woodbury, a retired military and law enforcement sniper expert and instructor gets credit for providing all of the technical aspects of sniper craft and weaponry. I have met no better sniper in my time than he.

Drone pilot Angelos Leiloglou was instrumental in relating the technical aspects of drone piloting which brought life to one of my support characters for all to enjoy.

I am immensely grateful to all of you for your generous assistance in making Border Justus a reality. *Now, on with the story!*

Cover photo courtesy of Dennis Dolezal.

CHAPTER 1

In the Weeds

IT WAS 03:00 am and even at this hour in mid-May it was eighty-five degrees. Gila County Sheriff's Department deputies Jessie Fremont and his partner Jacob "Tonto" Black Arrows were lying prone on the warm sand, deep in the tulles on the U.S. side of the Rio Brisas, a narrow tributary of the Rio Grande River. The deputies had covered themselves with a light-weight nylon desert camouflage tarp normally used for deer hunting. Only they weren't hunting bucks tonight. On this early morning their intended prey were transnational cartel drug smugglers.

Jessie and Jacob, who every deputy on the Gila County SD referred to by his nickname "Tonto," were wearing military issue high-tech night vision goggles, referred to as "NVG's" and camouflage battle dress uniforms (BDU's). On top of their BDU's they wore assault vests with heavy Threat Level III ceramic chest plates designed to stop all pistol, .223, AK-47, or .308 caliber rounds. The deputies were heavily armed with .223 caliber M-4 assault rifles mounted with green laser sights, and EoTec occluded-eye gunsights (OEG's) with side mounted Sure Fire tactical lights. Each of their assault vests carried six thirty-round magazines of .223 Caliber, 5.56 mm ammo for their rifles. For their Glock 23 semiautomatic pistols, they carried four additional .40 caliber eighteen-round magazines.

In addition to their side arms and rifles, Jacob who was a true Apache Indian, had brought his department approved, custom made, black, light-weight aluminum recurve bow. The bow was complimented with a quiver with a dozen black composite arrows with razor sharp broad tips strapped to the rear of his assault vest.

Jacob was probably the only law enforcement officer in the country who was authorized to carry a recurve bow and arrows as a lethal force weapon. This approval had been no easy task.

When Jacob first went to Sheriff Fremont with his request to carry a bow and arrows as an "alternate force weapon," the sheriff nearly laughed him out of the office. Jacob offered to demonstrate his skill with bow and arrow against other deputies using their firearms. He also explained to the sheriff that in some cases, the use of a bow and arrow as a silent, medium range force projection weapon had its advantages. In raids, or circumstances where the application of a silent weapon could prove to be tactically advantageous to deputies, a bow and arrow was an added and unexpected tool.

Sheriff Fremont was both curious and intrigued. He gave Jacob the opportunity to demonstrate what he was talking about, but there was a hitch. Jacob Black Arrows would have to first qualify on the range against deputies armed with pistols under the same distances and time constraints. Jacob smiled and enthusiastically accepted the challenge.

The day of the bow and arrows versus pistols competition was set for a Saturday morning. Every street deputy, half the corrections staff and their wives and kids showed up to watch.

Jacob had told the Sheriff he had no intention of using a bow and arrows at the initial distances of three and five yards. It was agreed that he would compete against deputies firing at the seven, ten, fifteen and twenty-five-yard lines. As a bonus, Jacob offered to compete against the deputies at the fifty-yard line as well. Sheriff Fremont told Jacob to, *"Go for it."*

The deputies were to qualify using their standard eighteen-round course of fire from the seven out to the twenty-five-yard lines. Three rounds would be fired in five seconds "on the move" from the various distances going back to the twenty-five-yard line. In a separate evolution, deputies would have ten seconds to fire three rounds at the fifty-yard line from a standing position. All rounds had to be within an eight-inch paper plate which had been stapled to the center of each "coke bottle" style target. The passing score was eighty percent.

Everyone was waiting to see how Jacob could possibly

pull off grabbing, drawing and shooting three arrows in only five seconds at each target. The crowd's curiosity was soon addressed. Mounted on Jacob's bow was a rack which held six arrows.

At the seven-yard line at the sound of the electronic beep, Jacob drew and fired one arrow. He immediately followed up by drawing two arrows at the same time and firing them together at the target. All of the arrows struck their mark within the allotted five seconds. The assembled crowd gasped in amazement.

As it turned out, as the distanced grew greater, Jacob maintained the drawing, aiming and firing of his three arrows. His competitors now had to pay much greater attention to the front sights of the pistols to hit their marks. By the time the deputies had completed their shots at the twenty-five-yard line Jacob, with his recurve bow and arrows, was even with them.

At the fifty-yard line, Jacob was definitely in his wheelhouse. He regularly practiced with his bow at distances of fifty to one hundred yards. Ten seconds was all he needed to methodically draw, aim and accurately fire one arrow at a time. All three arrows hit their mark. This time, Jacob scored better than all of his competitors and the crowd cheered.

Following the competition, Sheriff Fremont certified Jacob's score and approved his use of the bow and arrows on duty for special circumstances only. This stake-out was one of those occasions.

This morning, Jessie and Jacob were wearing what Jacob referred to as "war paint." Rubbed onto and across their faces was a combination of black and olive green camouflage grease paint in finger-wide stripes. The purpose of the face paint was to break up a pattern, as well as cutting any glare from the three-quarter moon above them at their 10 O'clock in the New Mexico sky.

The deputies were in their third hour of an all-night stake-out, hopefully waiting to intercept a band of fentanyl, meth and cocaine smugglers from the notorious and violent Tres Paises drug cartel. Tres Paises was a rising new drug cartel formed by former MS-13 members. The cartel's name "Tres Paises," was derived from the founding members countries of origin: Columbia, Honduras, and El Salvador.

Tres Paises was a cross-border drug syndicate whose base of operations was in the Mexican town of La Novia in the country's northern border state of Chihuahua. The cartel operated between the State of Chihuahua and Southwest New Mexico, extending east to El Paso, Texas and northwest to Denver, Colorado.

The syndicate controlled the flow of illegal drugs. It was also heavily involved in the human trafficking of illegal aliens that included women and children to serve the sex industry in Albuquerque, Las Cruces, El Paso, and Denver.

To avoid armed conflicts with the major Mexican transnational drug cartels, Tres Paises leaders had forged a tenuous agreement with the Sinaloa and Juarez cartels. This arrangement allowed them to ply drugs, as well as trafficking laborers, and women and children for the sex trade. In exchange, the members agreed to bear the brunt of the risk of imprisonment for trafficking the cartels' drug shipments. Tres Paises also provided the Sinaloa and Juarez cartels with hefty "commissions" on the profits from their various enterprises. So far, the agreement had been profitable for both sides.

Jessie and Jacob had been tipped off by a street-level dealer they caught selling meth near the Gila Independent School District High School the week before. The inexperienced dealer didn't want to spend the next ten years in prison as a sentencing enhancement for selling drugs within one thousand feet of a school in New Mexico.

In return for giving up the information that "packages" were coming across the river that evening, the deputies had worked out a plea deal with the county's District Attorney to amend the dealer's criminal charges. The dealer's charges of possession and distribution for sales would be reduced to mere possession with his promise to move out of Gila County. It was certainly worth the deal to get some "weight" and a couple of trafficker bodies whom they could interrogate and move up the drug trafficker chain.

Not knowing if anyone could be trusted in the District Attorney's Office as yet, the only person they had told and had obtained permission from to conduct the stakeout was Jessie's dad, Sheriff Matt Fremont. It was nice to have friends in high places.

The Gila County Sheriff's Department had only twelve

deputies to serve the rural Mexican border county and six of those were corrections deputies. That left only the Sheriff and five of his deputies to patrol an area of roughly 500 square miles with its entire southern side bordering the Rio Brisas River and Mexico.

Gila County was south of Luna and Dona Ana Counties and below or to the south of Las Cruces. It was only about sixty-five miles southwest from the busy Texas city of El Paso. El Paso was directly across "The Wall" from the violent Mexican city of Juarez.

Juarez, Mexico, located in the State of Chihuahua, was one of the most notorious and violent cities in all of Mexico. The confluence of the Sinaloa and Juarez cartels which were in reality transnational drug trafficking organizations had created this cauldron of violence. The State of Chihuahua bordered both New Mexico and Texas.

Seven major Mexican transnational drug cartels generated somewhere between twenty to thirty billion dollars in profits each year through the sale of illegal drugs and human trafficking operations. That was quite an incentive for aggressively moving forward in expanding their operations internationally.

The major drug cartels based in Mexico were the Beltran-Leyva, Gulf, Jalisco-New Generation, Los Zetas, Sinaloa, Tijuana/Arellano Felix and Juarez cartels. Perhaps the most powerful of the Mexican cartels was the Sinaloa cartel. This organization was also known by the names of the Guzman-Loera Organization, the Pacific Cartel, the Federation, and the Blood Alliance.

The Pacific Cartel was formerly run by drug lord Joaquin Guzman, who presently resided at the ADX Supermax federal prison in Florence, Colorado. Joaquin was housed there, awaiting trial on multiple homicides and drug trafficking charges.

It was believed that Ismael "El Mayo" Zambada García was running the Sinaloa syndicate that was based in the Mexican State of Sinaloa. The Sinaloa cartel made billions in trafficking illegal drugs to the U.S., Europe and Asia. It was also involved in human trafficking operations.

The Jalisco-New Generation cartel operated mainly in western Mexico and controlled the Tierra Caliente region.

However, this extremely violent organization was in competition with the Sinaloa cartel and was rapidly expanding its operational influence across Mexico. The organization which was run by a former Mexican police officer known as "El Mencho," was one of the world's most dominant transnational drug cartels, specializing in the distribution of synthetic drugs and methamphetamine.

The New Generation had been described as the most aggressive of all of the cartels in Mexico. It was responsible for the waves of violence presently terrorizing Tijuana, Juarez, Guanajuato and Mexico City. The waves of violence were the direct result of The New Generation warring with other cartels to expand its territories.

The Los Zetas cartel was founded by former members of Mexico's military Special Forces. This organization initially built its empire throughout the Gulf of Mexico, in the southern states of Tabasco, Yucatán, Quintana Roo, and Chiapas. Its territories also included the Pacific Coast states of Guerrero, Oaxaca, and Michoacán, as well as in Mexico City. The cartel had now expanded into human trafficking operations as well.

The Gulf Cartel operated in northeast Mexico around the State of Tamaulipas. This group trafficked in heroin, cocaine, and methamphetamine. However, the organization was also known for engaging in widespread political corruption, including bribing public officials.

Of all the drugs produced, traded and distributed by the Mexican cartels, the newest and by far the most dangerous drug was the highly addictive and deadly fentanyl. The opioid was one hundred times more powerful than morphine. Only a few micro grains of the drug could easily kill a human being. A pound of the deadly drug in its powered form could kill tens of thousands.

Not to put all of their eggs in one basket, the cartels also made billions of dollars in trafficking humans, including women and children used in the sex trafficking industry. The current United States Presidents' "Open Borders" policies now made the trafficking of human beings far less risky and nearly as profitable as smuggling narcotics. It was a win-win scenario for the cartels.

The combined cartels in Mexico were directly or indirectly responsible for murdering over 100,000 people in Mexico annually.

Their drug distribution network in the U.S. fed the voracious illicit drug appetite of Americans in one shape, manner or form. Drug overdoses and drug gang wars were responsible for an additional 120,000 overdose and drug gang war deaths annually on the U.S. side of the border.

Historically, on the Mexican side of the border, the Mexican government and its previous Presidential administrations were rife with corruption caused by a combination of cartel pay-offs at the highest levels of federal, state, local governments and their police. As a result, little to nothing had ever been done to fight against the cartel octopus which seemed to have their tentacles upon every aspect of Mexican and Central American life.

The newly elected President of Mexico was a populist who had come to power following an overwhelming vote of the people. His intention was to free them from the prior ineffective and corrupt governments which had unfortunately proven to be naïve as to the national security threat posed by the cartels to Mexico, the U.S. and Central America.

However, the Mexican President's current strategy of *"Abrazos, no balas,"* or *"Hugs, not bullets,"* had so far proven to be embarrassingly ineffective. Since the inception of the President's non-confrontational policy, the number of murders in the Second World nation had risen to 33,300 more than the previous year with over 40,000 people referred to as "los *desaparecidos*" or "the disappeared ones." The flow of drugs, immigrants, and sex trafficking victims from around the world through Mexico and into the U.S. continued.

Two years before, a large family that included a number of defenseless women and small children with dual American and Mexican citizenships had been slaughtered near the Texas border. A drug cartel was believed to be responsible.

The previous American President had had enough of this indiscriminate violence and had signed an executive order declaring the Mexican cartels as "terrorist organizations." The new "terrorists" designation had been a game changer because it suddenly brought to bear the entire might of U.S. military, financial, State Department and intelligence assets and resources to actively combat cartel trafficking and violence.

The United States' Center for Disease Control had estimated that there were 110,000 deaths the previous year in the U.S. from illicit drugs and prescription opioids. Of those, eighty percent of the overdose deaths were directly attributed to illicit synthetic fentanyl. Now, there was a new and even more deadly drug on the streets. This powerful synthetic opioid was referred to as "ISO", or isotonitazene. ISO was being smuggled into the U.S. by transnational drug cartels, mostly from Mexico. As a result of this huge influx of deadly synthetic opiates, the U.S. had experienced a two-fold increase in National Drug Overdose Deaths during the past ten years. Fentanyl and ISO overdoses were now the primary cause of death of Americans under the age of forty-five years.

To place these staggering statistics into perspective, in each and every year since 2009, the United States had lost the equivalent of two thirds of all military personnel killed in action during the fifteen year Vietnam War and nearly *nine* times the number all of our soldiers killed in the War on Terror since 2001.

As with all criminal organizations worldwide, the cartels in Mexico had divided up the country into territories where they operated. As a result, there were frequent violent conflicts between the various cartels including skirmishes between the small factions within the organizations themselves. Such conflicts resulted in incredible losses of life.

Jessie and Jacob's intel from their informant was that the gang trafficking across their southern border tonight were members of the newly formed and violent Tres Paises cartel. This made their assignment very high risk.

Jessie's and Jacob's informant believed that the "packages" might very well be cocaine, meth and perhaps a new shipment of fentanyl which had been promised for over a month. The last shipment of fentanyl had unfortunately been intercepted by ICE and DEA outside of Lordsburg the previous month. Drug addicts from Lordsburg to Las Cruces had been badly hurting for their drugs ever since.

It was now approaching 0330 hours and so far, no sign of anything nor anyone. The only sounds coming from the Rio Brisas were that of frogs and an occasional call of nocturnal birds that populated and roosted in the cypress trees near the riverbank. The deputies had concealed their Sheriff's Department Ford F-150 4X4 pick-up truck on the other side of the riverbank where it could not be seen by anyone crossing the Rio Brisas.

The deputies were engaged in a waiting game; not unlike fishing or sitting in a deer stand. Jessie and Jacob were born and bred country boys, so the waiting part was easy for them. Sometimes you catch something and sometimes you don't. It was what it was. Hours of waiting, occasionally followed by minutes of heart thumping, adrenalin rushing, intense excitement of capturing your prey. The one thing it wasn't was "Miami Vice" or "Bad Boys III." That was for sure.

As Jessie and Jacob were hunkered down in the tulles, they heard the call of a bobwhite quail coming from the opposing and Mexican side of the river and their ears perked up. *"Sounded like a bobwhite to me. That's weird,"* said Jessie to Jacob. Then another bird call sounded in the distance also across the river from their position.

"Yes, Kemosabe, Tonto knows that we haven't seen bobwhite quail around here for years. Me think bad men coming so time to lock and load," replied Jacob, playing their Lone Ranger game while smiling at Jessie.

Jessie keyed his throat mic and whispered onto the Sheriff Department's closed, tactical radio channel, *"One-Sam-10, we have possible smuggler contacts at our 20. Stand-by for confirmation. Restricted traffic. Will advise."*

Over Jessie and Jacob's earbud, they heard Sheriff's dispatch reply, *"One-Sam-10, copy. Standing by for confirmation, restricted traffic."*

Within a minute, Jessie and Jacob saw four men dressed in black clothing crest over the opposing side of the riverbank. The men were carrying a black rubber four-man raft filled with what appeared to be water-tight black bags. The two leading men in the front of the raft had AK-47's strapped to the front of them with forty-round extended "banana clip" magazines in canvas magazine carriers.

Jessie touched Jacob, keyed his mic and whispered on the tactical channel, *"One-Sam-10; confirmed contact with four armed subjects with large bags about to forge the river. Advise back-up to move in immediately to assist, ASAP."*

The Sheriff's dispatcher immediately responded, *"Expediting units to your 20. The Sheriff advises do not engage unless forced to. Be careful."*

Jessie only had time to whisper back, *"Copy. We'll try. No guarantees."* He then looked at Jacob and said, *"Well, this outta be interesting."*

Jessie and Jacob simultaneously switched the selector switches on the M-4's from "safe" to "fire." The deputies remained concealed in the thick tulles as the four heavily armed drug smugglers arrived at the riverbank and entered the slowly moving Rio Brisas. The river's depth was just short of chest-high, so the smugglers pushed their raft out into the river. They then removed the AK-47 assault rifles that were strapped to their chests and placed them into the raft. The four smugglers then waded into the river, holding onto the sides of the craft, as they directed it towards the U.S. bank.

Jessie and Jacob looked at each other and nodded. This was it. When the foursome reached the U.S. side of the river, both deputies stood up from the concealed positions in the tulles. Jessie and Jacob pointed their M-4 rifles at the drug smugglers and switched on their gun-mounted lights illuminating and blinding the smugglers. The deputies then painted the chests of the smugglers with their green laser designators and yelled out loudly, *"Sheriff's Department! You are all under arrest!"* followed in Spanish by, *"Departmentento del Sheriff; todos estan bajo arresto!"*

As anticipated, Jessie and Jacob had taken all four men totally by surprise. In response, the two smugglers near the bow of the raft immediately began reaching towards their weapons which were inside the raft.

Jessie yelled out, *"Stop! Don't move. Show us your hands!"* followed again in Spanish by, *"Détente! No te muevas! Muestranos sus manos!"*

Jessie's force warning was ignored. Both of the intruders responded by reaching into the raft and withdrawing their AK's. Once the men had retrieved their weapons, both began to swing the barrels of their AK's towards the sound of Jessie's voice and their gun lights.

"*Don't do it! Drop your weapons or we'll fire!*" yelled both deputies in unison.

There was no time for any bilingual translation of the deadly force warning. Jessie yelled to Jacob, "*Contact right!*" to which Jacob responded, "*Contact left!*" Both deputies opened fire with two controlled three-round bursts. The rounds crashed into the upper chests of both smugglers, dropping them immediately and causing them to sink under the water.

The distraction of the engagement between the deputies and the two forward smugglers allowed their two colleagues at the bow of the raft to grab their guns and open fire on Jessie and Jacob. One of the AK-47 rounds struck Jacob's M-4 which immediately disabled the weapon.

Jacob immediately transitioned to his Glock 23 and returned fire with a four-round burst. Jessie quickly engaged the man's partner armed with a pistol at the right rear of the raft. Jessie missed his mark, but his rounds penetrated the inflated rubber right side at rear of the raft. The bullet impacts resulted in multiple loud "pops," followed by air hissing out of the rubber fabric. This caused the raft to begin sinking from the stern under the weight of the heavy bags of dope. The two remaining smugglers were quickly losing concealment as the deflating raft began to partially sink into the river.

"Covering fire!" Jessie yelled out to his partner as he fired again. This allowed Jacob to quickly pick up his recurve bow. The Apache deputy drew an arrow from his quiver, pulled back and released a broad-tipped arrow, which flew towards its intended target. In less than a second, the arrow impacted square into one of the smuggler's chests from forty yards away. The man gasped and went down into the water head-first. The broad-tipped arrow's head and five inches of its black carbon fiber shaft emerged through the smuggler's back.

Seeing that all three of his friends were now dead, the remaining smuggler dropped his pistol into the river and yelled out in Spanish, "*No dispares, me rindo!*" or "*Don't shoot, I give up!*" The battle was over with a score favoring the deputies three-zip.

Suddenly in the distance the sound of multiple sirens rapidly approaching their position could be heard. Jessie ordered the remaining drug smuggler to pull the deflating raft to the U.S. side of the riverbank. He then proned the smuggler out on the sand at the water's edge. Jacob laid down his bow and provided cover to Jessie with his Glock pistol. Jessie slung his M-4 rifle behind his back, bent down and quickly handcuffed the smuggler. He finished up by conducting a quick cursory search of the man for additional weapons.

The handcuffed survivor was left prone in the sand. Jacob removed his assault vest, entered the water and pulled the damaged raft up to the shoreline. He then reentered the water, pulling each of the three deceased smugglers to the bank, one at a time.

Back-up deputies appeared over the crest with guns drawn. Jessie held up four fingers, yelling out, *"Code-4. We're good. Three down and one in custody. Advise dispatch."*

The two back-up deputies scanned both banks for additional threats and then looked down at the three dead smugglers. Deputy Marcus Carter saw the smuggler with the black shaft and broad-tipped arrow protruding out of the man's back and exclaimed, *"Holy shit! Don't ever fuck with an Apache. Just ask Custer."*

"Actually, the Sioux got Custer. They were Sioux; not Apache's," Jacob corrected the deputy.

"Whatever. I just want to read your use of force report. That's one for the records book," responded Marcus.

"Oh, and by the way Marcus, Jacob and I are just fine. Thanks for asking," said Jessie.

"Sorry, fellas. I was just a bit distracted by the whole fucking arrow through the suspect's back thing," replied Marcus snidely with a smile.

Jessie addressed Marcus, "OK, we got this for now. Go back to your unit. Grab some crime scene tape, your digital camera and your evidence kit. We need to secure the scene. In the meantime, I'll call the Sheriff, Border Patrol and DEA to report the incursion onto U.S. soil, our use of force and the suspected dope.

"By the way, there are going to be three AK's and one pistol in the

river just about over there. We're going to need BP's Dive Team to recover those weapons and any cartridges on the bottom. The river is hardly flowing, so it shouldn't be too difficult. The water runs pretty clean here.

"This incident also happened in our jurisdiction, so we've got the investigation. Since Jacob and I are the involved deputies, our involvement stops right now and we'll make our statements to the Sheriff when he arrives."

"Sure thing Jessie. You got it," replied Marcus who turned around and jogged back to his unit for the crime scene gear.

Jessie reached into one of the pockets of his assault vest and pulled out his cell phone. He then speed dialed his dad. Sheriff Matt Fremont picked up on the first ring.

"I'm heading your way, Jessie. Dispatch called me. My ETA is about ten. Copy you and Jacob are OK?" asked Jessie's dad.

"Affirm, Sheriff. Three bad guys down and we have one in custody. Got what we think is a pretty big load of dope, but it's still bagged. We haven't touched it. I was going to call Border Patrol and DEA next," said Jessie.

"I'll call State Police, BP and DEA. The call should come from me. I want State Police to handle the officer-involved shooting (OIS) investigation. So, get your thoughts together. You and Jacob can't be together or talk to each other from here on until after you're interviewed. Got that?" directed Matt.

"Copy. Sheriff. I'll just inform Jacob of your instructions. By the way, there are going to be three AK's, a pistol and some cartridges on the bottom of the river. Ask BP if their Dive Team can respond. I don't want anyone to think we shot these bandidos for no reason. See you when you get here," replied Jessie before hanging up.

By the time the sun broke over the eastern horizon, the crime scene was filled with law enforcement. First Responders, New Mexico State Police, Customs and Border Patrol, ICE, DEA and the County Medical Examiner were all in attendance.

The scene was being processed by the remaining Gila County Sheriff's Office deputies under the supervision of State Police OIS team Detective Sergeant Jimmy Velasquez. Everything was photographed in place. To keep things on the up and up,

Sheriff Fremont asked the DEA agents present to inventory and take possession of the narcotics found in the waterproof bags.

It turned out that there was ninety pounds of fentanyl, sixty pounds of cocaine, and thirty pounds of crystal methamphetamine. The fact that they had recovered enough fentanyl to easily kill four million people would definitely make the national news.

Matt Fremont surveyed the scene, including the bodies of the now deceased smugglers. He and Sergeant Velasquez saw the smuggler with a black arrow protruding completely through his body and looked over at Jacob Black Arrows.

"Jesus, Jacob. What the hell?!" exclaimed the Sheriff.

Sergeant Velasquez looked at the body and then Matt incredulously. "That's a fucking arrow, right?" the detective said to Matt.

"Yup. I'll give you the Readers Digest version when we get to the office," Matt replied.

Jacob was about to explain, but the sheriff cut him off. *"Nope. Don't even open your mouth to say one word until we get you back to the office."*

"OK, Sheriff," replied Jacob.

Matt Fremont looked over at his son Jessie and remarked, *"You neither, Deputy Fremont. Not one word."*

"I concur," said the detective.

Jessie only rolled his eyes and looked away from his dad.

"I'm remaining at the scene to supervise. My partner Detective Sergeant George Ramon will be meeting you at your offices. He's handling the interviews," the detective informed Matt before stepping away to keep his eyes on Matt's deputies who were processing the scene.

Matt, Jessie, and Jacob heard the sound of helicopter rotor blades coming from the west and looked up to see a McDonnell Douglas MD500 helicopter with Customs Border Patrol markings coming in low and pulling up sharply nearby in a cloud of dust and then landing.

Out of the chopper jumped a uniformed BP agent with silver plated eagles on her collar. The officer removed her helmet and tossed it into the rear seat of the craft and shook her collar-length blonde hair. The trio recognized the officer as Sector Assistant Chief and Executive Officer Katherine "Katie" Blackwater of the Southwest Sector.

Sheriff Fremont walked over to meet AC Blackwater and the pair shook hands.

"Hi Katie, didn't expect to see you here," said the Sheriff.

"Matt. Well you shouldn't be at all surprised you've got Border Patrol brass here. Incursion, firefight, three dead smugglers and a shit load of dope including what I understand from DEA to be about ninety pounds of fentanyl," replied AC Blackwater. *"Your guys OK?"* she added.

"Yup, thank God. Word gets around fast. The bad guys started it, but my guys finished it," replied Matt.

Katie Blackwater surveyed the scene, her eyes quickly fixating on the three dead bad guys including one who had the shaft of a black composite arrow with a broad-tip head sticking through his back.

"Is that a fucking arrow sticking out of that guy?" Assistant Chief Blackwater said as she pointed over at the dead drug smuggler. "How the H did that happen?"

"Ah, that would be the handywork of Deputy Jacob Black Arrows. He's qualified to carry a bow and arrows as an alternative defensive weapon. Long story," replied Matt.

"Well, I would hope so. That's a fucking broad-tip arrow, Matt. The guy's not a deer," replied AC Blackwater incredulously.

"Give me the short version of the incident. I can wait until I read your OIS after action report; which I'm sure you'll transmit over to me as a confidential read," Blackwater said.

"Well, I haven't spoken with my men yet. From what I was able to gather so far, my guys had an informant who gave them a tip about some dope that was gonna be smuggled across the river here. They got permission from me to conduct a night time surveillance. The smugglers showed up with that sunken raft over there, all of the dope plus AK-47s.

"We've got one survivor and we're going to turn him over to DEA to find out who these guys are. That is, if he's willing to talk a little. However, I want it clear to all the feds that this guy is our prisoner. Incursion or not, this happened in our jurisdiction.

"The way I see it so far is that my deputies attempted to affect an arrest, but the bad guys started shooting first. My guys were forced to engage. It appears that my deputies were better shots. So far I don't see as to how they had any other choice," explained Matt briefly.

"I should say so. Take it easy, Matt. I get it and I'm with you. I'm sure everything is going to be fine with your guys. No one at DHS or ICE is looking over your shoulder on this. I understand you asked for our Dive Team to assist in the recovery of some weapons?" asked Blackwater.

"Yeah, my deputies say there should be three AK-47's, one pistol and some empty cartridges on the bottom. Like I said, the smugglers were apparently heavily armed, and my guys were only defending themselves.

"To avoid conflicts, I've asked State Police to do the OIS investigation. No matter what the DEA wants to do, the survivor is our prisoner for now. I'm filing charges on him tomorrow. They can interview him all they want but we caught him and we're cleaning him so to speak. You understand, I'm sure," said Matt, making sure that the Border Patrol Assistant Chief understood who's dirt she was standing on.

AC Katie Blackwater smiled, "I get it Matt. We'll be all too happy to help out. Looks like a great dope pinch by your deputies. Please pass on my congratulations on a superior job, well done.

"Since State Police are already here, I'll tell my Dive Team to turn over the recovered weapons to them and write up supplementals to document the recovery. DHS and CBP are willing to provide any forensic resources State Police might need to assist you in their OIS investigation. I'm sure the detective will tell them but your deputies wanna make sure that they videotape the recovery of weapons from the river for your evidence as well. I'll write a report and send it up the chain."

"Sounds good, Katie. Thanks for the help. I gotta get my deputies back to the office so State Police can interview them," said Matt.

"Hey, isn't that one deputy your son Jessie? Was he one of the two deputies involved?" asked Blackwater.

"Yeah. Glad he made it out of this incident in one piece," replied Matt.

"Looks like a chip off the old Texas Ranger block. Gotta be the good gene pool. Be safe and I'll talk with you later," replied Katie Blackwater.

"Sure thing, Katie. You too," said the Sheriff as he turned around and walked over to Jessie and Jacob.

"Jacob, I'll take Jessie with me. You take your truck and follow us back to the office. Make sure you guys have all your gear," directed Fremont as he took his son Jessie in tow and headed for his patrol unit.

CHAPTER *2*

The OIS Interviews

SHERIFF MATT FREEMAN with his son Jessie and Deputy Jacob Black Arrows arrived at the Gila County Sheriff's Department in separate vehicles and parked in the Sally Port. All three men entered the building and walked directly to Matt's office.

"Jacob, you relax in the coffee room while I interview Jessie in the interview room. Remember that you can't talk to anyone about the incident. You will be interviewed by Detective Sergeant George Ramon from State Police. When he finishes with Jessie, I'll come get you. A lot of people from outside are probably going to look at what we do, so we are doing this by the book. State Police are the lead investigators on this, not us," instructed Sheriff Fremont.

"Yes, sir," replied Jacob as he headed off down the hall to the coffee room.

Matt walked over to a closet and removed a 35 mm SLR digital camera from a shelf. He turned towards Jessie, "OK, we're going down to the interview room where Sergeant Ramon is going to record your statement. I want zero criticisms on how this incident was investigated by outsiders or the media once it gets out that you're my son.

I'm going to photograph you in your uniform with all of the equipment you were wearing tonight. I'm also going to take your duty belt for now. You'll get a replacement sidearm and another rifle once we do the ballistics tests on your issued weapons. We are going to test the bad guys' weapons, compare any casings recovered from the river bed. State Police will conclude the investigation if all is good with the shoot," explained Matt.

Matt and Jessie walked down to the interview room. The Sheriff first had Jessie stand in front of a blank wall in the hallway and began photographing Jessie in his uniform from all sides. It was important to document his Sheriff's Office sewn on badge and shoulder insignia. Since Jessie and Jacob had been wearing their load-bearing tactical vests with Sheriff Office badges, and large embroidered 'SHERIFF' patches front and rear, the vests would be photographed as well. He wanted no issues with the surviving defendant saying that the deputies were not clearly identified as law enforcement officers.

After photographing Jessie's uniform and equipment, Matt took Jessie's duty belt and directed his son into the interview room where Detective Sergeant Ramon was waiting. Matt activated a video camera from a nearby desk and checked the computer monitor on the desk to confirm he had both video and sound before leaving the room. It was now the detective's turn.

An officer-involved shooting (OIS) interview was a serious, fact-finding, procedural and legal discussion. The interview provided critical information that needed to be thoroughly documented for the record as forensic evidence to be presented later in court if need be. Before the interview could begin, Matt fully briefed Sergeant Ramon on what the sheriff knew about the incident so far.

Sergeant Ramon had a yellow legal pad in front of him and drew a straight line right down the middle of it for notes. The key to being a good forensic interviewer was to not interrupt the interviewee and to let them do most of the talking. Before commencing the fact pattern portion of the interview, there were important legal issues to attend to as a matter of procedure. Jessie had rights; both criminal and civil that needed to be addressed.

Proper OIS investigations were "bifurcated," meaning that two separate investigations were actually conducted. One was criminal, to determine whether the shooting officer was legally justified. The second was administrative, to determine whether the involved officer had followed department policy and their training. A shooting officer could have a legally justified shooting but could still be disciplined including being terminated for violating department policy. State Police were handling the criminal side of the shooting. Matt would handle the administrative investigation afterwards. Matt clicked the "record" button on the video system and began.

"This is Detective Sergeant George Ramon, lead investigator for the new Mexico State Police's Officer-Involved Shooting Investigations Team. This interview pertains to an officer-involved shooting resulting in multiple fatalities that occurred this date at approximately 0315 hours within the jurisdiction of Gila County, New Mexico at the New Mexico – Mexico international border.

"The incident precipitated from an unlawful border incursion into the U.S. by four suspected Mexican national drug smugglers. Three subjects are deceased as a result of sheriff intervention. One unidentified Hispanic male surrendered and is in the custody of the Gila County Sheriff's Office. A sizable quantity of illegal drugs were recovered in the possession of the decedents and surviving drug smuggler."

Sergeant Ramon looked up from his legal pad at Jessie and continued, "Present at this interview is one of the involved shooting deputies. Deputy, please identify yourself with your badge number and assignment for the record."

Jessie replied, "Sheriff's Deputy Jessie Fremont, badge #15. I am assigned to patrol."

Ramon continued with the legal formalities, advising Jessie first of his Miranda Rights which Jessie waived.

The detective acknowledged Jessie's Miranda waiver, "Let the record reflect that Deputy Fremont has waived his rights to legal counsel, is here voluntarily and is willing to answer questions."

Now that the formalities had been concluded, Sergeant Ramon got right into the meat of the subject. He began by asking Jessie to explain his assignment that night. Next, he asked his deputy how and what information he and Deputy Jacob Black Arrows had obtained from their informant. Next was establishing how they obtained permission from the Sheriff to stake out the river that night to intercept the drug smugglers.

Sergeant Ramon was an experienced investigator. He knew that all uses of force, especially deadly force fell under New Mexico state statutes and separate federal guidelines of the 4th Amendment of the Bill of Rights. The detective knew full well that peace officers needed objective, probable cause to use force.

A mere subjective belief by Jessie and Jacob that their lives might have been threatened by the drug smugglers when they fired upon them wasn't going to cut it. This meant that each deputy independently had to clearly establish the circumstances of the imminent deadly force threats against them. This in turn would establish their probable cause in firing upon the subjects in self-defense.

Probable cause and an articulable objective life-threat were going to be critical components of testimony if the deputies were going to be cleared in the shootings. Later, establishing probable cause to believe that the smugglers posed an imminent life threat of serious bodily injury or death would be important in the criminal prosecution of the surviving smuggler.

Jessie went through the details leading up to the stake-out. It was important to explain that the sheriff had been thoroughly briefed and permission for the stake-out had been granted. Jessie also covered the contingency plans for back-up and the radio protocols they had followed in the minutes before the smugglers had first appeared on the Mexican side of the river.

Ramon listened intently, writing down only a word from time to time on his notepad. The words were to remind him of questions of clarification later in the interview.

"It went down quickly. We announced that we were law enforcement at least twice. We told them in Spanish and English to show their hands and not move towards their guns. They decided to fight. We were forced to shoot. You'll find that their guns had been fired. Their empty cartridges will be right where I said they were when we returned fire.

"One of their rounds struck and disabled Jacob's rifle. You'll see that too. I covered for him while he transitioned to his alternate weapon. Apparently due to the distance, which was about forty to fifty yards, Jacob used his recurve bow and took one of them out. I got two of them, Jacob got one and the last guy tossed his gun into the river and surrendered. It was what it was," explained Jessie.

Due to the distances involved in the engagement Sergeant Ramon already knew the answers to his next questions.

Procedurally he still had to address the issue of "preclusion," or what circumstances prevented or obstructed the deputies' ability to deploy less lethal force.

"So what other less lethal weaponry were you carrying last night and why didn't you use it?" Ramon asked Jessie.

"Well, Tonto…ah Deputy Black Arrows and I were wearing our TASERS and we also had some OC pepper spray. However, the smugglers immediately engaged us with deadly force. The imminent deadly force threat and extreme distances between us prevented us from even considering using our TASERs or pepper spray. We were just too far away, and we are trained not to use less lethal force against an imminent threat of opposing deadly force," replied Jessie.

Jessie's response led the detective to the ultimate deadly force question. "So again, why did you and Deputy Black Arrows make a joint decision to use deadly force?"

"Well, we began taking AK-47 rifle fire. At that point it was obvious to us that the smugglers posed an imminent threat to us of serious bodily injury or death. It was only until that point that we used our firearms to return fire. I personally believed that they were trying to kill us. Not wanting to speak for Jacob Black Arrows, I'm pretty sure he was thinking the same thing.

"We just had no choice. Our intent was not to shoot them but to get them to surrender peacefully. It was their decision to fire upon us. We were forced to protect ourselves and stop their threat," replied Jessie.

Addressing the forensic ballistics issues, Detective Ramon asked Jessie, "How many rounds do you think you fired in total?"

"Well, I know that Jacob and I each directed initial three-round bursts with our M-4's targeting the two lead smugglers of the four who engaged us. Our fire brought each of those men down.

"Jacob's M-4 was apparently disabled by their gun fire, so he transitioned to his Glock. I fired another three or four rounds of covering fire for him. I could hear Jacob firing his Glock pistol, but I have no idea how many rounds he fired. I was pretty busy myself at that point.

"I know that at some point, Jacob transitioned from his Glock to his bow and took out a third smuggler. I didn't hear it, but I saw the smuggler get tagged square in the chest with an arrow. I saw him fall backwards into the water. Then, the final guy threw up his hands, dropped his pistol into the water and surrendered. So I think in total, I fired six or seven rifle rounds. I never used my pistol," explained Jessie.

"How about the smugglers; how many rounds do you think they fired at you?" asked the detective.

"Shit, a bunch is all I know. They were on full-auto from what I remember. The rounds were whizzing all around us like angry hornets is what is sounded like to me. I really have no idea how many rounds they fired," said Jessie.

"OK, I get it. Did you sustain any injuries I need to know about?" asked Ramon.

"No, thank God. I can't believe that none of us got tagged after they fired that many rounds. St. Michael was definitely sitting on my shoulder last night," replied Jessie.

"Well Deputy Fremont, I think that's all that I have for you at this time. If anything comes up, I'll get back to you for clarifications should I need them. Do you have any questions for me?" Ramon asked.

"Well just the obvious like when can me and Deputy Black Arrows return to duty? When will we be able to get our weapons back and how long do you think this investigation process will take?" asked Jessie.

"Well Jessie, right now the investigation has just started. Administrative leave is up to Sheriff Fremont. Officially, I do have to inform you that you really can't discuss this incident with anyone, including Jacob. That also includes the feds. If they have questions for you, they have to come through me. CBP Assistant Chief Katie Blackwater and the DEA know this," explained Sergeant Ramon before rising from the table and shaking Jessie's hand. The detective then opened the door to the interview room so Matt Fremont could have a word with his son.

Matt put his hand on Jessie's shoulder, "I'm thinking that this incident is going to be pretty cut and dry. If there are no evidentiary problems, about five days of leave should do it. Take some R&R out of the county just in case the cartel you messed with is looking for revenge. You are to remain armed at all times. If you have any post-shooting psychological issues, I want to know about it right away. We'll hook you up with a psychologist who can help you if you need it. If you don't have any other questions, you're dismissed, deputy," explained Matt.

As Jessie walked out of the office and down the corridor, Matt found his Deputy Jacob Black Arrows in the coffee room.

"Hi Jacob, Sergeant Ramon is done with his interview of Jessie your partner and is ready for you. How about it? Do you feel up to discussing the incident tonight?" Matt asked.

"Sure Sheriff, that's why I'm here. The sooner I do the interview, the sooner I can get some sleep," replied Jacob.

"Well, hold on Jacob. If you are telling me you are too tired, we can certainly put this off for a bit. This is all about you. We are going to need you with all of your faculties when Sergeant Ramon interviews you about what happened," said Matt.

"I'm no different than Jessie and he just interviewed. Another hour in my life is not going to matter at this point in time. Let's get it done," Jacob responded.

Sheriff Fremont repeated the processing of photographically documenting the condition of his uniform and safety equipment. Then he brought Jacob into his office and invited him to sit down in in the interview room facing a video camera. Matt activated the camera and left the room.

Detective Sergeant Ramon entered the room, shook Jacob's hand and introduced himself. The detective advised Jacob of the nature of his investigation, and then went through many of the same questions he had asked Jessie earlier.

Jacob Black Arrows' observations, descriptions, and explanations as to what precipitated the officer-involved shooting was nearly identical to Jessie's except he was able to fill in much better what his actions and responses were to the drug smugglers firing upon him and Jessie.

"I'm curious as to why did you choose to use your bow?" the

detective asked.

"Distance sir. Distance," replied Jacob

"What do you mean, distance?" the Sheriff asked.

"Well, when one of the smugglers took my M-4 out of action, I needed to reach out further to stop the threat to Jessie and me. I estimated the distance to target to be roughly forty or more yards. That's a difficult shot to make with a pistol under the conditions I was faced with. I practice regularly with my bow at fifty yards, so I knew that I had to transition to my bow. I had a much better chance of stopping him at forty yards, so I went for it.

"As you observed, my force calculation was correct. After all, that's why Sheriff Fremont tested and certified me to carry the weapon in the first place. I believed and still do that my deadly force decision was well within policy and state statutes.

"The way I look at it, given the circumstances I was forced to deal with in a matter of only seconds, I really didn't see the difference between taking out the imminent threat with a bullet or a broad tip arrow," replied Jacob with confidence.

"Well, I sure can't argue with you there at this point in my investigation. I asked because a layperson would find it highly unusual that a deputy would be certified and entrusted to use a bow and arrow as a lethal force weapon," explained the detective.

"Well, that's all I have for you right now. I'll reach out to you if I need anything else. Like Jessie has been advised, you're on administrative leave with full pay and benefits until our office completes our investigation. Use your time off wisely. Decompress, relax, spend time with the family," Ramon advised. The detective then shook Jacob's hand and left the interview room to Sheriff Fremont who had been waiting outside.

The sheriff approached Jacob with an assuring smile. "Off the record, my advice for you and Jessie is that you get out of the county for the next five days but remain on standby with your cellphone. You guys no doubt took out some cartel soldiers and the cartel lost a lot of dope. They are going to be pissed off and maybe looking for a little payback.

"Remember that this is authorized leave; not a suspension

so you will remain armed at all times. Your leave starts immediately, but in an emergency, you are both subject to immediate call-back. Check in with me every morning and let me know where you are. OK, be on your way and remember, out of the county, got that?" directed the Sheriff.

"Yes sir. Will do," replied Jacob as he walked out of Sheriff Fremont's office.

CHAPTER 3

The Room

THE COUNTY OF Gila, New Mexico, population 5,700, was a dusty border county separating the United States from Mexico. The Rio Brisas was a tributary of the Gila River Rio which is a six-hundred and forty-nine mile long tributary of the Colorado River. The river begins at the western slopes of the mountains of Sierra County in western New Mexico. In Gila County, the river in places separates Mexico from the United States.

Gila County's southern border was of course, the State of Chihuahua, Mexico. It was surrounded by Luna County to the west and Dona Ana County on its north and east sides. The Rio Grande River in parts separated the county from Las Cruces, New Mexico.

Gila County's seat was the small town of Rio Brisas, population 2,200, which stood at the base of the Sierra Cielo Mountains in the Rio Brisas Valley on the northeast U.S. side of the Rio Brisas River. The mountain range on the opposite and Mexican side of the valley was the Montanas de Plata or the Mountains of Silver.

The Montanas de Plata range was marked by a prominent landmark referred to in Spanish as La Amante Durmiente or "Sleeping Mistress." The landmark was so called because the locals believed that whenever they gazed at the peaks of the mountain range, they saw the form of a woman with large breasts sleeping on top of the mountains. The Spanish myth was that the Amante was a mistress of a Spanish conquistador who after being scorned by her lover, climbed to the top of the mountain where she took poison and then fell permanently asleep.

Gila County was somewhat of a "dying" county. Its former claims to fame were its once highly lucrative silver mines, now depleted, and plentiful fields of Pima cotton, long gone with the reductions in water flow from its Gila River and Rio Brisas water sources. However, more plentiful than its human population were its beautiful saguaro cactus, a large tree-like cactus species that can grow over forty-feet in height, native to the Sonoran Desert in Arizona, the State of Sonora, Mexico, and the Whipple Mountains and Imperial County areas of California.

The region that Gila County found itself surrounded by was steadily becoming less inviting to businesses and residential living. All three counties, Luna, Dona Ana, and Gila were on the decline. Many of Gila's residents were just keeping their head above water as far as the U.S. poverty level was concerned.

Yes, the people of Gila County were definitely hurting economically. This was exactly why the Tres Paises Cartel had targeted it for infiltration and drug trafficking. People could be easily convinced that it was well worth their while to look the other way as drugs, sex-trafficked women and children and undocumented laborers were smuggled by traffickers across the Mexican border.

The town of Rio Brisas once had their own police department and Matt Fremont had been their Chief of Police. After retiring from the Texas Rangers, Matt had left the Great State of Texas to take the chief's job as a favor to his wife Esperanza so she could be closer to her folks.

Esperanza's parents resided in Rio Brisas and had not been doing well health-wise. Esperanza's father had worked in the silver mines and had contracted mesothelioma. At the time, her father's illness required considerable home care, which was too much for her mother. Matt accepted the low-paying chief's job so his wife and her sister Blanca could care for both parents. Then he and Esperanza packed up their things, sold their ranch in Blanco, Texas and moved to Rio Brisas. Matt and Esperanza always believed in "Family First." So instead of retiring after a long and distinguished career in law enforcement, Matt Fremont, a man now in his late sixty's began a new career as Rio Brisas' Chief of Police.

Matt worked as Rio Brisas' Police Chief for three years before the city council voted to defund and dissolve its police department in order to avoid bankruptcy. However, Matt saw it coming. Since it was an election year, the popular chief ran for the office of Sherriff of Gila County and was elected in a landslide. Matt was now well into his second term as Sheriff. Since being elected, Matt had worked tirelessly to keep the residents of Gila County safe.

Matt was well aware of the imminent threat posed by the Mexican transnational drugs cartels. Currently, it was the Tres Paises drug syndicate that his attention had been focused on since he had begun his second term in office. The previous night's violent and deadly engagement between the drug smugglers, his son Jessie and Jacob Black Arrows served to underscore just how serious the threat was increasingly becoming.

Matt arranged to have the DEA take possession of the sixty pounds of cocaine, the ten pounds of crystal meth and the ninety pounds of fentanyl that Jessie and Jacob had recovered from the smugglers' incursion onto U.S. soil. He picked up his phone and called his DEA liaison, Cecil McKenry, at the agency's El Paso Intelligence Center, known by the acronym "EPIC," to get an update on the drugs.

Special Agent McKenry recognized the phone ID and picked up on the second ring. "DEA, McKenry, What's up Sheriff?"

"Hi Cecil. Just checking up on the dope my boys recovered last night. Have you tested it yet?" asked Matt.

"Shit, I thought WE were the dope smuggling busters in this part of the territory. Great arrest by your guys last night. I heard your son was one of the deputies who made the pinch. I also heard that it was one hell of a gun fight too. How are your guys doing?" asked SSA McKenry.

"Well, a damn sight better than the smugglers, I assure you," replied Matt.

"Care to confirm the rumor that one of those assholes took a broad tip right through the ticker by one of your deputies? What the fuck!" exclaimed SSA McKenry.

"You know how it goes Cecil, I can neither confirm, nor deny. Have you tested the dope yet?" asked Matt, immediately deflecting and redirecting back to one of the reasons for his call.

"Yup, we confirmed the weight and tested it early this morning. Positive on coke, crystal meth and fentanyl. The big trifecta, Sheriff," said SSA McKenry.

"Well, that's much appreciated. Now let's talk about the sole survivor my guys collared who you guys have in pocket. I want first crack at him. After that, you guys can waterboard him all you want. Fair enough?" smirked Matt.

"Well, as you know, these are federal crimes, Matt. Under these circumstances, DEA interviews the smugglers," said SSA McKenry.

"Whoa, Cecil. Hold on one minute. Yes, they are federal crimes, but it happened in my county. My guys worked the case that led to the seizure of a ton of dope and the arrest of a key suspect. That ought to count for something. Besides, I'm willing to let your people sit in while I interview him. I only have a few questions pertaining specifically to my county and then the punk is all yours.

"All humility aside and no offense intended, after thirty years of rangering, I'm a much better interviewer than any of the DEA people I've met so far. I take the first shot and it's a win-win for all of us if he talks. You guys can have all the credit; I just need some intel for my county's safety. I've got nothing to prove to anyone. I neither need nor want to be the star here," explained Matt.

"Tell you what, Matt, let me run it by the Special Agent In Charge first. If the SAC says he has no problem with it, then we'll call you back and set up the interview here. I can let you know by noon. Sound fair?" asked SSA McKenry.

"Done. Just call me by noon," replied Sheriff Matt Fremont.

"Copy that," answered SSA McKenry before hanging up.

Matt Fremont's next call was to Border Patrol Assistant Chief Katherine "Katie" Blackwater. Matt had AC Blackwater's cell number on speed dial.

"AC Blackwater," the CBP administrator said into her phone.

"Katie, Matt Fremont. How is your dive team doing out at the scene?" asked Matt.

"Good news, Sheriff. I was going to call you in a few but you just saved me the trouble. Our dive team recovered the AK's, a semi-auto pistol and over fifty spent casings from the bottom of the Rio Brisas. We are sending all of the weapons and spent casings to the regional ATF office in Albuquerque for testing. So far, everything is checking out with what Jessie and Deputy Black Arrows told us at the scene. Looks good for your guys," advised AC Blackwater.

"Well, that's good to know, Katie. I never had a doubt that your people would be able to recover the evidence. I'm glad this incident didn't happen in winter with heavy rains, or everything could have been washed far down stream," said Matt.

"Well, we have everything packaged up to go. I'm going to do you a favor and have my pilot and one of my agents fly all of the evidence up to Albuquerque in about an hour. I'm putting a special rush on the exams. I'm thinking that we'll have results *in* about forty-eight hours," said AC Blackwater.

"Wow, that's great Katie. I really appreciate that. I'd like to keep the OIS investigation moving quickly so I can take it to the County's DA for a legal opinion. I'm working with DEA to interview the remaining suspect. I promise to share whatever I get from him with you. DEA is supposed to let me know about the interview today. I'll keep you in the loop," said Matt.

Just like clockwork at 12:05 pm, Matt Fremont's cell phone buzzed. He looked down at the phone and saw that the caller was DEA SSA Cecil McKenry.

"Cecil, I hope you have good news for me," said Matt.

"In fact, I do. My SAC says that in the spirit of mutual assistance and cooperation, blah, blah, blah, you get first crack at our lone survivor. BTW, after a lot of lying on his part, we confirmed his identity from both fingerprints and DNA as one Alfredo "Chuy" Montoya Guzman."

"Guzman, as in Adolfo Guzman, the head of the Tres Paises drug cartel?" asked Sheriff Fremont.

"None other. In fact, young Chuy is the nephew of Guzman, so he's definitely a big deal," replied SSA McKenry.

"Bingo! Then he's an up and comer for sure. We've never had contact with Chuy before. So, I'm thinking that Uncle Adolfo was giving him a chance to bust his cherry humping some large weight dope across the border and into my county. I'm sure that right now Adolfo's thinking, "So why doesn't he call?" laughed Matt.

"Well, my SAC says that both of our agencies really can't hold back much longer on giving up more of the story. Eventually, we will have to ID the kid because it's a big dope bust directly tied to Adolfo and the Tres Paises drug cartel. The old man is really going to have egg on his face and be super pissed once it gets out his nephew got pinched," said SSA McKenry.

"When can we schedule an interview with Chuy? The sooner, the better for all of us you know," said Matt.

"I'll run it past my SAC. For my part and in the spirit of exigency so you can complete your OIS investigation, I'll offer up early tonight around 6 pm, our place," said SSA McKenry.

"I'm on it. Just call me to confirm and I'll be there this evening," replied Matt, before hanging up.

Matt began typing out a chronology fact pattern of the events leading up to the confrontation between his deputies and the smugglers and the OIS for his investigative report. There were some obvious blanks in his chronology that he hoped his interview with Chuy Guzman would reveal.

At 2:15 pm, his cell phone chirped once, indicating a text message. He looked down at his phone and read the brief message from SSA Cecil McKenry that simply read, "Good to go w int. @ 6. We'll record."

Matt typed out a simple response, *"Copy,"* and resumed his typing, thinking about his interview strategy.

At 4:15 pm, Matt stopped typing and headed out to the Federal Bureau of Prison's La Tuna facility just outside of El Paso in Anthony. It was an easy drive on relatively deserted, dusty back country roads to Interstate 10, but he wanted to make sure he got through El Paso's infamous, horrendous traffic snarls on the I-10 through town where road construction never seemed to end.

Matt arrived at La Tuna at 6:30 pm and met with SSA McKenry to get a quick brief on Chuy's behavior since he had been arrested. He wanted to plan a seamless interview with the arrestee.

and how the interview was to be recorded.

"So how's our guy doing?" asked Matt.

"Guzman's the typical millennial. Entitled, overly confident and wise-cracking, "I'm a big shot," ahole type. More balls than brains. He's gonna be a challenge," replied McKenry.

"Has he made any calls out yet; his uncle, an associate, an attorney?" asked Matt.

"Well, the kid says that he doesn't need an attorney cause he ain't never going to trial," McKenry chuckled.

"Does he speak and understand English, or only Spanish," asked Matt.

"Both. Actually, his English is pretty good," said McKenry.

"That will make things a might easier. Well, where's the coffee? I'll get a cup and bring him one too and we can get going. How are you recording the interview?" asked Matt.

McKenry led Matt into a room with a large, mirrored bullet resistant plexiglass window. There was a video camera set up in front of the window that was facing a stark interview room with just a table and two chairs all bolted into the floor.

Seated at one of the chairs facing the camera was a young Mexican male in his mid-twenties, of average height and build with collar-length black hair and a mustache, dressed in a red jumpsuit. Chuy Guzman was wearing waist chains and his hands were cuffed in front through a D-ring. Both of his legs were shackled and additionally secured to a large O-ring screwed into the concrete floor directly beneath his chair. Guzman actually looked more like a college kid than an international drug smuggler.

"The usual set-up. Two cameras with one here and the other hidden in that light socket next to the door. See it? Two mics; one concealed in the overhead light and the other under the table on his side. We get great sound and HD quality video in that room," explained McKenry. "Let's get you that coffee."

SSA McKenry led Matt out to the small coffee room and Matt poured two cups of black coffee and brought them into the interview room. He then placed the coffee on the table and sat down matter of factly without even looking at Guzman.

Chuy Guzman looked quizzically at Matt.

Matt Fremont began after taking a sip of his coffee, "Real coffee, not that jail swill. Want some?" said the sheriff, offering Chuy a cup. Chuy didn't respond, nor did he reach of the coffee.

"Well, just about now your uncle Adolfo is probably saying to himself, 'Why doesn't my nephew Chuy check in?' What do you think?"

Chuy Guzman looked at the sheriff and his look changed to a smirk. "Well, I'm a big boy so I check in when I check in. You gringo federales ain't got shit."

"Well, Chuy, I'm not a fed. I'm the Sheriff of Gila County, New Mexico. That's the county where my deputies caught you and your pinche carnales humping some large weight dope into the U.S. and my county," replied Matt Fremont.

"Hijole. You're not even a fed? What the fuck. You ain't shit. You're just a fucking sheriff," Chuy laughed.

Sheriff Fremont looked directly into Chuy's eyes. "Wow, Chuy, that hurt. Look, puto. Here's the deal. First, I've got hemorrhoids older than you. Next, you tried to sneak a lot of dope not only into the U.S., but into my county. Here's the difference between the feds and me, a County Sheriff. They work for the President, but in my county, I am the President, so to speak. The only person who ain't shit in this room is you. I control what goes on in my county and since my guys busted you, that effectively means that I control what happens to you. Comprende, amigo?" The self-assured sheriff continued.

"So let me run this down for you and I'll speak slowly so your dumb ass can understand me. Right now, I've got you with smuggling enough dope into the U.S. to put you in a federal super max prison next to Pablo Escobar until you're so old, your tiny pecker won't even stand up and salute any more. Speaking of Escobar, how'd all that money and attorneys help him? He'll die in an American prison. Aqui no es Mexico, amigo.

"On top of that, I've also got you on two counts of attempted murder of two of my deputies with a weapon enhancement that will put you away for life. That means that you and your former La Vida Loca lifestyle effectively part ways. The only pussy you are going to see for the fucking rest of your life is if some feral cat walks past your quad in super max."

Sheriff Fremont continued as his fierce gaze began to burn out the retinas of Chuy Guzman, who's eyes were now as big as saucers.

"And speaking of sex, you're a young and nice looking guy. Some in the joint would even call you a 'pretty boy.' This means that you'll most likely end up as some gang leader's bitch and I'll venture to bet you'll become a pin cushion for all the inmates in D-Quad. After the first year getting punked by the vatos and white supremacists, your asshole will get so reamed that you won't even make noise when you fart. I think that about sizes it up, I'd say.

"Nope, you are definitely fucked in a major way right now. Even if Uncle Adolfo gets you a couple of high-priced attorneys to help you with the fed charges, Gila County and the State of New Mexico are going to hit you with so many felony charges that all the abogados and dope dinero in Mexico are not going to help you while I'm sheriff. Gila County is out of federal control. Sucks to be you right now, amigo," said Matt Fremont to Chuy as he continued to stare him down.

Chuy Guzman broke eye contact with Sheriff Fremont, averting his eyes and looking down at the cold metal table. Fremont, who was an expert forensic interviewer carefully gauged Chuy's physiological responses. Chuy's shoulders which were initially straight, now hunched forward, his breathing was slightly labored, his face was flushed, and light tearing was noticeable in his dilated eyes. The sheriff's "bad cop" tactic was working.

Matt Fremont knew that timing during an interview was everything and Chuy was beginning to psychologically collapse. The young and inexperienced drug smuggler was now ripe for a change in tactics and so Fremont transitioned to "good cop."

The sheriff looked at Chuy and smiled warmly and sympathetically. "Look Chuy, I'm not interested in anything the feds want to ask you. They are interested in dope. That's not my thing. I'm only interested in information that costs you nothing and could help your case.

"I'm not going to ask you anything about your drug operation or who you were going to connect with. That's DEA's thing. I just want to know who in my county gave you the information about the location you tried to cross at. Why you chose that location? That costs you nothing. If you help me out, I'll tell our DA that you cooperated with me and that can certainly help you out at sentencing. What do you say?" asked Fremont.

Chuy looked up from the table and back into Matt Fremont's eyes. "That's it? That's all you want?" asked the incredulous young man.

"Yup, pretty much," replied the sheriff who knew that DEA would eventually break Chuy to get all of the middle-level local dealers he was going to distribute the narcotics to. The DEA were trafficking chain people. They would interview Chuy to find out who he was distributing to and then walk up the supply chain to close down the cartel's operation in the U.S. Matt was careful not to step on the DEA's toes. His job was to soften up Chuy for the DEA.

In the end, Sheriff Matt Fremont got his wish. Chuy provided him with two county-level politicians who were in the pocket of Tres Paises. That's all he wanted for the time being. Best to know who your enemies were for intelligence purposes. The interview with Chuy Guzman was over in just a half an hour. Matt thanked Chuy for his cooperation and walked out the door.

DEA SSA McKenry met Matt in the hallway. "He's all yours, Cecil. My work here is done," said the Sheriff.

"Very impressive, I must say. You deflated Guzman pretty fast. I think he's still reeling and ready for round two," replied the DEA agent.

"Yeah, I wouldn't give him any time to recover. Psychologically, he's down. Get right in there before he catches his breath and begins to think about maybe now he needs a lawyer. You already Mirandized him and he waived. He can always assert his right to an attorney. Don't give him time to re-think that and lawyer-up," said the sheriff.

"Copy that. I'm going in. Thanks much for the boost and we'll talk if there is anything important I can share with you," said Cecil . The DEA supervisor shook Matt Fremont's hand and opened the door to the interview room to get started on double-teaming Chuy Guzman.

CHAPTER 4

"Manos arriba, placa!"

LIKE CLOCKWORK, TWO days after Sheriff Matt Fremont had interviewed Chuy Guzman, his cell phone rang just after lunch. Matt looked at the display and saw it was Border Patrol Assistant Chief Katie Blackwater.

"Katie, I hope you have some good news for me," said the sheriff.

"Well, as a matter of fact, I do," replied Katie. "All weapons tested out as functioning properly. Ballistics was able to positively identify and connect all of the AK and pistol cartridges to the bad guys, including Chuy Guzman who is in custody.

"Our crime scene techs had done a Forbus 360 scan of the crime scene. Thanks to the fact that the river wasn't moving swiftly and was low, the guns and the cartridges sank straight down to the river bed when they hit the water. Since Jessie and Deputy Black Arrows had provided us with their and the bad guys' positions in the river when the gunfight began, we were able to put together a pretty good forensic reconstruction of what took place with angles of fire from both sides.

"In short, the evidence and our reconstruction of the incident completely supports the statements you sent us from Jessie and Black Arrows. We are therefore closing our part of the investigation. I'll tell you this, your two deputies are two very lucky guys," said AC Blackwater.

"Well, thanks Katie. That's great news. No loose ends. I was just waiting for your report before I closed my investigation as well.

Looks like a justifiable shooting for both of my deputies. With all of the evidence supporting Jessie and Jacob, I can wrap this OIS up. If you can email me all of your reports including lab work, I'll take the packet over to the DA's Office tomorrow for a legal opinion. I'm pretty sure we won't need to empanel a Grand Jury to review this one," said Matt Fremont.

"Sure thing, Matt. You will have all of our reports by the end of the day. Do you want us to retain all of the weapons and evidence. It will be more secure with us than at your place," AC Blackwater offered.

"Yes, I'd like that, Katie. Much appreciated," replied the sheriff.

"Done deal. Let us know if we can be of any further assistance. Tell your deputies job well done from us," said the AC before hanging up. Sheriff Fremont called the Gila County District Attorney's Office and scheduled a 10:00 am meeting with the DA to review the officer-involved shooting.

The following morning, Sheriff Matt Fremont gathered up his investigations packet with all of the reports, photos, diagrams and scans on the OIS and headed over to the DA's office to brief the DA on the incident. He was out of the DA's office by noon with a legal opinion that the OIS involving his deputies was justified.

Matt Fremont called his son Jessie and Deputy Jacob Black Arrows to give them the good news and to tell each deputy to return to duty at the end of their administrative time off. He still wanted them to decompress after the incident.

One week after Deputies Jessie Fremont and Jacob Black Arrows had returned to duty, at approximately 10:30 pm, the Gila County Sheriff's Department received a cell phone call to their Emergency 9-1-1 line. A female driver reported that another female driver appeared to be stranded on the side of the roadway on Road 18 near the 9 Mile marker just north of Rio Brisas. The cell reception was poor, and the connection was lost. Attempts to re-contact the caller had been unsuccessful.

Deputy Jessie Fremont was working the Swing Shift in Unit Gila-10. Although Jessie was due to go off-duty at 11:00 pm, he took the call since his partner Deputy Black Arrows in Unit

Gila-20 was already engaged on a medical assist call twenty miles east of town.

"Control, Gila-10 copies the stranded motorist call on Road 18 at the 9 Mile marker. Enroute. ETA 10. Any more info?" radioed Jessie.

"Gila-10, Control. No further info. Contact broken with the RP. Negative on attempts to re-contact. Advise upon arrival," radioed back dispatch.

"Control, Gila-10 copies, will do," replied Jessie.

Road 18 was not a frequently traveled road. It terminated in an old silver mining village. There were scant occupied properties along the road, mostly dilapidated farm houses and falling down barns. There were no street lights along the road and only a quarter moon offered any ambient light along the way. As Jessie drove down Road 18, he wondered why some woman would be driving on that road at this time of night. She probably just got lost he speculated. It happens.

Jessie passed the 9 Mile marker and began to slow his speed. His highlights caught the reflection of faint taillights of a dark colored sedan off to the right side of the roadway pointing in the direction of the end of Road 18 about a half-mile further. On either side of the vehicle were tall berms about fifteen feet in height that had been formed by the discarded rock and gravel "tailings" of long abandoned silver mines.

As Jessie approached closer to the vehicle, he observed a single female who appeared to be in her late twenties exit the sedan and stand behind its hood. The young woman who was dressed in jeans and a dark hoodie sweatshirt, appeared to be holding a baby swaddled in a baby blanket.

"That's weird," It was chilly outside. Why not leave the baby inside the warm car where it was more comfortable," the deputy thought as he exited his patrol car to approach the woman.

"Hi Miss. Are you stuck or lost?" Jessie inquired as he walked to within six feet of the woman. Instead of responding, the woman turned slightly away from him to her left, appearing to be shielding the baby while fidgeting with the blanket. While Jessie waited for her to respond, the woman suddenly dropped what the deputy had thought was a baby wrapped in a blanket, while simultaneously producing a semi-automatic pistol and pointing it directly at his head. Jessie was caught flat-footed in surprise.

At the same time, a Mexican male suddenly appeared from his position of concealment in front of the sedan, holding and pointing an AK-47 at Jessie. Two other men armed with AK's on each side of the adjacent berms, both zeroed in on the hapless deputy. "Manos arriba, gringo!" The man from the front of the sedan yelled out at Jessie.

Deputy Jessie Fremont knew that there was no way he was going to survive if this turned into a gunfight. He was surrounded by four suspects, three of whom were armed with fully automatic AK-47 assault rifles, with 7.62 X 39 rounds capable of penetrating completely through his body armor.

"Calmese, amigos. No disparer. Relajate." "Calm down, friends. Don't shoot. Be cool," replied Jessie in perfect Spanish to his captors as he slowly raised his hands upwards above his head in submission.

The man with the AK who had been behind the sedan moved up to the female who was still pointing the pistol at Jessie's head. The two other men armed with AK's moved from their positions on the berms down to the street. All of the suspects now surrounded Jessie.

The first man who appeared to be the leader of the band motioned to the female, "Toma su pistola y damela," "Take his pistol and give it to me," he directed. The female immediately complied, placing her own pistol into the small of her back. Under cover of the others, she walked up to Jessie. The woman disarmed Jessie of his pistol and then spat in his face exclaiming in disgust, "Pinche, placa puto!"

The leader spoke to Jessie in English. "I think she doesn't like you, deputy. Could be because you killed her husband recently at the river. If it was up to her, you would already be dead now, but we have other orders. You will be coming with us. You resist, you die. Comprende?" the leader told Jessie.

"Yes. What do you want from me?" asked Jessie, realizing that these men were undoubtedly from the Tres Paises drug cartel.

Since this wasn't going to be a hit, they apparently wanted him for some reason and had been ordered to snatch him up and deliver him to someone higher up the chain. There was no chance of escaping alive at this point. Better not to give them any chance to kill him, especially the female.

The female delivered Jessie's pistol to the leader who directed her to use Jessie's own handcuffs to cuff his hands behind his back.

"You know the drill, deputy. Hands behind your back and no fucking around or you die right here, right now," said the leader to Jessie. The deputy complied so as not to provoke his captors.

As Jessie was being handcuffed, his handpack radio on his duty belt suddenly went off, "Gila-10, Control, 952. Are you Code-4?" asked the dispatcher.

"Is that for you? What are they asking you?" the leader asked Jessie.

"Yes. They want to know what's going on with the call and how I am," replied Jessie honestly.

The leader slung his AK-47 downwards, unholstered his pistol and put it up to Jessie's head as he removed Jessie's hand mic from the front of his load bearing vest and held it up to his mouth so Jessie could respond.

"You will tell this person that the woman is fine, she will be leaving soon and, you are OK. No radio codes or I will kill you right now, get it?!" instructed the leader.

"I get it," replied Jessie. The leader activated the radio mic and held it up to Jessie's mouth. Jessie reported back to the dispatcher exactly as he had been instructed.

"Gila-10, Control copies, I'm good. Thanks," replied the dispatcher.

After Jessie radioed back to dispatch, the leader removed Jessie's handpack radio from his assault vest. He walked over to the deputy's patrol unit, opened the driver's side door and tossed it inside. He walked back to Jessie, pulled a small portable radio of his own out of his back pocket and spoke briefly into it, "Bring up the trucks."

In less than a minute, two vehicles emerged from behind the tall berms. The first vehicle was a blacked out Hummer H-3 and the other was a camouflaged Toyota Tundra pick-up truck "mechanical" with a driver and a guy dressed out in camouflage BDU's in the back armed with a 5.56 M249 Squad Automatic Weapon or "SAW" light machine gun mounted in the truck bed.

"This was definitely a well planned and executed mission to kidnap him," thought Jessie just as a black cloth bag was suddenly tossed over his head and face, blinding his vision.

The leader directed the others to put Jessie into the back seat of the Hummer where his feet and ankles were shackled and attached to a D-ring that was bolted into the floor. He was then seat-belted in and secured with an armed guard sitting next to him.

The leader motioned to the female of the group and pointed to Jessie's patrol unit. "Quemalo y vete a casa," "Burn it and go home," he ordered. "Si, senor. Claro," the woman smiled.

The female walked back over to her car, popped the trunk and removed a 'Molotov cocktail" incendiary device from the bed. She then walked over to Jessie's patrol unit, opened the driver's side door, ignited the rag and tossed the device inside. The gas-filled bottle immediately exploded into a ball of orange fire.

"Vamos, amigos!" ordered the leader, as all three vehicles containing the heavily armed Tres Paises cartel members and their prize Deputy Jessie Fremont fled back across the border to Mexico.

As per the Sheriff's Office's dispatch officer safety protocol, the dispatcher checked in with her deputy after another ten minutes to make sure he was OK and finished with his call for service.

"Gila-10, Control, 952. Are you 10-8?" There was no response.

"Gila-10, Control. Are you still Code-4?" asked the dispatcher again. Again, no response.

Deputy Jacob Black Arrows in Gila-20 had completed his medical call and got on the air.

"Gila-10, Gila-20, do you copy? Are you Code-4, Jessie?"

Deputy Black Arrows asked over the radio. His inquiry was only met with silence. That immediately worried Black Arrows because Jessie had excellent radio protocol.

"Control, Gila-20. Confirm Gila-10's last 20 was Road 18 around the 9 Mile marker?" the deputy asked.

"Gila-20, Control affirm. I last heard from him about 20 ago. He said he was Code-4, but nothing since," the dispatcher replied.

"Control, Gila-20 copies. Show me enroute to his last reported 20," Black Arrows radioed back.

It took Jacob Black Arrows less than fifteen minutes to speed over to Road 18. At the 6 Mile marker, he immediately saw a faint orange glow of what appeared to be a fire down the roadway that led to the abandoned silver mines property. The deputy's officer safety antennae immediately went up. As Jacob sped faster up Road 18 passing the 8 Mile marker the orange glow loomed larger and the deputy knew something was wrong. He picked up his radio mic.

"Control, Gila-20, start rolling fire and paramedics Code-3 towards my location," the deputy directed.

"Gila-20, Control, what have you got?" the dispatcher asked.

"Not sure control, but we definitely have a fire a couple of miles up Road 18 probably around the 9 Mile marker near the abandoned silver mines village. I can't tell what's on fire, but we haven't heard from Gila-10 yet. He might have been in an accident so I'm not taking any chances right now."

Jacob Black Arrow's request for a fire department and EMS response was a smart move. If Jessie Fremont was alright, Jacob knew he could always cancel fire and the paramedics. However, if Jessie was injured, every minute counted in a rural area such as this and better to have medics on-scene treating Jessie than not.

"Gila-20, Control copies. Dispatching fire and paramedics to your 20 now. Advise your exact 20 upon arrival and status."

"Control, Gila-20 copies. Will do," replied Jacob who was now flying down the dark and dusty Road 18.

As Jacob reached the 9 Mile marker, he spotted Jessie Fremont's sheriff's patrol unit totally engulfed in flames and his heart sank. The flames from the intense fire were reflecting against the twin berms of rocky tailings on either side of the roadway.

Jacob stopped his patrol unit fifty yards behind Jessie's unit and radioed, "Control, Gila-20. Single vehicle fire" Jacob reported vaguely and intentionally. "Keep everyone coming quickly. I'm on Road 18 just a quarter mile north of the 9 Mile marker."

Jacob ran to his trunk and retrieved a fire extinguisher. He then ran towards Jessie's patrol unit which had flames pouring out of every window.

Although Jacob Black Arrows knew his small fire extinguisher was no match for the flames now devouring the vehicle's interior, he had to try. He approached the driver's side of the patrol unit and completely unloaded the extinguisher's chemical fire retardant through the fire shattered driver's side window. The flames briefly abated, but long enough for Jacob to see there was no one in the front compartment of the vehicle. The intense flames drove Jacob back and away from the patrol unit.

Jacob dropped his empty fire extinguisher in the roadway and pulled out his cell phone instead of his hand pack radio, "Control, Gila-20, keep 'em coming Code-3. I'm commencing an immediate area search for Gila-10. Will advise."

Jacob used his hand held flashlight to check both sides of the roadway and then he illuminated both the tall berms, looking for any signs of Jessie. Nothing, no Jessie. Jacob repeatedly called out for his patrol partner but received no response. Now he was really worried.

"Control, Gila-20, I've got no signs of Gila-10. His unit which appears to be empty," Jacob radioed as fire rescue and paramedics arrived on-scene.

The firemen immediately dismounted from their rig and ran a four-inch hose to the car. The engineer charged the hose while two firemen blasted the interior and exterior of the vehicle with water, quickly extinguishing the fire.

Jacob yelled out to the firemen, "Anyone in the unit?"

"No one inside, Jacob," the lead fireman holding the nozzle yelled back as he continued to hit the patrol unit with high pressure water.

Jacob approached Jessie's patrol unit and illuminated the interior with his flashlight. What he saw on the floorboard of the right front passenger seat confused and then worried him. It was Jessie's charred portable radio.

Instead of radioing dispatch, Jacob pulled out his cell phone again and called in. "Control, it's Jacob. Jessie is nowhere to be found and I spotted his hand pack on the floorboard in front. Call Sheriff Fremont and get him out here right away. We have problems. Don't put any of this over the radio from here on out, copy?" he instructed.

"You got it, Jacob. Will do. I'll have the sheriff call your cell and you can fill him in," replied the dispatcher.

Deputy Black Arrows then called out to the fire personnel and paramedics to meet with him over at his patrol unit. The first responders stopped what they were doing and gathered together.

"Listen up people. We now have an active crime scene. This is Deputy Jessie Fremont's unit. He's nowhere to be found. His handpack radio is melted and is laying on the front floor board. This is serious shit.

"As the lead investigating deputy right now, I'm ordering you to not put any of this over the radio. You go dark, got it? You put nothing out about any of our deputies being involved with a fire. Nothing. I'll tell dispatch by cell phone that you are all clearing the scene. We'll get a tow over here after we tape off and process the scene.

"Be careful where you step from now on. Use your flashlights to illuminate the ground. Be careful around other footprints. If you see other sets of prints, call my attention to them. I'm also going to need to photo the bottoms of all of your boots for sole comparisons. Same thing with your rigs. Nothing moves yet until I can photo and separate tire tread marks. Then I'll direct you out of here. Copy?" asked Jacob. The men all nodded affirmatively.

Jessie's head was covered by a hood, and he was effectively 'blind." He was attempting to keep track of time and terrain so that he would have an idea of the direction and type of terrain they were transporting him over.

They had been on the roadway for roughly ten minutes before turning off the paved roadway. Jessie could feel the Hummer he was in leaving the roadway and traversing over bumpy and harsh terrain. They bounced around for another fifteen minutes before the vehicle stopped. Jessie's feet and ankles were unlocked from the D-ring and his seat belt was removed. He was pulled harshly out of the rear passenger seat. He felt the barrel of a rifle in his back pushing him forward as someone grabbed onto his shirt collar from the left side and said, "Vamanos, puto."

Jessie could feel himself walking up the slight incline of a mound with waist-high brush and then down the opposite side. He nearly lost his balance more than once as he and his captors descended to a flat area once more. Then a relatively short walk to wet, sandy soil. He could smell and hear water moving slowly past him, so he knew he was at the bank of a river. He estimated that the walk from the Hummer had taken less than five minutes.

Jessie's thoughts were racing. His first thought was maybe this is where they are going to shoot him in revenge for he and Jacob Black Arrows killing the drug smugglers who had fired upon them. A symbolic execution. But then Jessie thought, these cartel members must have spent considerable time plotting his kidnapping. Their bosses undoubtedly had more important things in mind, but what?

As Jessie was pondering his fate, his English-speaking handler said, "Get into the boat, Gringo." Jessie responded, "Just how am I supposed to do that when I can't see a damn thing?"

Jessie's response was met with two sets of hands lifting him up off the ground and pushing him over the gunnel of *an aluminum flat-bottomed duck boat and into a flat metal seat.* "Sit still and shut up or I'll shoot your ass right here," ordered his handler who then directed his men, "Vamos a llevarlo al otro lado." "Let's get him over to the other side." Jessie understood enough Spanish to know that they must be taking him over to the Mexican side of the river. Mexico! This undoubtedly meant that they intended to use him as a hostage.

Jessie heard and felt at least two other men getting into the boat with him. He then heard paddling and felt the boat moving. The night was still and the river relatively quiet. He could tell that the river at the point they were crossing was not wide because they made landfall on the opposite side of the river within no time.

"Levantalo y sacalo del bote," 'Get him up and out of the boat,' his handler ordered the men. Again, Jessie felt himself being grabbed and lifted out of the flatboat. He was then prodded with the rifle barrel and physically escorted up another brush filled sandy berm and down the other side to another waiting 4x4 vehicle. As before, Jessie's feet and ankles were reattached to a D-ring bolted to the floor and he was resecured to a rear passenger seat with a three-point seat restraint with a guard sitting next to him.

Jessie heard three distinct engines start up and then they were off again on a bumpy and windy dirt road.

Jessie figured that they had been traveling only about thirty minutes more when the 4x4 he was in slowed to a stop. The driver shifted into a low gear and the vehicle began a slow climb up a hill for about two minutes before stopping. Jessie's door was opened, he was unlocked from the D-ring and pulled out of the vehicle.

Jessie felt the now familiar barrel of a rifle harshly pushed into his mid back and heard the commands to walk forward. He felt hands on both sides grabbing onto his biceps to support him as walked up a steep incline of ground which had the distinct feel of crushed rock like the tailings of a mine.

Even with the black bag over his head, Jessie could tell that his captors were taking him into a mine. He could see through the bag some illumination from powerful flashlights piercing the darkness. Next he immediately felt the distinct change in temperature as a cool current of air from inside the mine struck his bare arms. They were definitely entering some type of tunnel thought Jessie.

Jessie's captors escorted him into the tunnel for what seemed a relatively short distance before he was forcefully seated into a wooden chair. His captors affixed prisoner shackles to his ankles, which were then secured and locked to the legs of his chair. At this point the black bag was pulled off of his head. Jessie was immediately blinded by the lights, and he squinted to recover his eyesight. He was right. He was definitely inside an abandoned mine.

CHAPTER 5

"Welcome to your new home!"

"WELCOME TO YOUR new home, Deputy Freeman." I apologize for not being present earlier this evening to meet you, but please allow me to introduce myself now. I am Uberto Urias and as you police are fond of saying, you are in our custody."

Jessie thought carefully before he responded. He was definitely at the mercy of his captors who were no doubt cartel members based upon what he had been told by the gunmen who first took him hostage.

"Well, Mr. Urias, you have the advantage. Who are you and your group? You had an opportunity to kill me earlier, so there must be something that you want from me," Jessie said calmly.

Uberto "Toro" – The Bull - Urias, smiled grandly before he responded. Urias was the chief enforcer of Adolfo Guzman, head of the Tres Paises Cartel. He was only used when a high-profile dirty deed was to be done and he had the complete confidence of his boss.

"You are very perceptive, Deputy Fremont. May I call you Jessie? Jessie is your first name, que no?" asked Urias.

Jessie maintained his calm in responding. It would not bode well for him if he showed any sign of weakness before his captors, but he must be careful to show respect. It would be counterproductive to provoke his captors. His task right now was to remain alive as long as he possibly could since he was well aware that the life expectancy of cartel hostages was usually measured only in hours or days.

"Yes, it is, Senor Urias," replied Jessie smiling without showing the grave concern he was certainly feeling.

"Well, Jessie, I think given the circumstances, we should be on a first name basis. You may call me Uberto. As to your question, yes, my Patron does want something, but not from you. You are tangential in this game we are playing. We actually want something from your father, Sheriff Matt Fremont," said Urias.

"And what would that be, Uberto?" asked Jessie.

"Well, your father has something of great value to my Patron, Adolfo Guzman, who I am sure you know controls the Tres Paises Cartel," replied The Bull.

"Are you referring to the drugs we seized the other night?" asked Jessie.

"Well, Jessie, of course that would be nice, but is not what Senor Guzman wants. The drugs, although an unfortunate loss can be replaced. What my Patron wants is his nephew, Alfredo Montoya Guzman, who was captured during your encounter. You see, "Chuy, as we call him, is the son of Senor Guzman's sister and is his favorite nephew. He wants Chuy back," explained Urias.

"Well, if you already know that the drugs are in the custody of the Feds, specifically the DEA, then you also know that Senor Guzman's nephew is not in our jail, but in the custody of the DEA as well," said Jessie.

Urias again smiled, "Yes, Jessie. We do know that, but where Chuy is housed is not our concern. Our concern is how your father will deliver Chuy back to Senor Guzman. Your father's concern will be twofold. First, how he will get Chuy out of the DEA's custody and returned to us, and second, how he is going to keep his own son — that's you Jessie, alive."

"Second, we want your father's promise that he stops investigating or enforcing anything to do with Tres Paises in Gila County. It ends. No more interference with our activities," said Urias.

Well, there it was in a nutshell. *"I'm toast,"* thought Jessie. *"There is absolutely no way that is going to happen. The DEA and DHS are never going to trade such an important bargaining chip as Chuy*

Guzman for a small time rural county deputy sheriff like me."

Obviously, Jesse couldn't tell The Bull that. He had to stall for time. He was involved in a hostage negotiation and this time *he* was the hostage. Every hostage negotiator knows that no matter what you told the hostage takers, there were three things you never gave them: (1) transportation, (2) guns, and (3) trading one hostage for another. That was the rule, and no one knew it better than his dad, Sheriff Matt Fremont.

The second demand would never sit well with Sheriff Matt Fremont. His father would never give up his war against the Mexican cartels. That would never happen. This wasn't Mexico and former Texas Ranger Matt Fremont wasn't that kind of law enforcement officer.

Without showing any emotion, Jessie responded, "Well, Uberto, you've made it clear that my life may be forfeited if your boss doesn't get his nephew back. So, if you will provide me an opportunity, I'll call the Sheriff and inform him what has transpired and what your demand is. We'll just have to see how he responds.

"Of course, you do realize that since the DEA and Homeland Security are now involved, this will complicate things and it might take some time to arrange," explained Jessie, already trying to buy time."

"A wise offer, Jessie. Just understand that my jefe is not known to be a particularly patient man. He can be quite demanding and insisting when he wants his way. I'll give you that opportunity to reach your father. However, I'm sure that I don't have to remind you of the grave consequences of failing to please Senior Guzman," said Urias while purposefully displaying a look of serious concern, followed by another toothy smile.

Uberto "The Bull" Urias then motioned to one of his men, "Luis, dame una celular de la bolsa," "Give me a cellphone from the bag." The man immediately dug into a duffle bag which was on a nearby table and presented it to Urias. Urias flipped open the cheap "drop phone" which had no GPS function and could not be traced. He then checked to make sure it was activated.

"Remove his handcuffs only," Urias instructed another man who uncuffed Jessie. Jessie brought his hands forward and rubbed his wrists to get his blood circulation going again.

Urias handed the cell phone over to Jessie, "Call your father. No funny business, no police codes, or tricks. Keep the conversation on point." Urias directed.

"Understood," said Jessie as he accepted the cell phone and dialed his father's cell number.

Sheriff Matt Fremont was at the scene and talking with Deputy Black Arrows when his cell phone went off. Fremont looked at the display which only read "Anonymous." Fremont was going to let the call revert to voicemail thinking it to be a robocall but changed his mind and picked it up on the last ring.

"Who's this?" Sheriff answered curtly into the phone.

"Dad, it's Jessie," said Jessie.

"Jessie, what the hell? Where are you? What's going on? Are you OK, son? We're at the scene of your call. You unit was torched," asked Fremont.

"Dad, please listen. I don't have much time to talk, and I can't answer any of your questions. I've been taken hostage by the Tres Paises. They want to make a deal. Adolfo Guzman wants his nephew Chuy back. They want me to tell you that if you don't give Chuy back, they have orders to kill me," explained Jessie.

"Sons of bitches. Who's in charge there? I wanna speak to him," said Matt Fremont.

"Let me see, dad. Hang on a minute," replied Jessie as he motioned with the phone to Urias. "The sheriff wants to speak to you," Jessie said.

"I don't think so," said Urias, but then quickly changed his mind and took the cellphone from Jessie's outstretched hand.

The Bull spoke into the receiver, "I've got your pinche placa son, Senor Sheriff. He's not looking so good right now. The deal here is muy facil. Mi jefe wants his nephew Chuy back. Una vida, per vida. Your son's life for Chuy's life.

"Also, your pressure on Tres Paises esta terminado, comprende? Everything ends. No mas patrols, investigaciones, or arrests. You are looking the other way. Do you understand?" said Urias to Sheriff Fremont.

Sheriff Fremont listened carefully. He took a deep breath and chose his words carefully before speaking slowly back into the phone.

"You and your boss know that there are many moving parts here. Chuy Guzman violated not only New Mexico state laws, but federal laws too. I only have jurisdiction and authority in Gila County. I have absolutely no control over how the feds play things," replied the sheriff.

Uberto Urias chuckled over the phone and looked directly into Jessie's eyes as he spoke into the phone, "Sheriff Fremont, you are far too humble. Your reputation as a former Texas Ranger precedes you. I happen to know that the federales respect you mucho. Bit by bit you have been cleaning up your stinking county and they like that, yes? Well, now you need some motivation. Something to restore your confidence in your ability to make this deal happen. We will be in touch shortly and perhaps after that, you will think of a way to get Chuy back to us," said The Bull before abruptly closing the flip phone.

Sheriff Matt Fremont was thinking of a response when he suddenly heard the loud click on the other end of the line. "Hello? Hello?!" he exclaimed loudly into the phone to no one. "Shit!" he screamed so loud that the men at the scene heard him. Matt Fremont had an angry and worried expression on his face.

Jacob Black Arrows walked over to him. "You Okay, Sheriff?" the deputy asked.

"They've got Jessie. The Tres Paises have got my son, Jacob. He's a hostage and they want to trade him for Chuy Guzman. I don't know who I just spoke to, but I can tell you that these guys aren't fucking around," said Fremont.

"Holy shit. Those pieces of shit. What you gonna do, sheriff?" Jacob asked.

"Well, for one thing, we got keep a lid on this. We have to keep this in-house for now, except for the feds. That means just a need to know for our department. Nothing outside of that. You don't tell any of our guys right now. I'll hold a special briefing.

Absolutely zero outside people can know the cartel has Jessie, you got that?

"Next, I'm gonna have to talk with the feds right away. I have no idea as to how they would handle something like this. These things take time and the cartel guy I spoke with told me that his boss Adolfo Guzman is not a patient man. If we screw this thing up, I'm afraid Jessie's a goner," said the Sheriff.

"Copy that, sheriff. Just let me know what me and the boys can do and consider it done," replied Jacob.

"Well, for now, just handle the scene. Make sure that the scene stays frozen. I'm thinking we are going to have to try to track these guys out of here and try to establish in what direction they might have taken Jessie. Tire tracks and shoe prints, whatever you can find. How are your tracking skills?" asked Fremont.

"Hey, I'm Apache. I can track a rabbit over solid rock if I have to," said Jacob Black Arrows.

"Well, Jacob, you might just need to. You just might," said the Sheriff.

"Well then, I'm gonna stay here till daylight. Better to see the tracks then. Much better to track in daylight. OK if I keep one deputy with me here and we'll release everyone else?" asked Jessie.

"Just do whatever you need to do to make it happen. I'm outta here. I've got to wake a few feds up. We can't waste any time. Call me with any updates," said the worried Sheriff before getting into his unit and leaving.

As a Texas Ranger, Matt Fremont had worked a few kidnapping for ransom cases. While most had a happy ending with the hostage saved and the kidnappers in custody, a couple had not. He had ended up with a dead bank manager in one and dead teen in another. Real professionals could get away with it. It all depended upon the mindset of the kidnappers. Professionals knew the game and how to play it. Non-professionals tended to be desperate and impatient.

Matt knew he was dealing with a transnational cartel, so he was hoping he was dealing with professionals who would think twice before killing a law enforcement officer. However, he also knew that the Tres Paises were the newest, most competitive and therefore most reckless and violent of the border cartels. That gave him concern.

Compounding Matt's concerns were that this time was different. It was his own son who was being held hostage and this was not about money. It was about a trade for a high-value prisoner in federal custody, as well as his promise that he would cease all enforcement activity against the cartel. Matt knew that if he agreed to that, he would have surrendered his county and its innocent citizens to the lawless cartel.

As Matt Fremont sped back to the Sheriff's Office in the darkness, he pondered how he would make his pitch to his friends and colleagues at DEA and Border Patrol to save his only son.

CHAPTER **6**

The Meeting

IT WAS JUST after 0400 hours when Sheriff Matt Fremont returned to his office. He sat for a minute, decided he needed a strong cup of coffee and walked down the hall to grab some. Returning to his desk, Matt pulled out his cell phone and called his DEA liaison Cecil McKenry. On the last ring before going to voicemail, McKenry picked up.

"DEA, McKenry…and this better be important," a sleepy and obviously perturbed voice answered, without looking at the cell phone display.

"Cecil, Matt Fremont here. We need to talk," said Matt.

There was a pause, "Jesus, Matt. What the hell time is it? What's up, somebody dead?" said the agent, trying to shake the cobwebs from a deep sleep out of his head.

"Cecil, I've got serious problems over here in Gila. The Tres Paises have got my son, Jessie and they're holding him hostage," said Matt slowly and deliberately.

An immediate shot of adrenalin shot through Supervising Agent McKenry's body, waking him up. McKenry sat up in bed and turned on his bedstand light.

"Holy shit, Matt. I hate to ask but do you even know if Jessie's alive? Do you have a proof of life?" the agent asked.

"Yes, they let me speak with him, Then I spoke with their guy who made their demands," replied Matt.

"Demands, as in plural? They have more than one demand? Well, besides money, what the hell do they want?" asked McKenry.

"They don't want money, Cecil. Where the hell is a rural Sheriff in a dirt poor county like Gila, New Mexico going to get that kind of money? No, they want to trade Chuy Guzman for Jessie," said Matt.

There was a long pause before the DEA agent responded. "Geeze, Louise, Matt. They want Chuy? For real? Just how do they think that's going to happen?"

"Well, I was hoping that we could go to your people and see if we could work something out," said Matt in a low and measured voice.

"Well, Matt, we've done a lot of good work together since you were the Chief of Rio Brisas and then became Sheriff. The DEA is indebted to you. I also know Jessie, so you should know that I'll bust my hump to do whatever it takes to help you get your kid back.

"For my part, Chuy Guzman is simply a pawn in a chess game between DEA, the U.S. Government and Tres Paises. I play the long game, so while giving up Guzman would be a set-back, it's only a temporary one as far as I'm concerned. I'm all in. Let's talk to the brass this morning and get your kid back. When can you be here?" asked McKenry.

Matt breathed a sigh of relief, "Thanks my brother. It means a lot having your support. I owe ya one. I've got to make another call over to Katie Blackwater at Border Patrol. Then shower, change into a fresh uniform and then it's travel time to you from my office," said Matt.

"Okay Matt. I'll get up and get down to my office. The coffee will be on when you arrive. I'll set up a meet with my boss so we can hit the ground running. See you soon," said McKenry before hanging up.

To buy time before waking up Border Patrol Assistant Chief and sector agent Katie Blackwater, Matt grabbed a fresh uniform out of his closet and headed for the bathroom to shower and shave. He then poured a second cup of black coffee into a large to-go mug and sat back down behind his desk before dialing up Assistant

Chief Blackwater on his cell phone.

Katie Blackwater picked up on the second ring, "Matt? Katie here. What's up?" the Assistant Chief asked in a sleepy voice.

Matt Fremont took a deep breath and began, "Katie, I hate to bug you this early in the morning, but I think you know I wouldn't unless it was something serious. So I'll get right to it. I got a call this morning from my son Jessie. The Tres Paises cartel has kidnapped him, and they are holding him hostage somewhere. No doubt it's probably on their side of the border. Right now Jessie's okay. At least they haven't harmed him where Jessie would tell me. However, I spoke with their representative, and he's told me in no uncertain terms that if we don't trade Chuy Guzman for Jessie, they're going to kill Jessie," said Matt.

"They're not giving me a lot of time to get Chuy back to them, so I'm asking for your help. I've already spoken with SSA Cecil McKenry over at DEA. He's on-board, but I'm driving over to DEA's EPIC facility in El Paso to meet with his boss," explained Matt.

"My God, Matt. That's horrible. When and how did this happen?" asked Blackwater.

"It appears that our office got a 9-1-1 call from a motorist who said she was disabled out on one of our secluded roads. Jessie snagged the call and drove out there. That's all we know right now. Looks like the call was a ruse and Jessie was surprised and kidnapped. We have absolutely no idea where he is right now. What we do know is that Tres Paises has got him. They want to trade Jessie for Chuy Guzman who is the favorite nephew of Adolfo Guzman, who as you know runs Tres Paises," said Matt.

"Adolfo Guzman is bad news. Tres Paises is a renegade cartel made up of some of the worst sociopaths around. The key leadership are several former and very violent MS-13 gang bangers out to make a name for themselves. We've heard from our informants that the primary enforcer for the cartel is a hitman named Uberto "The Bull" Urias. Ice water in that guy's veins. Killed his own brother for skimming profits from the cartel a couple of years back," explained Blackwater.

"Good to know. Can you help me out with DEA, perhaps

some friendly influence. McKenry is on-board. He explained it as Chuy Guzman just being a pawn in the game. I don't want to play a game; I want my only son back," said Matt.

"Hell Matt, the way I see it is that we're all family in law enforcement. I got a son too. I'd be batshit crazy if they kidnapped my son and threatened to kill him. Of course I'll help any way I can. I'm down. Go meet with DEA and I'll call McKenry's boss and use whatever influence I may have to try to get them to agree to release Chuy," said the Border Patrol Assistant Chief.

"Thanks Katie. Appreciate the help. I owe you one. I gotta get going over to El Paso and meet with DEA. Let me know how their SAC and above feel about the trade-off. Always good to get the 4-1-1 from more than one source," said Matt before hanging up.

Sheriff Matt Fremont pulled out of the Sheriff's Office parking lot at 0530 hours and sped down two lane dusty country roads until he reached NM 81. Once he reached NM 9 after passing the town of Hachita, he continued north on NM 146 to the I-10 between Lordsburg and Deming. Matt then turned east towards El Paso, Texas which was about 100 miles away. He pulled into the DEA office compound at 0730 hours and went directly to DEA SSA Cecil McKenry's office. McKenry was waiting for him and directed him to a coffee machine in the lounge.

Once both men had poured their black coffees, SSA McKenry ushered Wade into his office, looked quickly down the hall and then closed the door behind them. The odd behavior did not escape Matt who sat down in a chair opposite of where McKenry sat behind his green metal government desk.

"Thanks for seeing me Cecil with such quick notice," Matt began.

"No problem, amigo," Replied McKenry. "Normally management doesn't waltz into the building until 0830 hours, but I called my new boss, Special Agent In Charge (SAC) Dick Vermillion, gave him a quick heads up on what happened to Jessie, and he's agreed to come in early to discuss the matter."

"McKenry then took a deep breath, furrowed his brow and continued. "As I told you when you called me, I'm all in and behind you 1,000%. Chuy Guzman is a total piece of shit and a drug smuggling enemy of America as far as I'm concerned and I'm not alone on that.

"However, in full disclosure, this may not be an easy negotiation to trade Jessie for Chuy. As you well know, there is a new administration in power that is in complete disagreement with our former President's border policies. It hasn't taken long for the powers that be to force out the Old Guard at several of our tip of the spear federal law enforcement agencies and replace them with lap dogs who will do whatever they are told in order to ascend to higher positions of authority.

"You know the layout since you preside over a what we refer to as a high-impact county. Both the DEA and DHS have been negatively impacted by policy changes," the DEA agent explained.

"The new administration has killed all future construction on the border wall making it as porous as an Italian pasta strainer. The border is wide open with tens of thousands of undocumented aliens – UDA's just walking, wading or swimming across from Mexico, the triangle of El Salvador, Honduras and Guatemala and one hundred and forty-eight other countries every month. DHS, Border Patrol and ICE are overwhelmed. Since the new administration came in, we already have nearly two million UDA's in the U.S. The current administration including the DHS Secretary have turned CBP agents into social workers processing hundreds of thousands of captured UDAs.

"Of course, now the cartels know that their coyotes and human traffickers can do as they please. So, now they are making almost as much money smuggling in people as drugs, But the difference is that no one is doing any time for trafficking humans, where drugs smugglers who bring in weight get twenty years just to start. It's not rocket science."

McKenry continued, "Now this has obviously got to stay between us, Matt. My new boss SAC Vermillion, is what we refer to tongue in cheek as "the New Generation of Leadership at DEA." The guy's got zero field experience. He's a former U.S. Attorney from USDOJ who got bounced when our former POTUS came into office and our Attorney General kindly suggested to all of the libtard U.S. Attorneys that it was time to update their resumes.

"Guys like Vermillion needed a parachute so they went into

private practice, corporate, or found a liberal state that would take them on as a State Attorney or prosecutor.

"Vermillion got picked up as a State Attorney in Virginia where he was from. However, he was also right next door to Washington DC, so he played the odds and became a political donor to candidates who have been since elected to power. His beneficiaries rewarded him with this nice SAC job, and he is already fast-tracking to become Assistant Administrator," said McKenry.

"But everyone in law enforcement hates drugs. Every two years opiates alone kill twice as many people than we lost in Viet Nam in fifteen years. Are you telling me Vermillion may not be on-board with trading Jessie for Chuy Guzman?" asked Matt incredulously.

"No Matt, I'm not saying that. I hardly know Vermillion. He's new here to us. He's an unknown. Seems like a typical paper-pusher. You know the type, "I've got no idea what's going on, so I better ask mamma first," type of boss. What I'm saying is that any trade of Jessie for Guzman might take time. It might be delayed while the consensus builders toss the idea around for a bit," said McKenry.

Matt now had a very worried look on his face as he listened to SSA McKenry tell him about the facts of life in the new DEA.

"Well, Adolfo Guzman's guy has already told me that the cartel boss is not a patient man. I'm really worried about Jessie. Right now, I've got no other choice but to make my case in front of your boss and hope that he sees what's at stake here," said Matt.

The phone on SSA McKenry's desk buzzed. The agent picked up the phone and answered, "McKenry. Yes, he's here. Be right down," and hung up the phone. McKenry looked at Matt. "He's here and ready to see you. Here we go."

McKenry and Matt left the building and walked across the parking lot over to a non-descript beige painted single-story building with a sign that read, "Administration." They walked down the hallway straight to a door with a plaque that read simply, "SAC Richard T. Vermillion." McKenry knocked twice on the door and the men heard a response from inside say, "Come." They entered.

Matt was surprised to find a man who was obviously not

yet forty years of age, dressed in a dark blue suit with a red power tie, sitting behind a large brown mahogany desk. SAC Vermillion did not rise as the men entered the room. He simply bade them to, "Please sit, gentlemen."

Matt offered his hand as McKenry performed the introductions. "SAC Vermillion, may I introduce Sheriff Matt Fremont of Gila County, New Mexico."

As Matt Fremont started to extend his hand, Vermillion responded by simply waving his right hand. Matt could see that Vermillion was not a guy who had been properly trained in gentlemanly etiquette. He quickly sized the SAC up as a Millennial.

"Supervising Agent McKenry informs me that you've got a problem involving your son but was circumspect in deferring to you to tell me what's up, Sheriff. So, exactly what's going on that involves the DEA?" said Vermillion.

Matt figured that he was not going to make any points with a young and inexperienced attorney who didn't even know how to shake hands, so he got right to the point.

"My son Jessie, who is a deputy sheriff in my department has been kidnapped by members of the Tres Paises drug cartel. Jessie had been instrumental in a large narcotics seizure on the border in Gila County. Members of the Tres Paises were smuggling a sizable amount of cocaine and fentanyl across our border river. When Jessie and another deputy attempted to take them into custody, the smugglers opened fire. This resulted in an officer-involved shooting where three cartel soldiers were killed and a player by the name of Chuy Guzman was captured," explained Matt.

"Chuy Guzman is the favorite nephew of Tres Paises Cartel boss, Adolfo Guzman. We believe that he led the smuggling team," offered SSA McKenry.

SAC Vermillion raised his hand like an elementary school crossing guard dismissively as McKenry spoke to interrupt him. The rude gesture was not lost on Matt.

"Continue, Sheriff Fremont," said Vermillion after abruptly silencing McKenry, as if his own agent was a child.

Matt continued, "Well, we have a small county and an even

smaller sheriff's department. I'm sure that Chuy saw Jessie's last name on his uniform and put two and two together to figure out he was my son. It's not a giant leap to figure out how to get that type of information out of any holding facility when you have the pull the Guzman's have. This is Adolfo Guzman's way of getting back at me and getting his favorite nephew back at the same time," he explained.

"Well, what does Guzman want? What are his demands?" asked Vermillion.

"He's got two. First, he wants Chuy back and second, he wants me to lay off of the Tres Paises in Gila County. Meaning they get a free ride to sneak in all of their dope and continue smuggling UDA's including females and kids for the cartel's sex trade," replied Matt.

"I'm surprised he also didn't demand all of his dope back too," cracked McKenry. Vermillion shot the "mad dog" look McKenry's way. Matt saw Vermillion's mean gaze and thought, "Not only an inexperienced kid, but intolerant too."

"So, what's your play, Sheriff Fremont?" asked Vermillion, either apparently oblivious to why Matt would have driven all the way out to El Paso to visit; or being coy and playing the authority figure to make the sheriff grovel.

Inside, Matt was pissed at this bureaucratic peacock, but he bit his tongue. He needed Vermillion's and the DEA's help, or Jessie was a goner. He played the respect, humility and mutual cooperation card.

"SAC Vermillion, the Gila County Sheriff's Department has always assisted DEA and have been at your disposal 24/7 during my tenure as sheriff. Adolfo Guzman will most certainly have my son Jessie executed if we don't trade Chuy Guzman for him. Chuy is a player and cocky. He's just a cog in the Tres Paises wheel. He's not their hub.

"If DEA will extend some professional courtesy and release Chuy, I'll get my son back. We will most definitely catch Chuy again and then it will be on our terms. I can promise you that I and my department will do everything in our power to assist the DEA in recapturing Chuy Guzman moving forward." offered Matt.

"Not to play devil's advocate," said Vermillion playing the devil's advocate, "But what's to prevent Tres Paises from just snagging and/or killing your kid again if we were to give them Chuy?"

Matt held his breath before he spoke. He wanted to get his blood pressure down. Right now, he had almost enough of Vermillion and just wanted to reach across the table, grab him by his red power tie and punch his lights out. He was just hoping that he still had his best poker face on so Vermillion wouldn't notice. Matt responded with the only come back he had,

"Well, I suggest that both of our agencies do our jobs and work together in the spirit of cooperation and focus on grabbing Chuy and knocking down Tres Paises. Then they will be so busy playing defense, they won't have time go on offense and come back on Jessie or any other of our men. What do you say? Can I count on you to help me get my son back home to his wife and family?" asked Matt.

True to form, Vermillion went into full consensus builder mode, "Well, that's a tall order. I'm hearing that Chuy Guzman is a major player. Because he's a favorite nephew of Alfonso Guzman, that gives DEA important leverage. I'm not sure my bosses will want to give him up just like that. I'll have to run this up the command ladder. I'll have to get back to you. You'll hear from us shortly," said the SAC gauging Matt's facial response the entire time he was speaking.

Mentally, Matt checked his poker face in concluding the meeting. One more talking point to press, the most important one of all.

"SAC Vermillion. Thank you for taking the time to hear me out. When you speak with your command, please remind them that time is of the essence. In fact, in this case it's literally a matter of life and death for my son. I've already been told twice by Tres Paises that Alfonso Guzman is not a patient man. I can probably stall them for a very short period of time, but certainly no more than that. I don't mean to time compress anyone, but we're talking my son's life here.

"Please call me 24/7 the moment you hear anything from your superiors. Anything you can do on Jessie's behalf is very much appreciated by our family and my department," said Matt as he stood up. Matt had no intention of trying to shake Vermillion's hand again. What would be the point, he thought.

SSA Cecil McKenry stood up with Matt and addressed his boss. "Boss, thanks for seeing Sheriff Fremont and I this morning. I sure hope we can help get his son back."

"Like I said gentlemen, I'll check with Washington and see what we can do. That's all that I can promise at this point," replied Vermillion in a less than enthusiastic tone of voice.

SSA McKenry showed Matt to the door and then closed it behind them after both men stepped through. Once the door was closed, he tugged on Matt's left arm and directed him back to McKenry's office.

Once Matt and McKenry were back in the agent's office, McKenry closed the door. Matt took one look at his friend and said, "Not the most welcome and supportive conversation. Certainly not a confidence builder. Vermillion's personality and charisma leave a lot to be desired to be sure."

"Once he knew that Jessie's life was at risk, I was hoping that he would have been keener on making a trade. He knows that Chuy's just a pawn in this power game," said McKenry.

"I think you profiled him to me pretty accurately before we even walked in there. I've got a bad feeling in my gut that all we are going to do is burn time and nothing is going to happen from up top. I'm more worried about Jessie than ever. I have to admit I held out hope that Vermillion would be in our camp on this," said Matt.

"Well, don't give up hope. Maybe Vermillion will surprise us and go to bat for Jessie. We'll know soon enough," said Cecil.

"Well, Cecil, that's my number one problem right now; time. I'm not so sure I have much left. I'm going to try to get ahead of this and call Guzman's guy. I'll update him on our meeting this morning and beg for some patience on Guzman's part. A good faith gesture. I'm going to ask him to give us a couple of days. Explain to him that DEA is a bureaucracy and the DEA Director himself is going to have to make the decision. He's got to understand that. I gotta run, partner. No time to waste now," said Matt as he shook McKenry's hand.

"God speed, Matt. I'm praying for you. I promise first thing I hear, I'm on the phone to you, pronto," said McKenry as he watched Matt turn away, walk down the hallway and out of the building.

CHAPTER 7

The Negotiation

AS MATT FREMONT headed back to Las Brisas from El Paso, he pondered his options. The meeting with new DEA SAC Vermillion had not been encouraging. While he tried to be optimistic, Matt knew the new administration's open border policies had significantly emboldened the drug cartels as well as enriched their coffers. Their trafficking of drugs and UDA's had increased astronomically. It was profiting them like never before.

The reality was that deaths of UDAs coming across the border and the amount of drugs entering the U.S. were at unpresented levels. Only the Kool-Aid drinkers and the disengaged public didn't see it. The mainstream media was aware of it but refused to report it. Stories like these just didn't fit their narrative.

The new, progressive administration needed to deflect and redirect negative messaging so the occasional press release of anti-drug trafficking "victories" in part served that purpose. How would giving up a major drug smuggler possibly be seen by the naïve public as a victory?

The murder of one deputy in rural south New Mexico these days was merely a blip on the radar screen. It was a ten second sound bite on the local news. It would never even be reported on CNN or MSNBC. Nope, the DEA would most likely play the odds. The world had changed in the last few years and not to the benefit of law enforcement. Today's message was all about restructuring and defunding law enforcement. Both Chuy Guzman and Jessie were pawns in a power struggle between good and evil. Right now, evil had the upper hand.

Matt was exhausted. He'd been up all night and morning. He decided to call the office to tell them that he would be in later and drive home to update Jessie's wife Josie and his wife Esperanza about his conversation with Vermillion. He would keep an optimistic face and attitude, while at the same time mull over his options. But first, he needed to call Adolfo Guzman's man who was holding Jessie captive.

Matt had saved Adolfo Guzman's representative's cell phone number from his recent calls file. He had created a contact that he simply listed as "Handler." Matt was sure it was a burner phone, without a GPS that couldn't be tracked or bugged. Once he had cleared El Paso and was on the eastbound I-10 with the Mexican city of Juarez over his left shoulder, Matt hit the "recent calls" button and hit the call that simply read "anonymous." A man who's voice he immediately recognized as the "Handler" picked up.

"Dime," (tell me) the man said flatly.

"It's Sheriff Matt Fremont. Are you the man who has my son?" said Matt.

The man's voice changed to a very distinctive and fairly well spoken English. "Ah yes, Sheriff Fremont. We have been waiting for your call. What have you to report?" asked the Handler.

"I want to provide you with an update, but I need proof of life first. Let me speak with my son first," replied Matt.

"Look Sheriff Fremont. That's not how this game is played. You give me the update and then I'll let you speak with your son," said the Handler.

Matt had had a long and stressful past twenty-four hours. He was in no mood to be trifled with right now. He took a deep breath, played the odds and abruptly hung up the phone.

The Handler suddenly heard a distinctive click, and the line went dead. He looked incredulously at his burner phone and swore. Then he called Matt back. Matt let the phone ring three times before picking up the phone again, but he said nothing.

"Sheriff Fremont. I don't think you get this. Tell me..." and then the line went dead again.

Matt's heart was pounding as his cell phone rang again. It was the Handler. This time Matt spoke, "What do I call you?" Matt asked.

"You may call me Toro," the man replied.

"Look Toro, don't for one second think that you have the only playing cards here. I'm trying to be reasonable and I'm tired of playing games. We both have something each other wants. I'm pretty sure that your Jefe Senor Guzman wants his favorite nephew back as much as I want my son back, so quit fucking with me.

"I have important information for you that you and Guzman don't have. I'm only asking for a proof of life. I want to speak with my son. Put him on the phone and we can move forward. Senor Guzman is going to be very angry if he learns that you were playing games and lost an opportunity of getting this information," said Matt.

Matt's boldness and tenacity paid off.

"Espere…Wait, senor sheriff. I will allow you your proof of life," said Urias

Urias was speaking from the abandoned silver mining cave in the Montanas de Plata range just across the border in Mexico. This is where they held Jessie captive. Urias told one of his soldiers to unshackle Jessie from his chair and bring him up to the entrance of the mine where there was better reception to speak on the phone.

After a couple of anxious minutes waiting on the phone, Matt heard Jessie on the other end of the line. Jessie was temporarily blinded by the light at the entrance to the mine. For the first time, he was able to see outside. His immediate view from an obviously elevated position part way up a mountain was a rocky, desert valley populated by scrub and hundreds of saguaro cactus. The closest saguaro to the mine's entrance was uniquely shaped like a cross. He quickly etched the landscape into his mind.

"Dad?" said Jessie.

"Son? Are you alright?" responded Matt.

"Yes, as good as can be expected," replied Jessie

"Jessie, I'm trying to work out an arrangement with DEA

to trade Chuy Guzman for you. We are going to get you back home, son. Can you hang in there a bit longer?" said Matt.

Urias abruptly took the cell phone from Jessie's hand and spoke into it, "Sheriff, you have your proof of life. Now it's time for you to give me the information you say is so important,"

Matt continued to play his hand, "Let me say goodbye to my son and you will have it," said Matt.

"Very well, but only a quick goodbye since it could be your last unless the information is good," said Urias in a veiled threat as he handed the cellphone back to Jessie.

"Jessie, I will tell mom and Josie that you are OK. I promise that I will do everything in my power including off the books to bring you home safely. I love you son," said Matt.

"Copy, off the books, dad," replied Jessie before Urias took the phone from him. "Take him back," directed Urias to his soldier who then removed Jessie from the mine's entrance.

"Now it is your turn, Sheriff. Give me the information and I will decide just how important it is," said Urias.

Matt related to Urias his conversation with DEA SAC Vermillion. However, the sheriff presented a more optimistic picture than he had actually experienced with the bureaucrat. Matt also told Urias to impart to Adolfo Guzman that not unlike the Mexican government, the U.S. DEA was a bureaucratic agency with several levels of command authority. Any deal to trade Chuy Guzman for Jessie would understandably take time.

Matt encouraged Urias to ask Guzman for a few days to get a trade for the men worked out. He reminded the kidnapper that Chuy was being treated well in custody and had not been out of pocket for long. Certainly a few more days would not be much of an inconvenience. Chuy had already invoked legal counsel, so he was not being interrogated by DEA agents.

"As I have already reminded you sheriff, patience is not a virtue of Senor Guzman. I will communicate with him what you have shared with me this morning. Expect my call again with his response shortly," said Urias before the line went dead.

Matt took a deep breath. He had accomplished his objectives for the call to "Toro" Urias and Guzman. Number one was that Jessie was alright and had not been tortured. Next, he had shown good faith to Jessie's kidnappers by keeping Guzman informed of his progress in trying to get Chuy Guzman released from custody. Hopefully, the last objective of buying Jessie more time had been achieved. A few more days for him to press his case with DEA command on trading Chuy for Jessie could end this thing if everything went right. That's all he needed, but would the DEA director agree to the trade? That was the sweat.

Matt Fremont called ahead to his wife Esperanza and asked her to have Jessie's wife Josie meet them at their ranch for an update. He arrived back at his ranch in Las Brisas just before noon.

Matt drove up the dusty, hard packed gravel driveway and through the gates of his compound and parked his Gila Sheriff's Department SUV. He entered the home and found Esperanza and Josie waiting for him in the living room. Esperanza had made coffee for everyone. Understandably, both women looked very concerned when Matt entered the living room.

"How is Jessie? Were you able to speak with him?" both women asked anxiously and simultaneously. Matt put forth his best smile and presented an air of reassurance which was important to do right now.

"Jessie is fine. Yes, they let me speak with him on the phone. Jessie has not been mistreated as far as I can tell," he said.

Esperanza began, "So tell us about your meeting with the DEA over in El Paso this morning. They have agreed to trade that drug smuggler for our boy, right?" she asked.

"Esperanza and Josie, yes, I did have a face to face meeting with the El Paso office DEA Special Agent In Charge. He's a guy named Vermillion. I had a three way meeting with Supervising Agent Cecil McKenry who I've known for years. Vermillion who is a new manager there. I made our case for a trade for Chuy Guzman for Jessie. Vermillion listened and I thought that our meeting was productive.

"It's pretty damn complicated. As you know, there is a new federal administration in place. The President has appointed his

VP "Border Czar" and made them responsible for all border issues. Literally all of the federal law enforcement agencies including DEA, DHS, Border Patrol, ICE and the USDOJ are under new management. The DHS, Border Patrol and DEA are the law enforcement components involved with Jessie's kidnapping. The President and VP have made sure that the heads of these agencies are all in lockstep with the President's Open Borders agenda.

"It's all very bureaucratic with multiple levels of command at DEA. So, a unique request to trade a heavy weight drug smuggler like Chuy Guzman for Jessie takes special consideration and time. DEA has to weigh their options. However, I didn't get any pushback so far from SAC Vermillion," explained Matt, trying to provide some optimism.

Jessie's wife Josie looked at Matt with tears in her eyes. "I don't understand why they have to weigh their options. People like Chuy Guzman are sleaze bags. The cartels have thousands of them in their employ and the DEA has hundreds of them in federal custody. One drug smuggler is nothing to the DEA when we are talking about my husband, an American and a law enforcement officer. Why can't they simply agree right now to a trade?" she asked.

Josie was a wonderful and very supportive wife to Jessie. Matt and Esperanza considered her almost like a daughter. To see the pain she was going through and tears in her eyes was rough. The emotional roller coaster they were all experiencing right now was traumatic, even for a tough former Texas Ranger like Matt.

Matt could see Esperanza's expression of anger and frustration. In reality, things right now were what they were. He replied, "With this new administration's open border policy towards immigration, they have emboldened the cartels. Not only UDA's but tons of drugs are pouring across our southern border that are killing tens of thousands of Americans . There is a lot of pressure to reduce drug trafficking, but DEA and DHS are overwhelmed with the UDA invasion of our southern border.

"DEA command has to balance releasing a known drug smuggler and any political and media blowback from that, against saving the life of a peace officer. In the end, it will be a political, not an ethical or moral decision. However Josie, I give you my solemn promise that I will do everything in my power to get our Jessie back. You can count on that," said Matt.

"I know you will Matt. I trust you. I just want my Jessie back home where he belongs," said Josie as she put her hand up over her mouth and broke out in tears.

Esperanza immediately went to Josie and embraced her while looking over Josie's shoulder at Matt. "Sweetheart, why don't you go into the bathroom to freshen up while I talk with Matt. I know Matt is doing everything he can do right now to help to get Jessie back to us." she said.

When the sobbing Josie left the living room, Esperanza approached Matt. Matt saw Esperanza's expression as she approached. Matt and Esperanza had been through a lot together. It was not easy being a law enforcement officer's wife. There had been trials, tribulations and sacrifices along the way during their marriage, but certainly nothing to compare with this.

Esperanza was a beautiful Hispanic woman who had a character that was uniquely strong and resilient. Matt had come to know that she had a long fuse, but once lit, there was little anyone could do to stop her fiery temper from exploding. His wife's expression told Matt that the match was dangerously close to that fuse right now.

Esperanza looked back towards the bathroom to ensure that Josie was still inside. She then came face to face with Matt and took both of Matt's hands in hers. Esperanza looked directly into her husband's eyes and spoke in a low, but assertive voice,

"Mi amor, I know that you are doing everything you can right now to return our son to us. But as your wife of many years, I also know that a sheriff can only do so much when dealing with this new government who has betrayed all of us. You have a good poker face, but I know your heart and soul. You are not optimistic about the DEA doing the right thing. I can see it. We may not get Jessie back as a result of anything they do. So as your wife and Jessie's mother, I will say this one time only.

"Do whatever you have to do to bring our son home. I don't care and I will never ask what you did. I don't care what you do or how you do it, but Jessie is our life. He is the future of our family and in this family, blood, love and loyalty to family is all that matters.

"I mean it Matt, do whatever it takes. Do whatever you have to do. Do you understand what I'm saying to you? And if so, we will never speak of this again," said Esperanza.

Matt looked directly back into his wife's eyes. This was the first time in all their years of marriage that he had ever seen this particular expression on her face or heard this tone in her voice. Esperanza had distinctly stressed in her tone the singular word, *"whatever."* Any Texas Ranger knew what that meant, and Matt was already prepared for the "whatever it takes" option.

"Mi amor, I understand. I promise you as God is my witness that I will do whatever it takes to bring Jessie back home. We will be a family once again. I promise you on my life," replied Matt as he embraced and kissed his wife reassuringly.

Matt continued, "I've been up for almost twenty-four hours, and I need to get some sleep for a few hours. I think I've bought us two or three days with Tres Paises. I'm going to give the DEA another day to mull this over and then make a decision on how to get our Jessie back.

"But understand this, after all my years of rangering, if DEA lets us down, things are going to move quickly, and it won't be pretty. You may not see me for a while, and you and Josie need to be prepared for some fallout. Let's see what direction things will go and we'll plan from there. Now, I've got to get some rest. You take care of Josie and I'll take care of our son. Wake me in four hours and please have a meal ready for me so I can hit the ground running," explained Matt.

Matt embraced his wife once more and headed off to the bedroom. As soon as his head hit the pillow he was out cold.

CHAPTER 8

Betrayal

OCTAVIA CABRAL WAS a 32 year old Hispanic firebrand Congresswoman who represented the 2nd Congressional District of New Mexico. This district was comprised of the southern border counties of Hidalgo, Grant, Luna, Gila, Dona Ana, Otero, Lincoln, Eddy and Lea. The easternmost border of her district shared state lines with the Great State of Texas at El Paso.

Cabral, who was known by her constituents, the media and her immense number of social media followers simply as "OC," had been elected two years before the new Progressive Left administration had come into power.

Cabral had made her bones as a university student revolutionary Marxist activist. "OC" had been a well-known political activist on campus at the University of New Mexico in Albuquerque. She had been elected as President of the UNM Student Union which she had ruled over with an iron hand. She had also become the self-appointed Chapter President and Chief Organizer of a group she founded called Students for Social Justice. OC was well-known to the Albuquerque Police Department and other law enforcement agencies along the state's southern border as an entitled, pain in the ass, unethical rabblerouser.

Octavia had obtained her bachelor's degree in political science and a Master's in ethnic studies from UNM. Trained and indoctrinated at an early and impressionable age by Marxist professors, OC had readily embraced Marxist ideology. She had learned well the lessons of Lenin, Fidel Castro, Che' Guevara and Saul Alinsky. She had practically memorized Alinsky's socialist treatise, *"Rules for Radicals."*

Octavia preferred the less regimented form of Cuban and Central American Marxism to the stricter and harsher Mao-based forms of Communism found in China and North Korea. Since she was Hispanic and her district was over eighty percent Spanish-speaking, the Castro Communist model, with the radicalism of Che' appealed to her. The talking points of Alinsky were easier to apply and sell to her Hispanic constituents. The revolutionary, radical communism of Che' resonated with the younger and more impressionable "Social Justice Warrior" students and millennials who followed her on Twitter, Instagram, Snap Chat, YouTube and Tik Tok.

"Politically astute," was an accurate description for Octavia Cabral. She was the youngest freshman Congresswoman ever elected to the House of Representatives. Fluent in Spanish, with a dedicated following of a similar minded leftist radical student population, OC had cleverly built up a base of community organizers. She had personally schooled her most ardent followers and community organizers in Marxist revolutionary activism.

Even though there was a minority population of blacks in southern New Mexico, OC had early on developed a strategic partnership with Black Lives Matter. This partnership was not because Cabral cared anything for black lives, but because the BLM movement was a radical Marxist-inspired movement that resonated for "social justice warriors" in need of a virtue signaling outlet.

Octavia Cabral had quickly adopted the BLM's "4-D's" anti-law enforcement strategy of Distance, Disenfranchise, Defund and Dissolve law enforcement. OC found the BLM's 4-D scheme perfect for her personal political goals to force the new administration to pull way to the left. Her goals in part included stopping the construction of the prior administration's border wall, so that more Hispanics from Mexico and Central America could gain illegal access to the U.S.

In order to unseat an older white male, moderate, four-term Democratic Congressman, Octavia Cabral needed money; lots of money. She knew that the impoverished Hispanics and students could not put together the funding needed to wage a successful campaign against an entrenched Congressman who had a well-established funding base made up of agri-businesses and wealthy donors.

However, during the very early stages of her campaign, Octavia was approached by representatives of the same international billionaire who was funding the BLM and other progressive leftist and Marxist leaning politicians throughout the U.S. This businessman who held dual citizenship in the U.S., was famous for funding Marxist organizations and revolutionaries world-wide. A meeting was arranged in New York City for OC and this "philanthropist" to meet, and a deal was soon struck.

Suddenly, out of seemingly nowhere, Congressional candidate Octavia Cabral's campaign coffers were overflowing with money. Octavia's campaign coffers quickly tripled the money in her opponent's campaign chest. Cabral quickly applied the new funds to hiring experienced political strategists referred to her by her international benefactor. The new funds allowed her to bring in hundreds of student and neighborhood campaign organizers and workers.

Octavia's Internet social media specialists quickly blitzed social media with campaign ads. After that, Octavia "OC" Cabral never looked back and was elected to office in a landslide victory. The poor white former Senior Congressman never knew what hit him. After the November elections, it was "Congresswoman Octavia "OC" Cabral."

The elderly Madam Speaker of the House was stupefied when Cabral had apparently come out of nowhere to unseat her Democratic rival. Immediately following the election, the Speaker arranged a meeting with OC. Historically, this was a self-serving get together with the newly elected members of the house. During these introductory meetings, the Speaker demonstrated the power of her office and set down the "ground rules of service."

Octavia Cabral was more than ready for her meeting with the Speaker. She arrived at the Speaker's office with two of the lesbian founders of the BLM movement and an internationally famous female singer worth half a billion dollars who had tens of millions of social media followers. Madam Speaker was completely caught off guard. OC made it abundantly clear to the Speaker that it was her army of radical, socialist followers, social media and money that would be setting the future tone of Congress and not eighty-plus year has-beens.

At the end of the meeting, it was the Speaker who was intimidated and Cabral who set the ground rules of service. The Hispanic firebrand walked out of her meeting with the Speaker with a bargained for plum assignment on the House's Subcommittee on Southern Border Relations.

Two weeks after assuming office, Octavia Cabral was invited to a meeting at one of Washington DC's poshest restaurants where she met with two very nicely dressed Hispanic men representing a multi-national venture capital conglomerate based in Mexico City. In reality, the "businessmen" were underbosses of the Gulf, Sinaloa and Juarez transnational drug and human trafficking cartels. An agreement was reached for Octavia to continue to press legislation needed to destroy the previous administration's border wall, as well as removing all of the past President's executive orders keeping undocumented aliens from entering the United States.

After the meeting with the two men, Octavia Cabral returned to her slick, expensive Tesla 300-S sedan which had been valet parked. In the trunk of her vehicle was a aluminum suitcase containing $200,000 in unmarked U.S. currency. Just a small down payment of things to come she was assured. Congresswoman Octavia Cabral had been in office just over two weeks and she was already bought and paid for by the drug cartels.

Octavia Cabral wasn't the only freshman Congressperson elected to office in the mid-term elections. Along with Octavia was another newbie up and comer from the socialist Progressive Left. Enter Charles "Chico" Silvers, youngest son from a wealthy and powerful oil family in Southwest Texas. Charles's path into politics wasn't much different from OC's.

After high school, Charles had attended the University of Texas – Austin, where he majored in political science and pre-law studies. Charles chose not to follow in his father's footsteps working in the family's oil business like his two older brothers. Instead Charles's radicalization to socialism drew him away from a lifestyle of wealth and privilege, to "social advocacy."

After graduating with a bachelor's degree in political science, and a hefty donation to Baylor University in Waco, Charles was accepted into Baylor's law school.

While at Baylor, Charles's many socio political causes

proved a bit too distracting for the law student. He had twice taken and failed the Texas State Bar Exam. While waiting to take the bar again, Charles had an epiphany. He moved into one of the family's homes in El Paso to work on homeless and immigration causes in the large border city.

Charles was an enthusiastic advocate for the homeless and undocumented aliens (UDA's) in El Paso. He quickly established a reputation in the media and in social justice circles in the city as a tenacious warrior for the oppressed masses. It wasn't long before Charles was being invited by various student groups and organizations at the University of Texas – El Paso to make presentations and speeches. By then Charles had adopted the Hispanic nickname "Chico," in an attempt "to blend in" with the Hispanic community. Since the majority of American voters were largely uninformed, the nickname "Chico" resonated with Hispanics as one of their own, even though Charles was as white as rice.

The newly branded "Chico," used his popularity among the student and Hispanic population, as well as a Progressive Left socialist platform to reform city politics as a political springboard to get him elected Mayor of Texas' third largest city. Following an uneventful two-year term as Mayor, Charles "Chico" Silvers announced his candidacy for Congressman in the 16th Congressional District which comprised El Paso and its outlying suburbs.

Of course Charles's family monetarily backed their son's campaign with some of the family's oil fortune. It just made good sense since oil and energy was big business in Texas and Congressmen in Texas legislate in favor of Big Oil. However, as campaigns go, Charles found himself in need of even more money to unseat another long- entrenched Republican opponent. His opponent would not go down without a fight and that made running for his seat expensive.

Unlike Octavia Cabral, the representatives of the Gulf and Juarez cartels didn't waste any time in contacting Charles through intermediates. Juarez shared the southern Texas border with the U.S. at El Paso and the current Republican Congressman Charles was running against was a "Build the Wall" and anti–illegal immigration advocate. A meeting was soon arranged at an expensive restaurant in Scottsdale, Arizona. This was neutral territory where it was doubtful that Charles or the cartel representatives would be recognized.

On the evening of the meeting over an expensive dinner and drinks, an agreement was reached that the cartels would heavily finance Charles's campaign through shell corporations in the U.S. Before even being elected to Congress which Charles eventually was, he had sold his soul and those of tens of thousands of Americans and UDA's to the international drug and human trafficking cartels for thirty pieces of silver.

Freshman Congressman Charles "Chico" Silvers was assured by the cartels that the money would continue to flow into his secret Swiss and Grand Cayman bank accounts as long as he played ball. The arrangement was that he would do everything he could to keep The Wall from being built and the U.S. – Mexico southern border wide open so drugs and UDA's could pass through.

Freshman Congressman Charles "Chico" Silvers and Congresswoman Octavia "OC" Cabral met while attending' the first Freshman Congressperson's Dinner and Dance at the upscale Lyle Hotel in downtown Washington DC and it was lust at first sight. After that, the conspiracy to obstruct and keep the southern border open and the flow of dark money into their secret bank accounts would continue. So would their betrayal.

CHAPTER 9

Package for Sheriff Fremont

SHERIFF MATT FREMONT had given the DEA two precious days to dialogue, consensus build, and all of the other bullshit federal bureaucrats need to do to cover their asses to make it appear that they were trying to do the right thing.

On the morning of the third day bright and early at 0700 hours, Matt hit DEA SSA Cecil McKenry's name on the speed dial of his cell phone. The special agent picked up on the second ring.

"Matt, not surprised to hear from you this morning," said McKenry.

"Well, your boss Vermillion said he needed 48 hours to present our case to the DEA command staff and I've given the DEA more than that. What do you know?" asked the Sheriff, knowing that if he hadn't heard from his friend, the news was going to be bad.

"I haven't heard anything as yet. You know I would have called at the first news of anything positive," replied McKenry.

"Thought so. Well, give me Vermillion's direct line and I'll call him as soon as he gets into the office. Will you buzz me when he gets in?" asked Matt.

"Sure. I know his secretary. She's cool. I'll call her and tell her to ring me when he walks into his office. I promise you'll be the first call he receives. He'll never know how you knew he was in," said the agent who then gave the Sheriff SAC Vermillion's direct line number.

"Appreciate it. Thanks for the heads up. I'll let you know what he says," said Matt before hanging up.

At 0835 hours, Matt's cell rang while he was working on his second cup of black coffee in his office. He saw it was Cecil McKenry and picked up on the first ring.

"He's in. Call him now," said Cecil before hanging up.

Matt had already put SAC Vermillion's direct line into his contacts on his cell phone. He punched up "DEA SAC-V" and the line rang. Vermillion picked up and immediately regretted it.

"SAC Vermillion," he answered.

"Sheriff Matt Fremont here. So this is the morning of Day Three SAC Vermillion. How did you make out with DEA command in DC regarding my son's hostage situation," asked Matt directly.

Vermillion could immediately hear the tone of Matt's voice and knew there wasn't going to be any preliminary small talk. The Sheriff had gotten right to the point. There was a brief pause, Vermillion cleared his throat and replied.

"First of all, Sheriff, I want you to know that we held extensive discussions within DEA at the highest levels of command, including with the Director. I pled your case to the best of my ability," Vermillion lied.

"In the end, it was the decision of the Director that Chuy Guzman is just too much of a high value target to release. Plus the fact that command does not believe that Adolfo Guzman can be trusted to keep his word. Unfortunately, it is command's belief that they would not release your son even if we kept our part of the bargain. I'm sorry," explained the SAC, adding a brief apology.

"Are you guys kidding me? You're refusing to trade that drug smuggling piece of shit for my son who is an American law enforcement officer?" said Matt incredulously, his patience nearly gone.

"Look Sheriff. I know and appreciate that you're upset. This is undoubtedly very stressful and frustrating time for you. I'm sorry for your situation. But I'm only one agent. I don't make the rules here. I have to follow orders like everybody else. The final decision was made way above my pay grade," said Vermillion, obviously trying to weasel out of it.

Matt Fremont was so angry on the other end of the phone, that he found it hard to respond. But he kept his anger boxed up for this useless conversation with the weak-kneed kiss-ass bureaucrat.

"This was not what I expected from a law enforcement agency of my own government. I expected better. My son put his life on the line doing DEA's bidding. If it wasn't for my son and our deputies, you wouldn't even have Chuy Guzman or literally a boat load of dangerous drugs. Just know this. This won't go down well with my men and my family. DEA is now forcing me to rely upon my own devices and that's exactly what I'm gonna do," said Matt without raising his voice.

"I'm sorry you feel that way, Sheriff. I would respectfully caution you against doing anything rash. If there is anything else I or DEA can do…," said SAC Vermillion over a dead cell phone line. Sheriff Matt Fremont had already hung up.

Matt Fremont set his cell phone down on his desk and took a couple of long, deep breaths. He momentarily felt sick to his stomach. He would have to tell Esperanza and Josie what Vermillion said.

However, first he had to think about how he was going to explain this to "Toro" who he had negotiated holding off any decision to harm Jessie for 48-hours while he worked with DEA to arrange a trade of Chuy Guzman for his only son. Matt had taken a sip of now tepid coffee and was staring up at the ceiling when his secretary rang his office phone.

"Sheriff, there's a package here for you that was just delivered," she said.

"Be right out in a second," replied Matt as he put his coffee cup down, took another deep breath and sighed despondently.

Matt walked out to his secretary's desk, and she picked up a small box packaged in brown paper bag type wrapping, scotch tapped up with a simple address written with a black Sharpie that simply read, "Sheriff Matt Fremont, Gila County Sheriff's Department." There was no postage nor any return address on the package which was very light.

"Who delivered this?" asked Matt.

"Never seen him before, Sheriff. Just an English-speaking Mexican fella in his thirties. Nothing special about him. He just walked in and asked if you were working today. I said you were, but you were on the phone and busy. Then he asked me to get this package to you and he left. I asked him his name, but he just walked out the door and was gone. Just like that," replied Matt's secretary.

"Thanks," replied Matt before walking back to his office with the curious package. The package was about a third the size of a shoe box, but not as high. The Sheriff was not expecting any packages so having someone unknown delivering it surprised him.

Matt sat down at his desk, took out his pocket knife and used it to cut through the tape and brown colored packaging material. Once the paper covering was removed, Matt found a white colored box similar to what jewelry would be packaged in.

Matt opened the box, looked inside and was immediately horrified. Wrapped carefully in white bloody tissue paper was a severed left ring finger. Also inside the box was a wedding ring and a black flash drive. A small card also inside the box provided a simple three word instruction, "Watch the video." Matt immediately recognized the wedding ring as Jessie's. His heart sank.

Matt used a pen on his desk to pick up and examine the bloody wedding ring. He didn't want to tamper with any forensic evidence just in case. He then carefully replaced the ring back into the box with the finger.

Next, Matt went back into his desk, pulled a pair of latex gloves out of one of the lower desk drawers and put them on. He found a long pair of tweezers in the top center desk drawer and used these to pick up and examine the black flash drive. The drive had no brand but was inscribed with "4.0 GB" which indicated that the device was a four gigabyte flash drive.

Matt left his office, walked down the hallway to a door marked, "Evidence/Property" and obtained a DNA test kit. He took the kit and returned to his office and then closed and locked his door. He then picked up his phone and simply told his secretary, "No calls or visitors for the next hour, please."

Even in his anger and despondency, Sheriff Matt Fremont

maintained his focus and professionalism. A serious crime had been committed, he had key pieces of evidence and this evidence needed to be processed immediately and properly before anything else. That's just the way it was. This was family, so no way Matt was going to trust anyone but himself at this point to process this evidence. Depending upon what he found, other forensic professionals could always expand upon whatever evidence he collected to identify any suspects involved in his son's kidnapping, torture, or God forbid Jessie's death.

Matt now regretted handling the package and its wrapping. But how would he have been expected to know what the contents within the package contained. He carefully photographed the brown colored packaging, the scotch tape, white jewelry box, tissue paper, Jessie's wedding ring and the black flash drive.

Next, Matt used several evidence Q-tips to swab each item of evidence separately and then package them separately for DNA. He was careful to only swab the bottom side of the flash drive so he could also attempt to retrieve a fingerprint off of the top side of the device if he was lucky. When this was done, he left his office and walked back down the hallway to the evidence/property room.

Once back at the evidence/property room, Matt prepared the Super Glue fingerprint booth and obtained a card board evidence box. Matt returned to his office, carefully placed all of the items from the package into the box and walked everything down to the evidence/property room. Once inside, he locked the door for privacy.

Matt obtained a UV light to first check the items for any oil-based fingerprints. It appeared that there might be some decent fingerprints on the paper bag packaging and a couple of partial prints on some of the scotch tape used to secure the lid of the white jewelry box and on top of the flash drive. Matt used his tweezers to painstakingly remove the tape away from the white box lid. Thankfully, the card stock of the white box lid was not as porous as its paper packaging, so he was successful in removing the tape for examination.

Next, Matt carefully placed Jessie's wedding ring, the white box, black flash drive and paper packaging into the glass "hood" compartment. He opened a fresh container of Super Glue and placed onto a dish in the glass compartment and closed the door to allow for the vapors of the Super Glue to be released to float around. The glue vapors would naturally adhere to any fingerprints found on the items where they would then be photographed. Any photos of the prints would then be enhanced for identification purposes. Matt's many years of forensic training as a Texas Ranger was definitely coming in handy right now.

After over an hour, Matt was able to successfully recover a couple of full prints off of the brown packaging material as well as a couple of partials off of the sticky side of the scotch tape that he had removed from the white card board jewelry box lid. Matt was especially pleased to find that he had recovered a fairly decent thumb print off of the top side of the black thumb drive. "I may have you now, you bastard," Matt thought as he looked at the white outline of the Super Glue vapors which had adhered and then dried, identifying the loops and swirls of two-thirds of a thumb print off the drive,

Finally, Matt used a 35 mm SLR digital camera to thoroughly enhance and photograph all of the fingerprints and items of evidence. The DNA swabs would have to be processed separately at the New Mexico State Police forensic lab in Santa Fe. He would assign one of his deputies to personally drive the swabs up there. Then he would call in a favor to make sure that the swabs were expeditiously processed. If there was any chance to identify anyone associated with Jessie's kidnapping, torture or murder, he would want to know that before anyone else.

Matt personally packaged, tagged and logged all of the items of evidence separately. The bloody tissue and Jessie's wedding ring were packaged in separate small card stock evidence boxes to further air-dry. One never placed bloody clothing or paper items into plastic where mold and other bacteria could grow and ruin the evidence. He placed the severed finger into a separate box which would be placed into the evidence freezer.

After processing all of the evidence, Matt returned to his office with the black flash drive. He donned yet another set of latex gloves and carefully inserted the flash drive into a laptop computer with anti-virus software to make sure that the flash drive was not a ruse to crash all of the Sheriff Department's computers, while at the same time retrieving and transmitting their sensitive information. The laptop anti-virus software advised that the flash drive was clear of any damaging viruses.

Next came the hard part; actually playing the singular video file on the drive. Matt took another deep breath, said a prayer and opened the file using Media Player. What followed was one of the most troubling videos he had ever watched in his law enforcement career.

As the video opened, his son Jessie, dressed in his Sheriff's Department uniform appeared. It was obvious that the video had been filmed using a cell phone camera. The video was hand-held, not stabilized and the sound quality was poor and echoed.

As the video began, Matt observed Jessie to be seated in a chair with straps restraining his upper body to the chair. Zip ties restrained his forearms and wrists to the arms of the metal chair. Jessie's ankles were shackled and additionally zip tied to the legs of the chair. Jessie had a black cloth bag over his head.

Two men with black balaclavas covering their faces except for their eyes were wearing load bearing military vests filled with 7.62 x 39 extended magazines and holding AK-47's. The men were positioned on either side of Jessie. A man speaking off camera had the voice which Matt immediately identified as that of Jessie's handler, "Toro."

The video began with Toro directing one of the men in Spanish to remove the covering off of Jessie's head, Matt saw that Jessie appeared understandably disheveled and obviously sleep deprived. Matt saw Jessie blinking into the artificial bright lights. He could hear the low but distinguishable sound of a gas powered generator in the background. The generator was obviously being used to power the lights and perhaps other electronic equipment. That was an important clue that indicated that Jessie was being held in some remote, rural location and was not within a small town or city with readily accessible electricity.

Toro began, "This video is for Gila County New Mexico Sheriff Matt Fremont. Pay close attention."

Toro next addressed Jessie with a brief instruction, "Tell them your name," he said.

Jessie responded in a low, strained and raspy voice, "Corporal

Jessie Fremont, Gila County Sheriff's department."

Toro continued, "Sheriff Fremont. The Tres Paises cartel has been patient in trying to work with you on the return of Chuy Guzman for your son here. We have given you more time than you deserve. Yet, you have failed so far to honor your word that you would convince your government to trade Chuy for your son. Is this not so?"

As Toro spoke, Matt stared at Jessie's face. Jessie was looking stoically directly into the camera. The lights appeared to be very bright, and Jessie was repeatedly blinking as he focused forward. Toro continued.

"Well, perhaps some motivation is needed so that you see that Senor Guzman is quickly losing his patience. He thinks that it is now time for a demonstration that will attract your attention," said Toro as he stepped forward.

As Toro spoke, Jessie continued blinking. Matt noticed that his son appeared to be sweating. Perhaps he was blinking to keep the salty sweat out of his eyes.

Toro was dressed all in black with a black balaclava over his head with just his piercing black eyes visible. He was holding a pair of one-handed stainless steel garden pruning shears in his right hand.

"Watch closely Sheriff Fremont," said Toro as he stepped in front of the camera. "The Bull" used his left hand to grab onto to Jessie's left hand which was secured to the arm of the chair with zip ties. He then spread Jessie's fingers apart, exposing the deputy's left ring finger. Urias moved Jessie's wedding ring down between the first knuckle and the hand, while he maneuvered the trimming shears blade open between the ring and the first knuckle. Jessie and Matt knew what was going to happen next. Matt could see he son tensing up, but strangely, Jessie continued to focus on the camera lens while blinking faster.

As a father, Matt had to close his eyes momentarily to keep from seeing his son tortured like this. He then heard Jessie scream out in intense pain as his son's captor cleanly severed Jessie's ring finger from his left hand. Jessie's wedding ring fell to the floor as the end of his severed finger spurted blood.

However, the torture wasn't over yet. As Matt opened his eyes, he saw Toro next take a white hot steel poker and apply the burning tip to the severed end of Jessie's ring finger. Cauterizing the end of Jessie's ring finger made his son cry out in even more pain. Jessie was now taking in deep breaths of air while groaning loudly. Yet, he continued to looking into the camera lens while blinking.

As Toro moved off camera, he resumed his instructions.

"Senor Guzman generously gives you three more days to reach an agreement with your DEA to trade Chuy Guzman for your son. After that time, we will mail your son home to you in small pieces. Do you like your gift? Remember, you have only three more days," and then the video ended abruptly.

Gila County Sheriff Matt Fremont sat for a moment gazing at a blank computer screen. He was trying to wrap his head around the events of the last five minutes as unveiled in the video of his only son Jessie being horribly tortured before his eyes. Matt then turned off the computer, removed the black flash drive, took a deep breath and slowly exhaled.

After a minute to recapture his senses, Matt picked up his cell phone, punched in the name "Wade Justus" and waited as the phone rang.

CHAPTER 10

When Left to Our Own Devices

IT WAS A bright sunny Spring morning on the banks of the Guadalupe River ten miles outside of Boerne, Texas, Wade Justus was on horse-back at the river's edge gazing across the river on his ranch at a couple of his bucking bulls who were munching on some tall grass. As always when he was at this location, he imagined his dear wife Helen at his side, and they were riding range together. His faithful dog Desi was hunting the cedar elm trees nearby for squirrels and any winged game she might flush.

Wade's thoughts were abruptly interrupted by his cellphone ringing from inside his saddle bag. He reached back to grab his phone and looking down at the display, he saw the name "Matt Fremont." Wade smiled and picked up.

"Well Matt, to what do I owe the pleasure of this call," said Wade as he smiled while taking the call from his old Texas Ranger senior partner and mentor.

"Hi Wade. Got a minute?" asked Matt Fremont.

Wade immediately noted the absence of Matt Fremont's usual friendly banter and the somber tone in his good friend's voice. "Sure Matt. I always have time for you. What's up," asked Wade.

"Wade, apologize for any bad timing but I've got something serious to discuss. I'm afraid I'm gonna be asking you for a big favor that you are absolutely free to turn down, cause it's a biggie," said Matt.

"Well, first of all, nothing I would do for you would be considered to be a favor. You really don't even have to ask me because whatever it is, you know I'm gonna say yes," replied Wade.

"Well, I appreciate that Wade, but you had better listen to this request first , because it's very serious or I would do it myself. It's about your God son Jessie," explained Matt.

"Has something happened to Jessie? Is he OK?" asked Wade with a serious tone.

"As a matter of fact, something bad has happened to Jessie. He's in deep trouble. Cartel kinda trouble. Jessie interdicted a big drug shipment coming across the Rio Brisas in our jurisdiction. There was a shootout and some of their guys were killed. Jessie captured a lone survivor; a guy by the name of Chuy Guzman. This Chuy character happens to be the favorite nephew of the cartel boss. This boss's name is Adolfo Guzman and apparently, he's a badass.

"A couple of days ago, the cartel set Jessie up on a ruse call and then kidnapped him. They've got Jessie stashed somewhere, but so far we don't know where. We had to turn Chuy Guzman over to DEA because of the amount of dope we recovered. With the cartel trying to sneak it over our U.S. border, it automatically became a DEA case, and I lost jurisdiction. Now Adolfo Guzman is pressuring me to work out a trade with the DEA for Jessie with Chuy Guzman.

"Chuy's just a pawn in the whole game here. He's definitely not a big player. But I think due to all the bad shit the current federal administration has created with their failed border policy, they aren't willing to work out a trade for Jessie with Guzman. My son Jessie's in the middle of this cluster fuck and they have been torturing him to how they say, "motivate" me to convince DEA to play ball with them," explained Matt.

"Sweet Jesus. They're torturing Jessie? How do you know that?" asked Wade.

"The bastards sent me a package today. It had Jessie's severed ring finger, his wedding ring and a flash drive with a video of them cutting off his finger. The video included a threat to send Jessie home in pieces if I'm not able to work out a trade with DEA for Chuy," explained Matt.

"Holy shit. They cut Jessie's finger off?" asked Wade angrily.

"Yes, as his father, it was hard to watch. I thought maybe I could see a clue; something that could tell me where he was being kept, but nothing leaped out at me. The video was short. They filmed only what they wanted me to see. Shock value sort of stuff," said Matt.

"So what cartel are we dealing with here?" asked Wade.

"A newer organization, Tres Paises. It's an offshoot of the Juarez cartel," replied Matt.

"I've heard of them. They've got some former MS-13 enforcers who decided to roll the dice and play with the big boys. Bad actors I hear. Crazy asshole killers, all," remarked Wade.

"Wade, in their video, they told me that I've only got three more days to make the trade or they're gonna kill Jessie," said Matt.

"First off Matt, no one is killing Jessie. Not if I have anything to do with this. I'm gonna pack some clothes and gear up with some weapons. I'll be on my way in two hours and head straight for your place. When I get there tonight, we can work out a plan. I wanna hit the ground running, so anything you can do to get me the intel and resources I need to get started would be appreciated," said Wade.

"Thanks Wade. I really can't thank you enough. Listen and this is important. By the way, the local DEA SAC named Vermillion has been handling this and what he tells me about their command staff, DEA won't be any help to us. The new administration is controlling the politics and the narrative here, so fuck them.

"No one's gonna save Jessie but us. This means that this entire operation is going to be done under the radar if you follow me. Bottom line is that I'm the sheriff in Gila County and anything and everything you or we do in my jurisdiction is going to be investigated by me. No one in my agency is going to do squat to assist the feds if they try to stick their noses into our business. I've got your back, brother. Promise," explained Matt.

"I figured as much. How's Esperanza and Jessie's wife Josie taking this?" asked Wade.

"Truth is, I haven't told Esperanza the latest. You're the only one who knows so far, so keep that in mind when you see her tonight. No mention at all about the package or the video. As for Josie, the wife and I are trying to keep her calm, so all she knows is that Tres Paises has got Jessie. The less she knows right now, the better," said Matt.

"Got it. See you tonight. I promise you that I won't stop until we have Jessie back home safe and sound," said Wade before hanging up.

CHAPTER 11

Gear Up!

AFTER TAKING MATT Fremont's disturbing call, Wade returned to his ranch house. He called over his main ranch hand Armando and told him that he was going out of town for a week or more. He asked his hand to make sure that the livestock and Desi were cared for, and to collect the mail. Desi was used to Wade being away and was pretty much an independent dog who had the entire ranch to wander around, so no worries there.

Wade picked out a week's worth of civilian and tactical clothes and placed them into a large duffle bag. He next went into his safe room to select the gear he figured he was most likely to use. His primary weapon would be his custom made Nichol's Combat 1911A .45 caliber semiautomatic pistol. He strapped the weapon into an Inside the waistband (IWB) holster with an open two-magazine holder on his left support side. He next opened a ballistic nylon 3-day pack and filled it with ten loaded .45 caliber mags, six boxes of Hornady Special Duty hollow point .45 caliber ammo, a small tactical light and holster and his Kydex outside the waistband (OWB) holster.

Wade opened his 32-gun safe and selected his favorite AR platform. This was his Nichols custom made, AR-15 "Commando" .556 tactical rifle with a short 10" barrel. The weapon boasted a telescoping shoulder stock, solid to strobe 600 lumens light, with an integrated green laser light system. The rifle was topped with an EOTEC occluded eye green dot gun sight for medium range to close quarter battle engagements.

Next came his shotgun. The Benelli M-2 12 gauge, 8-round semiauto would do the trick. Wade selected a number of 00 buck, slug and gas rounds for the weapon. The Gila County Sheriff's Department would provide any other ammunition he would need.

For a back-up pistol, Wade needed something reliable and light weight that would put a man down. He chose the Glock-48, 9 mm. semiauto pistol which had a thin enough frame and slide to fit into a cowboy boot or behind his back. The weapon, four mags of 9 mm Special Duty ammo and a leather IWB holster were also placed into his pack.

Finally, came body armor. Wade selected two types of body armor. First, under clothing wearable armor that had a front sleeve to place either flexible Threat Level 2 Kevlar or Threat level 3 ceramic plates. Next, Wade chose his standard Texas Ranger assault vest that incorporated Threat Level 3 ceramic with a chest holster and mags for his AR-15 rifle and his 1911A pistol.

He was now good to go.

It was 11:00 am by the time Wade had gassed up at the Walmart in Boerne. He jumped on the I-10 which would take him all the way through southwest Texas and into New Mexico. During his time with the Texas Rangers in Company F with Matt Fremont, the duo had traveled this way many times before. Wade could drive this way blindfolded. Boerne was about 570 miles or about eight hours from Las Cruces, New Mexico. From there, to Rio Brisas in Gila County where Matt lived was another seventy-five miles. Wade's gas stops were planned for Fort Stockton and El Paso.

Once one left behind the rolling hills, grass and trees west of Ozona, the landscape was pretty much dry flatlands and sage brush. Rows of gigantic white wind powered generators had been built upon the plains; monstrosities which Wade thought were a blight on the Texas landscape.

The plains were a good place for Wade to think about how he was going to approach this situation. Right now, he just had no context until he met with Matt and saw the lay of the land.

Wade was in a hurry to get to Rio Brisas, so he maintained a fairly constant speed of eighty-five, his eyes continuously scanning for Texas DPS State Troopers. Most of the land he was in now was fairly desolate. He gassed up in Fort Stockton, hit a drive-up fast food joint to stay fueled and was inbound to El Paso with Jason Aldean's "Fly-Over States" blasting on the radio.

Wade hit some end of day rush hour traffic in El Paso just before sunset, He wondered why that city had never really gotten its act together over the years on finishing the damn I-10. It seemed that Texas DOT had been either demolishing or building the freeway through El Paso for ten years.

Off to Wade's right and a stone's throw away across the border was the City of Juarez, Mexico, ruled by the violent Juarez drug cartel. Wade knew that the Tres Paises cartel couldn't possibly operate in New Mexico without the permission of the Juarez cartel. He was now a little more than two hours from Rio Brisas.

Wade gassed up again in El Paso and then topped off again in Deming. He then took the NM Highway 11 turn off at Deming and heading south towards Rio Brisas. It was getting dark as Wade entered the County of Gila. He was scanning for radio channels when a strong voice appeared on the airwaves out of the desert wilderness.

"And folks, that's exactly why the country is going to hell in a handbag. The current administration stopped The Wall in its tracks, we've got open borders, hundreds of thousands of illegals from over one hundred and forty-eight mostly Third World nations breaching in, and violent cartels trafficking drugs, women and children all over the USA.

"And so what's the DHS, Border Patrol, ICE and the DEA doing about this? Not much because their hands are tied due to this incompetent administration. Chew on that for a minute while we go to a commercial break. I'm Johnny Wake and this is Wake Up America at 103.5 FM, Rio Brisas, New Mexico."

Wade smiled somberly to himself as he listened to this apparently frustrated conservative talk show host sound off. The guy was right. That was the crux of the problem and more likely than not what was bringing him to Gila County. Wade selected the station for future listening and turned off the radio. He was now entering the dusty town of Rio Brisas.

Once in town, Wade used the Google Street app on his cell phone to find his way to Matt Fremont's place which he recalled was on a hill overlooking the town.

The Fremont ranch was on about fifty acres, with the main residence, guest quarters and out buildings on about three acres.

The main property with Matt's home was sort of half ranch and half compound. The main residence and detached guest house was built in New Mexico style heavy brick plastered in stucco with red Spanish tiled roofs. A nearby barn contained stables for horses and had an attached roofed area that stored ranch machinery and tools. Three sides of the main portion of the property were surrounded by ten foot stucco walls. The rear of the property without a wall looked out over the property.

Matt had chosen the property well. Strategically Matt had the high ground, so the main house and guest quarters were easily defensible. There was only one road coming up to the property which could be observed from CCTV cameras in the main house. Ten foot stucco walls meant that trespassers would need ladders to breach the thick stucco walls. Anyone coming in from the open area would enter interlocking fields of fire from the main house and guest quarters. Tactically, this was referred to as the "fatal funnel." Yup, Matt had a nice set up for sure.

When Wade got to the base of Matt's driveway leading up to the property, he stopped and called Matt on his cell phone to give him a head's up that he had arrived. Cops hated surprises. An electronic solar-powered metal gate opened to allow him access to the property. Wade drove up the hill and into the compound where he was met by Matt, Esperanza and Josie Fremont, along with a Native American about Wade's age with a weathered face.

Matt Fremont immediately approached and embraced Wade. Matt was followed by Esperanza and Josie who also embraced Wade as if he was family. The Native American waited to be introduced.

"Wade, you're a sight for sore eyes. Thanks so much for coming," said Matt as he grabbed Wade's right hand in a firm shake.

"Well, I'm happy to see you all again, only I wish it was under better circumstances," replied Wade who had not seen Matt and his family since the funeral of his wife Helen nearly five years before.

Matt turned towards the Native American gentleman and said to Wade, "This is our family's good friend Thomas "Fights with a Knife" Black Arrows. He's from the local Apache tribe and father to one of my best deputies, Jacob Black Arrows," explained Matt as Wade and Thomas walked towards each other and shook hands.

"I go by Tom," said Thomas Black Arrows.

"Nice to meet ya, Tom. Just call me Wade. That's an interesting name you have," said Wade.

"The pleasure is mine. Regards my name, it's an Apache thing. Long story. I heard a lot about you from the Fremont's. Heard you were once Matt's partner and did a lot of rangering," said Tom.

"As a matter of fact, I did. Like you, it's a long story. I try to raise bucking bulls these days. Emphasis on the word "try" Just a humble stock contractor these days," laughed Wade.

Matt took the lead, "Well, you've had a long drive and I'll bet you're hungry. Let's get your bags into the guest house, give you a chance to wash up and then get you a nice meal. Me and the gals have been cooking for the last hour in anticipation of your arrival and I can guarantee you some nice down home Texas-style bar-b-que and a beer."

Wade grabbed his bags and headed over to the guest house. He took a shower, changed his clothes and headed over to the main house where everyone was waiting. On the large center island in the kitchen Esperanza and Josie had placed bowls containing fresh salad, Mexican rice and beans, flour tortillas, and cut up fruit.

Matt entered the room carrying a large platter of BBQ beef ribs and sausage. "Wade and Tom, the beer's in the fridge. We don't stand on ceremony here so help yourselves."

After everyone had enjoyed the meal, Matt asked Wade and Tom to join him over in the guest house where Wade was staying. Matt was carrying an iPad. When the trio were inside the house, Matt looked outside to make sure the women were inside the main house. He then turned on the iPad.

Matt began, "What I'm going to show you is not pleasant and for the time being cannot be discussed with the women. But it's only fair that you see what you may be getting into. I know you guys are doing this as a favor to me and my family, but understand you are taking a serious risk here. The people we are up against are serious bad actors and at any time you want to change your minds about helping out, I will still always be indebted to you."

Matt then showed Wade and Tom the video of Jessie's torture that Tres Paises had sent him. Both Wade and Tom grimaced as they watched Adolfo Guzman's enforcer Urias sever Jessie's ring finger with gardening shears.

"Fucking piece of shit. I'm in all the way no matter what," said Wade after Matt turned off the video.

"Me too. That could have been my boy," said Tom Black Arrows.

"Looks like Jessie is doing a whole lot of blinking. Eyes burning or bright lights?" asked Wade rhetorically.

"Not sure, could be. I just don't know, but that's what I'm thinking," replied Matt.

"So, I'm sure you have had time to think about a response. What's the strategy so far?" asked Wade.

"Well, like I said, these are tough characters. Based upon the video which was obviously sent to me with Jessie's severed ring finger and his wedding ring for shock value and to motivate me, I fully believe that if we don't act asap, they will kill Jessie and then try to work out a separate deal with the feds. It makes sense to them.

"Chuy Guzman is in DEA custody and they're feds. The feds are making all the calls here. They're giving me an opportunity because they also want me to back off on enforcement and let them run around carte blanche in Gila County trafficking dope, UDA's and sex trafficking women.

"Tres Paises can't make that deal with the feds; only local law enforcement like me. Alfonso Guzman is all hyped up about Chuy because the kid is his favorite nephew and the guy's got egg on his face in front of his family and other cartel bosses because Jessie and Jacob dumped three of their traffickers and busted Chuy.

"Adolfo can't afford to lose face in front of the other cartel bosses because it makes him look weak. Remember that Tres Paises can't do shit without the permission of the stronger Juarez cartel. If Juarez thinks Adolfo is weak and can't deliver an area like Gila County to traffic dope, UDA's and women through, why the hell do they need him? They'll just replace him with one of their own and it's curtains for Adolfo," Matt explained.

"Makes sense. So how much time do you think we have before Tres Paises changes their original plan?" asked Wade as delicately as possible without mentioning the cartel murdering Matt's son.

"Well, I've done nothing but think about this since even before I got the package. No more than a couple more days max. That's all the time we have to find Jessie," said Matt.

"What resources do we have available to us? Based upon what you're telling us, it appears doubtful that we will be able to rely upon the feds. The clock is ticking, and we've got to hit the ground running," said Wade.

"Agreed. I'm gonna call a meeting with some of my deputies tomorrow, appraise them of the situation and then ask a couple of them I been thinking about with special skill sets if they want in on trying to rescue Jessie. FYI, no one but you two know anything about what was in the package I received. I've shared that with no one," said Matt.

Tom Black Arrows chimed in, "Well, if the clock's ticking as you say, then we are burning time right now. We need a lead quickly and I say we head into town to see what we can find out. The word I've had on the street for some weeks now is that a couple Tres Paises muscle people are already in town and trying to intimidate the locals. These gang bangers are all the same. It's a power and macho thing. They've also been poking around the res, trying to intimidate and recruit my people to mule dope. I think I know just the place to start asking a few questions."

"Sounds good. I'm your huckleberry. Give me a few minutes to gear up and I'll go with you," offered Wade.

"Sounds like a plan," said Tom.

"Agreed," replied Matt.

Wade was already anticipating the possibility of trouble.

Rio Brisas was a very small town where everyone knew everyone. Even an outsider like him who would ask some low-key questions was going to attract attention which automatically meant risk. Wade needed some additional confirmation from Matt that if Wade needed to take action to defend himself or get some intel, Matt would cover for him if things got dicey.

"Matt, I know we sort of covered this before on the phone, but if I have to take care of business, have you got this?" Wade asked.

"Like I said before, do what you guys got to do to get Jessie back home in one piece. This is my county which means that anything that happens here is a Gila County Sheriff's investigation. No feds involved. I got your backs. No one is going to come into my county, take and torture my son, fuck with me and my people and get away with it, comprende?" said Matt.

"Copy that, Matt. Tom, I'll be ready in ten. Let's take your ride," said Wade.

Matt and Tom left the guest house and Wade strapped on his Nichols Combat 1911 .45 caliber pistol, out of waistband holster just past his right hip with a double mag holster on his support side. He then secured his Glock 48 9 mm semiautomatic pistol into a Kydex inside the waistband holster behind his back on his dominate side as his back-up weapon. Finally, Wade secured two additional mags of 9 mm ammo into two mag pouches that were sewn into his leather range jacket that perfectly covered his .45. He was good to go.

Wade walked back into the main house and thanked Esperanza and Josie for a great dinner. Matt and Esperanza walked Wade back outside where Tom was already waiting in his pick-up truck.

"Don't wait up for me kids," joked Wade.

"Please be careful, Wade," said Esperanza.

"Always," replied Wade before climbing into Tom Black Arrows' truck and leaving the compound.

CHAPTER 12

"I got no rules. I'm retired."

TOM BLACK ARROWS' idea for seeking information was to head over to the Roadrunner Saloon in what was loosely referred to as "downtown Rio Brisas." The Roadrunner was a combination saloon and restaurant that served the region's customary fare of Mexican food, hamburgers and all things fried. It was also pretty much the only eating and drinking establishment open in downtown Rio Brisas after 8 pm when the town's dusty sidewalks were "rolled up."

The customer demographics of the Roadrunner were best described as "eclectic." The patrons were predominately locals of mixed ethnicities of Anglos, Mexicans and Native Americans. Like many saloons in equally small rural towns, the Roadrunner was a place to hook-up with friends, have a meal, suck down a few cheap beers and gossip about what was happening in the county. The perfect place to people watch and pick up any 4-1-1 from the locals.

For strategic reasons, Tom parked his pick-up truck two doors down from the saloon even though there was parking in front. Wade immediately noticed this and remarked to himself that Tom Black Arrows was no rookie in the personal safety department.

It was close to 9:30 pm when the men entered the saloon to find about ten patrons inside the establishment eating and drinking. Willie Nelson and Toby Keith were belting out "Whiskey for My Men and Beer for My Horses" on the stereo. Wade mused that for a very small town, this was a decent crowd. The former Texas Ranger immediately scanned the room for personal safety, looking for exits and quickly sizing up the people around them.

At one table against the right side wall sat two interesting looking men. One of the men could have been Willie Nelson's double; a grizzled guy in his late sixty's with long pig tails under a Viet Nam Vet baseball cap and tattooed sleeves on both arms. He was wearing a faded green short-sleeved T-shirt with a 1st Air Calvary logo. The guy sitting opposite of him was in his mid-thirty's with short-cropped hair, wearing a black T-shirt with the words "Question Authority" emblazoned on his chest. Wade noticed that this guy had double prosthetic legs sticking out from beneath his pant legs and into a pair of athletic shoes. Maybe two vets hanging out and having a beer together; maybe a father and son, Wade thought. Interesting.

At a table closer to the bar on the left side was a Hispanic Catholic priest, wearing the traditional black short-sleeved button down shirt with a white priest's collar, but with blue jean pants and cowboy boots. He was nursing a beer and had a plate of food in front of him.

At a table towards the center of the room were two Native Americans having a meal. The pair recognized and acknowledged Tom Black Arrows with upward nods of their heads.

A trio of obviously retired senior citizens including a woman were at a table against the left side wall with food and beers in front of them. It looked to Wade that beer was obviously the preferred drink at the Roadrunner.

Behind the bar was an attractive woman in her early fifties with a shapely figure. She seemed to have command of the place and Wade figured her for the manager or owner of the joint.

Out of curiosity, Wade and Tom took a table close to the Willie Nelson character and the guy with the Question Authority shirt. Wade figured these two obvious locals would be a good source of information.

Wade hadn't seen a server yet, so he offered to buy Tom a beer. He went up to the bar to meet the barkeep who he figured would be another good source of intel. As soon as he got up from their table, he noted that the bartender smiled and maintained eye contact as he approached the bar.

"What's your pleasure, cowboy? You new in town? Haven't seen ya before," said the bartender to Wade. Wade's white palm straw cowboy hat, range jacket and boots had given him away.

"Couple of beers, miss. What do you have?" replied Wade.

"Well, the Bud Light's on sale tonight. Three bucks a bottle. Helps to keep the place open a little longer during slow weekdays. And the name's Sally; Sally DuBois. What's yours?" she asked flirtatiously batting her long eyelashes.

"DuBois, is that French? Mine's Wade. Just in town for a few days and yeah, I'll go with two Bud Lights," replied Wade smiling back. Two could play this game he thought, all in the interest of information gathering of course.

"I see you're friends with Tom," said Sally demonstrating her knowledge of the locals. "And yes, DuBois is French; from the New Orleans DuBois'" she lied as she leaned over the bar to hand Wade his beers while purposefully revealing her more than ample cleavage.

Wade made it a point not to stare down and continued to maintain eye contact. "You worked here long? You seem to know people," said Wade.

"Well, I own the place so yeah, I know most all the locals who come in here. Why do you ask?" replied Sally.

In actuality, Sally DuBois was from New Orleans where she had established her reputation in her younger years as a stripper. Today the trade was referred to as exotic dancing. Sally had been smart and had invested her earnings, accumulating enough to quit the business. She had fallen head over heels for a musician who convinced her to relocate to Santa Fe.

When things eventually went sour with the musician, Sally saw an ad for the Roadrunner and bought the place, hoping to turn it into something, but that dream never really had quite materialized. Now the town was slowly drying up, but Sally kept it going by offering decent food, cheap beer and good customer service.

"Just cause you seem to know my buddy Tom," said Wade matter of factly.

"Easy to know Tom. As you probably know, he's born and bred here. Tribal elder from the local Apache reservation just outside the town limits," explained Sally.

Wade paid for the beers and told Sally that he was going to catch up with Tom and would come back for a couple more in a bit. Wade then walked back over to his table to find Tom engrossed in conversation with the two guys next to them. Tom beckoned Wade over to meet the men.

"Wade, I wanna introduce you to a couple of friends of mine," said Tom. Pointing to the Willie Nelson character, Tom said, "This older yet debonair gent is Jack, better known as "Black Jack" Stryker, and this younger fella is Johnny Wake."

Wade reached across the table and shook both men's hands. "How ya'all doing this evening? Pleased to make your acquaintance," replied Wade, smiling.

"Same here," said Stryker. "Me too," said Wake.

"Judging by the look of ya'all, you both served I take it. If so, thank you for your service," said Wade.

"Spot on, my hat give me away?" laughed Stryker.

"Well that and the Air Cav T-shirt. One badass unit in Nam. Did you fly?" asked Wade to Black Jack.

"Yup, mostly Huey's and 500-D's," replied Stryker, referring to the? Huey helicopter H1-D and the smaller reconnaissance 500-D models.

"How'd you guess that I served?" asked Johnny Wake.

"Well, I saw you got some iron sticking into your shoes and that Question Authority shirt sort of confirmed it for me. What was your branch and MOS?" asked Wade with a smile, interested in Wake's military operational specialty.

"Marines, EOD, IED finder, cept one day I found one that didn't agree with me in Mosul," replied Wake tapping one of his titanium prosthetic legs, referring to Explosives Ordinance Disposal, improvised explosive devices and his deployment to Iraq.

"I actually saw the guy who got me. He looked right at me and smiled from a second story apartment. Then I saw him raise up his cell phone, tap the display and wham! Next thing I remember is waking up in Regional Medical Center in Landstuhl, Germany. Only my legs didn't make the trip with me. Shit happens, he chuckled. I'm not bitter, I know what I signed up for," explained Wake philosophically.

"Semper Fi," said Wade acknowledging he had also served in the Corps.

"What'd you do in the Corps?" asked Stryker.

"Second Division Force Recon. Sneaky Pete's and LRRP's in Panama and Central America mostly, said Wade, referring to long range reconnaissance patrols and covert warfare. "Let me buy you vets another round when your done with those," offered Wade.

"I knew you guys would have stuff in common," said Tom Black Arrows, smiling as all the men clinked their beers bottles together as a toast to their service.

"So what are you guys doing for a living now?" asked Wade.

Stryker spoke up first. "I'm still driving choppers. It's in my blood. Agricultural, aerial spraying mostly. I also got a contract with the power company to check their towers and power lines after we have storms. It's a living and keeps me just busy enough," explained Black Jack.

"I got an internet podcast and pirate radio network called "Wake-Up America." Sort of a play on my last name. Allows me to vent, keep the locals informed and hold this fricking corrupt government accountable. Like the shirt says, I question authority like every patriot should be doing these days if you get my drift," offered Johnny.

"Geeze, I caught your show driving in here tonight. You hit a few cords with me. I liked it," said Wade as he held up his bottle for a toast, "God bless America," he said, and all four men clinked their bottles together again.

"Air Cav," said Black Jack as they all raised their bottles again. "To the Corps, Oohrah!" said Johnny as the men toasted their service again.

"So, what brings you into our dusty metropolis?" Black Jack asked Wade.

Wade and Tom looked around the room first before Wade answered. "Well, we've got a friend who's in a bit of a jam. A touchy situation. First, if it's okay to ask you fellas, have you seen any suspicious, new fellas from across the border popping up around here lately?" Black Jack and Johnny looked at each other at the same time and then scanned the room before Johnny answered,

"If you're referring to those drug smuggling, human trafficking, low-life sons a bitches who have been poisoning our people and prostituting women and children. Yeah we've seen 'em in town. More frequently now since the new corrupt federal administration came into power. Tom and his people have seen 'em too. Brazen lil' fuckers too. Seen 'em come into here recently hassling Miss Sally too. Looked to me like they were trying to put the arm on her for some dough, like the fricking Mafia. What specifically you wanna know?"

"Easy son, keep your voice down," said Stryker as he placed his hand on Johnny's arm to quiet him down a bit. Now all four men began scanning the room.

"What the fuck, Black Jack. These cartel assholes are pieces of shit. I hate all of them, coming over here trying to take over this county and this town. They're humping dope across the river all the time and driving our sheriff crazy. We heard on the QT that a couple of deputies shot it out with some POS drug smugglers the other day at the river and wasted a couple of 'em. Good for them. We should be taking them all out if you ask me. These fucks are invading this country and killing us with their poison. Damn government ain't doing shit to stop 'em either with this open border bullshit, " said Johnny.

"Tranquillo, amigo, calmate," said Stryker to Johnny while scanning the room again.

"What about you, Black Jack; had any interactions with these people," asked Wade. Stryker scanned the room again before answering. Satisfied that the music was covering their conversation he told Wade, "Look, full disclosure, I just didn't do time with Air Cav in the Nam. I was a good pilot and a bit crazy. I got noticed by our black ops people. When I was rotating out, they offered me a job smuggling dope, money and CIA spooks around the Golden Triangle. I made a ton more money than the Army paid me, and

I got to feed my adrenalin jones for a couple more years until I went back stateside. They offered me more work, but by then I had enough cash saved up to buy a spread out here, bought a couple of choppers and opened my business. Been here ever since living the dream."

"What about you, Wade. What's your story?" asked Johnny.

"Well, after the Corps, I went into law enforcement as you say, Black Jack, to feed my adrenalin jones. Started as a State Trooper with the Texas Department of Public Safety and then got appointed as a Texas Ranger. Did over twenty rangering and pulled the pin. Got a ranch in the Texas Hill Country northwest of San Antone and raise cattle and bucking bulls as a stock contractor. Good life when I get to spend time on my ranch," said Wade.

"You said you got a friend who's in a jam down here? Cartel entanglement?" asked Stryker.

"What makes you say that?" asked Wade coyly as Tom looked on.

"Well, you seem pretty interested about our amigos across the border. Not all that hard to figure out," said Stryker.

Wade looked around the room again and then back at Tom who slightly raised his head with a short "Go ahead and tell 'em" nod.

"As long as we have an agreement that what I tell you fellas is not for public consumption," said Wade.

"Deal," replied Stryker.

"Me too, deal," echoed Johnny.

Wade then took the next five minutes filling in Black Jack Stryker and Johnny Wake on the details of Sheriff Matt Fremont's son Jessie and Tom's son Jacob Black Arrows encounter and shoot out with members of the Tres Paises drug cartel, Jessie's kidnapping and torture and Matt Fremont's frustrating negotiations with the DEA's SAC in El Paso.

"That's some ugly, no account, rotten, cowardly bullshit by that DEA a-hole. That deputy is a fucking American. What the hell happened to leave no man behind?" said Johnny in a tone of disgust after listening to Wade's story.

"Wade, that's some pretty low down dealing. Knowing these cartel hombres like I do, I can tell ya they're gonna kill that kid just to make a point and leverage DEA to release Chuy Guzman. First they kill Jessie just to attract attention and then they threaten to plant a bomb to kill more Americans if they don't get Chuy released. It's a no win scenario for our government. Like you said, Chuy is just a pawn in this game," said Stryker.

"Afraid so," replied Wade. "But Sheriff Matt Fremont's my old Texas Ranger partner and my best friend. I owe him my life a couple of times over and I'm also Jessie's Godfather. Matt asked me for help and by God, that's why I'm down here with Tom. We're doing some intel work right now, but I gotta find a way to locate Jessie and bust him out of wherever Tres Paises has him stashed. I just don't have much time. Jessie's clock's ticking and they could kill him any day now," explained the retired Texas Ranger.

Stryker and Johnny looked at each other and then at Wade and Tom. "Well, we're in," said Stryker.

"What do you mean you're in. Nobody's asked you for anything," said Wade.

"Listen brother. You didn't have to. It's a righteous cause. Save an American hero, vanquish the evil dragon, save our country," replied Stryker.

"It's the patriotic thing to do. Strike a blow against these cartel a-holes," said Johnny assuredly.

Wade felt slightly overwhelmed at the response of his new found friends. "Look fellas, there are huge risks involved and zero money. I'm down here on my own accord to help family. You guys don't even know Jessie or Sheriff Fremont. You could lose everything. Hell, chances are pretty high you could both get yourselves killed," said Wade.

"Well, shit. This whole live a long life stuff is way over stated. I'm more for feeding my adrenalin jones," said Stryker laughing.

"Me too," laughed Johnny.

"Me three," said Wade who then raised up his beer bottle over the center of the table. "To feeding the jones," Wade toasted.

Stryker, Johnny and Tom clinked their beer bottles together with Wade's while loudly toasting, "Feeding the jones!"

At that moment, four rugged looking Mexican males in their thirty's and forty's entered the saloon and immediately surveyed the room and every person in it. All of the men wore waist-length jackets. None of them were smiling.

Stryker made eye contact with them and then with Wade and Johnny with a concerned look on his face. He whispered, "The two guys on the right are the cartel guys who hit me up to mule dope across the border in my chopper a few months ago."

Wade heard Stryker and slowly fingered off the safety on his Nichols Combat 1911a .45 caliber pistol that was holstered under his jacket. Slowly but surreptitiously Stryker, Johnny, and Tom were all checking their weapons as well. Not a good sign.

Wade felt like he was a sitting duck at the congested table. He stood up and said, "Well, looks like I'm buying the next round" and then moved towards the bar without looking at the foursome.

Tom took the hint, also stood up and began walking over to the priest, Father Marco Reyes, who he knew. Father Reyes was a Jesuit and a former Golden Gloves boxer from Mexico who had been naturalized many years before. He was the pastor of the town's only Catholic church. Father Reyes was also focusing on the foursome with a wary eye.

The four Mexicans separated as they walked deeper into the saloon. Three of the men approached the bar, while the fourth sauntered over to the alcove leading to the restrooms and stood against the wall without taking a seat. Wade noted that this man appeared to be focusing on the patrons and thought to himself, *"If this was a bank, that fella would be the tail gunner or back-up for the robbers."* Again, not a good sign.

Wade deliberately walked up to the far right side of the bar and took up a position just around its corner. The bar would provide him with a modicum of cover just in case.

Tom greeted Father Reyes with a broad smile, a handshake

and sat down at the priest's small table facing the fourth Mexican at the alcove. Black Jack Stryker and Johnny Wake remained at their table intently watching the suspicious Mexicans.

As the three Mexicans got up to the bar, Sally DuBois ignored them and walked over to Wade. "Miss me, handsome?" she asked flirtatiously, hiding her obvious anxiety.

"How'd you know? I'll have four more beers. Put it on my tab, miss. I'm feelin' like a big spender tonight," Wade joked as a distraction, noting the concerned look on Sally's face. Wade could tell that this wasn't Sally's first encounter with the rough-looking Mexicans now at her bar.

The man who appeared to be the leader spoke up in relatively good English, "Chica, my friends and I would like some service over here if you don't mind."

Sally turned from Wade to face the men. "What will it be gentlemen," she said.

"Mexican cervezas for me and my compadres, and then perhaps a bit of conversation, por favor," the leader said.

"Of course. Coming right up," said Sally as she left Wade and walked over to the glass refrigerator, pulling four long necked Modelo Especials and placing them on the bar before the men.

The leader who had jet black slicked back hair and a short beard placed his hand on Sally's as she placed the last beer bottle on the table. Sally reacted immediately by pulling her hand away. "Tranquillo, hombre. We got a rule in this saloon. Don't touch the help," she said to the man.

"Hey Chica. What, you no like?" he replied, faking surprise.

"That will be fifteen bucks, American, senor," Sally responded, ignoring the rude man's comment.

The leader pulled a large wad of bills from the front pocket of his jeans. He peeled off a fifty dollar bill and placed it on the bar. "Keep it for your trouble. Have you given any more thought to our last conversation about considering a partnership in this saloon of yours? My Jefe is seeking business investments in this town and would be willing to pay top dollar for half interest in your place," he said to Sally."

Sally looked the man in the eye, "Thanks for the tip. No offense, but I got the same answer for your boss as last time. Not interested. I like running things just the way they are. My answer's never going to change, so make sure you tell your Jefe that. Just not interested."

The leader was apparently not one to take no for an answer. "Senorita, I think perhaps you don't understand or appreciate my Jefe's magnanimous gesture. He is willing to pay you much more for this dump than it could possibly be worth. You could easily retire on what he would pay," said the man.

"Look fella. I get all of that. In fact, I got it last time too. I got no plans nor desire to sell any interest in this saloon. And certainly not to your Jefe nor anyone else like him, comprende?" said Sally assertively.

Wade, Stryker and Johnny were all closely watching the leader and his two companions. The leader gave Sally a broad smile showing his pearly white teeth, his eyes were a black as tar heroin as he leaned over the bar closer to Sally. It was a menacing gesture clearly designed to intimate the saloon owner. Wade slowly re-checked the safety on his 1911 and waited for the next response.

"Well, you know my Jefe can be very convincing when he wants to be. I really think you should reconsider his generous offer," said the man as he opened his jacket, revealing to only Sally a semiautomatic pistol heavily engraved with silver.

Now the man had pissed Sally DuBois off. Wade immediately saw fire in her eyes. Sally now raised her voice when she addressed the leader and his two companions. Things were getting dicey quickly.

"You think you shits can come into my place and threaten me in front of my customers? Get the hell out of here before I call the Sheriff. Tell your boss that he can stick it up his cartel drug smuggling ass! Now get!" said Sally who was now visibly angry.

The leader purposefully tipped over his bottle on the bar, spilling beer on its counter as he and his two companions backed away from the bar. At this point, then entire saloon went silent, with everyone looking at Sally and the three menacing men standing in front of her.

Wade took this gesture as a cue and stepped back from his position behind the corner of the bar, while checking behind and to the right and left of the three men for patrons. There were none.

Tom and Father Reyes had heard the commotion as well. Tom looked over this shoulder and saw Wade focused on the leader and the man closest to him. Things were quickly going to come to a boil. Tom turned back around to again face the fourth Mexican at the alcove. Stryker and Johnny Wake already had their hands on the grips of their pistols which were concealed in their waistbands. They were ready to fight.

"I think you need to clean up that beer and apologize to the lady before you and your amigos leave," said Wade calmly to the leader.

Stryker and Johnny looked at each other and then looked back at Wade and the Mexicans he was addressing. Knowing that Wade had been a Texas Ranger and the purpose of his visit to Las Brisas, they knew this would not end well.

"Oh shit. I've got the guy on the right, you take the ahole on the left. Looks like Wade wants the leader," whispered Stryker to Johnny.

"Copy that," replied Johnny, intensely gazing at the Mexican on the left with his hand on his gun.

The leader and his two companions looked directly at Wade. The man to the leader's left stepped away, closer to the table where Tom and Father Reyes were seated. Tom sensed the man's movement towards him, but instinctively never took his eyes off the fourth man at the alcove, who had placed his right hand inside his jacket. He was obviously armed.

The leader and the man closest to his right slightly separated, but not by much; only about four feet apart. The third man was eight feet to their right and now only four feet from Father Reyes' and Tom's table.

"My guy moved in front of Tom and the padre. I got no shot. I'll back Wade on the leader," Johnny whispered back to Stryker.

Patrons closest to the front doors immediately stood up from their tables and moved rapidly to and out of the front door. Others who were caught too far from the front door, quickly maneuvered to the far right corner. Wade noted that there was a clear field of fire between him and the leader and his companion.

"Sally honey, do me a favor and go behind the far end of the bar. Our amigo here can apologize to you just fine from there," said Wade calmly and assuredly as he looked from one man to the other.

Sally, seeing the look of concentration on Wade's face made no argument and did exactly what she was told.

Wade's next comments were directed to the bearded leader. "Now I know you're gonna want to apologize to the lady and clean up that beer you spilled and leave, right amigo?"

The leader looked Wade up and down and noticed that Wade had "the look" of a man who was or had been in law enforcement. He took a guess and then made a big mistake. He challenged Wade.

"Amigo, you must have confused me with some of those wetbacks who are afraid of you gringos. Yo no estoy este hombre (I'm not that guy)," the leader laughed. "I ain't gonna do shit except fuck you up, pinche placa," said the leader using the term "placa" or badge to indicate he believed that Wade was in law enforcement. The leader and his companion in unison moved their jackets exposing their semiautomatic pistols concealed inside waistband holsters.

"Amigo, you're a sheriff, right? Well, you ain't gonna do shit. You cops have rules. I know the rules. You can't do shit to us. We're gonna kill you, that bitch, and your family. We're gonna kill you all and burn this fucking place down to the ground tonight," said the leader smirking while he and the man next to him moved their hands onto the grips of their pistols. Hearing this threat, Stryker and Johnny both slowly and discretely unholstered and moved their guns next to their sides at the ready.

"Well, you're right about the law enforcement thing. But you're wrong about killing people. You aren't killing anyone tonight, my friends." said Wade.

"And why is that, deputy?" asked the leader, smirking again.

"Cause I got no rules, I'm retired," replied Wade.

In that second, both the leader and his companion went for their guns, but Wade was way ahead of them. Wade knew that an outside the waistband holster always had a faster draw than any inside the waistband holster.

Wade broke leather as he simultaneously shuffled to his right, using the cover of the bar. In the blink of an eye, he fired one round into center mass of each man, then shuffled again and dispatched another two-round burst, again one round directly into each man's upper torso. The man to the leader's left went down just as he cleared leather. However, the leader was more resilient. He managed to draw his silver plated pistol as he began to stagger forward. As he attempted to focus on raising the muzzle of his gun towards Wade, the former Texas Ranger again shuffled behind the bar to his right and fired a quick controlled pair which struck the right eye and center forehead of the cartel soldier. Down he went in a cloud of blood red mist. All in under four seconds.

As the third man started to go for his gun to engage Wade, Father Reyes quickly stood up from the table delivered a strong right hook to the right side of the man's head spinning him completely around. The priest then dispatched him with a left jab and a devastating upper cut which knocked him backwards over a nearby table.

With his three compadres down and out of the fight, the fourth Mexican at the alcove attempted to draw his weapon with his right hand from a cross draw holster concealed inside his left side waistband. Tom "Fights with a Knife," who had already stood away from his table, drew a flat-bladed throwing knife from a holster sewn into the back of the neck area of his jacket. The Apache flung the knife directly at the man's hand, completely penetrating through his hand as well as the man's thick leather belt, locking the hand into the belt and partially penetrating the shirt and skin at the abdomen. The last Mexican cartel soldier screamed, doubled over in pain and was out of the fight.

Black Jack Stryker and Johnny Wake had both drawn their guns, but the fight was clearly over. The men looked at each other incredulously and then looked back at Wade who now had his 1911 at the low-ready position, while alternately scanning his downed targets and the room for additional threats. There were none.

Tom "Fights with a Knife" moved quickly over to the wounded Mexican and disarmed him of his pistol. Stryker and Johnny got up from their table and covered Wade and Father Reyes to make sure all three Mexicans posed no further threat.

Under cover of Wade's 1911, Stryker checked the leader and his companion. Each cartel soldier had two perfectly placed .45 caliber rounds dead center in their chests that you could have covered with a playing card. The leader's forehead and right eye had been penetrated by .45 caliber rounds the force of which had taken out part of the rear of his head.

"Fucking dead as Julius Caesar. Nice shooting," said Stryker to Wade.

"I generally hit what I'm aiming at," replied Wade simply.

Father Reyes was checking out the Mexican he had punched out who was sprawled face up on the floor. "Still out like a light," said the priest.

"Well, keep your eyes on him. Roll him over and see if you can tie him up with something till the Sheriff gets here," directed Wade.

Tom called out from the alcove where the fourth Mexican was leaning up against the wall, moaning. "This one's gonna need to go to the hospital," he said. Tom's throwing knife was still stuck through the man's right hand and belt. "This might hurt some," said Tom to the Mexican. Without further notice, Tom suddenly and forcefully pulled the knife out of the man's hand which then began to spurt blood.

"Cover that wound with your other hand for a second, amigo," Tom instructed the Mexican, while he grabbed some napkins off of a nearby table and placed a stack of them over the wound to stanch the flow of blood. Tom then wiped the blade of his throwing knife off on the Mexican's pant leg and reholstered it behind his neck.

"Jesus Christ, Wade!" said Sally as she appeared up from the end of the bar. "It was just spilled beer for Christ sake. Now I got a bunch of dead Mexican cartel shits laying all over my saloon."

"You know it was far more than spilled beer, Sally. You wouldn't even own this place by next week if these bandidos had their way. Plus, they drew on me first," said Wade.

"I saw the whole thing. It was self-defense. You had no choice. You did what you had to do. Their fate was in God's hands. He protected you, my son," said Father Reyes.

"I saw the same thing. Self-defense. Wade had no choice," said Stryker.

"Exactly the way I saw it too. Self-defense," echoed Johnny Wake.

"Those Mexicans were fixing for a fight. The man over there was just defending himself. So was the Indian who threw the knife. Self-defense by both men," said a patron in the far corner of the saloon said.

"Sally, call 9-1-1 and get the Sheriff and an ambulance out here. No one here can leave until the Sheriff arrives. This is a crime scene now and we have to shut it down. Johnny, guard the door.

"No one in or out till the Sheriff says so. Sally, make sure you tell the dispatcher that there are two deceased, one wounded, two in custody and all of the suspects were armed. Make sure you also tell them that a retired law enforcement officer is the shooter. Tell them that I will meet the deputies outside unarmed when they arrive. Describe me for the dispatcher so the deputies will be able to identify me when they get here," directed Wade.

Sally went back behind the bar, still trying to catch her breath. What had just happened? Certainly, this man Wade Justus was no one to be trifled with, she thought to herself as she picked up her cell phone and dialed 9-1-1 for the Sheriff.

Black Jack Stryker and Johnny Wake were standing over the bodies of the leader of the Mexican cartel soldiers and the deceased companion closest to him and gazing down at the vicious wounds in the men's bodies.

"Did you see that draw?" Stryker whispered to Johnny.

"Shit, do you see these hits? Never seen nothing like it. Certainly not the guy you want to fuck with," Johnny whispered back to Stryker.

While Sally DuBois was calling 9-1-1 and explaining the circumstances, Wade pulled out his cell phone and told Stryker, Johnny and Father Reyes, "Guys, don't touch anything and step away from the bodies so I can document conditions." Wade then began methodically photographing the bodies, the men's exposed weapons and the condition of the scene including his expended cartridge casings. As much as possible, this shooting was going down by the book, and he wanted to clearly establish that this was a self-defense shooting.

In the distance, Wade heard the sounds of approaching sirens.

CHAPTER 13

The Clock is Ticking

AT THE FIRST sound of the approaching sirens, Wade unholstered his Nichols Custom Combat 1911A .45 caliber pistol and left it on the counter at the end of the bar where he had been when he shot the two Mexican cartel soldiers. The retired Texas Ranger then calmly walked out of the saloon and stood on the street. Wade raised his hands, holding his wallet with his ranger ID card and badge open in his right hand with his left hand palm open, showing that he was unarmed.

Two Gila County Sheriff's Department vehicles roared up Main Street with their emergency LED lights flashing and their sirens wailing. The units came to a stop directly in front of the Roadrunner Saloon in a tactical V-formation, using their bright takedown lights to fully illuminate Wade. This was an indication that the deputies were taking no chances, Officers would naturally be cautious with anyone reported to have killed two men and possibly wounded another, regardless that it was reported that the shooter was prior law enforcement .

One of the deputies to arrive was Blake Sheridan. Both were experienced officers. Sheridan was a former Marines Force Recon sniper who had previously served four tours in Afghanistan and Iraq. He had also done some black ops special assignment work for the CIA before leaving the service. Sheridan was an excellent shot and no one to be trifled with.

Sheridan had always wanted to enter law enforcement as a career, but due to his sniper and secret DOD background, no agency would hire him because it was believed that he would not be able to pass a psych background exam. However, Sheriff Matt

Fremont had interviewed him for the job of deputy specifically because of his USMC background. Sheridan's calm demeanor and honest responses to the psychologist's questions allowed him to pass the psychological exam. Sheriff Fremont had hired him on the spot. Sheridan was found to excel at his job and was grateful to Sheriff Fremont for giving him a chance to live his dream.

More sirens were heard, and the flashing lights of a fire rig and an ambulance were observed approaching the scene. The deputies on-scene radioed for fire and EMS to stage where they were temporarily until they scene was secure from any active threat. The approaching units shut down except for their flashing emergency lights and staged in place in the middle of the street.

Deputy Marcus Carter and Sheridan exited their marked units and carefully approached Wade with their guns drawn and at the low ready, scanning every inch of his body.

"Sir, we need you to raise your hands higher so we can see your waistband better," instructed Marcus.

In response, Wade spoke not a word and did as instructed.

The deputies could see that when Wade raised his hands higher, his waist-length jacket also rose up, exposing his waistband. The deputies could see Wade's empty holster, as well as a double magazine holster loaded with two magazines.

"Now carefully and slowly turn 360 so we can see what's behind your back. Then stop, facing us again," directed Marcus.

Again, Wade quietly did as instructed. He knew the drill. Just let the deputies do their jobs and remain calm.

The deputies could now see that Wade had nothing behind his back. Once Wade was facing towards them again, they concentrated on the Texas Ranger flat badge and ID he had exposed in the leather wallet he was holding in his right hand.

"Where's your weapon?" asked Jacob.

"Inside the scene at the end of the bar, right side on the counter," replied Wade simply.

"Current law enforcement or retired?" asked Jacob.

"Retired Texas Ranger here at the behest of your Sheriff, Matt Fremont," replied Wade.

Marcus kept watch on Wade as he spoke to Sheridan. "Moving forward to contact. Cover me, partner," said Marcus as he reholstered.

"Copy," replied Sheridan as he moved more to one side to keep Wade in his field of fire, while not pointing the muzzle of his weapon at his partner. This was the classic "contact-cover" technique used by officers working in pairs when encountering potentially high-risk subjects.

"Sir, go ahead and carefully extend your right hand outwards towards me so I can inspect your ID, while keeping your left hand raised," Marcus instructed Wade. Wade said nothing and complied, allowing the deputy to take and carefully examine Wade's Texas Ranger identification.

"Looks legit. You carrying a back-up weapon tonight, ranger?" Marcus asked Wade.

"I have a Glock 48 in my inside left boot. I also have a knife on a clip inside my right front pants pocket," replied Wade.

Jacob looked down at Wade's right front pocket, saw the clip and removed Wade's stiletto knife. The deputy placed the knife in the back of his waistband. He quickly checked Wade's waistband for concealed weapons and then reached down and pulled the Glock from his left boot. He then held up four fingers so Deputy Sheridan could see the gesture and said, "Code-4, partner," which was police lingo, for "everything is OK." Marcus told Wade he could put his hands down and relax. Deputy Sheridan reholstered his sidearm and approached Marcus and Wade.

Marcus radioed to the staged emergency personnel that the scene was clear of threats and to proceed in. The fire and EMS personnel came up the street and parked next to the sheriff patrol units.

As the crews dismounted with their first aid gear, Jacob instructed them, "Guys, be very careful what you touch and move around. Be wary of evidence and don't touch it. Leave the decedents in place after confirming medical status. We're gonna have to photograph and document everything. Don't make our job harder than it needs to be, understood?" The fire and EMS crews replied, "Got it," in unison and entered the saloon.

Deputy Carter directed Deputy Sheridan to enter the saloon with the fire and EMS crews.

Marcus began the initial shooting investigation in getting some quick initial details from Wade. This was called a "safety statement," but was not a comprehensive shooting interview.

At this point in the investigation and especially with a retired law enforcement officer involved as a shooter, the incident would be handled more like an officer-involved shooting. In such cases, the safety statement, also referred to as a "Walk Through," consisted of just asking very simple questions to identify safety issues, outstanding suspects, people who might be wounded or in need of medical attention, potential threats, shooting positions and the identification of evidence at the scene for documentation purposes. Nothing more.

Again, Wade was very familiar with the protocol and responded to anticipated questions in order of priority.

"You'll find two dead subjects, both armed in the center of the room near the bar. You have two other subjects, both who had been armed, but have now been disarmed. One guy has a knife injury to his right hand and will need medical attention. The other guy was just knocked out. People inside have those guys secured.

"There are three men inside who are armed and are guarding the subjects who are alive. No other active threats inside. The subjects are believed to all be drug cartel soldiers. Let me know when you want me inside to ID positions and evidence. I froze the scene and also took a number of photos of the scene and evidence. They are all on my cellphone. All of the people inside are witnesses to what happened," explained Wade.

Marcus immediately radioed to his partner inside everything that Wade had said and then addressed Wade.

"Sheriff Fremont has been contacted and he's responding. He should be here any minute. You say you're in Las Brisas at his behest? Can I ask what for?"

"Well, first understand that I want to cooperate with your

investigation and I'm going to make it easy on you. I won't be needing an attorney to respond to questions. I'm also ready to do the walk through the scene with you. I know what you've got to do and appreciate all of that. I've done a number of these in my rangering days. However, until Matt Fremont gets here, I'm really not at liberty to discuss why I'm here until I get his say so. I'm sure it's not going to be an issue, but I've just gotta wait until Matt gets here. You want to get inside and do the walk through before the scene gets torn up? There's important evidence inside," Wade suggested.

Deputy Carter was just about to take Wade's suggestion and go into the saloon when the sound of a wailing siren was heard. The pair looked up Main Street to see the flashing emergency lights of another marked Gila County Sheriff's Department unit approaching from the opposite direction. The unit parked in front of the saloon and Sheriff Matt Fremont emerged and approached them.

"Deputy Carter; Wade, are you involved in this?" the sheriff asked Wade.

"Afraid so, Matt. It's my shooting. Couldn't be helped, Tom either. He's inside, but OK," explained Wade briefly.

Sheriff Fremont addressed Jacob, "So what have we got so far, Marcus?" the sheriff asked.

"Well Sheriff, I haven't been inside yet. Deputy Sheridan, fire and EMS are in there. We contacted former Texas Ranger Justus outside and I was just getting a safety statement from him when you pulled up. Apparently we got a couple of dead guys inside, another guy wounded, and a fourth guy not wounded, but maybe knocked unconscious.

"Ranger Justus here says he helped to secure the scene and even took some photos. I don't have any more particulars than that, sir. Ranger, ah, Mr. Justus says he's in town at your behest. He's been very cooperative but wouldn't tell me why he's here unless you say so. That's all I got so far, Sheriff. We just got here," explained the deputy.

"OK son, I know former ranger Justus. We'll discuss why he's here later. Right now, I'm going to assume command of the investigation. I'm going to want you and Deputy Sheridan to assist in interviewing all of the witnesses. Once we identify the positions of everyone and the various locations of evidence, I'll want you to call Deputy Tristin Peters at home and have him respond down here to process the scene. Do brief interviews here first and then get everyone transported down to the station. I'm gonna do the walk through with ranger Justus and take his statement," said the sheriff.

"Copy that, Sheriff," replied Deputy Carter before he walked inside the saloon.

After Deputy Carter had walked inside, Matt Fremont turned to Wade and said, "OK partner, just what the hell happed tonight in there? Just give me the Reader's Digest version and we'll do a formal, recorded statement at the station."

Wade related the events at the Roadrunner Saloon to Matt Fremont, careful to mention that it appeared that the four cartel soldiers appeared to be extorting owner Sally DuBois. He explained that when he intervened, two of the four drew down on him and he was forced to defend himself. While dispatching the first two, a third man also went for his gun. Tom Fights with a Knife wounded him with a throwing knife and the last soldier was punched out by a Catholic priest.

"Sounds like you and Tom really had no choice," said Matt.

"Well, these punks were spoiling for a fight, and it appeared to me that they were scaring the hell out of the gal who owns the joint. I was actually surprised at how brazen these guys were. They came in like they owned the place. Seemed to be like this wasn't their first time extorting the owner for money, too. You might want to have a conversation with her about that. Just what the hell is going on here? I'd bet a month's pension these were cartel soldiers, with the main hombre being an enforcer. By the way, who's the padre with the awesome left hook who took out one of the survivors?" asked Wade

"That would be Father Marco Reyes. He used to be a pro boxer in Mexico in his younger days. He's the priest at our Catholic church in town. A good guy, fire and brimstone kind of holy man. Hates the cartels. He's seen enough cartel violence in Mexico. He's also been a naturalized U.S. citizen for many years and he's very proud of that," replied Matt.

"Gila County and Las Brisas have changed quite a bit since you were last here years ago when I took the Chief's job. The silver mining dried up and cotton is not as profitable as before. Cartel money and influence has been steadily creeping in and changing our way of life. Everyone used to get along on both sides of the border. Hell, like a lot of border counties in Arizona, New Mexico and Texas, it's hard to tell the difference where the border is culturally.

"What has always made the difference in keeping things calm has been law enforcement being honest and protecting the people. That's all changed now. With this crazy new progressive federal administration opening our border, the cartels now have the upper hand. Shit, they seem to be controlling everything now, drugs, illegals, sex trafficking and child sexual exploitation.

"I can guarantee you that there is not one person in the hundreds of thousands who have illegally entered into the U.S. who the cartels don't know about. Every one of those people must have permission from the cartels to cross over and every one of these illegals pay hefty fees to be personally escorted, smuggled in, or even to cross over by themselves.

"The cartels now make almost as much money smuggling illegals as they do trafficking narcotics. That's because the risk of going to prison for trafficking people is now almost non-existent compared to smuggling dope. The cartels have illegal alien trafficking down to a science, very sophisticated operations now. Hell, they even put colored wrist bands and electronic trackers on many of the people they sneak across the border. Different colors for the status of the people they smuggle in.

"As you already know from being a ranger or watching the news, we now have illegal aliens representing nearly one hundred and fifty nations being smuggled into the U.S. At last count, there are already over thirty-seven million illegal aliens in this country. Just in this year alone, nearly two million illegals have crossed into the U.S. The numbers are staggering.

"Getting back to the wrist bands, the cartels have fixed it so that if you are an Asian with a college degree you can pay up to $60,000 to be smuggled in; but if you are a simple uneducated laborer with no specific job skills, you're only paying about $5,000 –

$7,000 to the coyotes to be trafficked into the country. Women and men can also pay thousands extra to wear a colored band that tells everyone including coyotes that they are "protected" by the cartel, so they won't be robbed or raped," explained Matt.

"That's some operation they've got," replied Wade.

"There's far more to it than that, Wade. The cartels see to it that every illegal they smuggle in tells them who and where their family members are in the U.S. they will be staying with. When they get to where they are going, they must "check in" with the cartel so the cartel gets the rest of their money. If they don't check in, there are profound consequences for the illegal and/or U.S. family members. Same for the high-end people who are forced to wear electronic trackers. If they try to evade by throwing away their tracker, a family member suffers," said Matt.

"What about illegals who can't afford to pay and try sneaking across by themselves without a coyote," asked Wade.

"Simple, the cartels make public examples of them. We've had those before. We find them brutally tortured, mutilated, and/ or raped, executed and left out for public display as a message never to cross the cartel," explained Matt.

"Serious actors, but you already know that. In large part, this is why I asked for your help. Now these bastards have got Jessie and they are going to kill him if we can't find him and get him out of wherever the hell they've got him stashed," said Matt

"It's not just Jessie, it's taking back my county. I'm fairly certain they've got their hooks into a couple of our county commissioners and maybe more than that. Hard to tell who's taking cartel money on the fed side as well. My suspicions are that there's far more to this whole open borders advocacy by some of our federal politicians than meets the eye," said Matt.

"I don't doubt that for a minute. I promise you Matt that I'll do my very best to get Jessie back and to help you get your county back as well," replied Wade.

After a half an hour, Deputy Carter came outside with the witnesses and a now revived and handcuffed prisoner. They were followed by Deputy Sheridan, holding onto the wounded and handcuffed prisoner with the paramedics.

"All yours, Sheriff. We left the dead guys inside for the coroner. Deputy Tristin is still inside snapping photos and taking measurements," Marcus Carter said to Matt Fremont.

"Good deal, Marcus. You and Blake take everyone to the office for questioning. Get both of those perps processed. Book the first guy and have Blake take the wounded fella over to Urgent Care for stitches, then bring him back and book him as well. I'll do the walk-through with Ranger Justus, and we'll see you guys at the office later.

"Oh, and Marcus, absolutely no phone calls for these two until I clear it. We want to stay ahead of the cartel on this one for once. The least and later they know about what happened here, the better. Also stay off the radio. Use your cell phones and pass the word to our people, dispatch, Fire, EMS and the Coroner. I want a lid on this. Not even a word to the feds unless I say so," instructed Sheriff Fremont.

Sheriff Fremont surveyed the scene, paying close attention to the precisely placed four gunshot wounds in each of the two dead cartel soldiers' chests, as well as the two additional shots into one of the dead men's head. The sheriff also visually examined both of the men's pistols on the floor close to each body and noted that neither weapon appeared to have been discharged.

"I see that you haven't lost your touch in the gunfighting department. You don't have as much as a scratch," commented Matt.

"Well, Matt, I was lucky, that's all. These fellas really didn't give me much of a chance. I really don't know what they expected from me other than me dying. That certainly wasn't going to happen as far as I was concerned," replied Wade.

"Were their last words something like, "Oh, shit!" said Matt with a smirk on his face.

"I'm just a civilian trying to defend himself. I think you'll find out from the witnesses that they drew on me first," said Wade.

"I have no doubt the wits will say exactly that. Show me about where these two guys were standing when they pulled on you. Then take me over to where you were standing when you first drew and shot. I want to get an idea of distances," said Matt.

Wade spent a couple of minutes discussing and pointing to the positions where the cartel soldiers when they confronted him. Then Wade walked over to the far corner of the bar to point out his positions of movement and fire while Deputy Tristin Peters videoed, photographed and marked the various positions for a scene diagram he would construct later.

"Okay, I've seen enough for now. Let's get you down to the office where I can get a recorded statement from you," said Matt before turning to Deputy Peters who was documenting the scene.

"Tristin, take your time here with everything. Make sure that you get good photos of the decedents' weapons, the condition their weapons are in and their holsters. Did you get some good video and photos of the body positions in relation to where Ranger Justus said he was when he fired?" asked the sheriff.

"I think I'm good, Sheriff. I think I can have a good computer diagram for you by tomorrow afternoon," replied the young deputy.

"Great. Once the Coroner takes possession of the bodies, make sure that you get any ID's they have on them. We'll check any ID's, fingerprints and tattoos if they have them through NCIC, DEA, DHS and Interpol. I'll see if anything pops up. Same with the two survivors.

"Tristin, our bad guys undoubtedly drove here, so check them both for keys. Use your cell phone to call Marcus and Blake and tell them to search the two survivors for car keys too. Then find their vehicle and photograph it completely from the outside.

"Impound the vehicle and make sure that no one goes inside it. Have the vehicle towed to our place so I can search it later today. I'm going to get a telephonic search warrant for the vehicle. If I find anything inside, I'll want you with me to photograph and document anything of evidentiary value. Comprende?" instructed the sheriff.

"Copy that, Sheriff," replied Deputy Peters who immediately got on his cell phone to relay the sheriff's directions to all involved

Sheriff Fremont turned back to Wade, "Well, let's saddle up and head over to the office. I'm gonna need a short, recorded statement from you. I also have to photograph you head to toe, photo the condition of your weapon, holster, and any mags you have on you.

"I also have to remind you that I've got to hang on to your weapon to document its condition and functionality. You know the drill. I've got another 1911A .45 with three mags you can borrow until I return your pistol back to you. I'm not leaving you unarmed around here. Then you're free to go back to my ranch to get some sleep," said the sheriff.

"Yeah, I know the drill," replied Wade as he climbed into the sheriff's unit for the ride back to the sheriff's office.

"Looks like I'm going to be pulling an all-nighter, so I have a complete file ready for the DA including probable cause affidavits enough to hold our two survivors on felony charges. I'm not waking up the DA or a judge tonight for a search warrant. I'll get that tomorrow. Their vehicle's aren't going anywhere, and I don't know who I can trust these days if you get my drift," explained Matt.

"I'm beginning to see what you mean," replied Wade.

"Well, the good news is that if the witnesses support your version of events, it's going down as a clean self-defense shoot. No problems on our end. However, once the Tres Paises cartel bosses hear about you dumping two of their guys and two more busted, that's an entirely different story," said Matt.

"I'll take my chances. Way I see it, my work here has just begun. Next up is finding out where Jessie is and as you've reminded me, the clock is ticking," said Wade.

CHAPTER **14**

The Geek

AFTER WADE FINISHED his interview with Matt Fremont, the sheriff called Deputy Tristin Peters to take Wade down to the evidence room where he was photographed. The deputy accepted Wade's Nichols Custom Combat 1911A .45 caliber semiautomatic pistol, his holster and his magazines of ammunition and photographed their condition which included a round count in Wade's gun before booking everything into evidence. This was the normal evidence protocol in any shooting investigation.

Wade was allowed to keep his 1911a and double magazine holsters. The deputy then presented Wade with a replacement 1911A pistol and three freshly loaded magazines from Sheriff Fremont's personal arsenal.

Wade inspected the replacement pistol, racking the slide to clear the weapon and then checking the safety and trigger pull. He inserted a fresh magazine into the well of the weapon, racked and pressed checked it before engaging the safety and holstering the weapon. "This should do for now," he told Deputy Peters before inserting both magazines into his magazine holster.

"We just have to run the standard check for functionality. The sheriff wants this investigation by the book. But, from what I saw at the scene and what I'm hearing, you'll be getting all your gear back very shortly. I'm detailed to give you a ride back to Sheriff Fremont's ranch. I'm sure you're pretty tired," explained Deputy Peters.

"I'm ready when you are, deputy," replied Wade.

Driving the short distance back to Matt Fremont's ranch, Wade looked over Deputy Peters. Tristin Peters appeared to be an unlikely candidate to be a deputy sheriff. He appeared to be very young, slight in frame at about one hundred and forty pounds five feet nine inches in height. The guy looked more like a techno geek than a rural deputy. Knowing Matt Fremont's conservative bent in law enforcement, Wade was naturally curious. In his eyes, Deputy Peters looked out of place. Wade really didn't see this young man surviving a fight in bar while making an arrest.

"So, no offense if I might ask," said Wade, "This looks like a pretty tough neighborhood for someone like you. What's your story?" asked Wade.

Tristin Peters smirked back at Wade with a look that said, "Well, I was wondering how long it was going to take before you asked me the 'someone like you' question.

"Well, Ranger Justus, since you asked, I'll give you the Readers Digest version. I'm twenty-four years old and I've wanted to be in law enforcement all my life. I've got a degree in computer science with a minor in criminal justice.

"My grandfather was a State Police officer, and it was he who gave me the bug. Unfortunately, he was shot and killed on the job a number of years ago. I always wanted to follow in his footsteps. I just loved all his stories about the job and have always been community service oriented. Understandably, my parents were completely against me entering law enforcement, but they have supported me none the less.

"I'm sure that you see me as the last guy who gets picked to play on a flag football team. However, we all have our special skill sets. Mine is technology; especially anything electronic.

"I tested for several agencies but could never make it past the final oral board. Chiefs and sheriffs would look at me and say to themselves, 'This kid ain't got it. He looks like a geek without the man bun'.

Sheriff Fremont looked past what I look like. He let me demonstrate my skill set, gave me a chance and here I am. Maybe while you're here, I can show you that police work isn't just muscle and guns," explained Tristin.

"I learned a long time ago not to be judgmental. If you're working for Matt Fremont, that's good enough for me. He's a great judge of character. I'll look forward to it," replied Wade as they pulled up into the Fremont compound.

Wade bade Deputy Peters a good evening. He walked over to and entered the guest cottage. He was understandably exhausted after a very long day. He unholstered the 1911A with the two additional mags that Matt had loaned him and placed them on the night stand next to his bed. He went into his travel duffle, removed a small tactical light and placed the light next to the pistol and mags. Always important to be prepared he mused. On the nightstand was a TV remote. He turned on the TV and caught the late evening news.

"Breaking News Tonight – The U.S. Border Patrol estimates that over 1.7 million undocumented aliens representing over 140 nations have now been arrested while illegally entered the U.S. since January of this year when the new administration took over. This is the largest increase in illegal border crossings in U.S. History. This month, in the states of Texas and New Mexico, BP and ICE report that there were over 200,000 apprehensions, with another 60,000 'get-aways'.

"In related border news, the Departments of Homeland Security and the Drug Enforcement Administration report that seizures of dangerous drugs especially the deadly drug fentanyl are at levels ten times what they were only one year ago. The DEA estimates that currently in the U.S. there is enough illegal fentanyl on the streets to kill every man, woman and child in the country.

"In the small rural county of Gila, New Mexico, law enforcement authorities last week intercepted ninety pounds of the deadly drug during a border incursion by the Tres Paises drug cartel. During this smuggling operation, three heavily armed cartel smugglers were killed in a shootout with Gila County Sheriff deputies. The DEA says that only a couple of micrograms of the drug are enough to kill a human being. During the past two years, over 110,000 Americans each year have died from opioid and fentanyl related drug overdoses. And in the world of sports...."

Wade clicked off the set. He didn't need to be listening about something that he was living right now. Within two minutes he was sound asleep.

Wade slept in a bit late and woke up at 0700 hours. He hit

the floor, banged out a quick 100 push-ups, 100 sit-ups, did some twisting and stretching exercises for flexibility. He took a quick shower, shaved and made himself a cup of coffee.

Matt had texted him to meet him at the Sheriff's Office at 0800 hours. Wade looked outside the window and saw that Matt's Sheriff's SUV was gone.

CHAPTER 15

The Briefing

SHERIFF MATT FREMONT had called for a mandatory, confidential special briefing of all patrol deputies at 0800 hours sharp. The sheriff was explicit that no one – absolutely no one outside of the five remaining patrol deputies was to be informed of the briefing. His administrative secretary Lisa Owens had made cell phone calls to each deputy advising them of the meeting. Nothing had gone out over the radio and even dispatch had not been informed. The two day-shift deputies were directed to make up an on-view call and to place themselves out on this call for one hour for purposes of the Computer Aided Dispatch or "CAD" system. There would be no other paper trail of the deputies' absence.

The confidential briefing involving all patrol deputies was a highly unusual step. No one could remember the sheriff ever doing this since he had become their sheriff. By 0750 hours, everyone was gathered in the small briefing and report writing room awaiting the sheriff. In attendance were Jacob Black Arrows, Tristin Peters, Blake Sheridan, Marcus Carter, and Pete Vasquez. You could cut the tension with a knife.

At 0759 hours, Sheriff Fremont walked into the briefing room with Wade Justus who was strapped with his 1911A .45 caliber pistol and three magazines of ammo and looking every bit the picture of a Texas Ranger. All of the deputies had heard of Wade either by reputation or had met him during the recent shooting investigation at the Roadrunner. Seeing him with the sheriff in this confidential briefing only added to the suspense.

Sheriff Fremont wasted no time and got straight to the point.

"Men, I need to begin by giving you an order that everything we are about to discuss in this briefing must be held in the highest level of secrecy. None of you may discuss, even with members of your own family what we will be talking about from here on out. Our lives and the lives of others will literally depend upon this, is that understood?"

The deputies respond affirmatively in unison.

"Thank you. As all of you know by now, my son and our fellow Deputy Jessie was recently kidnapped by members of the Tres Paises drug cartel. I greatly appreciate your maintaining secrecy in this matter. So far, there have been no press inquiries. I need to keep it that way.

"Since Jessie was kidnapped, I have been negotiating in secret with the DEA to make arrangements with the Tres Paises for Jessie's release. The main condition as set by Tres Paises is the release of Chuy Guzman, who was arrested by Jessie and Jacob Black Arrows during the recent drug interdiction and officer involved shooting. After holding two meetings with the regional DEA SAC in El Paso, I regret to inform you that it looks like the DEA will not be cooperating in Chuy Guzman's release.

"Adolfo Guzman, who heads the Tres Paises cartel has directed that if Chuy is not released very soon, they will execute Jessie. To motivate law enforcement into releasing Jessie, I recently received in a package Jessie's wedding ring complete with his left ring finger."

The assembled deputies responded with a gasp as the sheriff continued.

"For obvious reasons, I have not shared that information with Jessie's mother or his wife. It is extremely clear to me that Tres Paises will kill Jessie soon. Since the DEA will not cooperate, nor can we depend upon any of the federal law enforcement agencies for help directly due to the open border policies of this administration, I am left with only one alternative and that is to mount a plan to extract Jessie ourselves."

The deputies looked at each other as the tension grew.

"With us today is retired Texas Ranger Wade Justus. In case you don't know, Ranger Justus and I were partners back in the day and have remained close friends. Wade is Jessie's Godfather and has volunteered his services in the effort to rescue Jessie from the hands of the Tres Paises."

All of the deputies looked at Wade, who made eye contact with each and every one of them. This was quickly going to get very serious and dangerous each deputy thought.

"There is another thing Adolfo Guzman has demanded that affects all of us. He is demanding that this department and that means each of you are to stand down with regards to any enforcement actions against members of the Tres Paises cartel. That is not going to happen while I am your sheriff. Las Brisas and Gila County are not going to become another Juarez, Mexico where drugs flow, humans are trafficked, cops are bought, and innocent people are exploited and murdered indiscriminately.

"The plan we will be developing to save Jessie will require cunning, commitment, stealth and audacity. It will be extremely dangerous and potentially deadly for those involved, albeit not all of you will be directly involved.

"Another thing is that at this point, we really don't know exactly where Jessie is, but we believe that it might be inside Mexico. If that's the case, then you need to know that by being involved in the raid party, we would be breaking U.S. and federal and Mexican laws.

"Breaking international laws could easily get us arrested, convicted and imprisoned most probably in a Mexican prison where we would be unlikely to survive a cartel hit. This is why I am only taking volunteers. Therefore, anyone who for personal reasons including family concerns wants out, please take a moment and tell me now. I promise you that you will continue to receive my deepest thanks, appreciation and respect. I'm going to let that set in for a minute and then I need a show of hands of all those who want to volunteer for this mission."

Matt Fremont took a deep breath and looked at Wade. Matt knew that this was the most difficult and demanding decision he had ever made in his life. Undoubtedly the same can be said for his men, none of whom had anywhere near the experience of he and Wade. The deputies looked at each other and then at Sheriff Fremont and at Wade. Both men looked back at the assembled deputies stoically and silently as the clock on the wall ticked.

After only fifteen seconds, Jacob Black Arrows hand went up, immediately followed by Blake Sheridan's and Tristin Peters. Deputies Marcus Carter and Pete Vasquez's hands soon followed. In less than a minute it was a unanimous decision to volunteer for the deadly rescue mission.

Matt Fremont took another deep breath, let out a quiet sigh of relief and then displayed a smile of great pride in the heroic courage of his band of rural deputies. "Men, you honor me and Jessie. Thank you in advance for this sacrifice," said the sheriff.

Matt walked over to the large flat screen TV in the video room that was attached to a USB cord affixed to a laptop. "Now, I have something that I need to show you. This is a video that was sent to me on a thumb drive that accompanied Jessie's wedding ring and ring finger. It is very troubling to watch but there is a purpose to it. I want you to watch this video closely. We will play it as many times as you want. Your first response like mine will no doubt be an emotional one because it records Jessie under extreme duress.

"However, I need you to look past what you see and compartmentalize your emotions. I need you to have a forensic, rather than an emotional response to the video. It's important that you to pay close attention to everything that is said, every behavior you see and the environment where this video was shot.

"What intelligence information can we gain from this video? Where have the Tres Paises screwed up? What if anything does this short video tell us and how can we exploit that information for our benefit?"

Sheriff Fremont hit the play button and introduced the video matter of factly as if he was teaching a class on evidence.

Immediately on screen appeared Jessie, secured to a chair in zip ties with a dark hood over his head. Two masked men with assault vests filled with magazines and holding AK-47's appeared immediately behind Jessie. From the right side of the screen a man dressed all in black with a black balaclava over his head with just his piercing black eyes visible. Urias was holding a pair of one-handed stainless-steel gardening, trimming shears in his right hand.

The man harshly pulled the hood off of Jessie's head revealing his distressed face. It was an ominous sight to behold, surreal like a movie.

"We believe this man who narrated the video, and we refer to as "Toro" is Uberto Urias, aka "The Bull." Urias has been identified by the DEA as Adolfo Guzman's chief enforcer. We believe that he spearheaded the op that kidnapped Jessie in Las Brisas."

The video began with the Urias directing Jessie, "Tell them your name," and Jessie responding by identifying himself as a Gila County Sheriff's Department deputy.

Urias continued, "Sheriff Fremont. The Tres Paises cartel has been patient in trying to work with you on the return of Chuy Guzman for your son here. We have given you more time than you deserve, and you have not honored our agreement that you would convince your government to trade Chuy for your son. Is this not so?"

As Urias spoke, Jessie was looking stoically directly into the camera with bright lights focused upon Jessie's face. Jessie was repeatedly blinking as he focused forward. The Handler continued.

"Well, perhaps some motivation is needed so that you see that Senor Guzman is quickly losing his patience. He thinks that it is now time for a demonstration that should attract your attention," said Urias.

As Urias spoke, Jessie continued blinking. Was it the lights or sweat dripping into Jessie's eyes that caused him to blink so much?

"Watch closely Sheriff Fremont," said Urias. "The Bull" used his left hand to grab onto to Jessie's left hand which was secured to the arm of the chair with zip ties. He then spread Jessie's fingers apart, exposing the deputy's left ring finger. Urias moved Jessie's wedding ring down between the first knuckle and the hand, while he maneuvered the trimming shears blade open between the ring and the first knuckle. It was a foregone conclusion what was about to occur next. The assembled deputies could see Jessie tensing up, but strangely continuing to focus on the camera lens while blinking faster.

Jessie cried out in pain as Urias cleanly severed Jessie's ring finger from his left hand. Jessie's wedding ring fell to the floor as the end of his severed finger spurted blood. But the torture wasn't over yet. As the deputies winced, Urias next took a white-hot steel poker and applied the burning tip to the severed end of Jessie's ring finger. In response, Jessie cried out from the intense pain as a couple of the deputies looked away. Jessie was now taking in deep breaths of air while groaning loudly. Yet, he continued to look into the camera lens while blinking.

The video continued as the camera now focused upon the masked Urias who said, "Senor Guzman generously gives you three more days to reach an agreement with your DEA to trade Chuy Guzman for your son. After that time, we will mail your son home to you in small pieces. Do you like your gift? Remember, you have only three more days," and then the video ended abruptly.

As Matt had anticipated, the deputies were initially angered by the video and expressed it openly, but he let that slide. It was a natural, visceral response to witnessing a man being tortured. However, to the deputies' credit, they stayed on mission and began to express some thoughts about what they had seen in the video.

"Well, it sure looks like they got Jessie in some type of cave," said Jacob Black Arrows.

"I'm hearing the sound of a generator in the background, hear it? Let's play it again," said Blake Sheridan.

Sheriff Fremont replayed the video as the men intensely began to parse out and isolate certain aspects of what was being shown.

"Yes, definitely a generator in the background. That means they have no other source of electrical power. Got to be a remote rural location," said Sheridan.

"Agreed," replied the sheriff.

"Me too," said Wade.

"Why do you think Jessie keeps blinking so much?" Marcus Carter asked to no one in particular.

"Probably those lights in his face along with sweat irritating his eyes," replied Pete Vasquez.

Tristin Peters was fixated at the TV screen. "Play it again, Sheriff," he said. Matt Fremont started the video over.

Tristin stared intently at Jessie as he was speaking and later as Uberto "The Bull" Urias was severing Jessie's finger. It was difficult to watch, but Tristin was not watching The Bull severing the hapless deputy's finger. Tristin was watching Jessie's facial expressions, especially his blinking eyes.

"Sheriff, can you please play it again?" Tristin asked. None of the deputies had anything else to offer, so Matt accommodated the deputy.

As the video played through, Tristin watched intensely and then began tapping his pen on the table as Jessie was blinking. The annoying behavior attracted the attention of everyone in the room. though, no one said anything because Tristin appeared to be locked deep in thought, transfixed to the video.

As the video ended, Tristin stopped tapping. "Again, Sheriff. Please," said the geeky deputy.

Matt said nothing and simply hit the play button on his laptop and the video commenced again. This time, Tristin wasn't tapping his pen, he was watching Jessie's eyes blink and was writing on a notepad he had removed from his uniform shirt pocket before suddenly and loudly announcing with a broad smile, "Morse code! Morse fucking code!"

"Morse what?" said a young Marcus Carter.

"Morse code. An old form of communication dating back to the 1800's. You know, like in the days of the telegraph. Like on ships. The military also used it and might even still use it for all I know," replied Tristin.

"You know Morse code?" asked Sheriff Fremont.

"Yeah, I learned it to get my shortwave radio license," replied Tristin.

"Figures the geek would know shit like that," laughed Blake Sheridan.

"Fuck you, Sheridan, you jarhead, neanderthal, bonehead," replied Tristin.

"Ouch, that smarts computer boy," smirked Sheridan.

"OK, just hold on fellas. Tristin, you telling us you can decipher what Jessie is trying to tell us? How?" asked the sheriff.

"Yes, sheriff. First of all, I noted that Jessie was blinking his eyes far more than he needed to even though he's got lights and sweat in his eyes. The key for me was he even continued to blink his eyes after that guy cut off his finger. Who does that? The excruciating pain would be extremely distracting.

Jessie was intensely focused on blinking his eyes even through all that pain. Next, after watching the video these few times, I saw that the blinks of his eyes were repetitive. He was using a series of repeated blinks. That was critical for me. It's a short sequence of a burst of blinks, repeated over and over again," explained Tristin.

"Well, what's Jessie trying to tell us?" asked Sheriff Fremont?

Tristin looked down at his note pad. "I'll need to check it over again a couple of times, but here's what I've got so far. "Old mine, cactus cross, sleeping lady." He blinks that three times during the video. "Old mine, cactus cross, sleeping lady." I'm pretty sure that's it," replied Tristin.

"That's absolutely amazing, kid. Nice job," offered Wade.

"It certainly is," echoed Sheriff Fremont who beamed with pride at his young deputy. "Are you pretty sure that's what Jessie is telling us?"

"Yes, sir. I'll watch it again, but I tapped it out as he was blinking and then wrote it out and I'm sure that's what your son is telling us," replied Tristin.

"OK, then what it appears that we are looking for is some type of abandoned mine where they are holding Jessie. Now, what about the words, "cactus cross and sleeping lady." What's that all about?" asked Wade to everyone in the room.

"I have no idea," said Tristin.

"Well, since you are our electronic and technology guru, why don't you begin Googling "sleeping lady" and "cactus cross,"

Tristin. As for the rest of you, put your heads together and see if you can come up with anything relating to a cactus cross and a sleeping lady. What do those terms mean? I need to know pronto; Jessie is running out of time. That's your assignment for now while Ranger Justus and I plan our extraction operation. Stick around and work on this.

"Deputies Vasquez and Carter, you're here until a radio call comes up. Put yourselves both 10-8 and available to shag calls but work here as long as you can. Let's not make dispatch any more curious than they need to be.

"Also, Deputies Blake and Black Arrows, I want to see you two in my office now. Briefing adjourned," directed the sheriff.

Matt immediately left the briefing room followed by Wade with Deputies Blake and Black Arrows in tow. The four men walked into Sheriff Fremont's office. Matt shut the door, picked up the phone and told his administrative secretary Lisa Owens "Hold my calls for the next two hours."

Deputies Black Arrows and Sheridan were trying to figure out why they had been separated from the pack. Before being sworn in as a deputy in Gila County, Blake Sheridan had been a USMC Force Recon sniper who had served tours in Afghanistan and Iraq. On the record, he had a well-recognized service-wide reputation of establishing a very high body count. Marine snipers joked that Sheridan had killed more men than cancer.

While in the Corps, Sheridan had been loaned out "TDY" (temporary duty) to the CIA where he had done some black ops work as a sniper, providing overwatch for CIA assets during high-risk missions. Blake had all of the qualities of a good sniper, he was patient, persistent, tenacious, fearless and deadly accurate. His call sign as a sniper in the field had been "Archangel."

Sheridan had always wanted to be a cop but due to his sniper background, high body count and secret DOD background, no one would hire him. Sheriff Matt Fremont hired Blake due to his USMC background and solid personality.

Sheridan and Black Arrows looked quickly at each other when Sheriff Fremont shut the door. Matt Fremont asked the men to take seats around his desk and began.

"Blake and Jacob, first up, I thank you and my family thanks you for volunteering for this mission. I asked you to come into my office because each of you have unique skill sets as trackers and shooters that are definitely going to come in handy on this mission to extract Jessie. Each of you know how to stealthfully track and approach a target covertly under cover of darkness, set up sniper or ambush positions and take out the enemy without hesitation if need be.

"Former Ranger Justus and I believe that Tres Paises have Jessie sequestered somewhere near the border on the Mexican side. This makes sense since Adolfo Guzman wants to facilitate the release of his nephew Chuy in trade for Jessie. That transaction would go down quickly. It makes total sense that Tres Paises wouldn't drive long distances across Mexico to make that happen. They would want to make the trade directly on the border, grab Chuy and vanish as quickly as possible into an area of Mexico they feel comfortable with. That means more likely than not to be within just a few miles from our U.S. border here in Gila County.

"Taking into consideration optimistically that we will shortly be able to identify the place where Tres Paises has Jessie, we assume that the location will be well protected by some of Guzman's best fighters. Again, we need to also assume that they will be well armed and provisioned with ammo and night vision.

"Ranger Justus and I will be involved with drawing up the extraction plan. Blake, you have worked on and been involved in a number of similar extraction or assassination plans. We will want you to check our work and offer suggestions wherever necessary. Specifically, I will want you to draw all weaponry, accessories and ammo you think you will need to provide both intelligence and overwatch to and for the extraction team. That means your own sniper rifle system, silencer, NVG's (night vision goggles), optics and ammo. We'll work on comm gear for the op suitable for the location we'll be deploying to."

"Copy that, Sheriff," replied Sheridan.

"Jacob, since stealth and surprise are the key components of this op, once the location of Jessie and the cartel members is identified, we will need your expert tracking abilities to plot the best insertion point to the target. You will guide the team to the location, identify their best lines of approach and protect the team members both entering and extracting from the location.

"Blake and Jacob listen up; the rules of engagement are simple so you both have to be mentally good with them. This is a completely stealth black op. It is off the books. These assholes are going to kill your fellow deputy who is your friend and my son. They won't hesitate taking out our entire team to protect their hostage. Then they may even kill Jessie anyway in retribution for us trying to rescue him. This will most definitely involve proactively mitigating the risk of deadly force against us. That means you will be taking out their scouts and guards so the team can enter, find and secure Jessie, and extract him from the site.

"Another thing, we are not shooting to wound anyone. We are killing people here without prejudice and never reporting it. This is war. We didn't start it, but we sure as hell are going to finish it. Do you understand and are you OK with this? I need to know now," explained the sheriff.

"I'm good, sheriff," replied Jacob Black Arrows.

"Where do I sign?" said Blake Sheridan.

Sheriff Fremont looked both men in the eyes.

"Remember that in agreeing to go on this op, none of us will be going as LEO's. You will be civilians in a foreign land. You will be subject to Mexican laws and a corrupt justice system. If the U.S. feds decide to take a piece of you, you'd be dealing with our own morally bankrupt and politically biased justice system.

"We are off the books and this mission can never, ever be discussed with anyone. If we are successful, afterwards, we will destroy all evidence of our incursion into Mexico and all actions we have taken. Is that clear?" asked Sheriff Fremont.

"Sir, yes sir," both men said in unison.

"Okay, then you are dismissed. Take the remainder of the day to gather up all of the gear you need. Stay next to your cell phones for my call. We will most probably spin up within the next twenty-four to forty-eight hours," said the sheriff. Matt Fremont and Wade shook each man's hand before they quietly left the office.

Matt Fremont looked at Wade. "So, what do you think?"

"Well, this is a tall assignment for everyone involved. I've got no worries about Sheridan. He's been there before and has the T-shirt. As for Black Arrows, from what you've told me, he did well during the drug smuggler's incursion and dumped at least two bad guys. Jessie is also his best friend, and the loyalty factor is there. He'll do whatever it takes to get Jessie back home. I think mentally, he can handle taking out some bad guys who pose an imminent deadly force threat to the team. I think you correctly chose the two strongest men on your department for this job. I wouldn't want to be the gangster to stand in their way," said Wade.

"Good to know from another pro who's also been there and has the T-shirt," smiled Matt. "Let's go back to the briefing room and check on our boys to see what if anything they've come up with."

Sheriff Fremont and Wade re-entered the briefing room to find Tristin Peters, Marcus Carter and Pete Vasquez busy on department PC's, looking for any references to a "sleeping lady" or a "cactus cross."

"Well, how's the searching coming, fellas?" Sheriff Fremont asked.

Deputies Carter and Vasquez replied that they had not found anything for either term in the various search engines they had queried.

Deputy Tristin Peters picked up his notebook which had about four pages of notes scrawled and engaged the sheriff.

"Well, just like Marcus and Pete, I couldn't find anything even remotely approaching the term "cactus cross." With regard to a "sleeping lady," I initially found nothing. Then I started thinking about the areas in New Mexico and across the border into Mexico within one hour from Las Brisas. I queried the term "sleeping lady" associated with the names of mines and found nothing. Then I began thinking about where silver mines are located because silver mines constitute about ninety percent of all of the mineral mines in this region within my one-hour travel circumference of Las Brisas, but again found nothing.

"Then I did some research on the topography where silver

mines in this region are most likely found. My research found that silver mines are most commonly found on flat surfaces like those in Gila County but are also found dug into mountain sides. Silver mines dug into the sides of mountains are most commonly found in Mexico. Apparently, there are quite a number of those within an hour of Las Brisas. So, extrapolating that information, I began querying mountainous areas within that area, using the word "sleeping" as my search word and bingo, I found a fairly well-known mountain referred as the Amante Durmiente, or 'Sleeping Mistress.'

"The Amante Durmiente mountain is found just half an hour from our southern border with Mexico in La Plata County of the Mexican State of Chihuahua. The mythology of the Amante Durmiente is that the mountain takes its name from a story about the despondent and pregnant mistress of a wealthy Mexican caballero landowner. As the folklore goes, when her caballero lover refused to leave his wife to marry her, the woman went to the top of the mountain and poisoned herself. Back then, the mountain's ridge looked to Mexican peasants as the mistress having fallen asleep on the mountain top as she passed away. Hence the term, "Sleeping Mistress," which is pretty close in translation to "sleeping lady." I think this is what Jessie was trying to tell us by blinking Morse code," explained Tristin.

"Fascinating. You found this all on your own?" asked Sheriff Fremont.

"Yes sir. It seemed a logical course in my brief investigation. In fact, here is a photo image of the Amante Durmiente. See for yourself," said Tristin as he transferred the image of the mountain from his laptop onto the big screen TV in the briefing room.

"It sure looks like the image of a sleeping woman if you ask me, but of course you have to use your imagination," said the deputy.

"Yeah, I can see that," said Wade.

"Yup, me too. Nice going Deputy Peters. I think you found our mountain where the mine is. Now all we have to do is to figure out what Jessie's term "cactus cross" refers to, replied the sheriff.

"Well, sheriff if I may add something," said Tristin.

"Sure, you're batting 100% in my book so far. What are you thinking?" asked the sheriff.

Tristin adjusted the TV to accept the screen from his laptop and then turned on the Google Maps Pro application which immediately popped up on the screen.

"Since the Amante Durmiente is a known historical location, we can easily pull it up on Google Maps."

Tristin typed in the name Amante Durmiente and hit the "enter" button and a map of the world that was displayed immediately began to rotate towards the North American continent. A small red dot appeared on the country of Mexico near the U.S. border and the map rotated to a position over that red dot with the GPS coordinates appearing at the top of the screen.

"Okay, we now have the accurate GPS coordinates in Mexico. Next, let's go down a bit and off to the northside of the mountain so we can look over to its ridge and compare the outline of the ridge to the image I pulled off the internet," said Tristin.

Tristin worked the cursor down to the 2,000-foot level of the mountain on its east side which allowed everyone in the room to look directly over to the mountain's ridge. It was a near match to its internet image.

"That's amazing, son. Clear as day," said Sheriff Fremont.

"Alright, now watch and hear me out for a minute," said Tristin as he kept the image on station at 2,000-feet and then placed his cursor over the compass superimposed over the image on the upper right of the screen and began to rotate the compass. When he did that, the view transitioned to one looking directly down at the hillsides and ground surrounding the north, south and east sides of the mountain.

"Tell me what you see?" Tristin asked the men in the room.

"Dirt," said Marcus Carter.

"Tons of rocks, dirt and scrub," replied Pete Vasquez.

"Lots of cactus," said Wade.

"Yes, lots of cactus," replied Sheriff Fremont.

"Cactus!" replied all of the men spontaneously at once

"Yes, lots of cactus. In fact, saguaro cactus. And we have tens of thousands of them in the southwest region of the U.S. and Mexico. And what do saguaro cactus look like sometimes?" Tristin asked.

"People," said Marcus.

"Yeah, people with their hands up or down," replied, Pete Vasquez.

"Or maybe, just maybe crosses," said Wade.

"Bingo. Exactly," replied Tristin.

"Makes complete sense. What if Jessie is in fact inside a mine and had a brief opportunity to look outside? He could see the area where the mine was located and maybe spotted a unique landmark near the mine. Then he gives us the lead and a landmark by blinking his eyes and using Morse code to transmit that information?" said the sheriff.

"I've heard of worse far-fetched ideas," said Wade.

"What are the odds we are wrong here? Just look at the scientific method and see how things are matching up. How we arc connecting the dots," said Tristin.

"Success favors the prepared mind," said Wade.

"Agreed," said Matt.

"But like Tristin said, there are literally thousands of saguaro cactus in the region. How the hell do we find a single cactus that is shaped like a cross? Even so, just how many of those might there be, hundreds? We can't check them all out," said Marcus Carter.

"Yes difficult, but far from impossible. First, we now have a very good idea that the place where they are hiding Jessie is a mine. Next, we have Jessie's clue that the mine is located on or near the Amante Durmiente mountain. That narrows things down quite a bit," explained Tristin.

"So how do we narrow things down further given the severe time constraints?" asked the sheriff.

"Well, these Google Pro images were taken from an aircraft from above as you can see. They are no ground images. The planes do not remain on station, so there is only so much I can do with something like this. There are no Google Street images because Google cars cannot and do not access these remote areas. Satellite images are too far up there and even though you can greatly enhance satellite images, we can't get down low enough to see what an actual cactus really looks like. A helicopter would be too noisy and too conspicuous. It would immediately alert the bad guys and if so, game over.

"So, what we would need is something like a drone that cannot be seen, remain quietly on station and be maneuvered to select and enhance various cacti of interest," explained Tristin.

"A drone," Matt Fremont said to no one in particular.

"Yeah, a drone that could be tasked to fly around on station, searching for a saguaro cactus that looked like a cross. This is in Mexican territory, so I pretty much doubt we are calling on the Mexican Air Force to help us out on this one," replied Tristin.

"So, based on your own experience as our department's drone pilot, do you think a drone is the ticket?" asked Matt.

"Absolutely," replied Tristin.

"Okay, I'll work on that. Everyone is dismissed. Return to your assignments or go home if you're on your time off but stay close to your cell phones. Ranger Justus will be working on the op plans. Most likely, we will spin up in the next twenty-four hours. Remember, not a single word to anyone. If anyone asks, we worked on a new department budget today. That's all we did. You're all dismissed. Thanks for your involvement and input," said Matt.

As Deputy Tristin Peters was packing up his laptop, Matt Fremont and Wade approached him.

"That was one hell of a piece of work you did today, Tristin. I'm glad I hired you and pleased that you're on the team, son," said Matt.

Tristin blushed. "Well, thank you sheriff. I just want to do my part," replied the young deputy.

"Great work, deputy," said Wade patting the young deputy on the back. "Real Texas Ranger work today."

"Gosh, thanks Ranger Justus. That's a real compliment coming from you," said Tristin.

Matt and Wade left to plan the mission. They would be up all night. Tomorrow was going to be a long day.

CHAPTER 16

Operation "Off the Books"

ONCE INSIDE HIS office, Matt Fremont picked up his cell phone and called Border Patrol Assistant Chief Katie Blackwater who picked up on the second ring.

"Matt, what brings you to call me on a lovely day like today?" said Katie.

Matt's only response was, "Katie, call me on a secure line ASAP," and he hung up.

Katie Blackwater could tell by the tone of Sheriff Fremont's voice and the abruptness of his call that their next conversation would be extraordinary. She put down her department issued cell phone, retrieved her personal cell and immediately called Matt back. The sheriff picked up mid-ring.

"Okay, I give. Why all the cloak and dagger, Matt?" she asked.

"Thanks for calling me back, Katie. This is about my son Jessie. It's extremely critical that we meet in person ASAP today. How's your schedule, can you do that?" asked Matt.

"Nothing important on my end that can't be put off a bit. Just budget stuff. Any news of Jessie?" asked Katie.

"Yes, lots, but none of it good. Listen Katie, I know that this might be a bit of an imposition, but can you meet me in Gila County using the fastest form of transportation?" asked Matt.

"Sure, that should be no problem. I'll take the chopper,"

replied Katie noting that Matt Fremont's tone sounded dark and ominous.

"Great. This is definitely going to sound weird, but if you take the chopper, use your most trusted pilot and turn off the transponder. I'm going to give you the GPS coordinates for the meet. Got something to write them down?" asked Matt.

"Yes, go with coordinates," replied Katie.

Matt provided the assistant chief with the coordinates and then said, " Listen Katie, the cloak and dagger as you call it hasn't even begun. This meeting is off the books, are you OK with that?"

"Of course," replied Katie.

"One hour from now, see you there. Thanks, Katie," and all Katie Blackwater heard was a click and Matt was gone.

"What was that all about?" asked Wade.

"Tristin said we would need a drone to surveil the Amante Durmiente mountain area and I'm going to try to get us one," replied Wade.

"Well, who besides the federal government has a drone?" asked Wade skeptically.

"Exactly. I'm about to ask for a big favor from a dear friend and because it's a high-risk request, I'm not so sure they will help. But I owe it to my son and this county to try," replied Matt.

"Well, get going and I'll work on our plan," said Wade.

Matt Fremont left his office, got into his sheriff's department SUV and headed off to his meeting with Katie Blackwater.

On Assistant Chief Blackwater's end, she called her personal pilot and told him to prepare the chopper to spin up in thirty minutes. She had checked the GPS coordinates Matt had given her with her electronic map. The meet with Sheriff Fremont was not going to be far away, but just far out enough for their meeting not to be observed.

Katie pulled up to the tarmac where the observation helicopter assigned to her had been rolled out. Her personal pilot Lt. Burt Medina, who had been doing his walk-around of the aircraft walked over to her. Lt. Medina snapped to attention and delivered a crisp salute.

Katie had chosen her personal pilot well. Medina was formerly of the U.S. Army Airborne's famous 160th Special Operations Aviation Regiment (SOAR), also known as "The Nightstalker's" based out of Ft. Campbell, Kentucky.

The SOAR is the unit that flies, inserts and extracts elite spec ops teams like the Navy SEALs to their covert high-risk assignments. The unit was instrumental in the op that killed Osama Bin Laden. Medina was well known within the ranks of Border Patrol and DHS aviation as a skilled and very accomplished helicopter pilot. He was intensely loyal and because of all of his prior covert military missions, Katie knew that Medina could be trusted to keep a secret.

"Good morning, Chief. Your carriage awaits," smiled Medina.

"Knock off the bullshit, Burt. How's my bird?" Katie asked with a smirk.

"Just now completed my interior and exterior check list. I'm ready to spin her up for a ride. Since you directed me not to file a flight plan, I still gotta ask, where we off to?" Medina asked.

Normally, the Border Patrol flew the Sikorsky UH-60 Blackhawk helicopter, but for administrative and observation uses, the BP also used the Hughes 500-D series light observation helicopters, also referred to by Special Operations groups as "Little Birds."

Katie handed Burt Medina a small piece of paper that had the GPS coordinates of the planned meet with Sheriff Matt Fremont.

"Here's where we're going. Got enough gas for a round trip flight?" Katie asked.

"Absolutely, we are all gassed up, Chief," replied Medina.

"Great, let's go," Katie directed.

Katie and Lt. Medina got into the Hughes 500-D and Burt handed Katie her flight helmet with integrated com gear. Before the pair donned their helmets Katie told Medina, "Before we get strapped in, a couple of additional directions. First, this flight and meet is strictly off the books; never happened. Next, don't turn on our transponder. You OK with that?"

"Sounds like secret squirrel, cone of silence stuff, eh?" Medina replied.

"Exactly, I'm not so sure what we are about to get into, but just in case, we both need plausible deniability. I can only tell you that we're gonna meet with Gila County Sheriff Matt Fremont. You already know Matt. He and I go way back to my rookie days in CBP. Whatever he wants to discuss, it's apparently completely confidential and we will be holding that confidence.

"To keep you out of any potential conflicts, your job is to simply get me to the meet site and back. You'll remain in the bird while I speak with the sheriff and then you'll get me back to base. On the way back, fly over the border and we'll check out the border wall. That's our excuse in the event that anyone saw us take off. We were just checking out illegal alien incursion spots. There are plenty of those to choose from so we should be good there. Absolutely no radio traffic for the duration, copy?" directed Katie.

"Copy that, Chief," replied Medina.

"Also, if you got a cell phone with you, turn it off or leave it here. Spin us up and let's go," directed Katie. Within three minutes they were airborne and headed for a very remote part of Gila County about thirty minutes' drive time out of Las Brisas.

It was a short twenty-minute helo ride to the meet site. Burt Medina kept the Little Bird at two-hundred feet to stay just under the radar. He approached from the west and spotted the Gila County Sheriff SUV already there. He did a quick aerial, circling and then dropped down quickly, feathering to just about five feet off the ground. Medina then set the bird down with just a slight bump.

Matt walked out of the rotor dust as Lt. Medina was powering down and greeted Katie with a firm handshake. They walked back towards Matt's SUV, out of hearing range.

"Thanks for coming. Sorry for the clandestine preface to the meet. Is that Burt Medina I see piloting the Little Bird?" asked

Matt.

"Yup. You said to pick a trusted pilot, so that's always gonna be Burt," replied Katie.

"Solid warrior and patriot. Good choice," replied Matt who continued.

"We've kept the news and information about Jessie's disappearance under wraps for good reason. No one outside of certain members of the department and our family know that he was actually kidnapped by members of the Tres Paises drug cartel. The only other people who know that are DEA Supervising Agent Cecil McKenry and his SAC who functions as the El Paso regional director. That's a guy by the name of Dick Vermillion," explained Matt.

"Holy shit, Matt. You mean to tell me that Jessie's been kidnapped by Tres Paises and he's still alive?" asked Katie incredulously.

"Yeah, but it gets much worse and that's why I need your help, Katie," replied Matt.

"Well, I can tell you one thing. This DEA SAC Vermillion is a total woke Kool Aid drinker of the administration. A total ho and an asshole to boot. He used to be a U.S. Attorney with USDOJ but got canned from the last administration when our former President and his AG came into office. Real career climber. He's got his head so far up the rear end of the DEA Director, I wonder why he's not tanner than he is for a white boy. We've had more than a couple of run-ins with Vermillion regarding drug seizures," said Katie.

"Well, I can tell you that I'm not in his fan club either. After Jessie was kidnapped, I received a phone call from a person who refers to himself as "Toro." I'm pretty sure this guy is Uberto Urias aka "The Bull." Intel is that Urias is Adolfo Guzman's chief enforcer and henchman. Toro told me in no uncertain terms that Guzman wanted to trade Jessie for his nephew Chuy Guzman. That's the surviving dope smuggler Jessie arrested during that big drug seizure and OIS we had.

"Toro told me that Guzman is only giving me a couple of days to work out the trade or they are going to send Jessie back to me in pieces. Well, I went to Vermillion to negotiate a deal and trade for Jessie, but the SOB refused to give Chuy up.

"Even though Chuy Guzman is relatively small potatoes as a drug smuggler, Vermillion wants to use him as a trophy. Probably wants to throw the media a bone in order to show that the administration has got a handle on illegal drugs coming over the border from Mexico. It's total bullshit and my Jessie has become a pawn in this stupid and deadly chess game," explained Matt.

"So how do I fit in?" asked Katie.

"Adolfo Guzman only gave me a couple of days to work out the trade with DEA; Chuy for Jessie. Well, I spent those two days trying to get Vermillion to listen to reason and arrange for the trade. He told me he approached the DEA director and the administration to agree to the trade. It was no dice.

"When I tried to buy more time through Toro with Adolfo to work out a trade, Adolfo apparently directed Toro to "motivate" me more. The result was that they tortured Jessie. They fucking cut off his ring finger on camera and then mailed it to me along with his ring finger and a video of the torture. They gave me only three more days and I've already used up one of them trying to figure out where they have Jessie sequestered," said Matt.

"They fucking cut off Jessie's ring finger?!" exclaimed Katie.

"I'm just lucky it wasn't his hand," replied Matt.

"Here's where you come in. We studied the video and one of our guys who is very tech savvy discovered that while being recorded, Jessie managed to silently communicate where he was being held. We've determined that it's most probably inside some abandoned mine on or in the immediate vicinity of the Amante Durmiente mountain. That's over on the Mexican side of the border, in Plata County, State of Chihuahua.

"Jessie communicated that right near this mine there is apparently a saguaro cactus shaped like a cross. That's our landmark. However, when our guy used Google Maps to look out over the area, there are hundreds, if not thousands of saguaro cactus all around and in the hillsides of this mountain. He suggested that we would need a drone to fly over the area high enough where it would not be spotted, then task the drone to remain on station, looking down and enhancing the mountain hillsides and immediate surrounding area in search of the cactus shaped like a cross. Once we are able to find this cactus, then a search of the immediate area around this particular cactus will reveal the mouth of the mine or cave where Tres Paises has Jessie.

"I'm asking for a big favor here, Katie. One that could get you into a lot of hot water, maybe lose your job, maybe get you a prison term for violating not only CBP policy, but international laws. You need to know that. You know I would never ask this of you, but Jessie's life is at risk here. I need a drone and a drone pilot to help us," said Matt.

"Matt, as you know, I've been doing this job all of my adult life. I see myself as a patriot and a defender of these United States. I, like my colleagues, have been proud of our accomplishments protecting this nation, but recently, that feeling has subsided. All we feel now is complete frustration, extreme disappointment and anger about what is happening due to this completely non-sensical Open Borders BS. In thinking naively that they are helping immigrants, this woke administration's misplaced compassion is really complicit in killing thousands of them. This is not to mention potentially hundreds of thousands of Americans as a direct result of drug and human trafficking and drug and gang-related violence.

"Now they have put Jessie in the crosshairs, and I won't stand for it. Count me in, of course I'll help," said Katie as she put her hand on Matt's shoulder in a gesture of empathy and support.

"Thanks a lot, Katie. Your support means everything. How does this work? I have less than twenty-four hours left," replied Matt.

"Well, I already know where Amante Durmiente, the "Sleeping Mistress" mountain is. It's easy to get the GPS coordinates for a search of the area. I have a contact who can be trusted for a covert search. Tasking might be a bit more difficult because our drone would be flying over Mexican airspace. It's pretty stealthy and we could turn off the UAV's transponder, but I'm not an expert.

"Let me reach out to my contact. We'll use burner phones to communicate. I'm sure we each have them in our respective evidence rooms that we have confiscated from drug dealers. The perfect irony. Give me four hours to get this thing set up. No guarantees, but I promise to do my best. We'll use our department hardlines to communicate burner phone numbers. We talk frequently, so that won't arise any suspicions. After that, everything regarding the transfer of intel is strictly via the burner phones, got it?" asked Katie.

"Done and thanks, Katie," replied Matt.

"You'd do it for me if I were in your shoes," replied Katie.

"Definitely," said Matt. Assistant Chief Katie Blackwater smiled at Matt, then raised her arm up in the air and made a swirling, circular motion indicating to Burt Medina to spin up the Little Bird. The rotor began to spin and in less than two minutes, Katie was up, up and away.

After leaving the meet with Matt Fremont, Lt. Burt Medina and Katie headed straight for the border where Burt flew a sweep directly over the Gila and Rio Brisas Rivers to "check on border incursion areas." They then headed back to base.

Before parting, Katie told Burt to write up the "faulty transponder" in his maintenance log discovered during a morning flight and then update the log that the transponder issue had been resolved so that they were additionally covered.

Katie Blackwater returned to her office. She used her burner phone to reach out to an old friend from her younger days in the Air Force, Major Miranda Prescott. Miranda Prescott had taught drone pilots at the U.S. Army's drone pilot training facility at Ft. Huachuca, in Sierra Vista, Arizona. The major was now stationed somewhat nearby at Holloman Air Force Base, New Mexico where she commanded the drone UAS wing there and also supervised the DHS's drone "fleet" of two drones.

Ft. Holloman, AFB was established in 1942 to train U.S. Army Air Corps pilots during WWII. Now it was used in part as a military and DHS drone base. The base was located just six miles southwest of Alamogordo in Otero County on Highway 90/82 north of El Paso. The base was about sixty miles east of Las Cruces, NM which was only seventy miles northeast of Katie's area of operation.

Major Prescott picked up on the fourth ring with an inquisitive, "Major Prescott, who's calling?" she asked.

"Miranda, it's me, Katie; Katie Blackwater," Katie said.

"Katie? Oh my God, it's great to hear from you. It's been about a year since my change of assignments out to New Mexico, right? What brings you to call me? This phone says, 'unidentified caller,' that's not your regular cell phone," said the major.

"It's great to hear your voice too. In short, I've got a favor to ask you in person and I need to do it in person today. I'll come to you. When are you available today?" asked Katie.

Major Miranda Prescott could immediately tell by the tone of Katie's voice, her use of an unidentified phone number, the obviously clandestine nature of her call and the exigency in wanting to drive all the way out to Alamogordo that her friend's request was both important and urgent.

"I can take some time off at meet you at 1400 hours. My place good?" Miranda asked.

"Perfect. See you at 1400 and please don't mention this to anyone. It's got to be off the books," replied Katie.

Now the Air Force major knew something was definitely up and her dear friend was in dire need of her help. She just couldn't imagine what that help might consist of.

"Copy that, girlfriend, off the books," Major Prescott agreed before Katie hung up.

Katie Blackwater told her administrative officer that she wasn't feeling well and was taking the remainder of the day off on sick time. She drove to a nearby Circle K gas station with a store and changed from her uniform into some civilian clothes she had in the trunk of her personal vehicle. She filled up the gas tank and was off to Alamogordo while listening to FOX NEWS.

"FOX Breaking News! The U.S. Border Patrol reports that this quarter, they detained a record 225,250 undocumented aliens who crossed over the border between the El Paso, Texas and Tucson, Arizona stations. This marks the 5th consecutive significant quarterly rise in UDA interdictions since the new administration took office and commenced their Open Border and sanctuary policies towards illegal aliens. To date, it is estimated that over two million UDA's from over one hundred and forty-eight nations have snuck into the United States since the new President

came into office.

"In addition, CBP and DEA report that they have interdicted and recovered over ten times the amount of deadly fentanyl, methamphetamine and cocaine as they had seized during the last year of the previous administration. The DEA estimates that just this year alone, they have seized enough fentanyl to kill every man, woman and child in the U.S. three times over.

"The Center for Disease Control – CDC – estimates that during the first year of the current administration, over 110,000 American lives were lost in opioid-related overdose deaths. This is an all-time high in opioid-related deaths. The federal law enforcement agencies further report that the staggering numbers in drug seizures constitute approximately only one tenth of the amount of deadly drugs being smuggled into the U.S. And in entertainment news...."

Katie Blackwater switched the radio to a country western channel so she could get some respite from the anger and frustration she was feeling.

The federal administration had managed to politicize and compromise the nation's safety and security to cater to its liberal base. The country was literally being invaded by hordes of drug smugglers, MS-13 gang bangers, terrorists, sexual predators and human traffickers. Tons of deadly drugs were being smuggled across the border, killing tens of thousands through overdose. Drug gangs were killing each other over territory and drug profits with innocents frequently caught in the crossfire.

The lives of Americans, law enforcement officers and UDA's were being lost on a daily basis and all the current administration wanted Americans to focus on was climate change and renewable energy. It was almost more than one could bear. She had to help Matt Fremont get his son back. It was now her mission to do her part. How could she live with herself if she didn't at least try to help?

Katie Blackwater arrived at the condo of Major Miranda Prescott just before 2:00 pm and knocked on the door. She was immediately greeted by her old friend with a warm embrace. Katie sat on a couch in the living room while Miranda got them both ice cold beers. They toasted their long friendship and then Katie got down to business.

"Miranda, sorry for all the clandestine backdrop here. You were the only person I could come to for this. Before I begin, I need to tell you that I've potentially taken quite a risk coming here and what I'm about to tell you could also get you into a lot of trouble as well. It could really be a career-ender for both of us and maybe worse. So, if you ask me to not discuss anything serious with you, I'll simply enjoy a cold beer with you, talk about old times and I'll be out of your hair. I promise all will be good between us," said Katie.

"Good gracious, girl. What could be so serious that would destroy both of our careers or worse as you say?" asked Miranda.

"If you promise me that this conversation never occurred and can hold that promise, I'll tell you. Otherwise, we'll just have beer and shoot the shit for an hour and then I'll blow out of here," said Katie.

"What conversation? Never happened. Off the books," replied Miranda.

"Off the books," repeated Katie as both gals toasted to Miranda's promise.

"I'm here representing a small group who are developing a covert plan to save a LEO's life. He's the son of my dear friend and colleague Matt Fremont who is the Sheriff of Gila County. The deputy's name is Jessie Fremont. Jessie was kidnapped and tortured by the Tres Paises drug cartel four days ago."

Katie explained to Miranda about the drug smuggling and officer-involved shooting incident that Jessie was involved in. She shared how the deputy was kidnapped by Tres Paises. Katie explained how Adolfo Guzman, the head of Tres Paises was demanding that the DEA trade Adolfo's nephew Chuy Guzman for Jessie.

Katie described how Sheriff Fremont had attempted unsuccessfully to convince the SAC of the El Paso office of the DEA to convince the DEA director to trade Chuy for Jessie. She told Miranda how members of the Tres Paises had tortured Jessie, cut off his ring finger and mailed it back to Matt Fremont with his son's wedding ring along with a video of the torture to motivate him to make good on the trade.

"Holy shit. Those vile pieces of shit," exclaimed Miranda.

Katie explained how Matt Fremont's deputies had figured out from the video and Jessie's Morse code eye blinking message that Jessie was most probably being held somewhere near or on the "Sleeping Mistress" mountain just over the Mexican border in Plata County, State of Chihuahua.

"I know that mountain. It's called the Amante Durmiente. So why come to me? Like you said that mountain is in Mexico," said Miranda.

"Well, that's the dicey part. Jessie actually blinked out two clues. The first was what they believe is the Sleeping Mistress, but his second clue was 'cactus cross.' Matt's people strongly believe that Jessie must have seen this unique cactus from the mouth of the mine or cave they have him held in. They think it's a key landmark in finding the entrance to that place," said Katie.

"When Matt's deputies did a Google Earth Map search of the mountain, there were literally hundreds of saguaro cacti on the mountain's base and surrounding it. Their tech guru suggested that the only way to scope out the area and locating this cactus shaped like a cross without being seen by the Tres Paises guarding Jessie is by high altitude drone," explained Katie.

Major Miranda Prescott looked incredulously at her old friend.

"Wait, wait, just wait a minute young lady. Let me get this right. You got a deputy who was kidnapped and tortured by a bunch of drug cartel thugs in some fricking cave or mine. This deputy, while he's being tortured has the presence of mind to blink out some Morse code to tell you that he's somewhere's on the Sleeping Lady mountain in fricking Mexico. You do realize that Mexico is a whole other fricking country, right?

"Then your deputy blinks out the words "cactus cross," and the deputies use Google fricking Earth Maps and see a shit load of saguaro cactus. They think that this cross-shaped cactus could be a landmark pointing to the entrance of this shit hole they have your deputy in.

"Then some techy deputy suggests in his delusional state that the best way to identify this one single, fricking saguaro cactus shaped like a fricking cross is to just go to Costco and snag a high-altitude drone? Are you all on drugs?!" replied Miranda in amazement.

"Well, we're not actually going to get a high-altitude drone from Costco, we were thinking more of a military grade high-altitude drone," replied Katie with a sly smile.

"What the frick! A military drone. A fricking military drone, for Christ's sake. That's all you need? Well, why the hell didn't you just ask? Let me get right on the phone and dial one up for you. And just where were you thinking to put your hands on a military drone?" laughed Miranda.

"Well, as Assistant Chief of my region, I just happen to know that DHS-CPB received two retired Predator drones from you guys last year and you personally supervise their tasking," said Katie confidently.

"Hey, that's not fair. I shared that confidential information with you the last time we saw each other," replied Miranda.

"So, it's not really like they are "military" or Air Force drones. They actually belong to my team," said Katie wryly.

"At ease Assistant Chief, you of all people know that both of us work for the feds. The same federal administration that has an Open Borders President, a Vice President who laughingly is in charge of border issues. Plus a Secretary of the DHS who also runs Customs and Border Patrol who agrees with these two idiots.

"There is no way in hell anyone from this administration or your agency is going to grant permission to use an important high security asset like a high-altitude Predator drone. You're talking about an invasion of Mexican air space to conduct covert surveillance operations. Hell, your own CBP director is a total Open Borders whack job.

"In case you cut class the day 'Spying and International Incidents' was taught at Assistant Chief's School we don't fly our drones over friendly nations without their permission. No way the Mexican government under your circumstances is going to give their permission for the Air Force, CBP or anyone else to fly over Mexican airspace and Mexican nationals "looking for cacti," said Miranda.

"With all due respect Major wiseass, the U.S.A. flies covert missions over friendly nations 24/7. Those assets are called satellites and drones. Hell, even private companies like Space-X and Big Tech have hundreds of satellites flying all around the globe looking at all sorts of stuff and that doesn't even count scores of weather satellites," said Katie who continued,

"Look Miranda, all we are asking for here is a clandestine donation of one hour or less of flight time from one of those two Predators. Hell, the people you are supervising are already flying over the border. Just one hour or less to potentially save a LEO's life. That's all we are asking here.

"We've got nowhere else to go and Jessie's time is up in less than two days for sure. This creep Adolfo Guzman is one serious motherfucker. He will off Jessie just to make a point. How about it?" asked Katie in her best pleading voice.

Major Miranda Prescott put her beer down and gazed out the living room window at nothing in particular. She was deep in thought for a minute before she spoke.

"I hate all this open borders bullshit. I hate the games being played with people's lives. I despise the moral and ethical blindness. I and my people are patriots. Our nation is going to hell in a hand basket and most times I feel powerless to stop it. I've always been taught to fight the good fight, but this border debacle and everything that goes with it is nothing less than pure insanity.

"I'll be damned if I'm gonna let a brave deputy die because our current administration is too woke and naïve to even care about the sacrifices we and people like your deputy have made. It might cost me my career, but if you're in, I'm in, sister. I'll get you your drone," said Miranda.

Katie got up from the couch, walked over to Miranda and hugged her close friend.

"What's your plan and how much time do I have to get ready?" asked Miranda.

"Get out your laptop and let's start with some GPS coordinates for Amante Durmiente. We are already time compressed. Let's call this mission *"Operation off the Books,"* said Katie with a smile.

"Love it. Let the conspiracy begin," replied Miranda.

For the next half hour Katie and Miranda conspired on accessing and tasking one of the CBP drones. By 3:30 pm, the women parted ways with Major Prescott returning to Holloman AFB and Assistant Chief Katie Blackwater returning to her office.

CHAPTER 17

All We Need Now Is A Chopper

ON THE WAY back, Katie used her burner phone to call Matt Fremont to tell him the good news. She had arranged for a high-altitude drone to surveil the "Sleeping Mistress" mountain in an attempt to locate the cactus cross Jessie had coded to them via the video.

"Outstanding news, Katie. I am eternally grateful," replied Matt.

"How are your plans coming for a rescue?" asked Katie.

"Wade and I have been working all afternoon on them," said Matt.

"So have you figured out how you guys are getting out there. It's Mexico you know," said Katie.

"Well, we can't drive out there. The Tres Paises would see us coming for miles in that desert dust, even at night if they have NVG's. I'm planning for a helo insertion and hiking in. I was just about to call Uber. I know a guy. Tell ya when it's confirmed. When do you think we'll have word on a possible location for Jessie?" asked Matt.

"My contact is very good. They will have the drone over the Sleeping Mistress easy two hours before sunset. If we get a confirmation on the cactus cross landmark, I'll be given the coordinates and I'll pass those on to you. How many people you taking?" asked Katie.

"Only four not counting the pilot due to weight and

equipment limitations of the chopper," said Matt.

"Shit Matt, that's pretty slim considering Tres Paises might have twenty bandidos guarding Jessie. You sure about that?" asked Katie.

"It is what it is. I can't afford to take any more people and I can't trust anyone other than my own patrol deputies to keep a lid on the op," replied Matt.

"I got it. I'll call you as soon as I know the coordinates. If it's bad news and my contact reports "No joy," that will unfortunately mean that your op is off," said Katie.

"I'll be praying for good news. Talk later," Matt said before hanging up.

Matt Fremont immediately called Jack Stryker.

"Valkyrie Helos, Stryker speaking. How can we be of service?"

"Jack, Matt Fremont here. Got a minute? I've got something urgent to discuss with you," Matt said.

"Absolutely, What's up?" Stryker asked.

"It's better if we talk in person. You at your place? I can be there in fifteen minutes," said Matt.

"Nothing going on right now. I did my power line checks yesterday, so I'm in what we call a lull," laughed Stryker.

"Great. See you in fifteen," said Matt before hanging up.

Matt left his office and drove out to Valkyrie Helos on the outskirts of Las Brisas. The one-man helicopter operation was owned and operated by Jack Stryker.

"Black Jack," as he was affectionately known to his close circle of friends, was a unique man with a colorful history. Stryker was a seventy-five-year-old Viet Nam vet who had an infamous history piloting helicopters as a Warrant Officer in the U.S. Army's First Air Cavalry.

Stryker was the spitting image of Country Western musician Willie Nelson, pig tails and all. A decorated pilot, Stryker was absolutely fearless in battle and had been certified to literally fly every helicopter in the Army's inventory. He had several helos shot out from under him in the war. Stryker had flown both overt and covert special operations missions while assigned to Special Forces Green Beret "A-Teams." His work with the Green Berets introduced him to the CIA where he volunteered to fly covert missions in "no-go zones" of Cambodia and Laos. Stryker's favorite aircraft was the Hughes 500-D "Little Bird" of which he owned two of the helicopters.

Matt knew that the 500-D Little Bird was the perfect aircraft to literally fly under the U.S./Mexican border radar screen and insert and extract a covert mission with four operators.

The Sheriff was keenly aware of Stryker's personal family tragedy involving a drug cartel. Before Matt was Sheriff, a Mexican transnational drug cartel had tried to recruit Stryker to smuggle dope across the border in his helicopters. The Viet Nam vet had turned them down. One day while he was gone on a run checking power lines for the regional power provider, members of the cartel had invaded his home. They raped and murdered his wife and teenaged daughter in retribution. The crime had never been solved. No one was ever brought to justice.

Matt knew that Stryker was hungry for pay back and this type of mission would no doubt resonate with him. He also knew that the pilot was a true patriot who would be up for helping to rescue Jessie. This was a crazy operation. Therefore, a crazy, fearless pilot was just the person to fly them in and out of the Amante Durmiente.

Matt pulled up in front of Black Jack Stryker's hanger and office. The doors to the hanger were open and he could see Stryker standing on the mobile platform upon which the Hughes 500-D was perched. Matt walked inside to greet Stryker.

"So, what brings the Sheriff of Gila County out here to speak with the unwashed masses?" Stryker asked.

"Jack, in short, I need a favor, a big one. I have need of your unique skill set," said Matt.

"Hence, the private meeting out here instead of telling me what you are in need of on the phone, right?" Stryker replied perceptively.

Matt proceeded to fill Stryker in on the history of his department's interactions with the Tres Paises drug cartel. This included Jessie's recent deadly encounter with the drug smugglers, his kidnapping and torture. Then, Adolfo Guzman's demand that DEA trade Chuy Guzman for Jessie, or they would mail Jessie back piece by piece to his family.

Matt told the pilot all about how Jessie using Morse code, had blinked out a couple of clues on where he was being held by the cartel while he was being tortured. Then how Deputy Tristin Peters had brilliantly figured out the general vicinity of where the Tres Paises was holding his son.

Matt informed Stryker that he had arranged through a federal contact to have a drone tasked to fly over the Amante Durmiente mountain to locate and confirm the most likely location where the Tres Paises was holding Jessie. They believed that Jessie was in an abandoned mine or cave.

"Motherfucking scum bags. These assholes will never stop. You gotta put them all in the ground. How can I be of service, Sheriff?" Stryker asked.

"Here's the difficult part of the favor, Jack. You might or might not know it, but the Amante Durmiente is in Mexico. It's just about a thirty minute car ride south of the border. Obviously, I'm planning an op to rescue my son. We can't drive over the border to the mountain. We'd be seen in a minute. As soon as the Tres Paises saw us and figured out we're not tourists, we'd be in their gun sights. Then they'd kill my son, so vehicles are definitely out.

I'm looking for a helicopter pilot skilled and crazy enough to fly under the radar screen and insert a team of operators. The pilot would need to wait on station for a signal. Then come in hot to extract our team and Jessie and blow out of there probably under intense gunfire. It's very high risk.

Plus you gotta know that we would be breaking all sorts of U.S. and Mexican laws. If we were caught, it would easily get us all prison time. You could lose everything you have built here. Like me, you're no Spring chicken. With a twenty-year sentence in a U.S. prison, you could die there. In a Mexican prison controlled by drug cartels, you wouldn't last a week. This is serious shit," explained Matt.

"Black Jack" Stryker looked at Matt long and hard before responding.

"You know before you came to Gila County, one of the cartels who had heard about my flying skills came to me with a very lucrative offer to fly dope over the border. I'm not poisoning American kids with that shit, so I turned them down. They told me to think about their offer because they were only going to make it once. In my stubborn bravado, I told them I didn't need any more time to consider their offer, my mind was made up.

"The greasy haired, gold chain wearing asshole who came to me only smiled and said, "No problem. You're mind's made up. It is what it is. But I think you will regret your decision, amigo." Then they left. I thought that he was referring to me turning down all of that money, but I was wrong. They returned a week later when I was on a flying job. They invaded my home and raped and killed my beautiful wife, who was the love of my life, and my daughter.

Before you came here to be the Las Brisas Police Chief, the policing here was lazy and stupid. Neither the Chief, the Sheriff, or the feds did anything to find out who raped and murdered my family. The local yokels back then weren't smart or courageous enough to identify, arrest and convict those barbarians.

I've wanted an opportunity for pay back ever since. It's just that no opportunity ever presented itself until now. I'm willing and able to do whatever you need me to do. Fuck breaking the law and/ or going to prison. Just ask," said Stryker.

"Well, I have a four person extraction team that needs a ride in and out of the site. If they are successful, they'll have my son and that will make five, not counting you as their pilot. I was thinking that your Little Bird would be the perfect helo for the op. I just need you to fly the op," said Matt.

"Well, you know your aircraft. The Hughes 500-D over there is the best aircraft to do this job. It's pretty quiet, very maneuverable and easy to control. Problem is the weight on take-off if they manage to free your son. You see, the empty weight of the Little Bird is about 1,590 pounds. The maximum take off weight is really no more than 3,500 pounds. That means I can't safely carry more than 1,960 pounds. I would need to know the combined weight of your team with their equipment. Then I'd have to factor in the weight of your son. Can you do that for me? Then all I need is a go time.

"Everyone would have to meet here for lift-off. If we become weight heavy, that's gonna mean that we got to jettison equipment immediately before take-off," explained Stryker.

"I can do that. After I leave here, I'm gonna call the team in and we can do a combined weigh-in. I can call you with those numbers. My son Jessie weighs about 190 pounds. One of the team members is a light weight, maybe no more than a buck-forty. That ought to help," said Matt.

"Geezus, you got a deputy who only weighs one hundred and forty pounds? Kinda scrawny, eh," laughed Stryker.

"Trust me, what he lacks in weight, he more than makes up in brain power. He's the guy that knew Morse code and figured out where Jessie might be," replied Matt.

"Just in case, I'll check out the bird and see if there is anything I can possibly remove to lighten its weight a bit more. Even fifty pounds less makes a difference," said Stryker.

"Once we get the confirmation on where they are holding Jessie and the coordinates, I'll ring you. Do you have a burner phone? This op is definitely off the books," said Matt.

"Hell yes, I could sell you a burner phone," laughed Stryker.

"I want to hit these guys at a time when they are very tired with their guard down and maybe already asleep. How long would it take you to fly from here to Amante Durmiente?" asked Matt.

"Not long. It's gonna be a straight shot flying low initially at under a hundred feet to clear the radar. Nap of the earth sort of shit. Once we're in Mexico, I'll climb a bit and approach from their blind side, once we establish what side of the mountain the mine or cave is on. From take-off to insertion shouldn't take more than thirty minutes tops," explained Stryker.

"Alright, then let's set assembly time here at 0300 hours

with lift-off no later than 0330 hours. That puts insertion at roughly 0400 hours. The bad guys ought to be pretty bored, tired and even asleep by then," said Matt.

"Let's set our watches. See you guys at 0300 hours if we are a go. Now get going cause I got a lot of work to do. Thanks for the opportunity, brother," said Stryker as he shook Matt's hand firmly.

As Matt began to walk away Stryker exclaimed, "Oh, and one more thing. I'm gonna need your contact at Border Patrol. I'm gonna need a favor."

"And what might that be?" asked Matt inquisitively.

"Something mission specific. Better you don't know so you have plausible deniability," replied Stryker, winking.

Before getting into his SUV, Matt provided the pilot with Katie Blackwater's burner phone number, but not her name or rank.

While driving back to his office. Matt called Katie Blackwater on his burner phone. He told Katie to expect a call from his pilot. "He wouldn't tell me what he wanted you for. I'll leave that up to you. I'm not going to tell you his name, but I'm sure you can figure out who we're using. You don't need to tell him your name or rank either."

Matt then began calling back the team members he had chosen for the op, Jacob Black Arrows, Blake Sheridan and Tristin Peters. Matt told each man that weight was going to be a challenge and to bring only that amount of gear that was absolutely essential for the mission. He also directed each man to weigh themselves, their equipment and to have that combined weight number ready when they showed up at the department.

Wade was already in the office when Matt arrived. The Ranger had been diligently working on the op. Wade had the plan all mapped out except for the final confirmation on the location of where the Tres Paises was holding Jessie.

"How's it going, Wade?" asked Matt.

"Thanks to your boy Tristin, I got most of this doped out. Using the Google Earth Map photos of the Amante Durmiente, I've diagramed possible insertion, staging and extraction points for all sides of the mountain. Optimistically, once we get confirmation and coordinates for the location, I'll reconfigure the points for insertion, staging and extraction. Did you secure a bird for the op?" asked Wade.

"Stryker is all-in. You guys are riding in his Hughes 500-D Little Bird. Weight is going to be an important factor. You will have to be as light as you can possibly be, yet bring enough gear to surveil and fight a prolonged battle if it comes to that," explained Matt.

"What's your idea of an execute time if we get the coordinates for the site?" asked Wade.

"I was thinking no later than 0330 hours, with us getting over to Stryker's by 0300 hours. Then it's lift-off. Stryker estimates a thirty minute flight to the site with insertion. I wanna catch those bastards bored, tired, hopefully asleep and not ready to fight. If we all do our jobs, you'll be on them like white on rice before they even know it. You have my permission to take out without prejudice anyone and everyone who gets in your way. You grab Jessie and extract with everyone intact," explained Matt.

"Okay, I like that. While you are waiting for your guys, I need to gear up. I'm gonna need to get over to your place, pack my stuff and return. If I can borrow a car, it shouldn't take me more than forty-five minutes to do that and return. I'll keep in mind that weight is an issue," said Wade.

"I'll ask my secretary Lisa if you can borrow her car for an hour. Shouldn't be a problem," said Matt.

Within five minutes, Wade was enroute to Matt Fremont's ranch just outside of town.

Matt Fremont walked out of the briefing room and entered his office. This was going to be the hardest and most important decision of his life. For the first time, he was actually sending men into what would most likely be heated battle where some might not return. It mattered not that they were all volunteers. Matt would stay behind and could only offer his leadership, his confidence in their abilities and then pray for their survival. He would also pray for his son Jessie's survival as well. The grizzly Sheriff sat at his desk deep in thought, staring at a photo of Jessie at his law enforcement academy graduation. "We'll get you home son. I promise," Matt said to Jessie's photo.

CHAPTER 18

Spinning Up

BACK AT HOLLOMAN AFB, Major Miranda Prescott returned to base in uniform. She told her administrative sergeant that she was feeling much better. She had decided to finish her shift and do some additional work. At 5:00 pm, she informed her admin that she was going to make the rounds of the UAS flight modules to check on her drone pilots and walked out of the building.

Major Prescott walked down the row of tan colored air conditioned sixteen by thirty-foot corrugated metal modules. Each small building was identified by the letters UAS with a number identifying each drones' patrol region. Miranda arrived at the last building in the row. This module was marked "DHS/CBP UAS NM/M-1," translated to mean Department of Homeland Security – Customs & Border Protection New Mexico-Mexico patrol region.

Miranda opened the door into a much cooler, darkened environment. The room was only illuminated by the lights coming from electronic consoles and several large flat-screen television monitors. At the back of the module sat a CBP officer maneuvering a joystick while staring intensely at the large monitor in front of him. Miranda immediately recognized Agent Cedrick Tucker as one of her students from drone flight school at U.S. Army base Ft. Huachuca, in Sierra Vista, Cochise County, AZ. Miranda had been there TDY as a drone flight instructor.

"Agent Tucker how goes the shift?" asked Miranda.

Tucker, a young man of twenty-six looked surprised to see the major so late in the day. "Good afternoon Major. Just the usual border incursions by scores of UDA's. I've been vectoring BP agents to various incursion sites to intercept and detain. No smuggling to report so far today. I'm scheduled to go Code-7 shortly at 1800 hours," replied the agent.

Agent Tucker was piloting one of the two older MQ-1 Predator drones that had been retired from the Air Force in 2018. The Air Force had given the Predator to the DHS-CBP for aerial reconnaissance along the border. It had been replaced by the more modern MQ-9 "Reaper" model.

The MQ-1 Predator had come into the military's arsenal in 1994. Back then, it had been primarily used by the Air Force and the CIA for high altitude surveillance and intelligence gathering. The UAS had been converted to also serve as a weapons platform. The drone had been highly successful in targeting and taking out high-value terrorists. The Predator had seen service in Afghanistan, Pakistan, Iraq, Syria and Serbia. The aerial platform was also assigned to more covert operations the CIA would not identify for "reasons of national security."

The Predator model was still an excellent platform for high altitude aerial surveillance. It had a maximum operating altitude of 50,000 feet, although it normally flew in the 25,000 foot altitude range and had a flying range of 770 miles. The bird could stay aloft for a maximum of forty hours. Its maximum speed was 135 mph, but the Predator could remain on station at speeds as slow as 80 mph. It was perfect for the Border Patrol's mission of UDA and drug smuggling interdiction.

"So, Tucker, in what area are you flying right now?" Miranda asked.

"Right now, I'm just west of Las Brisas in Gila County, just doing border sweeps. Pretty quiet right now. I'm just flying grid patterns. As you know, we shut down these days at sunset," the agent replied.

"Tell you what. I'm getting rusty, so why don't you let me take the stick for an hour while you're having chow. In fact, take ninety minutes on me. I'll hand her over to you when you get back and you can finish the shift and land her," offered Miranda.

"Serious Major? That would be swell; the bird's at Angels 25 and coasting in east to west parallels. You can see the Rio Brisas just below. You can run the same pattern or deviate if you want. Your choice. Here you go. I've put her on autopilot," said the young CBP agent getting out of his seat and offering the joystick to his supervisor.

"Angels 25, east to west pattern, copy that. Take your time and enjoy your chow," said Major Prescott as the happy agent left the room.

As soon as the drone pilot left, Miranda Prescott removed a small sheet of note paper from her pocket with the coordinates of the Amante Durmiente mountain. She turned off the transponder to the Predator drone and punched in the coordinates.

Miranda took a deep breath, cast her military career aside and took hold of the joystick, tasking the bird to climb to Angels 50, the drone's maximum altitude. *"Here we go sweetie,"* she said and just like that, crossed over the U.S./Mexican border, violating Mexican airspace and international law.

Miranda knew that she had less than ninety minutes to complete her mission. She was only going to get one shot at finding a saguaro cactus shaped like a cross on or near the base of the Amante Durmiente. It was going to be like looking for a unique needle in a stack of needles. Only ninety minutes to find that damn cactus or Sheriff Matt Fremont's son was toast.

Miranda flew the Predator at its maximum speed of 135 mph. She was over the mountain in ten minutes doing aerials at 50,000 feet. The sun was dipping towards the horizon which allowed her to drop the drone down to 40,000 feet. The bluish-grey color of the drone allowed for it to blend into the sky. Miranda knew that from this altitude the Predator would never be seen by anyone on the ground, even if they were staring right up in its direction. Technology was cool.

Miranda had the drone's camera on maximum enhancement as she began slow aerials around the mountain at the Predator's slowest speed. With the sun setting in the west, the cacti cast their shadows eastwards. She noted that there were hundreds of saguaro cacti below. However, she was able to quickly remove many of them because they had multiple appendages. Miranda was only looking for cacti that had two shaped like a man's arms, or more accurately, like a Christian cross. A "cactus cross" like Jessie had coded.

Miranda was on her fifth aerial when she suddenly spotted a cactus of interest on the north side of the mountain about two hundred yards up the hillside. She maneuvered the joystick to tighten her circle around the cactus of interest, studying it closely. It looked pretty damn good.

The major then began a sweep on the hillside proximate to the cactus and damn if she didn't spot what were definite wheel tracks leading up the hillside. These were the only tire tracks on the entire north side of the mountain. Miranda followed the tracks to a point where they suddenly stopped. As she zeroed in closer with her camera, she saw what appeared to be an object about the size of a pick-up truck that was definitely concealed by a desert camouflage tarp. *"Hello,"* she mused.

Miranda began scanning the immediate area near the truck and up another one hundred yards she spied the tailings of a mine and then the dark opening of the mine itself. She pulled the camera back to get better context and observed that the entrance to the mine was in line with the cactus shaped like a Christian cross Immediately next to the mine's entrance. At that moment, she spotted a sentry in desert camouflage armed with an AK-47 automatic rifle.

"Eureka! Got you, you little bastards," Miranda exclaimed out loud.

Miranda did a quick photo and video survey of the area, writing down the exact GPS coordinates of the location. She put a thumb drive into the console's hard drive, downloaded the photos and video file and removed the thumb drive. She then deleted the file she had created and then re-deleted the entire trash file just to make sure there was no record of the event.

Miranda tickled the joystick immediately climbed the Predator back up to 50,000 feet and flew it at maximum speed back across the U.S. border. Once there, she dropped back down to Angels 25, turned back on the Predator's transponder and returned to an east to west search pattern. Five minutes later Agent Cedrick Tucker returned.

"How you doing, Major?" the agent asked.

"Like riding a bike Agent Tucker. Something's you never

forget. She's all yours," Major Prescott replied handing the joystick over to the drone pilot.

"Yes ma'am, I got it," the agent replied, accepting control of the drone.

Miranda walked out of the module and back to her office. Inside her office, she placed the thumb drive into her personal laptop and emailed the photos and video file to Katie Blackwater's personal computer. Then she called Katie on her burner phone.

Katie Blackwater's burner phone vibrated in her pocket indicating a call. She picked up and heard Miranda's simply say,

"Target positively identified. Prepare to receive GPS coordinates, now. Check your email for photos and video file. Good luck and happy hunting." Katie's phone went silent as Miranda hung up.

Katie's heart was thumping in her chest. *Miranda had scored!* Now the team had a real change. *Game on!* She immediately opened her laptop, found the photo/video files from Miranda and immediately forwarded them to Matt's laptop.

After Major Miranda Prescott completed her brief call to Katie she erased all evidence of her email and deleted her trash file. She removed the flash drive and flushed it down the toilet of the ladies restroom in her office building. Major Miranda Prescott's part of the mission was done. Now she would spend the evening praying that her work would have meaning, and a life would be saved.

After Katie forwarded the drone photos and video file to Matt Fremont, she used her burner phone to dial the Sheriff. Matt picked up on the second ring and simply said, "Go."

Brevity with such communications was the key. All Matt heard on his end on his cell was, "Target ID'd. Texting GPS coordinates. Check your emails for photo/video files. Advise upon mission termination. Good luck, prayers out," and Matt's phone went silent.

Wade had just walked into Matt's office. The sheriff walked over to Wade, punched his shoulder and gave him a two thumbs up.

"They found it. Positive ID on the site. I'll have the GPS coordinates in a minute. Katie sent a photo/video file. I'll connect my laptop to the flat screen in the briefing room and pull up the files. Get your map ready to update. The guys should be here any minute," said Matt.

Matt downloaded a series of enhanced photos and one video taken by the Predator onto the desktop of his laptop. He then connected the HDMI cord to the flat screen TV in the briefing room.

Both men were amazed by the quality and clarity of the photos and videos. Major Prescott had placed target squares over the saguaro cactus shaped like a cross, the entrance of an abandoned mine and the vehicle covered by the desert camouflage tarp. The drone video footage also showed the elevations exact compass directions and GPS coordinates for everything, as well as a camouflaged cartel soldier armed with an AK-47 guarding the entrance.

Matt and Wade stared intensely at the photos. "Absolutely amazing. That damn cactus really does look like a Christian cross. Jessie was right on by giving us that landmark," said Matt.

"Definitely an abandoned mine, look at the tailings downwards from the entrance," remarked Wade as they switched over to the real time video and stared intensely. Wade was looking for lines of approach and attack.

"Look on the hillside northeast corner, you see that? It's a guard and he's armed with an AK, see him?" asked Wade.

"Yes, about fifty yards above and to the right of the entrance as you face it. Sentry for sure," replied Matt.

Knowing that the team would need a place to insert, Major Prescott had provided them with a 360 degree aerial video of the mountain from two miles out, complete with moving compass headings and GPS coordinates.

"We'll have to run all of this by Stryker, but to me, it looks like we'll have to insert about two miles northwest of the north side of the mountain and hike in. We can't afford to call the sentry's attention to any rotor noise from the chopper. Definitely have to calculate time to stealthfully hike in and set up a sniper position first. We'll need sniper overwatch to protect the team," explained Wade.

"Agreed," replied Matt as the team members began to assemble with their gear in the briefing room.

It was now 10:00 pm and dark. Jacob Black Arrows and Blake Sheridan were there with all their gear. Deputy Tristin Peters was missing.

"Where's Tristin?" asked Sheriff Fremont.

"He's here. He's out in the parking lot checking out a portable drone he's taking with him," replied Jacob.

"Well, I gotta see that," replied Matt. "Wade come with me for a minute. Let's see what Tristin's bringing" and both men walked out into the parking lot to find the deputy holding an iPad that had some type of attachment with a joy stick. A small drone no bigger than a shoebox was hovering just about twenty feet off the ground above the deputy.

"Is this the gear you're bringing? asked Matt.

"Yes, sir. This is the drone. I have it accessorized with a gyro-stabilized with night vision video camera. It has a range of over a mile, a maximum altitude of 1,000 feet and can remain aloft for twenty minutes. I also brought two back-up batteries. Just the thing we'll need to gather additional intelligence once we're on site.

If there are sentries guarding the site, this drone will spot them before Blake does. Plus, with the night vision, I can even look into the mine's entrance for any sentries guarding from that position. Wanna see what I see? Look here," offered Tristin as he shared his iPad screen which displayed what the drone was videoing using the night vision function. All three men were clearly shown in the greenish hue of the night vision camera.

"At twenty feet, you can hear the four rotors, but at one hundred feet, it's quiet as a mouse. I'm going to be flying it at an altitude of between four to five hundred feet, so there is zero chance of anyone picking up the drone even when it's flying directly over them."

"Excellent. Perfect for the op," remarked Wade.

Tristin landed the drone, folded its wings and rotors and placed it with the iPad into his backpack.

"How much does your backpack weigh, drone, batteries and all?" asked Matt.

"About 10 pounds. I weighed everything on a scale at home," replied Tristin.

"And how much do you weigh with your body armor, assault vest and weapons," asked Matt.

"I think close to 160," replied the deputy.

"Good, that's manageable. You saved us some important weight. Sometimes being skinny comes in handy," laughed Wade.

The three men returned to the briefing room where they found Deputies Jacob Black Arrows and Blake Sheridan dressed in USMC style digital desert camos, doing secondary checks of their gear.

Both men greeted the sheriff, Wade and Tristin.

"Hey, you guys had better suit up. I found BDU's for you, Wade and a small women's size set for you 'geek'" Sheridan said to the men.

"Well, I'll wear mine with pride knowing that they came from you, you big brute," Tristin joked back.

Sheridan handed over the Battle Dress Uniforms to Wade and Tristin who excused themselves and headed over to the locker room to try them on.

Jacob and Blake had been told to bring only what was essential to them for any possible extended engagement with the heavily armed cartel sentries. They were advised that their method of insertion and extraction was going to be a Hughes 500-D "Little Bird." Weight was going to be a critical issue since the aircraft could only carry five people and gear with a maximum weight of 1,157 pounds. That included Jessie if they were able to extract him as well which was the sole objective of the op.

The men had their gear spread out on the floor and long briefing table.

Blake Sheridan had brought his custom built Remington 700 style bolt-action .308 sniper rifle made by AllTerra Arms, considered by true precision riflemen as the sniper's "connoisseurs rifle." The weapon was matched with a single point cut Hawk Hill Custom barrel. Blake had accessorized his rifle with an Asset suppressor made by Elite Iron. Next to Blake's rifle were his "NOD's" or Night Observation Devices. The sniper had carefully chosen an AN/PVS 24 along with the Trijicon SNIPE-IR as his thermal option.

Matt saw that besides his M-4 .223 cal. urban carbine with OEG optics with ten thirty-round magazines and his Glock .40 cal. were six eighteen round mags of ammo.

Jacob had brought a compound bow and a quiver with 20 black broad-tipped carbon fiber arrows. But not any compound bow. Jacob had a subdued black Hoyt Carbon RX-7 bow. This light weight bow was specially engineered for long-range accurate shooting. It had an integrated Picatinny sight mount which kept weight off of the side of the bow and in line with the riser to maintain its balance and stability for long-range shots.

Affixed to the Picatinny sight mount Jacob had mounted a Garmin Xero A-1 two-inch auto-ranging digital bow sight with LED pins. To a skilled archer like Black Arrows, the Hoyt RX-7 in combination with its Garmin Xero A-1 sight was the perfect silent deadly weapon.

Blake Sheridan was checking out Jacob's compound bow. He had seen a couple of the Apache deputy's shorter tactical bows before during his quarterly special qualification shots with his bows.

"That's some serious shit there, "Tonto." Just how far can you accurately punch out with that beast?" asked Sheridan using Jacob's respectful nickname among the deputies.

"I can punch straight through a melon at a hundred yards under the right conditions, Kemosabe. Hitting a white man in the dark, not so hard. Apache's know they glow in the moonlight," joked back Black Arrows just as Tristin and Wade walked back in dressed in their BDU's.

"Totally rad!" remarked Tristin as he spotted Jacob's compound bow.

"Spoken like a true twelve-year-old, drone boy," joked Sheridan.

"Hey Blake, do these BDU pants make my ass look fat to you cause I see you staring at it," joked Tristin to Sheridan.

"Okay, pipe down you two," said Sheriff Fremont who looked over at Wade.

"Wade, can you brief the team on the updated information we got from the drone and how this intel fits into your operational insertion, engagement and extraction plans?" asked Matt.

"Sure sheriff," replied Wade as he switched on the flat screen TV which was connected to Matt Fremont's laptop.

For the next two hours, Wade displayed the videos and enhanced still photos taken from the MQ-1 Predator drone earlier that afternoon. He outlined the positions of the team's insertion LZ via Little Bird and how they would approach the mine. Then he discussed the team's positions of surveillance, their approach options. Depending upon whether or not they were able to rescue Jessie and if they came under attack, Wade had chosen two different extraction LZ's for Stryker to land his Little Bird.

"So, we will insert here on the west side of the mountain about 1.5 miles out. Our Little Bird pilot, 'Black Jack' Stryker who you all know, tells me that this side of the mountain will conceal the rotor noise. However, that also means that we hike in to the site as stealthfully as possible. Jacob is our best tracker, so he'll be on point with me behind him. Sheridan will follow behind me and Tristin bringing up the rear.

"Tristin, how far can you get that drone out in front of us?" asked Wade.

"I can get my drone out about a half mile in front of us at 400 feet. With the night vision and IR cameras, we'll be able to see 360 degrees around us, all the way in once we get a half mile from the site. We won't need it before then and I only have three twenty-minute lithium batteries. That will exhaust the first battery and I will need the remaining two for surveillance and intel once we get near the place," the deputy explained.

"Good idea, that makes sense," replied Wade.

"Blake, after seeing the videos and enhanced stills, have you given any thought to your overwatch position for the team?" asked Wade.

"Blake walked up to the flatscreen TV that was displaying an enhanced front or north facing shot of Amante Durmiente. He pointed to a spot about two hundred yards up and to the right or northwest of the entrance to the mine.

"From here, I've got tactical advantage. I'm just above them and I can shoot and hit anyone below, on either side or even at the entrance if they are stupid enough to show their faces," he explained.

Tristin added, "I'll also have my drone up around 500 feet about 100 yards out from the mouth of the mine. I'll help Blake and Jacob as their scout observer to spot any targets they haven't identified. If anyone is near the entrance, I should be able to spot them and advise their position and range. No one will hear or see the drone from that height," offered Tristin.

"I like that," said Blake.

"Me too," replied Jacob.

"What's the best position for you to operate the drone?" Wade asked Tristin.

"Well, if Jacob and you can clear the area where that covered truck is, I'd like to use that truck for cover. I can launch and recover the drone from there," replied Tristin.

"Okay, we'll see if we can make that happen," said Jacob.

Wade knew the answer to the question he was going to ask Matt but asked it anyway to make sure the directions were clearly heard and understood by the team members.

"Sheriff, can you go over the rules of engagement for the team, please?"

"Men, you are all volunteers on this mission. Once we cross the U.S./Mexico border, our law enforcement status ends. You immediately become civilians. More than that, you will all become criminals in violation of federal, Mexican and international laws. I've named this op, "Off the Books," because that's exactly what it is and will be forever – off the books.

"You know who we are dealing with. Our adversaries are cold blooded killers without conscience. If they spot us, they will not hesitate to kill us all and Jessie. This is a rescue mission. We do not want a war with these people, even though they attacked, kidnapped and tortured one of our own. But by God, they started this thing and if forced to engage, we are going to finish it.

"The ROE's are simple, do whatever you think you need to do to accomplish the rescue mission and to protect your life and the lives of your teammates. That means whatever active or proactive steps you need to take, you take them.

"This is not a shoot only if fired upon directive. This is don't even allow these assholes to get into a position where they can harm you or your teammates and that includes Jessie. It is what it is. Any questions?" asked Matt.

There was no response from the team who clearly understood the seriousness of the mission, the imminent threat to their lives once they began their approach, and the consequences of failure.

"Okay, now let's go over the extraction plan," said Wade using the same enhanced drone photo that Blake Sheridan had used.

"Blake and Jacob will identify and eliminate all visible sentries. After that, Tristin remains in place here at the covered truck with his drone up. He can communicate to us if and when he spots anyone at the mouth or inside the mine entrance.

Jacob and I will be making the final approach under protection of Blake who will continue to maintain overwatch with Tristin as his scout observer. Blake, what was your USMC sniper designation when you were in the field?" asked Wade.

"Archangel, after Saint Michael, the patron saint and protector of soldiers and cops," replied Sheridan.

"Okay, Archangel it is for this op as well. Everybody got that?" Wade asked the team. Everyone nodded affirmatively.

"So, Jacob and I will approach and make entry into the mine. Blake and Tristin, at this point you will lose visual, and we'll be on our own. Once inside, it will undoubtedly go down fast, furious and bloody. Jacob, I don't I have to tell you that the ROE's are simple. Once inside and if we are forced to engage, we quickly take out anyone and everyone who gets in our way and/or threatens Jessie. I mean everyone.

We grab Jessie and get out of there as quickly as we can. We must consider that Jessie may have mobility problems and may need to be carried out and to the extraction site.

"Blake and Tristin, this means that you guys have to be really on your toes, surveilling for and taking out secondary threats as the team retreats to the extraction point. Everybody got that?" asked Wade.

"Where's the extraction point?" asked Blake.

Wade walked back over to the flatscreen TV.

"Well, we're gonna let Stryker suggest that site after he gets to see these videos and photos. Obviously, we don't want to be exposed for a prolonged period of time, especially if Jessie's non-ambulatory, or has difficulty walking.

I'm hoping Stryker will pick a spot in this flat area without any cacti at the base just 100 yards east of the covered truck. That's the fastest and easiest spot from what I can tell, but it's his decision. He's the pilot. However, in case we are fired upon or a force approaches to engage us, I've also chosen an alternate LZ we can extract from," explained Wade as Sheriff Fremont stepped back up in front of the TV.

"That's a very good briefing, Wade. If anyone's got any questions about anything, now's the time to bring it up. If not, I've got a large scale over here and let's get everyone weighed in with all your gear.

Jessie weighs about 190 pounds, so we really can't be over 1,700 pounds combined weight if Black Jack is going to extract with all of you including Jessie," explained the Sheriff.

Each one of the team members approached the scale with their gear and weighed in while Matt read off the weights. Wade wrote them down and then used a calculator to get a combined weight.

"Counting Jessie's weight, that makes 1,670 pounds," Wade announced to a collective sigh.

"Man, that's cutting it close. We'll see what Stryker has to say. We might have to dump gear to make it out of there. Just in case, start thinking about what you can afford to lose. We don't want to leave weapons behind that can identify us, so think about dumping vests, body armor, magazines, stuff like that. Also, start removing any and all patches on your vests and BDU's that ID you as law enforcement," said Matt.

Wade spoke up and passed around a plastic tray.

"Also, because this is a black op, none of you can be identified as Americans, so that means that anything that identifies you in any way gets left here. That means no wallets, ID's, cell phones, or jewelry. Nothing with your name on it goes. Leave anything that ID's you as well as your cell phones and jewelry on and in this tray. We'll secure everything in the evidence locker. That way, the GPS trackers will all show you here at the department. That's gonna be our alibi if we need one.

Your alibi is that you were all in a training session learning about how to conduct night time surveillance for drug interdiction. Please check each other to make sure that each of you are clean and good to go. "

The team members began digging into their pockets, assault vests and backpacks, shedding all items that might identify them if they were killed or captured.

"Reminds me of my TDY ops with the CIA," said Blake Sheridan.

"And mine with Force Recon," replied Wade.

By this time, it was 02:30 am and they needed to be at Black Jack Stryker's hanger no later than 03:00 hours.

Matt Fremont gathered all of the team members together.

"Men, just a few words. First, no matter how this ends up, I just want you to know that my family and I will never be able to repay you for your courage and audacity in volunteering for this mission to free my son and your brother Jessie. Words can't possibly describe how I feel right now. Just know that I am forever in your debt.

If I may, let's join hands and bow our heads for a moment of prayer."

As the four team members joined hands with the Sheriff and Wade bowed their heads, Matt gave a short prayer.

"Dear Lord, please bless these brave men and look down upon them and protect them from the evil they will soon encounter. Grant them the righteous victory they have prepared for and deserve.

"Dear Lord, please bring our brother Jessie and these men back to us without injury. Lord, should any of these men fall in battle, lift them up and transport them to Heaven and into your heavenly embrace. For you Lord are the truth, the power and the glory. Amen."

"Amen," all of the men responded in unison as they lifted their heads back up and looked at their sheriff and Wade.

"Okay, you are leaving all of your personal vehicles here and we're taking the unmarked van to Stryker's. I'm driving and I'll pick you all up after the op. Time to go," said Matt.

The team members grabbed their gear and backpacks and filed out of the briefing room, down the hallway and out into the rear parking lot silently. Matt pulled the van up, the men stowed their gear, got in and drove off for Stryker's compound just across town.

CHAPTER 19

Engage & Extract

SHERIFF FREMONT AND the "Off the Books" op team arrived at Valkyrie Helicopters just before 0300 hours. Matt spotted the Stryker's Hughes 500-D "Little Bird" already rolled out of the hanger and waiting. He pulled the Sheriff's department's unmarked van containing the team just to the right of the hanger to avoid any rotor wash when the helicopter lifted off.

Wade, Blake Sheridan, Jacob Black Arrows and Tristin Peters climbed out of the van. The men immediately went to its rear and began pulling out their gear.

Black Jack Stryker was up on the Little Bird's rolling platform and stepped down to greet them. Matt and Wade noted that Stryker was wearing his old Air Cav trooper's hat with a desert camo pilot's jumpsuit absent of any identifying indicia. His only jewelry was a digital pilot's watch. His hair was split into two long pigtails, all held down by a red bandana headband.

Matt Fremont and Wade looked over Stryker's Little Bird and noted that the aircraft's identifying numbers had been painted over.

"No numbers, nice touch, Stryker," Wade remarked to the pilot.

"Well, you guys told me the op is off the books so what helicopter would you be referring to?" Stryker replied smiling back.

Matt asked the pilot how he was going to deal with the DHS-CBP radar system crossing the border into Mexico.

Black Jack responded, "Well, you have certainly posed an interesting question. Yes, it's gonna be a challenge but I think I've arranged for us to have an edge.

"Ever since we got surprised on 9-11, the U.S. Government and DHS have been working on various radar systems to identify low-flying aircraft flying below 15,000 feet.

"The DHS's Science & Technology Directorate or S&T launched what they refer to as their "Small, Dark Aircraft Project." Research from this project has led to the development of what they refer to as a "Multi-Static Radar Project," referred to by the acronym "MITRE."

"The MITRE system is essentially a portable, low-cost 24/7 aerial surveillance system that is pre-positioned to identify and intercept nefarious aircraft. Here's how it works; multiple ground-based acoustic sensors will detect the sound of a low-flying aircraft and using a real-time AI - deep learning model, will identify the type of aircraft and determine the aircraft's position using multilateration.

"Once the sound of a suspected aircraft is detected, a transmitter floods the area with radio frequency signals and the radar receivers detect reflections off the target creating a comprehensive air picture of the entire area. Agents can then select and then track the targeted aircraft with GPS coordinates, review its flight path and note specific activity.

"Spectrographic analysis of the audio file data then allows the agents to identify the type of aircraft. The DHS-CBP agent in control radios directions on all frequencies to the aircraft to identify itself to determine friend or foe. For instance, an airplane pilot would be asked to toggle their wings, a helicopter pilot might be asked to climb and descend quickly. Obviously, those pilots who do not respond are automatically considered to be unfriendly's and/or smugglers. If that's the case, then DHS can immediately arrange for the feds or military aircraft to intercept. In our case, if the aircraft crosses into Mexican airspace, DHS will call their Mexican counterparts and advise of a suspicious aircraft entering their airspace. Simple, right?"

"Well, that's a nice explanation of the DHS/CBP radar system, but you still haven't explained how you're planning to get across the Mexican border without being detected. You dropping chaff?" pressed Matt.

Deputy Tristin Peters, overheard the conversation and chimed in, "Sheriff, modern radar can distinguish between chaff and an aircraft by measuring what's called the Doppler Shift. Chaff quickly loses its speed compared to an aircraft and therefore displays a characteristic change in frequency that allows it to be filtered out."

"Who's this whiz kid?" asked Stryker who then looked at Tristin and exclaimed, "Exactly right, nice job kid."

Tristin beamed with the compliment and replied, "Thanks Mr. Stryker, dying to learn how you worked this out."

Stryker turned back to Matt and answered his question, sort of.

"Well, remember when I explained to you that the MITRE radar system is acoustically based?"

"Yup," replied the Sheriff.

"Well, I practice the KISS Principle, "Keep it Simple, Stupid." I've made arrangements to mess with the system's acoustics. It can't identify what it can't hear, it can't transmit. So it really can't see us either. It ought to work, but nothing is for certain," said the pilot.

"Well, I think I get it. Like you suggested, I really don't need or want to know any more than that. Plausible deniability," replied Matt.

Stryker asked Wade to have the team members line up in front of him with all of their gear for his personal inspection before lift-off. Once the men had done that, the pilot went down the line visually checking out each man and the gear they were bringing for any issues. As he got to Jacob Black Arrows, he looked down at the Apache Indian's sophisticated compound bow and asked,

"Is that a fucking bow and arrows set-up?! You know you ain't going deer hunting, kid," said Stryker.

"Yes, sir, I know that, but I've found this weapon system to be both silent and very effective. I'm qualified to use it, so it's coming with me," replied Jacob.

"Well, I've seen some badass shit in my time, but this is a first for me. Just don't count coup and scalp anyone out there," joked the politically incorrect pilot.

"Have you weighed in everyone plus their gear?" Stryker asked Wade.

"Affirmative. Total weight with all gear is 1,670 pounds and add 190 pounds for Deputy Jessie Fremont," replied Wade.

"That's cutting it close. We might have to jettison some gear quick to lift-off for extraction, especially if we are under fire. This bird is no spring chicken. I bought her used and she's got plenty of hours on her," said Stryker.

"I've already planned for that contingency and alerted the team. They'll know what to do. You give the order, and they'll do it," replied Wade.

It was getting close to Zero Hour. Stryker walked one more time around the Hughes 500-D. He had pretty much stripped out everything not essential for the mission. Stryker beckoned the team to come closer to him.

"Okay fellas, here's how it works. The rear where you sit is completely stripped down for weight purposes. No seats, but you'll see that I have rigged up four harnesses with safety straps, two on each side for you. You'll be sitting inside with your legs and feet out the doors, operators' style. Make sure you strap in tight and double-check your harness and safety strap. I'm gonna be flying fast under the radar screen and will be zigzagging in and out of our target area. I don't want anyone falling out.

You've already been told that in case we have trouble lifting off upon extraction, you may get an order from me to jettison some gear. You should have already assessed what you're gonna dump if we need to. That means all excess ammo, your ceramic body armor, and anything else that is not essential for defense or survival. You'll have to do it quick, especially if we are taking fire. I want to blast out of there if we are going to have any chance of all coming home in one piece. And another thing, I've only got enough comm gear for two of you back there, so you two will have to communicate my orders and directions to the two without comm gear, got it?" said

Stryker.

All of the men nodded.

Stryker then turned to Wade, "Ranger, you're up front with me. There's a flight helmet on your seat with NVG's and comm gear. Go take a seat and strap in. I'm gonna give you a quick lesson in autorotation just in case something happens to me when we're up."

Wade and Stryker shook hands with Matt Fremont, who went down the line and shook the hands of his deputies. Matt stopped at Tristin Peters, "You gonna be OK, son?" the Sheriff asked.

"I'm good to go, Sheriff. Thanks for letting me go," said the young deputy.

"Well, Tristin, we wouldn't have been able to do this without you figuring out Jessie's Morse code message," replied Matt, putting his arm on Tristin's shoulder.

"Mount up, men. Time to fly. Air Cav!" Striker yelled, with his hand in a raised fist with forefinger high, then making a circle, indicating it was time to kick the tires and light the fire.

"Uoorah!" Yelled out Blake and Wade in unison.

The men climbed in the back and secured themselves in their harnesses and safety lines, half-way in and half-way out of the Little Bird. Stryker and Wade took their positions in the cockpit.

Stryker tested the aircraft's comm gear to make sure the team members could hear him.

"Welcome to Valkyrie Airlines, I'm your pilot and tour guide. I appreciate you using your frequent flyer miles today. Unfortunately, due to the short duration of this flight and perhaps some zig-zag turbulence, we will have to forego our customary beverage service. Please lock your seats and tray tables in the upright position. Don't forget that your luggage may shift slightly in the overhead bins during our flight. Now show me thumbs up if you copy."

Wade, Blake, Jacob and Tristin raised their thumbs up indicating that they could hear Black Jack over the comm.

Stryker rolled the throttle to the ident position, then used his right hand to push the ignition button on the end of the collective. There was a second or two of ticking sounds from the engine, and then a soft roar as the turbine began sucking life.

Once all instruments were in the green, Stryker began pulling pitch. The Hughes 500-D responded immediately, moving slowly upwards to a height of 3 feet. Stryker then *slowly pushed the cyclic forward, added collective,* and off into the black night they disappeared as Sheriff Fremont watched.

"God speed, men. God speed," Matt uttered to himself.

Black Jack Stryker headed due south at an altitude of 500 feet at a near maximum speed of 150 mph. The U.S./Mexican border was only five minutes away. The Little Bird was completely blacked out.

It had been Stryker's plan to cross the U.S./Mexican border over the Rio Brisas at 0345 hours. It was a pretty rugged area that might only be patrolled by the CBP agents on horseback. However, there had been a high-profile media driven controversy the previous Fall involving false allegations against members of the CBP Mounted Unit that riders had chased down and whipped Haitian UDA's sneaking across the border. In response, the woke President and DHS Secretary had ordered that the CBP could no longer use their Mounted Unit to patrol the southern border. Now, except for the occasional DHS-CBP or DEA surveillance aircraft, there were no assets in the immediate area watching for low flying aircraft, or ground-based smugglers entering the U.S. there.

In place of a CBP mounted patrol or aircraft, the DHS S&T had placed a single portable MITRE acoustic sensor system. CBP Assistant Chief Katie Blackwater had personally supervised the installation of this system and had its GPS coordinates.

At exactly 03:00 hours, Katie arrived in her Jeep a half-mile from where the portable MITRE system had been installed. She parked her Jeep in the brush, confident that she would not be encountering any of her agents patrolling the area.

Katie was wearing a helmet affixed with NVG's. She removed a backpack containing only a compact battery powered stereo receiver and large Bluetooth audio speaker used by kids disturbing neighborhoods when they drove through blasting their radios.

Katie used her GPS to fix on the coordinates of the MITRE system and began her hike to the system. She had to move quickly to arrive on station by 0330 hours as planned. She would only remain on station ninety minutes to avoid any chance of detection by CBP patrols.

The path to the MITRE site was a bit more rugged than Katie had recalled. She arrived a bit late at 0335 hours but in plenty of time to set up her equipment. Katie removed the stereo receiver and Bluetooth speaker and placed them on the ground about four feet from the solar powered MITRE system's acoustic array. She then removed a small thumb drive containing a file of two musical selections that Black Jack Stryker had emailed her the previous afternoon. Katie inserted the drive into the system and waited, searching the skies and listening. The time was now 0342 hours and she heard nothing.

As instructed by Black Jack, Katie put on her Bose noise-cancelling headset and activated the stereo system with its first selection turned on full blast at a ground shaking 150 decibels. The Rolling Stones *"Paint it Black"* blared from the speaker in front of the acoustic array, causing the system to go haywire. Katie recoiled from the blast of 60's music. Back at the DHS/CBP surveillance, a young half asleep agent monitoring the MITRE array system suddenly hearing the mind blowing music jumped out of seat and threw off his headset exclaiming. *"What the fuck?!"*

At exactly 0343 hours, four miles north of the border Stryker keyed his intercom, "Hold on fellas, dropping down. Nap of the earth for a bit." The pilot then pitched the Little Bird down to 100 feet, streaking across the Rio Brisas towards the Mexican border. One mile from Katie Blackwater's position and using his NVG's, Stryker dropped the Little Bird down to only fifty feet above the sage brush covered terrain as the bird crossed over the Rio Brisas.

At that moment, Katie's stereo switched from *"Paint it Black"* to Wagner's *"Flight of the Valkyries"* with its females sopranos singing at a level that could shatter a champaign glass. The blast of Nordic opera music further over loaded the radar system, causing it to shut down and go into a re-boot for its own protection.

The MITRE radar system was activated by lower decibel sounds produced by aircraft flying under 15,000 feet. It was unable to withstand the over-riding, extremely high decibel levels of the music Katie was blasting directly towards its acoustic array. The system was unable to communicate the information to its transmitter that was intended to sweep the area with high frequency signals its radar might be to identify as an aircraft. The high-pitched music in effect "blinded" the radar system. The concept was both simple and brilliant!

The Little Bird cleared the Rio Brisas at an altitude of fifty feet at exactly 0345 hours and Stryker got on the comm, "We're in Mexican airspace from here on in. We are all officially criminals."

Stryker had already inserted the GPS coordinates for the Amanté Durmiente. At the speed they were going the mountain was only twenty minutes away straight line of sight. Eight miles from the mountain, Stryker turned the chopper right and ninety degrees west to give the mountain wide birth to conceal rotor noise. He and Wade switched to NVG's. When Stryker was four miles out, he came around heading north-west and slowed down measurably to ease into the insertion zone he had chosen.

"Get ready to bail, fellas. Insertion in sixty seconds. Get out quickly and stay low for the rotor. Do not, I say again, do not go to the rear of the chopper. I gotta a blade running there too.

I'll wait for your call and meet you at extraction Zone Alpha unless things change; then it's Zone Bravo. Good luck and God speed," said the pilot.

Wade pulled his comm plug, quickly removed his helmet and dismounted. He quickly moved low to the rear compartment to help anyone out who needed help. All three team members exited quickly with their gear.

Blake Sheridan who was on the pilot's side stood outside Stryker's door. The sniper gave Stryker a thumb's up and whirled his finger in the air advising Black Jack that everyone was out and clear of the chopper and to lift off. Stryker returned the thumbs up gesture. He pulled pitch while applying left pedal, and took off, heading west and out of sight. He would find a place to set down a safe distance away, but close enough to immediately blaze in for the extraction.

Wade gathered the team together. Everyone was wearing NVG's affixed to their helmets. Tristin was not using his because they interfered with him watching the video feed while his drone was up.

Wade addressed his team. "Okay boys, that wasn't so bad, was it?" he asked.

"Well, I'm sure glad I didn't go for the big burrito plate tonight. That was an interesting ride," remarked Blake as the other team members chuckled.

"Alright, by my GPS reading, we are about a mile and a half from the north side of the Amanté Durmiente. Lock and load with safeties on. Maintain weapon safety. I don't want any accidental discharges if you trip on this uneven terrain."

Wade turned to Tristin, "When we get a half-mile out, we'll stop and give you time to unpack that drone and get her up. We're gonna need its eyes.

"Jacob, you take point and I'll be behind you.

"Blake, you and Tristin have got the rear. Tristin, if your drone sees any sentries or anything unusual, I want you to tap Blake's shoulder. Blake, you tap mine and I'll call a halt.

"Once we get on the northwest corner of the mountain, we stop. Tristin will fly the drone all around the front from the base and up the hillside to the mine entrance. Let's see if we can clear the area where the covered truck is first so you can set up there.

"Jacob and Blake, once you get the go ahead from Tristin that the area look clear, you can move to your positions. Blake, you are taking the high ground. Jacob, you are going left of the entrance at the base and waiting for me. We will slowly make our approach under protection of Archangel. Remember our discussion about ROE's. We protect each other at all costs. You all do what you need to do to keep us safe on this mission.

"Complete radio silence unless absolutely necessary to report threats or safety directions. Stealth, surprise and audacity will be the keys to our success tonight, remember that. Okay, Jacob take point and let's get moving. Everyone switch on your NVG's," said Wade.

Jacob Black Arrows walked to the point position approximately thirty yards in front of the team members. Jacob, Wade and Blake Sheridan were all armed with fully suppressed weapons. Jacob's immediate weapon was his M-4 .223 carbine, but he also had his subdued black Hoyt RX-7 compound bow with his quiver of carbon fiber arrows strapped to his back.

Jacob moved without making a sound. Wade and the deputies behind Jacob marveled as to how quiet the Apache Indian deputy was while walking through the bone dry, brittle sage brush and uneven, rocky terrain. The sweet scent of silver sage filled the air. Jacob methodically scanned the area in front of him left to right, right to left. He occasionally stopped when he encountered the occasional coyote, desert fox or jack rabbit who were night inhabitants of the area.

Little by little, the team moved stealthfully towards the northwest corner of the Sleeping Mistress mountain. When they got a half mile from where the covered truck in front of the mine was located, Jacob Black Arrows stopped. Wade immediately raised up his left hand in a fist. In response, the team held in place, the men immediately taking a knee to lower their profiles. Wade crouched down and walked back to Tristin.

"Okay Tristin, we're about a half mile from where the covered truck is. Time to unpack your drone and get her up so we can see what and who's out there."

Tristin dutifully removed the Skydio X2D autonomous, carbon fiber drone and controller from his backpack and began his pre-flight checklist. He first checked the drone's battery pack to confirm it was powered up. He had blacked out the drone by covering its running lights with black tape. He unfolded its arms and inspected the quadcopter's rotors and props to make sure there was no visible damage, and they were functioning properly.

Tristin then connected the controller and had Wade hold the drone in his hands so he could inspect the hybrid night vision payload which included both night vision and FLIR thermal cameras. Lastly, Tristin verified the 360° obstacle avoidance,

8-camera optical system and AI assistance were all operative.

Tristin directed Wade to hold the drone in his palm out in front of him in preparation for launch. The deputy activated the drone, and its four "stealth" props immediately began to whirl. With a push of a button the drone launched straight up from Wade's open hand and hovered twenty feet overhead. On the controller, the deputy brought up the side-by-side night vision/IR live view and confirmed that the drone and cameras were operational.

"We are good to go, sir. All systems are fully operational," said Tristin.

"Okay, take her up and move her forward of us about one hundred yards out at four hundred feet. That should give you a pretty good line of sight for you to identify any threats. I want you next to me for this part. I want to know what you know and when you know it," directed Wade. Tristin flew the drone into position and Wade directed the team to continue onto the site.

When the team was about two hundred yards from the site of the covered truck, Tristin took the drone to five hundred feet. Using the AR (Augmented Reality) view, he began to define a waypoint mission to perform slow aerials. Tristin swept the entire north face of the mountain proximate to the mine's entrance. Using the drone's computer vision and real-time 3D mapping, he then swept the hillside below the mine and all around the covered truck. The deputy next switched to full IR view to locate and confirm heat signatures. Then he tapped Wade on the shoulder to show him the live view on his controller screen.

"Sir, look here at the screen. I've confirmed three definite targets on the north side of the hillside, here," the deputy said pointing to the bright targets on the screen. Wade stood next to Tristin, looking down at the screen.

"Okay, here's the first guy next to the covered truck on its west side. See, he's sitting on the ground with his AK next to him. He's not moving, so possibly asleep," explained Tristin. Wade saw the man and acknowledged.

"Next, we have what appears to be two sentries up near the entrance to the mine, but off to the sides. This guy here is about fifty yards west of the entrance. See him? With the video in IR mode, Tristin zoomed in and said to Wade, "See the heat signature? He's smoking a cigarette. Can you see that bright light for a second as he takes a puff? That's the hot end of the cigarette. He's also armed with an AK," explained the deputy.

"Yes, I see him. Man, that's pretty good," replied Wade.

Tristin continued, "Okay, let's move over to the left or east side of the entrance. Here's the third guy about another fifty to sixty yards east of the entrance. Looks like he's armed with some type of high powered rifle. See him?" asked Tristin as he zoomed in the camera closer.

"Got him. Yes, he definitely has a long gun. Do you see anyone else, especially at the entrance of the mine?" asked Wade.

Tristin quickly tasked the drone using the AR waypoints, "Let's take another look. I'm going to move and drop the drone down to a position about two hundred feet above and seventy yards out in front of the mine's entrance so we can have a look," said Tristin.

"Are you sure these guys are not going to be able to hear the drone?" asked Wade.

"No chance, sir. We're good," replied the deputy as he tasked the drone and gazed carefully at the controller screen for a couple of minutes.

"I'm sorry sir, but I can't see anything but a very faint light. I even tried IR for any heat signatures, but nothing," replied Tristin.

"Okay, thanks," said Wade gathering his team together before he continued.

"Tristin, I want you to show Blake and Jacob exactly where their targets are," directed Wade. Tristin then redeployed the drone to the initial mission as Blake, Jacob and Wade gazed down at the screen of his controller.

Directing his comments to Jacob and Blake, Wade asked,

"So, how do you guys want to handle this?"

Jacob deferred to Blake Sheridan, the team's experienced sniper. Blake took the lead on the plan of engagement.

"Well, the way these three guys are positioned, I think the plan should be that I take a position of cover behind that covered pick-up truck. I can easily take out the two sentries east and west of the entrance to the mine. Each shot is less than four hundred yards so easy pickings for me. I'm used to taking out bad guys at two to three times that distance.

However, first, I'd like Jacob to sneak up on the guy next to the truck and take him out. He can then advise me to move up to the truck where I can get my work done. In that position, I'll have a great line of sight and I can quickly take out anyone who emerges from the mine's entrance.

Jacob, I'll give you two clicks on my mic to let you know I'm in place. When you take out the guy at the truck, give me three clicks on your mic. When Tristin and I hear that, he can recover his drone.

After I take my sniper position at the covered truck and take out the two targets, Tristin can recover his drone. He can then come over to me to provide me with some immediate cover.

Tristin, I'll just need you watch my back and act as my scout. All you have to do is warn me, give me the threat's position and an approximate distance. I'll do the rest. Then Wade and Jacob can assault the mine and free Jessie. I'll provide overwatch during your approach and extraction," explained Blake.

"That sounds like a solid plan. Let's go with that," said Wade.

"Tristin, hover your drone over the guy at the covered truck. I want you to also keep eyes on all three sentries, so Jacob has no surprises. You can communicate directly with him if you think he's been spotted by anyone.

Blake, I want you to follow Jacob for a bit and then find a place where you can preliminarily provide overwatch. I need you to take out those two sentries who have the higher ground in case they spot Jacob moving in on the guy at the truck. Are you guys ready to move out?" asked Wade.

Jacob and Blake gave Wade a thumb's up signal. Jacob left first, followed by Blake fifty yards to his rear. Wade stayed with Tristin, intently watching the controller screen for any signs of movement by the snipers.

Approximately one hundred yards away from the sentry at the covered truck, Jacob gave Blake Sheridan a hand signal to peel off to his right. Blake moved to a position about eighty yards to Jacob's right side. From there, he could easily observe each of the two sentries positioned to the left and right of the mine's entrance. Jacob Black Arrows heard two mic clicks over the comm indicating that Blake was in position.

Jacob began to stealthfully approach the sentry who was still seated next to the truck. The soldier had his AK-47 cradled in his arms across his abdomen with the weapon resting on his thighs.

Jacob got about eighty yards from the sentry. He quietly removed one of the black, carbon fiber arrows with a razor-sharp broad tip arrowhead. He then placed the slotted plastic tip into a pre-selected "nocking point" on the bowstring. He activated his Garmin Aero A-1 auto-ranging digital bow sight which illuminated his range to target. It showed seventy-nine yards and provided an LED pin, identifying the sentry.

Jacob began to slowly approach the sentry with the man in his sight. Suddenly, a desert grouse launched into the air chirping loudly almost like a pheasant. Jacob froze like a statue in place as the sentry stirred and then stood up. The man peered into the darkness, holding the AK-47 waist-high. It seemed as if he was looking directly at the deputy, but he was searching for movement where there was none.

The sentry panned the terrain to his left and away from Jacob's position. Jacob aimed center mass at the sentry, placing the LED pin square on the man's sternum before releasing his arrow from seventy-five yards. The arrow ran true and penetrated completely through the man's chest mid-sternum with a subdued and sickly "thunk." The sentry fell backwards against the covered truck and silently collapsed to the desert floor.

Wade and Tristin were observing Jacob's approach to the sentry from Tristin's video feed. They watched as Jacob with bow in hand suddenly stood up and fired upon the sentry just as the man stood up. Then the sentry dropped to the ground and remained motionless.

"Holy moly, that was quick," whispered Tristin in utter surprise as he watched the sentry being neutralized.

Jacob quickly removed a second carbon fiber arrow and placed it into the bowstring's nocking point ready to re-engage the sentry just in case. The Apache Indian deputy moved to within fifty yards of the downed sentry and noted that one half of the arrow's shaft was sticking out of the man's sternum, and he had not moved an inch. Jacob keyed his mic three times. Target neutralized.

Black Sheridan, Wade and Tristin heard the distinct three mic clicks confirming that Jacob had effectively taken out the lower sentry. All three men began moving towards the covered truck to join Jacob.

Blake arrived at the scene first. He looked at the deceased sentry with the arrow sticking out of his chest. "Nice work. I ought to take up archery someday," he whispered. Blake wasted no time. He began quietly setting up his suppressed sniper rifle using the covered hood of the pick-up truck as his aiming platform.

Wade and Tristin arrived at the truck together. Both immediately saw the dead sentry lying on the ground with the shaft of a black carbon fiber arrow sticking out of his chest. It was obvious that young Tristin had never seen a dead person before because he kept staring at the dead sentry. Wade noted this and immediately broke Tristin's focus on the dead man.

"Come on, Tristin. Get into position to support Blake while he's setting up and providing overwatch. Me and Jacob have got to hump up the hill to the mine."

"Blake, what do you make the distances for those two up there?" asked Wade indicating the sentries above them.

Blake looked through his Terrapin X range finder and ranged both sentries. "Left four-hundred-twenty, right three-fifty." Then he switched to the Terrapin survey mode and measured from the sentry closest to Black Arrows to a large rock he believed was two-hundred yards away. "Two-twenty-five" he whispered under his breath. It was more than requested but he would go to work when they got close to the rock.

"Allow me and Jacob to get within two hundred yards of the entrance to the mine if we can, then take 'em out. Obviously, if you note either of them getting hinky, you're free to engage both targets at will," directed Wade.

"Copy that, two hundred yards it is. If you hear two clicks, that will be the guy on the left; three more clicks means I got the guy on the right," replied Blake.

Wade and Jacob stayed together with Jacob taking the lead because he was the quieter of the two. The men carefully climbed up the slanted hillside among all manner of brush and rocks while occasionally looking upwards towards the two sentries. One slip would immediately alert the suspicions of the sentries and foil the mission.

The men climbed slowly and methodically upwards. It seemed like it was taking an hour just to go the two hundred yards they needed to move to before Blake sent the sentries to their rightful places in the netherworld.

Blake remained focused on his rifle scope, occasionally moving his support hand to the gain control knob. The light from the mine's entrance made it impossible to see anything but the sentry's silhouette as they were moving around the area. Blake changed his focus to a pole he was using as his reference point. From this position, he could see when Wade and Jacob were close to their positions.

Blake slowly increased the gain's intensity until he could see the area in front of the pole. He quickly checked his dope card and rolled 1.5 mil onto his elevation turret. The experienced sniper knew that he would have to transition quickly between his shots on the sentries and wouldn't have time to dial his DOPE for each one. One point five mils required him to aim a little high for the left sentry and a little low for the right sentry.

Trained as a tracker, Jacob Black Arrows was a very good judge of distances. He suddenly stopped and raised a flat bladed left hand, telling Wade to stop and wait. Wade watched as the skilled Apache deputy got as low to the ground as he could. Wade mimicked the posture. Both men waited in place watching the sentries and listening on their comm gear.

"Archangel, we're in position," Jacob whispered over the comm. A single mic click was the only response from Sheridan.

Blake centered the reticle on the head of the furthest sentry on the left side of the mine's entrance. *Slowly squeezing the trigger… compression…break.* The weapon's muzzle hissed and recoiled with a hard thump against Blake's right shoulder. One second later, the sentry's head literally exploded as the .308 Federal Gold Dot Match 175 grain round penetrated the sentry's right eye and exploded out the back of the man's head. Blood, bone and brain spatter decorated the rock wall in tight circle behind the fallen sentry. The sentry went down silently, never knowing what hit him.

Archangel keyed his mic, *click…click.* Left target down.

Blake quickly transitioned his weapon system to the sentry on the right and verified range to target at three hundred and fifty yards. The soldier had heard the thwack of the bullet violently striking his partner's head. He just didn't know what the sound meant. The sentry looked over towards his colleague's direction. Blake took a breath, slowly exhaled and then stopped exhaling. *Trigger set, slow squeeze…compression…brake.* The rifle hissed a second time. Less than a second later the round impacted the bridge of the sentry's nose, taking out the entire left side of his head.

Just as before, Archangel keyed his mic, *click…click…click.* Right target down. Jacob heard the clicks and knew it was time to move towards the mine's entrance.

"Check entrance," Wade whispered over his mic. Blake instinctively knew that Wade wanted him to check the mine's entrance for secondary threats.

Blake carefully scanned the entrance to the mine for any signs of additional sentries and keyed hic mic, *Click…click.* All clear at the entrance.

Under cover of Archangel's lethal sniper rifle, Jacob Black Arrows and Wade covered the final two hundred yards of the hillside. They opted to make their approach to the left side of the mine's entrance. The men stopped just about twenty yards from the dark opening. They listened for two full minutes, trying to pick up any ambient sounds from within. The air was deathly silent.

Wade touched Jacob's shoulder and whispered,

"Okay, here's where it gets dicey. No doubt there is at least one sentry inside with Jessie. This will be close quarters, so no rifles. Leave 'em here. Use your bow and I'll use my side arm. I'll take everything left and you've got the right side. As we enter, we slice the pie on the left side with you off my right shoulder. Immediately engage any threats on your side and I'll do the same on mine.

Once we clear the corner and enter, we proceed with purpose slowly and deliberately. If you see a threat, immediately engage without hesitation. If they surrender, we secure them, tape their mouths with duct tape and move on. Just remember that we can't allow any of them to alert the others or we're all dead. We do what we need to do.

Also, we've got no idea how long this mine travels or where Jessie is. Hopefully, like Tristin said, there's some illumination inside to identify our targets and Jessie. Remember to stay away from the sides of the tunnel to avoid ricochets. You ready?"

Jacob nodded affirmatively and the men quietly laid down their rifles. Jacob withdrew not one but two broad-tipped arrows from his quiver and placed the notches of their shafts into the bow string next to each other. Wade unholstered his 1911A .45 and screwed a suppressor onto the end of the muzzle. He automatically press checked the chamber, ensuring that a round was indeed in battery. Jacob assumed a position immediately behind and to the right of Wade. He tapped Wade's shoulder indicating he was ready to move.

As a pair, Wade and Jacob began pivoting the left corner of the mine's entrance in unison, slowly and deliberately. The purpose of the "slicing the pie," also referred to as "sneak and peek" tactic is to use linear physics to identify any potential threats before the target can see you.

The men cleared the mine's entrance. They could see a dim light emanating from what appeared to be a recessed area to the left of the tunnel, thirty yards down from their position as the mine continued straight. It was a good chance that this is where Jessie was, and the action would go down.

Wade and Jacob slowly closed the distance to the recessed area. Wade was on the left side of the tunnel, so it was his job to sneak and peak the corner. Since the entry to the recessed area was narrow, Wade peeked quickly around the corner and pulled back.

Wade spotted two additional men guarding Jessie who was restrained in a chair and asleep. Everyone was on the left side of the small area less than fifteen yards from their position. Jessie was in the middle, his guards on either side of him. Both men were leaning against the wall and appeared drowsy. Their AK-47's were leaning against the wall next to them. Wade saw that the guard on Jessie's left was holding a Glock semiautomatic pistol in his right hand.

Using sign language, Wade tapped Jacob and then held up his left hand using two fingers to point to his eyes. He then held them vertically to indicate *"I see two guards."* Wade then made a circle over his heart using his thumb and forefinger indicating a badge which referred to Jessie. Wade signed that the guards were to the right and left of Jessie. Finally, he signed for Jacob to take the guard on the right, and he would take the guard on the left who was armed with a handgun.

The moment had arrived. Wade held up his left hand in a fist and then outstretched three fingers to signal the countdown. Jacob silently pulled back the bow string with the two broad-tipped arrows affixed to it and stood ready. Wade brought his .45 to chest level and began the short count…*three…two…one!*

Wade and Jacob pivoted the corner simultaneously offset by five feet and faced the two men who were immediately taken off-guard by their sudden presence. As the guard on the right began to move towards his AK-47, Jacob aimed center mass and let fly his arrows. The deadly missiles simultaneously struck the guard's chest with a sickening double thump, one at the top of the sternum and the other mid-sternum. Both broad tips penetrated completely through the man's chest and partially through his back. The shock of being hit with such force from so short a distance catapulted the guard violently against the wall before he collapsed to the dirt floor.

Wade's target was quicker. He raised his pistol up to Jessie's head, looked at Wade and screamed, "I kill! I kill! Drop gun!"

Knowing that a human being usually cannot talk and pull the trigger of a gun at the same time, Wade quickly responded by taking a bead on the guard's head while he was yelling and depressed the trigger, firing a single round from the suppressed pistol.

The silencer hissed and a single .45 caliber Critical Duty jacketed hollow point round struck the guard in the middle of his forehead. The projectile traversed the man's brain and exploded out of the back of his skull. The guard collapsed silently to the floor consistent with the effects of a central nervous system shot. The violent confrontation was over in less than five seconds.

The sounds of the brief engagement awoke Jessie who looked with wide eyes at Wade and Jacob with a combination of disbelief, joy and then relief.

Before Jessie could say anything, Wade placed his index finger over his mouth, motioning to Jessie to keep quiet. Wade then whispered, "How many more around?"

Jessie replied, "There are at least three outside. What time is it? There is a change of the guards just before dawn. Sometimes sooner."

"We took care of the three guys who were outside. No one further down this mine tunnel?" Wade asked.

"Not tonight, but my captor told me yesterday that in the morning I was going to see my last sunrise. They were going to video my execution and send it to dad. I think there will be a bunch of guys coming for that," replied Jessie.

"Okay, well this is certainly going to mess up their plans. Let's bail. Can you walk?" asked Wade.

"Just watch me. Get me out of this damn chair and I'll race you down the mountain," replied Jessie smiling.

Wade keyed his mic, *Click…click…click*, indicating all targets down. In response, Blake Sheridan keyed his mic a single time, indicating confirmation that all guards had been taken out.

Since all of the threats had been eliminated by the team, Wade got on the comm to Blake.

"Archangel, all threats neutralized, package in hand and ambulatory. We are extracting…now. Advise bird to 87 at extraction zone Alpha, repeat, LZ Alpha and get an ETA. Watch our backs, here we come."

Sheridan keyed his mic, "Little Bird, Little Bird, all threats down, package in hand. 10-87 at extraction zone Alpha, need ETA, copy?"

Black Jack Stryker keyed his mic, "Copy package in hand, Extraction Zone Alpha, no threats, ETA less than five."

Stryker had been sitting at idle. To have shut down would have required him to wait an extended period of time until the engine had significantly cooled down in order to prevent a hot start. In an emergency, Stryker knew that would have compromised the mission, so he sat on site with the engine running.

Stryker rolled in power, applied left pedal, and lifted to a hover. He then applied slight forward collective, and the little bird shuddered through transitional lift and flew into the black void of night.

Wade, Jacob Black Arrows and Jessie emerged together from the mine's entrance. Wade and Jacob picked up their M-4's and Jacob secured his compound box behind his back. The three men began to quickly descend the hillside to the extraction point below under protection of Archangel.

The men had just reached the base of the hillside and could hear Stryker's Little Bird flying towards them. At that moment, Tristin suddenly spotted a single lifted and camouflaged 4x4 pick-up truck rapidly moving towards them from the south east. In the back bed of the truck was a mounted machine gun manned by a Tres Paises soldier. This was serious trouble.

Tristin slapped Sheridan on his back, pointed to the mech and yelled, "Oh shit, we've got company on our left."

"Copy contact left," said Sheridan. In response, the sniper immediately spun his rifle to the left towards the vehicle. He immediately recognized its configuration as a "mech." Mechs were mechanized armed vehicles popular with terrorist groups in war zones like Somalia, Afghanistan and Syria. They were now used by drug cartels throughout Mexico and Central America.

Sheridan keyed his mic, "This is Archangel, contact left. I say again, contact to the south east. Mech with a heavy machine gun heading our way fast. Suggest you move immediately to extraction zone Bravo, I say again, contact to the south east, a mech with a heavy machine gun. Change LZ to Bravo. I'll attempt to engage. Copy?"

Sheridan dropped his standard duty magazine and grabbed a magazine containing his 196 grain bullets with tungsten cores for armor penetration.

Wade, Jacob and Jessie had just passed behind Blake and Tristin. The trio were only fifty yards from their original extraction point when they heard the radio traffic. "Copy contact to the southeast. We see 'em. Moving to extraction zone Bravo, now," yelled Wade.

Stryker was coming in low and fast to extraction zone Alpha. He heard Archangel's warning and keyed his mike, "Little Bird copies enemy contact to the southeast. I can confirm one armed mech heading our way. Looks like it's armed with a Russian NSV."

From his time in Viet Nam, Stryker was aware of the lethality of the older NSV 12.7 millimeter heavy machine gun adopted for combat by the Soviet Army in 1971.

Stryker keyed his mic again, "Moving to Bravo. Haul ass, fellas cause those cartel assholes can tear me up with that fucking gun!"

Blake Sheridan was now tracking the quickly moving mech with his scope. His auto-range finder was rapidly changing distances as the vehicle moved closer to them. Blake could see two cartel soldiers in the front besides the one manning the NSV on a swivel stand in the truck's bed. The sniper got on the comm.

"Little Bird, Little Bird, this is Archangel. What's the effective range of that gun?" the sniper asked.

"On the ground, 1,500 meters at 700 − 800 rounds a minute. It fires 12.7 Mike-Mike's" the pilot responded, referring to the weapon's devastating 12.7 mm projectiles.

Sheridan looked at his scout observer, "Time to haul ass, Tristin. I don't need you anymore. I got this. Get the fuck out of here!"

The worried sniper knew this was going to be some very difficult shooting. He immediately changed out his ammo, replacing the magazine with Lapua 165 grain AP rounds. The core of these bullets contained a tungsten penetrator allowing them to pierce through light armored vehicles.

"Good luck, Blake. We'll be waiting for you at the chopper," Tristin replied confidently. The young deputy shouldered his backpack with his drone, grabbed his M-4, then turned and took off like a bat out of hell towards extraction zone Bravo.

Stryker flared the Hughes 500-D, kicking hard left pedal to turn the little bird sidewise so as not to plow the tail rotor into the ground. He knew the LZ might immediately become hot. The Little Bird kicked up all manner of dust, dirt, small rocks and desert sage as Wade, Jacob and Jessie approached. The men ducked low to avoid the whirling rotor.

"Get the fuck in and strapped down! Where's the kid?" yelled the former Viet Nam Air Cav pilot.

Wade looked backwards as Jessie and Jacob dove into the rear compartment. "He's coming. He's out another hundred yards," Wade yelled back over the sound of the spinning rotor.

As Wade looked back to follow Tristin's progress, he could see the bouncing headlights of the fast approaching mech 1,200 yards southeast of their position. Wade pulled back the bolt of his M-4 slightly to perform a press check. He was re-confirming that he was still locked and loaded in the event that the mech got past Archangel.

Back at the covered pick-up truck, Blake Sheridan was intensely focused on tracking the mech. He scanned the road in front of the vehicle and found an area that offered a long exposure of the vehicle driving. He grabbed his terrapin and ranged the area the vehicle would first appear to be 920 yards. The last exposure would be 850 yards.

Blake transitioned to the survey mode on his Terrapin and measured the distance between the two points to be 258 yards. This was plenty of room to work out his lead. He knew that waiting for the right range would enhance his ability to accurately engage the enemy cartel soldiers bent on stopping their extraction with Jessie. Blake scanned the route and found several tall saguaros that he could use as aiming references.

As the mech approached, Blake knew it would take some time until the driver reached the area where he intended to engage. To approximate the distance, he split the difference between the two exposure points, estimating it to be 885 yards. He next checked his DOPE card and determined his bracket elevation would be 8.9 mils. The Zero Compromise scope had 1.5 mils of rotation on the elevation. To assist him while dialing at night he had attached a felt tab at every 5 mils for easy reference points.

Blake reached up and rotated past two felt tabs listening as the elevation turret ratcheted up and rotated as he spun through the turret. As the clicks echoed back to him, he stopped when the second piece of felt faced him. He then methodically reversed his turret five clicks and then another five plus one for a total of eleven clicks. This gave him the desired 8.9 mils he needed to engage. He was ready.

Blake went to the first saguaro, selected a reference point and settled the vertical portion of the crosshair on it. He intended to use the ambush method for engaging this moving target.

In order to take out the driver and rear gunner while the mech was moving towards him, Sheridan needed to determine its speed. The best way to do that was to use his rangefinder to first range the target. Then he needed to get a distance, wait three to five seconds, and range the target again based upon the distance reduced during his wait time. As a rule of thumb, a vehicle moving ten yards every one second was traveling at roughly twenty miles per hour.

Sheridan watched his Terrapin X or TRPNX rangefinder determine the mech's reduced distances. He was mentally calculating the dope for the most accurate placement. He would use the dope from the last range he got from the rangefinder and then hold low on the target. The Max Point-Blank Theory should allow the bullet to still strike his targets in their upper torsos, even though any armored glass windshield.

Ranging was one thing, but the use of night optics to identify and neutralize targets was an entirely different and even more challenging skill. It had been easy to take out the two sentries using his AN/PVS 24 NOD. However, this was a vehicle moving towards him in the dark. This meant going to a thermal option.

Like all experienced military Spec Ops snipers, Blake was prepared for all sniping scenarios including moving people or vehicles. Once he had seen the mech, he had quickly switched from his AN/PVS 24 to his Trijicon SNIPE-IR thermal option sight. This sight employed white phosphorous to see into the night.

If Blake had stayed with his PVS, his view of his targets would have washed out since there was already a lot of light coming from the moving vehicle. The light sources such as headlights and roof mounted LED spotlights would be directed towards the objective lens of the PVS scope. The light wash from the vehicle would have not only made it near impossible to use the optic but could harm his vision.

Blake knew that his Trijicon thermal sight would not wash out in the light. But the optic could be confused due to its use of thermal energy for distinction. This was the challenge since through the sight, the vehicle's headlights would be constantly moving. Therefore, Blake would not be able to detect the driver's position to accurately engage.

Blake moved the muzzle of his rifle between the man on the NSV and the driver. He pondered, *"Should I stop the driver, or try the more difficult shot which was trying to take out the gunner?"*

Even though it was going to be an extremely difficult and time compressed shot, Blake decided to take out the driver first. His thinking was that perhaps if hit, the driver would lose control and crash. This would most likely take out the gunner as well. Blake's Terrapin X continued its countdown as he whispered to himself, *"1,200 yards…1,150…1,100…1,050…1,000…"*

As the mech continued to approach, the wheel track in the desert's sandy and rocky surface suddenly smoothed out, causing the vehicle to stop bouncing so violently. The vehicle was now heading directly for the helicopter. This provided the gunner in the rear bed of the vehicle with an opportunity to begin tracking the muzzle of the heavy machine gun towards the aircraft. He was aware that the machine gunner could engage the Little Bird and its occupants with the NSV out to 1,500 yards. The question right now was did the gunner know that?

"Now or never," thought Blake.

Sheridan used the armored vehicle's headlights and the silhouette of the vehicle as an aiming reference for the target. He figured that the driver was probably sitting six to eight inches inside of the driver's side headlight for a vertical reference. For his horizonal reference, Blake guessed that the driver would most likely be positioned about one third the distance from the top of the vehicle's silhouette to the bottom of it.

As the mech continued towards him, Blake centered the Trijicon thermal sight on the driver's side of the armored front windshield in the center of his points of reference and held steady. The experienced combat sniper began to adjust his breathing pattern while lightly squeezing the trigger rearwards.

"Nine-hundred and fifty yards... 900... 850... squeeze... compression brake...now!"

Archangel's Remington 700 barked a single time, its recoil delivering a solid thump of the butt of its stock against his right shoulder.

Blake waited and watched through his scope as the single armored-piercing Lapua 165 grain tungsten round penetrated through the driver's side of its armored windshield. He observed the 4x4 pick-up truck to immediately veer sharply to its right and roll to a stop.

Blake immediately cycled a new round into the chamber. He noted that the rangefinder indicated 795 yards to target. The sudden out of control veering of the mech had knocked the NSV gunner off-balance. This caused him to fall backwards into the bed of the truck. The heavy machine gun was now temporarily unmanned. Blake now switched his attention to the right front passenger who was trying to move the dead driver out of his seat.

"Oh no you don't, asshole," said Blake as he adjusted his two points of reference to the right side of the and depressed the trigger once more. The weapon barked, recoiled and sent a second Lapua 165 grain AP projectile through the windshield. The bullet penetrated through the passenger's right ear, skull, seat and cab, before ricocheting into the bed, narrowly missing the gunner. For the time being, the mech was going nowhere. The sniper cleared the spent cartridge and quickly chambered a new round.

Blake now scanned back towards the bed of the truck. He found the rear gunner standing, using the metal stand form the NSV machine gun to support himself. He could see through his scope that the cartel soldier was dazed but goal-oriented enough to attempt to engage the Little Bird.

Blake aligned his sights on the center of his adversary's head. As the gunner raised the muzzle of the heavy machine gun and began to point it in the direction of the small helicopter, Blake fired. The gunner's skull exploded in a red misty cloud of blood, hair, flesh and bone. The headless gunner stood strangely still for a brief moment, before falling backwards into the bed of the truck.

Blake Sheridan keyed his comm mic, "This is Archangel, all threats neutralized. I repeat, all targets down. I'm heading for extraction zone Bravo, copy?"

"All threats neutralized, copy Archangel. We're waiting for you at zone Bravo, nice work," replied Wade. Hearing the news, Jacob Black Arrows, Tristin Peters, Jessie Fremont and Black Jack Stryker cheered loudly in unison.

Blake Sheridan wasted no time hustling to the alternate extraction zone. Upon his arrival, he found Wade waiting for him outside the bird with Jacob. Jessie and Tristin already inside and strapped down.

Wade kept low as he moved over and into the co-pilot's seat. Once inside the aircraft, he gave Black Jack Stryker a thumb's up. Wade then donned his helmet and belted himself in. He looked at Stryker and rotated his right index finger to indicate they were ready for the pilot to get them out of there.

In response, Stryker, keyed his mic and said, "Hold onto your corsets, ladies. Here we go!" The pilot then hit the "play" switch on the 1970's boombox stereo system he had strapped next to him. Jimmy Hendrix's *All Along the Watchtower* blared out throughout the cabin.

Stryker applied full left pedal as he pulled in maximum pitch, yanking the Little Bird into the air. The blades slapped the air as they grasped for lift. There was less than thirty minutes of darkness left. The Little Bird pitched forward and tore through the Mexican darkness at one hundred feet, heading north for the U.S.

border and freedom.

Back at the MITRE radar station, Katie Blackwater remained concealed as she repeatedly glanced at her watch. She had no comm gear and was operating solely on specific time directions that Black Jack Stryker had provided her with. At exactly 0450 hours, Katie turned on her stereo system full blast belting out Steppenwolf's *"Magic Carpet Ride"* at one-hundred and fifty decibels.

"Damn, again?! What the hell!" exclaimed the DHS/CBP MITRE operator as he pulled off and tossed his headset onto the floor.

The MITRE radar system's acoustic array was again completely overcome by the sudden blast of hard rock as the Little Bird containing the team piloted by Black Jack Stryker streaked back across the Rio Grande and the U.S./Mexican border at tree top level.

Katie could hear the Hughes 500-D pass overhead; she just couldn't see the chopper. Thirty seconds later, the sounds of Steppenwolf's *"Born to be Wild,"* blasted out of her speaker causing the radar's system back at DHS/CBP to suddenly stop and begin a re-boot, again frustrating its agent operator. Katie laughed out loud imagining what was going on in the CBP operations room right now.

Katie allowed the music to play out, then packed up her gear. The Border Patrol Assistant Chief hiked back to her Jeep and drove off as the eastern sky was just beginning to display a hint of pink with the arriving sunrise.

CHAPTER 20

Aftermath

ADOLFO GUZMAN'S CHIEF enforcer Uberto "The Bull" Urias had been trying to radio the point vehicle of Tres Paises soldiers heading to the mine for ten minutes. The sun was rising, and his own armored vehicle was rounding the east side of the Amante Durmiente mountain. The frustrated Urias was now yelling over the radio, *"Donde estas, tontos, digame?! (Where are you idiots? Tell me!)* There was only silence in response.

The Bull was riding in a desert camouflaged Improvised Armored Fighting Vehicle (IAFV). These vehicles were often referred to by the cartels as narcotanques or "narco tanks." As the vehicle turned the northeast corner of the mountain, its driver spotted the first mech diagonally off to the right side of the road track. The driver called out into the back of the vehicle to his boss, "Jefe, Ahi ellos estan por delante!" *(There they are ahead).*

The Bull's AV pulled up behind the first mech. Urias dismounted with his crew of four cartel soldiers and cautiously approached the mech with their guns raised. Upon getting to the cab, they immediately saw the two bullet impacts through the front blood and brain spattered windshield. One of the soldiers opened the driver's side door and its deceased driver poured out onto the desert floor. The right front passenger was slumped over and onto the driver's seat. The remains of both men's heads were plastered all over the backs of their seats and partially shattered rear window.

One of the soldiers looked over the side of the rear bed where the NSV heavy machine gun was mounted and found its headless gunner dead in the back. Amazingly, there was only one round in each man, and all were head shots. The obvious struck

Urias as if he himself had been shot.

"Snipers!, Cubranse en nuestro vehiculo!" *(Snipers! Take cover in our vehicle!)* the enforcer yelled out as he ducked and ran for the cover of his armored vehicle. The Bull's soldiers immediately looked up and around and also ran for the cover of the armored vehicle and clambered inside after their boss.

"Get me the fuck out of here! Head for the mine!" Urias yelled to his driver. Immediately complying, the driver floored the accelerator and began zigzagging down and across both sides of the dirt roadway. This caused the armored vehicle to violently bounce up, down, back and forth. The vehicle reached the base of the hillside leading up to the mine's entrance where the covered truck had been stored. The now woozy, motion sick Urias ordered the driver to stop.

The Bull and his soldiers peered out from the armored glass windows for any traces of an enemy but saw nothing. Not being a fool, Urias ordered one of his men to get out of the vehicle to survey the area first. The man reluctantly emerged from the vehicle and began to cautiously work his way around the covered truck. Urias and the other three men watched the Guinea pig from the safety of the armored vehicle.

It was light out now and Urias and his men could see that the point man had not been harmed. As the soldier turned the corner of the truck, he suddenly stopped and looked down towards the ground. The man then crouched low and ran back to the vehicle yelling, "Pablo is dead! He is dead, Jefe!"

Urias immediately thought they had driven directly into a trap but saw no evidence of any enemy presence. Surely, if this was an ambush by the Mexican Army, or worse yet, the feared Mexican Marines, they would have been attacked by now. Yet, nothing was happening.

Urias was processing the situation in light speed. *"It couldn't be the Mexican Army,"* he thought. The Army's regional battalion commander was on the cartel's payroll and Adolfo would have certainly been warned. On the other hand, the Marines could not be bribed, and they would have been inserted by helicopters. Yet, they had neither seen nor heard any aircraft.

There was clear evidence that precision shooting had killed his men. This meant snipers. But how had these assets arrived? There was no evidence of the presence of any other vehicles at the scene. Certainly, a rival cartel would not have chosen this time or location for an attack. There was no sense it. Adolfo and his captains would not take the risk of coming so close to the U.S./ Mexican border. There were no drug caches or money to steal.

The Bull got on his radio and called out to the sentries and guards watching over the American sheriff deputy. Neither team responded to several calls out to them.

Urias picked up a pair of binoculars and carefully surveyed up the hillside to the mine's entrance where the sentries had been stationed. He saw no one, nothing. It was time to take a chance. Adolfo would need to know the status of their deputy hostage and the men guarding him.

"Get out of the vehicle. We need to investigate," Urias ordered his men. He then directed his point soldier, "Take me to where Pablo is."

The enforcer and his men carefully exited their armored vehicle, weapons at the ready, looking in all directions. The point soldier directed Urias to the far side of the covered truck. Upon making the turn, what Urias saw both confused and surprised him. Lying on the ground was Pablo, the distal, feathered end of a black carbon fiber arrow shaft protruding from the center of his chest.

Urias cautiously walked over to the deceased soldier and turned him over onto his side. He observed three inches of the arrow's remaining shaft ending in the razor-sharp broad tip.

"What the fuck is this, a fucking arrow? My soldier was killed by a fucking arrow? Who kills with a fucking arrow?!" Urias exclaimed to no one in particular. He touched and rubbed the arrow's black shaft again. The shaft was made of carbon fiber. This was no normal type of arrow. This was professional grade. A professional had killed his man.

Urias called his four soldiers together for a quick briefing,

"I can't reach anyone up there. We are going to spread out and ascend the hillside to the mine. You three spread out, one to the left, one up the middle and one to the right side. Enrique and I will provide cover for you. When you arrive up top, radio the status of the sentries outside of the mine. If it's clear we will come up. When I arrive, we will enter the mine together. Be careful. So far, all of your brothers are dead so don't add to it."

The three soldiers reluctantly and cautiously climbed the hillside feeling that at any time they could meet the fate of their companions. The men reached the top, located the two deceased cartel sentries and radioed back with the information Urias feared.

"Jefe, they are both dead," said one of the men.

"How, bullets or arrows?" The Bull asked.

"Headshots," replied the soldier. The response caused the now paranoid Urias and his guard to immediately duck down and get low to the ground. Urias and the man looked around three hundred and sixty degrees for snipers. The environment remained deathly quiet.

"Fucking pinche putos!" declared the angry and concerned enforcer who at this moment, felt entirely powerless to control his immediate environment.

"Okay, don't enter the mine. Wait for us. Try your best to provide cover for us as we climb up to meet you. Look for snipers. It is better that we enter the mine together, understood?" directed Urias.

"Si, Jefe, comprendido," the senior of the men replied.

Urias got back on his radio and again attempted to reach the two men guarding the sheriff deputy hostage. There was no response. He knew this was a very bad sign.

"Vamanos. Nosotros excalamos!" (Let's go. We climb!) The Bull ordered his personal guard.

Urias and his man reached the left side of the mine's entrance. He then directed all four men to enter the tunnel with their AK-47's at the ready. "Kill everyone you see who is not ours except for that pinche deputy. Leave him to me. Radio your findings," ordered the enforcer. If there were enemies inside, better for a much lower level cartel soldier to die than he.

All of my men are expendable, he mused.

The Bull's men entered the mine's dark tunnel while he remained outside in a position of safety. There was a hint of light coming from the recessed area to the left where Wade and Jacob had earlier encountered and killed the two guards and freed Jessie.

Uberto Urias waited anxiously for the gunfire that never came. Within three minutes his portable radio crackled with the news from one of his soldiers that both guards were dead, and the deputy hostage was nowhere to be found.

"Putas!" Urias exclaimed angrily. Urias entered the mine tunnel and worked his way to the illuminated recessed area. There he found the two deceased guards in a grisly scene. Observing their bodies, The Bull found that one man had a bullet hole square in the middle of his forehead, the back of his skull missing. The second guard had the shafts of two black carbon fiber arrows spread only four inches apart penetrating through his sternum and heart. The razor-sharp broad tips protruded a full six inches out from the man's bloody back. Both men had died with their eyes open, a look of shock and surprise on their faces. Both bodies were also still warm.

"Single kill shots and carbon fiber arrows. Obviously skilled professionals like himself," thought Urias. Inexplicably, the deputy sheriff hostage that Adolfo Guzman wanted to be executed on video was gone. He had apparently been freed by the killers.

The puzzle at this point was difficult to solve. Urias was confident that none of his men were moles. He was also certain none of them would dare to open their mouths in any way revealing that Tres Paises had an American law enforcement officer hostage, or where that hostage was being held.

"So how the hell had this happened?" he thought.

Right now, the issue that most concerned Urias was that he would have to call his boss. Explaining the circumstances and troubling news that Adolfo's main leverage against Gila County Sheriff Matt Fremont and the American DEA and USDOJ was gone would not go down well.

The Americans still had Adolfo's favorite nephew Chuy in custody, and they had nothing to leverage his release. The Gila County deputy was his responsibility. His boss would no doubt certainly see his failure to secure his hostage as a breach of duty; perhaps even a sign of disloyalty. In the Tres Paises world, disloyalty could be punished by death.

"I need a moment alone," Urias said to his men as he walked out of the mine to call Adolfo. His men understood the gravity of the situation and looked down at the ground, avoiding all eye contact. No one right now wanted to be in The Bull's shoes.

Once outside, Urias dialed Guzman's cell with an unusually shaky hand. Adolfo answered on the second ring.

"Mi patron, por favor, disculpame. I am afraid I have some very bad news to tell you," Urias began.

"You are calling to tell me that something bad has happened to the deputy before you had a chance to kill him?" Guzman inquired impatiently.

"No senor, I'm afraid worse than that," replied Urias.

"What could possibly be worse than that, Toro?" asked Guzman.

"I am afraid that in my absence, people came to the mine and killed all of our men guarding the deputy. The deputy has vanished. There is no trace of him, so we don't know if he is alive or dead senor," explained Urias.

There was a long, uncomfortable pause on the other end of the line. Urias simply waited for a response. There was no way he was going to speak unless spoken to right now. The silence was deafening. Then The Bull heard Adolfo take a deep breath and exhale.

"Toro, you are my chief enforcer, a man whom I have trusted above many others even at the highest levels of our organization. Is this not so?" Guzman asked.

"Si senor," Urias replied briefly.

"You are also the man I personally delegated this most important assignment to. One where the very life of my most favored nephew, the son of my sister depends upon the success of the assignment I entrusted to you. Is this also not so," asked Guzman, his voice rising.

"Si, senor," replied Urias softly. The last thing he wanted to do was say anything that would increase the frustration and anger he sensed building in his boss.

"And now, you call to tell me that not only several of my men have been killed, but an important hostage…our only leverage against the Americans is missing? That he might have been freed by whomever murdered my men. My fucking men, in my fucking territory! Is that what you're telling me, Toro?" Guzman screamed over the phone.

Urias held his tongue, trying to conjure up the right words to assuage his cartel boss.

"Are you fucking hearing me, Toro? Are you hearing my questions? Speak to me! Is this a sign of your incompetent disloyalty to me. Your Padron who has given you everything!" Guzman shrieked over the phone.

Urias knew that his next words would have to be very carefully chosen or they might be some of his last. If any of his men's cell phones went off after this call, it was surely an order by Adolfo to kill him.

"Mi Padron, knowing how important it was to you have the sheriff's son kidnapped, I personally planned and executed a perfect kidnapping. I chose an excellent site on our side of the border, in your territory and under our control. A place close enough for us to quickly facilitate the exchange of Chuy for this deputy. I can promise you that none of the men I chose for this mission gave away its location.

"If you allow me some time, I will do everything in my power to find out who killed our men and took the deputy. But moreover, I promise you that I will devise a plan to recover your nephew Chuy from the Americans. I swear on my life, senor that I will not fail. I have faithfully served you well all these years. Please give me a chance to prove myself again to you," pleaded Urias.

Adolfo Guzman listened to his chief enforcer begging for his life. This was indeed a different side of the killer who had no conscience. With Chuy's time running out, Adolfo knew that he needed his most experienced and trusted enforcer engaged. Right now, he could not afford an emotional response that would cause

Urias to end up buried out in the middle of the desert with a bullet in his head.

Guzman remained purposely silent for a full minute, allowing time for Toro Urias to consider his possible fate. The excruciating waiting was a punishment in part. If his enforcer failed again, he could always order his death and train a new enforcer from a stable of enthusiastic cartel assassins.

As the phone remained silent and time ticked away, beads of sweat rolled down Urias' face, the salty water entering his eyes and stinging. *Tick…tick…tick…*

Guzman responded in a tone of voice that was lower and more understanding. The voice of remediation, of potential redemption.

"Perhaps this incident was not your fault. Perhaps it was no one's fault. Perhaps our new enemy who has yet to be revealed simply got lucky. I do not believe that the American federales, or the sheriff in Gila County are smart enough to pull off something like this right under our eyes.

"You tell me that you can find out who took out our men and stole the deputy from us. You also say that you can devise a plan to get my Chuy back. In consideration of your prior service to me I will give you this one chance to redeem yourself. I owe you this much. However, I also give you a stern warning that this one chance is all you get. If you fail to get Chuy back, then you will force me to exercise other options," said Adolfo calmly and deliberately, letting the subdued threat sink in.

Uberto Urias, sighed silently in relief. His carefully parsed words had spared his life and bought him some time. However, he also understood Guzman's meaning behind the words, *"fail and you will force me to exercise other options."*

The coveted position of chief enforcer was highly competitive. Urias knew that there were a number of ambitious young warriors who would be more than happy to take his place. A younger generation who would kill him without even blinking an eye to earn Adolfo Guzman's favor. Urias knew that he had just made promises to his boss that he might not be able to keep. However, the desire not to be killed was a great motivator. *"He must not fail; he would not fail,"* he thought.

CHAPTER 21

"Mi Jefe, I have a plan."

AS UBERTO URIAS and his soldiers were arriving at the Amante Durmiente to discover the death scene, the Hughes 500-D "Little Bird" carrying the team and their package Sheriff Deputy Jessie Fremont was landing back at the Valkyrie Helicopters compound. Sheriff Matt Fremont was already out of his SUV and waiting for them.

As the helicopter's rotors wound down, Wade, Jessie and the team emerged, crouched down and headed for the sheriff. Matt and Jessie embraced as father and son as the team surrounded them and applauded. Black Jack Stryker dismounted from the chopper and joined the team. Matt Fremont shook every man's hand and embraced Wade.

"Thank you all from the bottom of my family's hearts for returning my son to us. You are all heroes in my book. You all look pretty tired. Get some rest and we will debrief later. I'll call you. Now I'd like to call my family to let them know that our Jessie is safe and home again. Then I want to get Jessie over to the hospital to get his finger taken care of," said the grateful sheriff.

The men returned to the helicopter for their gear and left in the Sheriff's unmarked van. Wade shook Stryker's hand and thanked him for his plan and excellent flying. He promised to get together for a beer soon. Wade then climbed into Matt's SUV with Jessie and the trio left for Matt's ranch.

On the way back to Matt's ranch, the sheriff asked his former Texas Ranger partner, "I know we are going to de-brief later, but is there anything I need to know about? Any problems I need to deal with?" Matt inquired.

Wade wanted to maintain the sheriff's plausible deniability status, so he simply replied, "We did what we needed to do. Nothing that the team couldn't handle. I'm not sure that we need a debriefing, but I can fill you in on a couple of things we saw over there."

Matt had trained and worked with Wade in the rangers for many years. Knowing how he had handled himself at the Roadrunner Saloon, the sheriff was perceptive enough not to pursue the matter further right now.

On the afternoon of Jessie Fremont's rescue, the shaken enforcer Uberto Urias gathered twenty of his best soldiers together for a meeting. He wanted to discuss how he was going to move forward to make good on his optimistic promises to his Jefe Adolfo Guzman.

The Bull began the meeting by somberly informing his men that the mission to trade the kidnapped deputy sheriff son of the Gila County, NM sheriff for Chuy Guzman had failed. An unknown force had been able to identify where Tres Paises had been holding the deputy. They had infiltrated the hideout at Amante Durmiente and had eliminated the entire protection force guarding the deputy. It appeared that this element had apparently rescued their hostage and had vanished without a trace.

"Men, I need your full attention and commitment. These people killed your brothers. They have disrespected Tres Paises and thwarted our plan to return our Jefe's nephew Chuy back to his family. Such things do not happen to us. This is a black stain on our organization. Needless to say, Senor Guzman is angry beyond belief.

I have been given permission by our Jefe to use all of Tres Paises' resources to identify the bastards who rescued this deputy and killed our brothers. That means putting all of you into play. I am devising plans to accomplish two objectives. First, to identify who is responsible for this incident and kill them all. Second, a more sophisticated plan to rescue Chuy.

I will be calling upon each of you to do your part in gathering intelligence and neutralizing this new enemy. However, our first priority must be to get Chuy back. These plans will require your one hundred percent commitment and personal sacrifice.

We must all be willing to do anything and everything to successfully complete these separate, but related missions. Success will mean your elevation within Tres Paises as well as monetary rewards. Are you with me?" Urias asked.

"Si, senor!" yelled out his men in unison.

After briefing his men and receiving their commitment to his two plans, Urias visited his boss to discuss his plans and resources he would need for success. The Bull actually began the meeting with discussing his second plan which was to free Chuy Guzman.

"Senor, I have a plan to free Chuy, but it is slightly complicated. The plan's success depends upon the cooperation and assistance of the Las Cruces congresswoman on your payroll. Perhaps even the Tejano congressman from El Paso as well," said Urias.

"What will be needed from our assets, Toro?" Adolfo asked.

"Well, most importantly our influence with the government, specifically with the American Department of Homeland Security and Customs and Border Patrol," replied Urias.

"Digame. Tell me how our congresswoman Senorita Cabral and the Tejano Chico Silvers could be of assistance to you. What is your plan to free Chuy?" asked Guzman.

The head of the Tres Paises cartel was referring to Octavia Cabral, the Congresswoman who represented the 2nd Congressional District of New Mexico.

Charles "Chico" Silvers was the Congressman representing Texas' 16th Congressional District.

Urias still had not worked out all the details of his plan but provided enough information that would resonate with his boss.

"Well, we know that the American DHS and DEA have Chuy in custody at the La Tuna Federal Correctional Institution in Anthony, just outside of El Paso. Obviously, this facility is well guarded so assaulting the facility is out of the question. Therefore, the only way to gain access to Chuy would be to arrange for the federales to move Chuy to somewhere else; to bring him to us so to speak," said Urias.

"And why would the federales want to move a high value prisoner from a place of high security and risk taking them to a place of lower security?" asked Guzman.

"Ah, this is a good question, Senor. The answers are ego, notoriety and most of all, politics. Let me explain further.

"Presently, the President's approval ratings have been going steadily downhill. His policies have failed in literally every area both nationally and internationally. The President's worst ratings are in dealing with America's immigration problems.

"The U.S, President has tried to enhance his party's political base by offering millions of illegals amnesty and the ability to vote. In doing so, his policies have created an unprecedented revenue source for all of the transnational cartels due to our ability to smuggle both immigrants and drugs into the U.S.

"This new illegal alien smuggling revenue source is worth scores of billions of dollars to us annually. We now make nearly as much money smuggling illegals as we do drugs. When our people are caught smuggling people across the border, the American criminal penalties are far less than when they are caught smuggling drugs.

"The American President's political problem is that in enabling us to smuggle in millions of illegals, he has also angered many Americans. His own DHS secretary who we own just told his own Border Patrol agents that it wasn't against the law to illegally cross into the U.S. He also stupidly remarked in public that the border was secure. Of course, this is what we want him to say," laughed Urias.

"The drugs we smuggle in like fentanyl, ISO, methamphetamine and cocaine have killed over one hundred thousand Americans annually. Eighty percent of these deaths are fentanyl opioid deaths. China provides us with the fentanyl powder, but since the President has covert business relationships with the Chinese, he takes no actions against them. The result is that Americans are now turning against him, and his party is suffering as a result.

"The President, his party's Congress and the Senate may lose the next election. If that happens, it is really going to cut into our business. To bolster his polling numbers, the American President is going to have to showcase something positive that he can claim credit for. My plan is to offer him just that. A victory in his so-called war on drugs," explained Urias.

"And just how do you propose to do that?" asked Guzman.

"Well, they already have Chuy in custody. Your nephew is someone who they can present to the American media and the public as a major drug smuggler. What they don't have are two things, a venue to showcase their victory and timing.

"My sources tell me that the DEA have no plans right now to do anything with Chuy. Timing is everything in politics. My plan is to change both paradigms by offering them both a venue, and the timing to showcase Chuy as their victory trophy. In effect, your nephew becomes an important political pawn," said The Bull.

"Go on. Explain to me how you plan to accomplish this feat," directed Guzman.

"Jefe, con tu permiso, what I propose is that we use Congresswoman Cabral and perhaps her cohort the Congressman from El Paso, "Chico" Silvers. Both are on our payroll. We will need to have Cabral and Silvers convince the President's staff that with his poll numbers dropping, what is needed is to parade Chuy in front of the television cameras during a court arraignment on drug charges at the federal courthouse in Silver City. This town is in Grant County which is 110 miles west of Las Cruces and just thirty-five miles from our Mexican border. This area is within the Tres Paises territory," explained Urias.

"And your plan is to assault the federal courthouse and free Chuy?" asked Guzman.

Adolfo Guzman's chief enforcer pulled out a map and spread it out over a nearby table.

"No Senor. What I propose is less risky. I intend to deploy a well-trained tactical team to surprise and assault the law enforcement convoy carrying Chuy as they enter the Customs and Border Patrol Station referred to as Checkpoint Delta. This station is just ten miles east of the town of Deming. My team will then free Chuy. From there, we will evacuate south and cross the U.S./ Mexican border with your nephew," said Urias.

"And how do you propose to take the convoy carrying my nephew at the Border Patrol station? What of the officers guarding that station?" asked Guzman.

"You leave that up to me, Jefe. I am confident that my plan will work. I will personally train all of the men on my team. What I need from you is to make the arrangements with Cabral and Chico Silvers to do their parts. They will undoubtedly ask for a lot of money but pay them. Even if they ask for a couple of million American dollars each, it will be more than worth it to get your nephew back safe and sound. Then it is we who claim victory!" exclaimed Urias with confidence.

Adolfo Guzman looked down at the map spread before him and then back at his henchman, considering his proposal.

"Toro, your audacious plan is both simple and logical. However, it will all initially depend upon our Congress stooges managing to convince the American President's people that showcasing Chuy will elevate the President's stature among his people. What do you think our chances are?" asked Guzman.

"Jefe, I believe that getting our congresspeople to do our bidding will depend upon a couple of things. First, their greed, so you must give them a sizable bribe. Next, they are already deep in our debt. They have become millionaires because of us. In tasting the candy, they have not only become addicted, but directly tied to us. So, if they baulk at the money, a little hint of extortion is also a great motivator. Offer the money first and see how these putas respond. If they are reluctant, then remind them of their ties to Tres Paises. That ought to do it. My bet is that the offer of a lot of money will be sufficient," explained Urias.

"Alright, I will make the arrangements. How long will it take for you to train your team," asked Guzman.

"One week for reconnaissance and training. It will take that long for you to negotiate with Cabral and Chico and allow them to convince the President's advisors to parade Chuy in front of the TV cameras," replied Urias.

Congresswoman Octavia Cabral was just getting into her

car when a text message "55263" popped up on her personal cell. The cryptic numbers corresponded with "Llame" or "Call me" in Spanish. According to a previous agreement, there was only one person who would contact her in this manner.

The Congresswoman got into her $130,000 Tesla 300-S four-door sedan. She reached into her purse and produced a burner cell phone. She then punched in the letter "L" which speed-dialed a matching burner iPhone belonging to a Mexican attorney working for Adolfo Guzman.

"I'm responding to your text," said Octavia.

"Good. My uncle is in need of an urgent favor. Are you in Washington or Las Cruces?" asked the attorney.

"We are out of session, so I am in Las Cruces. What is needed?" replied Octavia.

"A meeting tonight where this matter will be discussed. Can you bring Chico with you?" the attorney asked.

"We were going out to dinner tonight anyway so yes I can bring him. How urgent is this favor and when and where is the meeting?" asked the Congresswoman.

"I'll text you the location and time on this phone. Call Chico and make the arrangements. My uncle wants both of you there. You will be met by Senor Guzman's point man in Las Brisas, Sancho Villegas. This is important so don't be late," replied the attorney abruptly before hanging up.

One minute after the call, Octavia received another cryptic text message on her burner phone that read, "Rosa's, Deming, 730, 2M." Octavia looked down at the text in surprise. It meant "Rosa's Cantina, Deming, NM, 7:30 pm. You will receive a payment of $2 Million."

"Two million dollars for going to a meeting and doing an urgent favor for Adolfo Guzman? That was a lot of money. What did the head of the Tres Paises drug cartel want from her now? What would he also need Chico for?" thought Octavia.

After a joyous greeting with his wife and mother, Matt Fremont took his son Jessie to the small Gila County Memorial

Hospital to be examined by the ER physician. The doctor determined that Jessie's left ring finger had been cleanly severed and cauterized. He said that only removing the brunt skin, cleaning, suturing and a shot of strong antibiotics was needed. The physician also provided Jessie with a prescription of amoxicillin to further guard against any infection. He also recommended that Jessie take a couple of weeks off work to let the amputation heal properly

The physician's young ER nurse's assistant bandaged up Jessie's severed finger and he was discharged from the ER to return home.

As Jessie and his father were driving back home, Jessie asked his father, "So when can I return to duty? The missing finger won't hamper anything I do on the job, dad."

Sheriff Matt Fremont anticipated this question and responded.

"Look Jessie, you've been through a lot in the past few days. Thank God you only lost a finger instead of your life. Your wife and mother have been frantic about your absence. I purposely didn't tell them that those bastards had tortured you.

"The kidnapping by Tres Paises alone was more than enough to scare the living daylights out of them. As your boss and your dad, I'm going to order you to just take it easy and kick back at home for at least a week. This will allow everything and everyone to decompress and give your finger time to heal. The last thing your family wants right now is for you to get back into the thick of it. Remember that more than likely, Tres Paises has no idea who killed their men, rescued you and even where you are.

"Keep a low profile at the ranch for the time being. Just give yourself and the family a break. There were a lot of moving parts involved in getting you home safely and I still don't know what the repercussions(,) if any might be. Just lay low for now, Okay?" asked Matt.

"Alright, dad. I'll abide by your wishes. However, after a week off, I want to return to full duty status I already miss the guys," replied Jessie.

Matt and Jessie returned to the Fremont ranch. They walked over to the guest house to visit Wade and found the former

Texas Ranger busy packing up his gear.

"What's all this about?" Matt asked, surprised to see his old partner packing and apparently getting ready to leave.

"Well, as I recall, you brought me in to do a job. I'm looking at the live results of that assignment, so as they say, "My work here is done.""

"It's time for me to get back to my own ranch in Texas. The place won't run itself, and I've been gone a week. There are bulls to feed and train. I've got plenty of chores to do and I'm sure my dog Desi misses me. Plus, I can use some downtime. I'm a retired Texas Ranger, remember? The key word in that last sentence being, "retired.""

"You're the law dog here, Matt. I'm just a stock contractor these days,. Repeat after me, "stock contractor," replied Wade, smiling at both men.

"Okay, I get it, but just stay a few hours more. Let's have a celebratory early supper BBQ. I'll call over the team, Black Jack Stryker, Johnny Wake; get them all over here for a nice TexMex style meal. We can all celebrate Jessie's safe return and a job well done. Afterwards, you can say your good-byes to family and new friends and head back to Texas at sundown. Fair enough?" asked Matt.

Jessie broke into the conversation. "Yes, Wade. Please stay for just a few more hours. It won't hurt nothin'. Texas will still be there. It's gonna take you a day to get there even if you're speeding. You'll just be a few hours late. How about it? It would make mom and Josie happy to spend some extra time with you before you go."

"Well, how can I possibly turn that offer down? Okay, I'll stick around for the party, but after that, I've got to head out," replied Wade.

"Early supper at 4:00 pm this afternoon. You'll be out of here by 6:00 pm with the sunset at your back as you drive out," said Matt.

"Perfect," replied Wade as he continued packing.

Matt and Jessie left Wade to finish his packing and headed

off to the ranch house where Matt began calling up members of the team. Esperanza and Josie Fremont made up a grocery list and headed off to the local market.

Uberto "The Bull" Urias' was at the Tres Paises gun range. He was teaching his assault team the finer points of close quarter battle and disabling armored vehicles using automatic weapons when his cell phone rang. Over the gun fire, Adolfo Guzman's chief enforcer picked up.

"Digame!" He yelled out over the discharges as he stepped further away from his men who were practicing firing at vehicles.

"Jefe, we have located the deputy you kidnapped," said Sancho Villegas, his chief operative in Las Brisas on the other end of the call.

"Donde es?," asked the surprised Urias.

"A cousin of one of our men works as a medical assistant. She called and told him that this deputy was at the hospital in Las Brisas earlier today to get a severed ring finger treated. She personally bandaged his hand. This girl read the medical chart and saw that the patient's name was "Jessie Fremont." She heard that there was a reward for this information," replied the soldier.

"Is the deputy still at the hospital?" asked Urias.

"No, Jefe, the deputy was brought in by the sheriff himself whose name is also Fremont. The deputy was undoubtedly his son. The deputy was discharged late this morning. The girl asks can she get the reward," explained Villegas.

"Of course, Sancho. Give this woman $1,000 and tell her that she is not to say anything about this man to anyone," ordered Urias who then hung up.

Urias now knew that Deputy Jessie Fremont was already back in Las Brisas. He also knew that his father the sheriff had personally brought him into the county hospital to be treated. This meant that the sheriff himself was in some way involved with his son's rescue.

"But who else could have facilitated the son's rescue? An American county sheriff would never risk crossing the border and kill multiple

civilians. That would be considered by both the Mexican and American governments as a serious breach of international law," he thought.

Thinking back, Urias recalled that his man in Las Brisas had recently reported that three Tres Paises soldiers had gotten into a skirmish with a gringo at a saloon in the town. The gringo was apparently a pistolero who had killed two of the men in a resultant gunfight. The third man had been injured with a knife yielded by a local Apache Indian who had accompanied the gringo into the saloon. The information had been confirmed through a criminal defense attorney on the Tres Paises payroll who was representing the third wounded soldier.

The defense attorney had spoken in confidence with the wounded soldier while in jail. The man had heard the jail deputies mentioning that the gringo who killed the two Tres Paises soldiers was a former Texas Ranger named Wade Justus. This ranger was apparently a good friend of the Gila County Sheriff. The wounded soldier had provided his defense attorney with a physical description of this Texas Ranger wearing a brown Stetson cowboy hat.

This made total sense. Undoubtedly, the sheriff had employed this former Texas Ranger as a mercenary.

"Who else could plan an operation that resulted in the death of several of his men and the rescue of a hostage without having been observed? Mercenaries!" Urias said to himself, believing that he had solved the puzzle.

Urias called Sancho Villegas in Las Brisas. When Villegas picked up, The Bull directed him to commence surveillance on the Gila County Sheriff's Department. "Photograph anyone matching the unique features of this Texas Ranger wearing a brown Stetson cowboy hat," ordered Urias. The enforcer's order was immediately obeyed.

At 3:00 pm, Wade called Matt at the sheriff's department. The sheriff had finished his investigation into Wade's self-defense double homicide over at the Roadrunner Saloon. Wade wanted his pistol back.

"Hey, can I get my gun back?" asked Wade.

"Sure thing. Come on down now and I'll sign it out to you," replied Matt Fremont.

"Great. See you in a few minutes. I feel naked without it," replied Wade.

Ten minutes later, Wade pulled his pick-up truck into the parking lot of the sheriff's department. Wade emerged from his truck, donned his brown Stetson cowboy hat and walked into the front lobby.

The Tres Paises soldier maintaining surveillance on the sheriff's department spotted Wade immediately. Wade had appeared too quick to snap a photo of him, so the soldier readied his camera and long range lens, awaiting Wade's return to his vehicle.

Wade entered the lobby and was warmly greeted by Matt Fremont's personal administrative secretary Lisa Owens.

"Afternoon, Lisa, I called the sheriff about my gun," explained Wade.

"Matt already told me, Wade. Go on back to his office," directed Lisa.

Matt already had an evidence box laying on his desk containing Wade's 1911A .45 caliber Nichol's Custom Combat semiautomatic pistol.

"Here you go. Just sign here to release your pistol from evidence. Figured you'd never leave town without this baby. Just keep the box," said Matt with a smile.

"You're right. Thanks partner. See you back home," replied Wade who then left Matt's office. Wade walked back out towards the front lobby and said good-bye to Lisa Owens before clearing the front lobby and walking back to his truck.

This time, the cartel soldier with the camera was ready and waiting for the former Texas Ranger. As Wade walked the twenty yards to his truck, the cameraman zoomed in. *Click, click, click, click, click, click, click...* went the speed shutter of the 35 mm SLR digital camera. Wade's full features had now been captured close-up.

Wade entered his pick-up truck, started it up and headed for the front gate of the sheriff's department. The truck was pointed directly towards the concealed cartel cameraman. *Click, click, click, click, click...*whirled the SLR camera's high-speed shutter again, capturing Wade's pick-up truck and its Texas license plate number.

The cameraman uploaded the camera's SIM card into a digital file which he then transmitted directly to Sanchez Villegas' cell phone. In turn, Villegas relayed the photos to Uberto Urias' cell phone as a text message. Now Urias, Adolfo Guzman and all of Tres Paises hitmen would soon know exactly what the former Texas Ranger named Wade Justus looked like.

Wade arrived back at the Fremont ranch compound. He went directly into the guest house, grabbed his gear and stowed it in his pick-up. Now he was all set to leave at the conclusion of the get together. As Wade was walking over to the ranch house, Matt Fremont pulled up in his marked Gila County Sheriff's Department SUV.

The scents of spiced Mexican beans cooking filled the air. The men entered the residence to find Matt's wife Esperanza and Jessie's wife Josie busy in the kitchen. Matt and Jessie greeted their spouses with big hugs and kisses.

"Cerveza frio, Wade?" Esperanza asked Wade with a bright smile.

"I think I'll have an iced tea for now if you have one. I'm driving a long way tonight, so I'm gonna only have one beer with supper with the guys," replied Wade.

"Bueno, I'll bring you one. Go relax outside with Matt and Jessie," said Esperanza.

"Matt, I've got the ribs, sausages and carne asada laid out for you. The guys will be here soon, I'd start grilling the ribs and then the sausage. Save the asada until last in case anyone wants tacos," directed Esperanza.

Matt picked up the large platters of ribs and sausage. Jessie and Wade ventured outside to the porch where Matt's grill was already fired up, courtesy of Esperanza. Matt laid the meat on the grill to slowly cook, while the men conversed, awaiting the arrival of the team members.

Tristin Peters arrived first, followed by Blake Sheridan. Then came Jacob Black Arrows in the company of his father Thomas Fights with A Knife. Lastly, Jack Stryker made his appearance with

Johnny Wake in tow. It was a lively family affair with Jessie making a short speech of thanks to the men who had saved his life.

Matt, Esperanza and Josie offered their thanks to Wade and the team for bringing Jessie back safe and sound. The entire group ate great BBQ and toasted Jessie and the team on their amazing success in rescuing Jessie from the hands of the brutal Tres Paises drug cartel. Finally, Matt asked the group to come together for a prayer and then asked the Lord to protect Wade on his journey back to Texas.

The group was enjoying the evening and the New Mexico sun was just above the horizon, ready to set. Wade said his good-byes to the team, shaking each member's hand. Esperanza and Josie bestowed the former Ranger with loving hugs and kisses. Jessie gave Wade a hug and shook his hand, again saying thanks. Matt was the last and followed Wade outside to his truck to say a personal thanks and good-bye.

Matt and Wade walked to Wade's truck. Matt took Wade's hand and shook it warmly while looking into his former partner's eyes.

"Well, compadre, I knew you were the right man for this job. Thank you for bringing Jessie back home to us. It's a debt we can never repay," said the sheriff.

"You owe me nothing. You'd do the same for me. I was all-in from the beginning. Jessie is my God son, and I would never allow anything bad to happen to him. It was my pleasure and honor to be here for you and your family," replied Wade.

"Ve con Dios, amigo. Safe travels" said Matt, giving Wade a brotherly hug.

Wade got into his pick-up truck and drove out of the Fremont Ranch compound while waving to Matt Fremont. Wade watched Matt disappear in his rear view mirror with the reflection of the blazing orange New Mexico setting sun. He then began the long journey back to Boerne, Texas and his Shady Creek Ranch.

CHAPTER 22

Deadly Deming

WADE HAD HIS truck's radio tuned to Johnny Wake's "Wake Up America" radio show. The news podcast he had heard when he had first driven into Las Brisas. As he turned on his radio, he heard some border news mid story,

".... and the Texas Department of Public Safety reports today that in the city of San Marcos, just off of Highway 35, a tractor trailer containing the bodies of over fifty-three suspected illegal immigrants was discovered in the parking lot of a large shopping center.

"According to the Texas DPS and the Texas Rangers, the UDA's were found inside of a parked tractor trailer which had been locked from the outside and abandoned by its driver.

"The DPS spokesperson states that it is possible that all of the UDA's perished from heat exhaustion and a lack of water. Customs and Border Patrol have been notified and the investigation is on-going. This brings the number of dead UDA's to well over eight hundred during this last fiscal year. This figure does not include the number of deaths on the Mexican side of the border.

"The District Chief of the CBP also reports that so far this quarter, his agents have interdicted and detained over 150,000 each month in their sector alone. This amazing number does not even include over six hundred thousand of what Border Patrol refers to as "got-aways" so far this fiscal year that they could not capture due to severe manpower shortages along the border.

"The problem is that agents who would normally be guarding our border have now been tasked to administrative and humanitarian duties

caring for tens of thousands of UDA's detained in hastily constructed detention shelters. This is not what they were trained for. These are front line law enforcement personnel, not social workers and babysitters.

"With the President's anticipated removal of the Federal Title 42 medical restrictions, DHS/CBP admits that with the mild weather we are currently experiencing and low water levels on the Rio Grande River, an estimated three million UDA's representing over one hundred and sixty nations are anticipated to breach our southern border from Texas to California by the Fall.

"What kinda crap is this? This is certainly not what Americans signed up for. Get engaged, people! You can change this!

"This is Johnny Wake, and this is Wake Up America on 103.5 FM. Now for a word from our sponsor, Tractor Shed, Las Brisas. The only place to buy your new and used tractors."

"Damn Johnny Wake raising cane on the radio again," Wade laughed to himself. Since he had just finished having dinner with Johnny, he knew that Johnny had evidently taped the broadcast earlier that afternoon. Unfortunately, everything Johnny was reporting was true. In fact, they were far worse than even the shocking statistics revealed.

Wade needed a change of pace from the depressing drug cartel-related news. He changed the station to Highway Country-56 and proceeded down the roadway towards Deming. The sun had set, and the pink hued twilight had arrived. Wade rolled his window down and listened to a repeat rendition of Jason Aldean's *"Fly Over States."*

"Just a bunch of square cornfields and wheat farms,

"Man, it all looks the same,

"Miles and miles of back roads and highways,

"Connectin' little towns with funny names…."

It was 7:45 pm by time Wade reached the dusty New Mexico town of Deming. He wanted to fill his tank and a get a large cup of strong coffee that would carry him to El Paso. In the populated border town next to Juarez, Wade planned to gas up again to make it to Fort Stockton where he would bed down for the night.

Deming, with a population of nearly 15,000 people was the principle town and the county seat of Luna County. To a traveler on the I-10, it was merely a speck of dusty, worn out streets in sad need of repair between Lordsburg and Las Cruces. The town's two notable facilities were the county courthouse and a CBP station referred to as "Station-Delta." "Delta" was the military alpha designation "D" for Deming. Station-Delta was located on the I-10 just eight miles east of town before the Highway 180 exit to Silver City.

Wade drove through the Station-Delta checkpoint and stopped briefly for the Border Patrol Agent manning the gate. The agent spotted Wade's Texas license plates and saw that he was a Caucasian American. The agent quickly assessed Wade and his truck and simply asked him the required salutation, "Are you a U.S. citizen?" to which Wade replied in his Texas drawl, "Sure am."

The Border patrol agent waived Wade through the check point, and he headed down the I-10. From the highway, Wade could read the reflective signs displaying the town's sleeping, eating and gas station offerings, Wade selected the W. Pine Street exit and left the interstate.

Wade drove past the Best Western and Comfort Inn Hotels in search of a sit-down restaurant so he could stretch his legs. Right now, he needed a cup of coffee and afterwards he'd get a large cup to go. He passed by the Taco Bell and Subway fast food joints. Then he spotted a Circle-K gas station on the corner next to a Mexican restaurant with a brightly lit red neon sign that announced, "Rosa's Cantina and Café."

"That's my stop. Gas and coffee all in one place," Wade said to himself.

Wade gassed up at the Circle-K and looked over at Rosa's. The four cars in the front of the establishment confirmed the restaurant was open. Wade drove into the parking lot and parked away from them.

Wade entered Rosa's and noted that it was a relatively small, typical family run operation with less than fifteen tables and a small bar. The joint was manned by only one waitress who appeared to multi-task as a hostess, waitress and bartender. He observed a cook in the back.

The restaurant was occupied by only four patrons who were sharing a booth in the back left side. Three were males and one was a female. Two of the men were military-aged Hispanic males. The third was a tanned Caucasian male. The fourth party was an attractive Hispanic gal in her early thirties with long dark hair. Wade noted that she was dressed in a business suit, and clearly looked out of place. The waitress had been speaking with the foursome when Wade entered. She finished her conversation, excused herself and walked over to Wade.

"Dinner?" she asked.

"Just a cup of black coffee for now," replied Wade.

"Fine, please sit anywhere you like," replied the waitress.

Wade chose another booth on the opposite side of the restaurant facing the foursome. Consistent with his normal routine, he put his back to the wall, in line with the cash register with his gun side facing outwards. This was the typical tactical position of safety experienced LEO's would choose. No one is behind you, and you've got an unobstructed view of the cash register. You can easily access and draw your weapon if you needed to, but also make a quick escape in case of trouble.

Wade glanced from time to time at the foursome while he waited for his coffee. There was something familiar about the white guy sitting next to the attractive woman. The man was well groomed with a fresh haircut. He was wearing pressed chinos with a form fitting golf shirt and had a businessman look about him.

In contrast, the two dark complected Mexican men sitting with the man and Hispanic woman wore close-cropped dark hair and looked rough and muscular. Wade made them for ex-military, perhaps even Special Forces. Formerly of the USMC Force Recon Division, Wade knew the look well.

Like all experienced LEO's, especially Texas Rangers, Wade was an expert in behavioral profiling. The body language between white guy and the Hispanic woman was telling. Rather than sitting apart when there was room in the booth for them to do so, their bodies were touching each other. *"Interesting,"* Wade mused.

When Wade's coffee arrived, he took another opportunity to sneak a peek past the waitress at the three men and the woman.

The two Mexicans definitely looked out of place in the company of the better dressed and groomed couple. *"What's this all about?"* thought Wade.

Wade looked under their table. Both men were wearing black military boots. *"Former military for sure,"* supposed Wade. The former Ranger spied two small black sports duffle bags under the table next to the Mexican men. No one at the table looked like they were coming from or going to the gym, and they didn't look like travelers. *"So why the sports duffels?"* Wade asked himself.

Wade wanted to keep a low profile, so he now avoided eye contact with the foursome. But the white guy looking so familiar bothered him. *"I know this guy. Where have I seen this guy before?"* he kept thinking.

It suddenly dawned on Wade that the white guy was a politician. Wade had seen him on television before, several times in fact. *He had been running for office….Senate?....No, Congress! This guy was a Congressman from southwest Texas, maybe El Paso,"* he thought.

Wade asked himself, *"Why the hell was a Texas Congressman and an attractive female meeting with these two goons in a dusty, dried up town in New Mexico like Deming? Something was definitely wrong about this, but what?"*

Wade pondered the puzzle as he drank his black coffee. He then beckoned for the waitress to return to his table. It was time to go. Perhaps Matt Fremont could help solve the puzzle. But how would he explain or better identify who was at the table for Matt?

"One large cup of black coffee to go and a check, please" said Wade when the waitress arrived.

When the waitress left him, Wade placed his cell phone on the table. He covertly selected "settings," and from there selected "ringtone." Wade then touched the ringtone button causing his cell phone to ring.

Wade picked up and pretended to be taking a call. As he did so, he shifted his body sideways with the phone in his right ear facing the foursome and touched the photo button on the side of his phone which allowed him to quickly take a series of photographs. Silently the phone quickly clicked off fifteen photos. Wade then put the phone down as if he had completed the call without looking towards the foursome.

As Wade was making his pretend phone call and surreptitiously snapping photos, one of the two Mexican Tres Paises soldiers at the table was curiously staring at him. This soldier was Sancho Villegas, Adolfo Guzman's point man in Las Brisas. Villegas had been directed to meet with the Congresspeople and provide them with directions and a two million dollar bribe each by Adolfo Guzman. Looking intensely at Wade Villegas thought, *"Where have I seen this gringo with the cowboy hat and boots before?"*

Villegas reached into his left side shirt pocket and pulled out a photo of a man that Uberto "The Bull" Urias was looking for. This man named "Wade Justus," had been described by Urias as a high value target. He looked at Wade drinking coffee, looked at the photo and back to Wade again. *"It is the gringo!"* Villegas said to himself excitedly.

Villegas placed the photo of Wade on the table top, slid it across to his partner and tapped him on the forearm. The partner looked down at the photo and then up at Villegas for a cue. Villegas darted his eyes towards Wade and then tapped the photo.

The partner looked over at Wade and then again at the photo, confirming it was the gringo. The men's silent communication was also observed by Chico Silvers and Octavia Cabral who also gazed down at Wade's photo and then at Wade.

Wade observed the subtle, silent communication between the two smarmy Mexicans and noted that the foursome was now staring directly at him.

"Jigs up, I'm outta here," he thought and immediately arose from his table to leave. Instead of waiting for the waitress to bring him his coffee, Wade walked directly over to the front cash register to pay the bill. He would be closer to the front door now.

"Come on…come on…walk over here, senorita," Wade thought anxiously.

"Who is that man and why are you so concerned about him?" Cabral asked Sancho Villegas in Spanish.

"This gringo is trouble for all of us. Urias and Guzman believe he is a former Texas Ranger, turned mercenary who was involved in freeing an American deputy sheriff we had taken as hostage. He has also killed several of our men," Villegas replied.

Immediately panicking, Chico Silvers whispered to Villegas, "Shit! You mean a fucking Texas Ranger?! I'm from fucking Texas! No one can see us meeting with you here like this. You need to stop him. You need to take care of him, now!"

Octavia Cabral now chimed in, speaking again in Spanish, "Do whatever you need to do with this Texas Ranger. We can't afford to be identified or tied in any way to your organization. Follow him out of here and take care of it quickly.

You've told us what Senor Guzman wants and you have paid us. Now leave immediately and take care of this business. We will leave right after you. Text me when it is done."

The waitress with Wade's coffee in hand saw him at the register.

"Sir, you almost forgot your coffee," she said handing the paper cup of black coffee to him.

"I see that I'm gonna be late on my trip. Just keep the change," replied Wade handing the waitress a ten dollar bill.

Gratified to receive a sixty percent tip, the waitress happily handed Wade his coffee, wishing him a safe journey. Wade was quickly out the door and making a beeline for his pick-up truck, coffee in hand.

As Wade started up his truck, Villegas and his partner emerged through the front door. They spotted Wade in his truck and quickly headed for their two identical black Ford Bronco's. Wade saw the men enter their vehicles. *"Not good,"* he thought. He quickly opened his driver's side window and tossed his coffee into the parking lot.

Observing Wade toss his coffee, both soldiers knew that Wade had burned them. Wade left the parking lot and made a right turn onto the I-10 frontage road paralleling the interstate. The two cartel soldiers were right behind him, following him one immediately behind the other at a distance of one hundred yards.

Testing to see if he was indeed being followed, Wade made

a right turn onto N. Iron Street which was the opposite direction as one would head to get onto the I-10. Both vehicles remained behind him. Wade drove two blocks and made another right turn onto W. Maple St. and then a quick left turn onto S. Zinc St. The men responded in kind, speeding up, but remaining a safe seventy-five yards behind him. The men were professionals who suspected that the Texas Ranger was armed. After losing a number of their brothers, they were not taking any chances with this dangerous gringo.

As Wade drove ahead, he kept checking the side streets for an opportunity to engage. Jumping onto the freeway would be a mistake because it would be easier for them to ram him. Wade needed to take them on at a much closer distance and on his terms. Villegas and his partner were in two separate vehicles. This made Wade's task much more challenging, but not impossible.

Wade remembered how he had taken out terrorists during a vehicle pursuit in downtown Florence, Italy. He was looking for an alley. While driving on S. Zinc St., he looked to his right and saw his opportunity. He sped up quickly to provide the bait and emotionally capture the men following him. Then Wade made a sudden right turn down an unpaved alley between W. Birch and W. Ash Streets.

Villegas was in the lead Bronco and took the bait. He managed the quick turn into the alley behind Wade. Seeing this, Villegas's partner sped up, turning right on W. Birch. He then circled the block to enter the alley from its opposite end to cut Wade off. *"Perfect. Gracias, amigos. Now set the hook,"* said Wade to himself.

Wade slowed down mid-way down the alley. Then stopped and shifted into neutral so as not to betray his rear back-up lights. Believing that he was now going to easily catch Wade, Villegas sped up, closing the distance to only thirty feet.

As Villegas closed the distance, Wade immediately shifted into reverse and floored it. His heavy duty pick-up truck flew backwards at thirty miles per hour in a giant cloud of dust that obscured his truck.

Action is always faster than reaction. Due to the action-reaction perception lag time, Villegas had no time to react defensively. The heavy iron bumper welded onto the frame of the rear of Wade's pick-up truck with its extended trailer hitch smashed violently into the front of the Bronco. The impact completely obliterated the Bronco's front end, causing all of the Bronco's air bags to deploy, trapping the seat-belted Villegas into the driver's seat.

Wade unholstered his .45 caliber 1911A pistol as he quickly exited his truck. He immediately fired two rounds through the center of the Bronco's driver's side windshield and the deployed the white airbags.

Wade ran past the driver's side of the Bronco, so he was now in a tactical position behind the door post and driver. Without hesitating, he aimed at Villegas' head and upper rear seat and double-tapped two more rounds. The first round entered the rear of Sancho Villegas' head, exploding out of his forehead. A bloody cone of brain tissue and skull fragments painted the driver's side airbag. The second hollow point round impacted the upper rear seat ten inches below the first, penetrating through Villegas' back and heart. *One down, one to go!*

The second man entered the alley in his black Bronco facing Wade's pick-up truck. However, the scene and vehicles was now enveloped in a large cloud of dust. The man sped up the alley braking to a sudden stop just yards from Wade's pick-up truck.

The dust cloud only worsened the hitman's ability to see anything. Wade took the vision obscurement as an opportunity to run past the man from the opposite side of the alley. He emerged behind the Bronco on the driver's side. The hitman exited his vehicle armed with a short barreled, commando AK-47 assault rifle with an extended forty-round magazine. However, in his haste to confront Wade, the soldier found himself standing in front of and sandwiched between by his own headlights and those of Wade's truck.

The vehicles' lights blinded the heavily armed hitman, providing Wade with an excellent tactical advantage over his adversary. Wade used the left rear of the Bronco as cover as he took careful aim center mass of the man's upper back. Then he yelled out, *"Hey, Pendejo, I'm over here!"*

The surprised hitman turned around 180 degrees to face

Wade and his own blinding blue-hued Halogen headlights. Wade's front sight was now covering the center of the man's chest. As the hitman began to raise up his AK, Wade double-tapped two quick rounds to the center of the man's chest with a third round entering his mouth. The cartel hitman dropped to the ground in a large puff of desert dust, eyes wide open in a look of total surprise.

Wade walked forward to check the man status. *"Dead as Julius Caesar,"* he mused satisfactorily.

Wade reholstered his .45. He quickly checked the man's pockets for ID but found none. However, the guy did have a thick wad of U.S. hundreds and fifty's in his pants pocket. Wade never touched the man's AK-47. *"No reason to leave any prints or DNA evidence here for the cops to find,"* he thought.

Wade walked back to the first black Bronco and found Sancho Villegas slumped forward between his seatbelt. Wade checked Villegas' pockets as well. Inside the hitman's left front shirt pocket, he removed a bloody photograph of… *himself! "Oh shit, not good,"* the former Texas Ranger thought.

As with the second hitman, Villegas also had no ID, but had plenty of U.S. cash wadded up in a pants pocket.

"Cartel goons for sure," thought Wade.

As Wade was just about to close the driver's side door, he spotted a cell phone on the floorboard. He picked it up and put it into his pants pocket.

"Might come in handy," he thought.

Wade quickly returned to the second man's Bronco. He got into the driver's seat and drove the vehicle around the deceased hitman to the far side of the alley. This would provide sufficient room for his own vehicle to pass. Wade wiped down the surfaces he had touched. He used a nearby dried up silver sage plant as a broom to obliterate his cowboy boot tracks at the scene. He then entered his truck, discarded the plant and sped out of the alley. Wade headed back to W. Pine St. and then onto the eastbound I-10 towards Las Cruces.

As Wade drove towards Las Cruces, he unholstered his pistol, dropped the mag that had only one round remaining and reloaded with a fresh mag. He steered the truck with his knees briefly while press checking the Nichols Custom Combat .45 to ensure that a round was still chambered.

Wade had a lot to think about. He had fallen into some pretty serious shit. An El Paso, Texas Congressman and some other Hispanic wench meeting with obvious cartel hitmen. These guys most likely had Spec ops backgrounds. They were undoubtedly transferring duffel bags full of money to the couple. The hitmen had unsuccessfully attempted to kill him.

Now Wade had left more dead guys in his wake. *"Certainly a justified self-defense shooting, but still not good,"* thought Wade. This was the second time in less than a week where the retired Texas Ranger had killed men in gunfights, all in New Mexico. There was an old saying that cops hate coincidences, but this was far more than a coincidence. This was a clear attempt by the Tres Paises drug cartel to murder him.

"Someone in Tres Paises has connected at least some of the dots. Now I'm a target," he thought.

As Wade headed east on the I-10 back toward Texas, two Sheriff Department Units running Code-3 with sirens wailing passed him traveling westbound in the opposite direction. No doubt the units were heading to the crime scene in Deming.

Wade was playing it safe. He maintained the seventy-five mile per hour speed limit while considering his next move. He spotted a Pilot Gas station ahead and pulled off the interstate and into the parking lot of the station. He looked around and parked away from any surveillance cameras at the pumps in the darkest area he could find.

Wade pulled his cell phone out of his pocket and checked his photos application for the most recent photographs taken. He examined a series of fifteen photos he had rapidly snapped off back at Rosa's Cantina & Café. Although most of the photos were blurred from movement, four photos were of good enough quality to identify Charles "Chico" Slivers, the unknown Hispanic female in the business suit and the two cartel hitmen. The photos also depicted two bulging black sports duffel bags under the table between the foursome.

A simple enhancement of the photos would certainly get the female identified. Photos of the two hitmen could later be compared with the two dead bodies with bullet holes in them in the dusty alley back in Deming. Maybe CBP would have the men in their facial recognition database.

Wade's right side pants pocket began to vibrate. He realized that it was the cell phone he had taken from the lead hitman's vehicle. *Someone was calling the hitman.*

Wade pulled out the phone and looked at its illuminated dial. The message display had a text message in Spanish from a 202 area code, *"Esta muerto el Texas Ranger?"*

Wade pulled out his own cell phone and took a photo of the message and the 202 phone number it came from. He then used the Google app on his own cell to query what area code 202 came back to. The response was *"Washington DC."*

"The plot thickens," Wade said to himself.

Wade thought carefully. He finally determined that there was no way he could simply return back to Texas after what he had just observed and experienced. He hit the speed dial on his cell phone to call Matt Fremont. Matt answered on the third ring.

"How's the trip so far, miss us already?" asked Matt.

"Matt, I'm calling because I just left Deming. I really got into the shit over here. It appears that the Tres Paises cartel know who I am and tried to hit me tonight," replied Wade.

"What, how?" replied the sheriff.

Wade recounted how he had pulled into Deming for gas and coffee and how he had accidentally observed a covert meeting between Texas Congressman Charles "Chico" Silvers, a Hispanic gal and two Tres Paises pistoleros.

Wade related how he had been followed by the two cartel hitmen after he had left the restaurant. He explained his violent encounter in the dusty alley. He finished the story by telling Matt that he had just received a text message on a cell phone he had recovered from one of the assassins. The message that came from a Washington DC area code asked if the Texas Ranger was dead.

"Jesus, Wade. You mean the person who sent the text message to the hitman was from Washington DC? Are you okay? " Matt asked, showing genuine concern.

"I'm fine, but I can't say the same for those two fellas. They're a bit banged up," Wade replied.

"Banged up how?" asked Matt.

"Well, I was forced to defend myself. I killed both of them."

"Did you contact law enforcement?" asked Matt.

"Are you kidding me? Even if they see me as the victim here, I'm definitely losing my guns, all of my tactical equipment and my truck while they investigate. That would strand me unarmed in Luna County where I don't know or trust a soul. That's why I called you!

"I have no idea who is on their payroll here. Hell, it's pretty obvious that the El Paso Congressman is playing footsies with Tres Paises. So why not the local Mounties getting paid off too? It's also pretty obvious that someone with a Washington DC area cell phone wants me dead," said Wade.

"So, what's your plan now, partner?" asked Matt as he considered Wade's situation.

"Well, after this I'm certainly not going back to Texas. I've got plenty of gas. I figured that I'd turn around and head back to Las Brisas where we can figure out some options. By the way, I also got cell photos of Chico Silvers, the Hispanic chick with him and the two cartel hitmen. I thought that maybe you could get the gal and the hitmen ID'd. That would be a start," explained Wade.

"Sure thing. Message me with your photos. Then turn around and come back. You're staying with me while we work on a plan. We can always contact the locals later. It's not like any real honest citizens were killed here. Better to get you into a reasonably safe location for now. I think that the State Police will understand that." said Matt.

"Copy that. I'm less than two hours from you. I'll see you before midnight, easy," replied Wade.

"Watch your back, compadre. Safe travels," replied Matt

before the pair hung up. Matt selected the four best cell phone photos and messaged them to Matt Fremont. He then turned his pick-up truck around, heading west on the I-10 for Las Brisas.

When Matt Fremont received Wade's text message containing the foursome, he was shocked. Low and behold, the attractive female in a business suit with the Texas Congressman and the two cartel hitmen was no other than his own Congresswoman, Octavia Cabral!

"Holy shit! Things just got a lot more serious for me, Gila County and Wade Justus," thought the sheriff.

CHAPTER *23*

Not Exactly As Planned

OCTAVIA CABRAL TRIED for over an hour to contact Sancho Villegas to find out if the former Texas Ranger Wade Justus was dead. There was no response from Villegas. Now worried, Cabral called Chico Silvers who was already back in El Paso.

"Chico, I've messaged and called Sancho three times and he doesn't answer my texts or calls. I'm concerned," Octavia said.

Chico downplayed Octavia's concern. "Look, there were two of them and they looked like a couple of bad asses. I'm confident that those guys are quite capable of taking care of themselves and this former Texas Ranger. Maybe they are busy hiding the body. I wouldn't worry too much right now," he replied.

"Call Sancho again in another two hours. If he doesn't respond, then call Urias. They are his guys. They would have called him first to report that they had killed the ranger." said Chico who was not nearly as concerned as his lover was.

"Okay, you're probably right. I'll wait and call Sancho again in a couple of hours. If he doesn't get back to me, I'll call Urias," said Octavia.

Two hours later, Octavia Cabral still had not heard back from Villegas. Now she *was* seriously worried. Using the burner phone provided by the cartel, she texted Urias *"55263, Call me"* in Spanish. Ten minutes later, Cabral's burner phone rang.

"Did you and Chico meet with Sancho to get your orders and the money?" asked Urias.

"Yes, we have the money, thank you. We understand what Guzman wants, but this is a tall order. I'm not so confident that we have sufficient influence to pull it off. The Vice President and President are experiencing many distractions with detractors right now. Lots of what we call "noise." I'm not sure she would even make time to take my call right now," said Cabral.

Uberto Urias's voice suddenly became gruff and demanding,

"Listen to me, senorita. Senor Guzman has given you and Chico a lot of money over the past two years. You have enriched yourselves greatly for completing only simple tasks. So don't talk to me about "noise." You have now each been paid a very large sum for this one important task. Mi Jefe's expectation is that you will use your combined influence to do this favor as well, entiendes? Do you understand?

"What if we experience problems or pushback from the Vice President? We can only do so much," the Congresswoman pleaded.

"If this is the case, then you approach her with a side offer as you have before. Senor Guzman says that money is no object to get his nephew back. His offer is $5 million to your Vice President and another $3 million to your Secretary of Homeland Security. The money can immediately be provided to speed things up. This needs to happen early this week. There can be no delays.

"Just call the Vice President, have a quick meeting and make the offer. Report back to me after your meeting and our people will do the rest. Now why have you contacted me?" asked Urias.

"It's about our meeting with Sancho earlier this evening. As I said, Chico and I met with him and another man in Deming earlier as directed. However, a man came into the restaurant I think by coincidence who Sancho recognized. This man who he said you were looking for saw both of us. Sancho even had a photograph of the man who he said was a former Texas Ranger. Chico freaked out when he heard that. After the man left, Chico told your men to kill him. After the ranger left the restaurant, your men also left, presumably to take care of him.

"Sancho was supposed to call me to advise that they had killed the man. It's been over two hours now and Sancho hasn't called back. Now I'm worried," explained Cabral.

Urias immediately realized that the man Octavia Cabral was referring to was the former Texas Ranger known as "Wade Justus." He pulled out a photo he also carried and looked down at it.

"Describe this man for me," said Urias.

"A white man in his early fifty's, tanned, fit and good looking. He had silver hair, was six feet tall and about 190 pounds. He was wearing a brown cowboy hat, with a tan shirt, jeans and brown cowboy boots," replied Cabral.

The man in the photo identified to him as "Wade Justus," exactly matched Cabral's description. Urias swore under his breath.

"You say this man came into the restaurant? What did he do in there? Do you think you were followed?" asked the enforcer.

"Well, we had already been inside for a while when he just walked in. I don't think we were followed. The man just sat down and ordered coffee. Nothing more. He didn't look like he expected to see us in there. There was nothing really distinctive about him or his behavior.

"Then Sancho looked at the man, pulled out a photo and showed it to his partner. Chico asked the men why they were interested in this guy. Sancho said he was someone that you were looking for and that he used to be a Texas Ranger. That's when Chico lost it.

"I think that since Chico is from El Paso and the man apparently used to be a Texas Ranger, Chico got scared. Obviously, Chico did not want to be recognized. He told your men that he could not be compromised. Like I said, Chico directed your men to follow the man and kill him. Sancho was supposed to check in with me, but I haven't had a call, nor have I been able to reach him," explained Cabral.

Now it was Urias who was concerned. He had already lost several of his own men since this former Texas Ranger had mysteriously appeared in Las Brisas.

"What was this Wade Justus doing in Deming?" he asked himself.

Not wanting to further distract the worried Octavia Cabral, Urias now attempted to assuage her. He needed her to concentrate on the plan. Being worried was an unneeded diversion.

"Now is not the time for worries. Sancho is supposed to call me in the morning. I'm sure they took care of that man and just got distracted. I'll call you after I hear back from Sancho. Just concentrate on getting your Vice president on board with ordering the immediate arraignment of Chuy Guzman at the courthouse in Silver City. That's your sole mission, the arraignment, and it has to be in Silver City, at the federal courthouse," said Urias.

After speaking with Octavia Cabral, Urias' next call was to his Las Brisas point man Sancho Villegas. Villegas didn't pick up which was odd. When your boss calls you, you pick up. Urias could not contact the soldier who Sancho had chosen to accompany Villegas because he didn't know that man's name. He tried texting Villegas in code, *"55263, Call me."*

One hour had passed and still no call from Sancho. Urias called him again, but he still didn't answer.

"This was a problem," thought Urias who now called another one of his English speaking soldiers in Las Brisas. The enforcer directed the man to drive over to Deming to find out anything he could about any problems in the town that evening.

"Take a scanner in the event that this has become a police matter. Take someone with you and be careful. Call me immediately if you find out anything," Urias advised.

It was just before dawn the following morning when Urias' cell phone buzzed. He picked up, "Digame," said the enforcer into the phone.

"Jefe, bad news. Sancho y Tomas estan muertos," Urias' soldier replied.

"How?" the enforcer asked.

"Both killed… shot," replied his man briefly.

"And you know this, how?" asked Urias.

"As you directed, Jefe, we drove to Deming. I had the scanner on, listening for the police radio traffic. We heard that a coroner had been sent to a location in the town. We heard radio traffic from the local and state policia who were at this same location in an alley. When we drove over there, the entire alley was blocked off and there was a crowd of people there. They had bright portable lights to illuminate the alley.

"We managed to enter a side yard to get closer to the middle of this alley. We saw our two black Broncos. There were police all around the vehicles, so we had to be very careful. When we got closer, we could see a body covered by a yellow plastic tarp. We saw that one of the Bronco's had been in an accident.

"When we got closer to look at this Bronco, we saw that Sancho was inside. He was strapped in the driver's seat, and he had been killed. There was blood all over the front windshield. Sancho did not die in any accident.

"Eventually the coroner arrived. The policia first led him over to the body that was covered with the tarp. When the officers lifted the tarp for the coroner to examine the body, we saw that it was Tomas. Both men had been shot," explained the soldier.

"There were no other bodies? What of the gringo you have a photo of, was he not there? Could he have been talking with the policia?" asked Urias.

"No senor. We did not see this gringo, only Sancho y Tomas who were dead," replied the soldier.

There was silence on the soldier's end of the phone for a few moments. Then Urias replied, "Alright. Your work there is done. Return to Las Brisas," and abruptly hung up.

"Again, the pinche Gringo!" Urias screamed to no one as he returned to bed. This former Texas Ranger seemed to be popping up everywhere. His actions were thwarting Tres Paises efforts to take over Gila County and further expand their territory.

Tres Paises' audacious plan to actually be the first transnational drug cartel to obtain a major foothold in the U.S. was in sight. Their goal to freely control the distribution of illegal drugs and greatly expand human smuggling, sex trafficking and child exploitation operations was in sight as well. The ability to meet the growing demands of their American and Canadian customers and gain unfathomable profits was certainly achievable under this new

Presidential administration. But now their plan was in jeopardy.

Adolfo Guzman's first component of the plan had been working. The bribing of greedy, impressionable young, rising politicians with an "Open Borders" agenda had been successful so far. The bribing of the Vice President and the Secretary of the Department of Homeland Security was allowing millions of new undocumented aliens to enter the U.S. These UDA's would eventually obtain amnesty as they had over the past forty years. Amnesty meant voting rights. It was a foregone conclusion that the new voters would favor the political party that granted them citizenship and free benefits that Americans themselves had difficulty obtaining.

In America, large voting blocs equated to political power. The game never changed. Power and control over the people equated to big money. Political contributions by lobbyists and dark money from globalist billionaire influencers put hundreds of millions of dollars into campaign coffers. In turn, politicians legislating social entitlement programs created fraud that funneled the money into so-called "foundations" and Non-Government Organizations (NGO's) that enriched the ruling political elite.

Greedy politicians craved money and personal enrichment. Donations into their political foundation accounts could be easily laundered through family members hired as campaign advisors. "Black" covert PAC's funded from the laundered money allowed corrupt, "bought" politicians to pedal influence both nationally and internationally. This was the cartel-style organized criminal enterprise model at its most basic level.

Guzman's paid Americans politicians had indeed opened the U.S./Mexican border. The enhanced enforcement policies of the previous administration had put a serious dent in their drug smuggling profits. Conversely, the Open Border policies of the current administration had created an entirely new and extremely profitable revenue source – the smuggling of illegals and the trafficking of women and children for sex.

The overburdened DHS and U.S. Customs and Border Patrol agencies were unable to provide sufficient manpower to protect the U.S. border. So, Tres Paises and other transnational cartels were able to greatly expand their drug and human smuggling operations.

It was a brilliant plan!

The cartels had become so sophisticated that literally every single illegal alien crossing into the U.S. had to pay a fee to enter. Those who didn't pay the cartel were killed as a warning to others to pay up.

While the current administration either refused to or were incapable of tracking the UDA's, this was not so with the cartels. The cartel's had the sophistication, money and technical resources to track them all. They even provided the UDA's with colored wristbands to indicate to the coyotes in their smuggling operations the level of protection each UDA had paid for. Depending upon the color of the wrist band, UDAs were protected from being robbed, sexually assaulted or having their children molested, raped or sold off to other traffickers. Some high profile UDA's were even provided with GPS tracking devices to follow their progress.

The cartels vetted every illegal who wanted to enter the U.S. by getting information on their relatives who were sponsoring them. Once the UDA was smuggled into the U.S., they had a certain amount of time to check in with the cartel point man in their area. Then, either they or their family had to pay up or there would be violent repercussions to the UDA and/or their sponsoring family.

UDA's who owed a lot of money to the cartel smugglers were often provided with cell phones so that they could be tracked and communicated with to ensure timely payments. Everyone paid on time because no one wanted to be visited by a cartel enforcer. The cartels ran their human smuggling operations like a well-oiled money making machine.

Unlike U.S. Immigration that had absolutely no idea of who and where the UDA's had gone to once entering the country, the cartels knew exactly where every single UDA they smuggled into the U.S. was. The cartels had an excellent, sophisticated, highly organized and profit-based incentive business model.

The final and perhaps most important component of Guzman's plan was locating and gradually taking over a very small, rural border county. The plan was to anchor and expand their U.S. distribution operations from there. The aggressive cartel leader had chosen the small, underprivileged County of Gila, New Mexico for this purpose.

However, now because of the unanticipated pushback from the county's Sheriff, Matt Fremont and this new former Texas Ranger turned mercenary Wade Justus, the cartel's plans to move forward had been stymied.

Urias now had to develop a plan to get rid of both Sheriff Matt Fremont and this Wade Justus character. The operation needed to be well thought out, brutal and decisive.

CHAPTER 24

"We're definitely in the shit, now."

IT WAS MIDNIGHT when Wade arrived back at Matt Fremont's ranch. Matt greeted his old partner in front of the guest house and walked inside with him.

"Well, that was a quick trip. Just what the hell happened in Deming?" the sheriff asked.

"It was pretty much just like I told you. Not really much to add. I pulled off the highway to get some gas and coffee. Got the gas and there was a Mexican restaurant next door. I walked in just to stretch my legs, have a cup and get one to go. There were these four people in a booth across from me. No one else in the place but us.

"There was this well dressed, attractive Mexican gal and this well-groomed white guy sitting in a booth with these two rugged Mexican guys who looked ex-military to me. The gal and the guy just didn't fit in. The two men looked like rough customers. Short-cropped hair, in good shape, wearing black military boots. I made them for former spec ops guys. Like I said, to me it just didn't fit.

"The guys had identical black sports duffels on the floor next to them under the table. They were all conversing together when I walked in. I was across the room so I couldn't hear what they were saying. The white guy looked familiar to me, but I just couldn't place him. Then it hit me. I'd seen the guy on campaign commercials on TV. He's a Congressman from El Paso for Christ's sake. Not good. I'm figuring why the hell is this guy meeting with a couple of Mexican goons in the middle of New Mexico at night?

"Then they started to focus on me, especially the two Mexican guys. I had the gut feeling that it was time to go. Everything looked wrong to me, so I used my cellphone to covertly snap some photos of the foursome. I thought that maybe you could connect the dots. After that, I was outta there.

"So, the two Mexican guys follow me outside and I take off. They followed me in a couple of black Broncos. I thought about making it to the freeway but considered against it. I figured that my best odds were side streets and picking my place and time if things were going downhill, which they did pretty quick.

"I went down an alley and they tried to block me in. I rear-ended the first guy and took him out. Then the second guy blocked me in and got out of his car with an AK. I circled around behind him and got him too.

"Here's the kicker. Before I took off, I searched both guys. No ID's but each had plenty of U.S. cash. I recovered a photo and cell phone off of the first guy. The photo he had was one of me for God's sake. How the hell did the guy have a photo of me? Also, the black duffels they had with them…gone. So I figure it was a hand-off to the white Congressman and the Mexican gal.

"The guy's cell phone has gone off three times so far, each time from a 202 area code. I looked it up and it's from the Washington DC area. Maybe the Congressman. Look here, what do you think?" asked Wade as he handed both the cell phone and the photo to Matt Fremont.

Matt Fremont keyed the messages app on the burner and looked at the single message written in Spanish from a 202 area code, *"Esta muerto el Texas Ranger?"(Is the Texas Ranger dead?)*. Then he hit the recent calls button. It showed that the same person from the 202 area code had tried to call the owner twice in the past three hours.

Matt concentrated on the bloody photo Wade had handed him. "Well, whoever these people are, they were definitely cartel hit men trying to kill you. You don't need to be a master detective to figure that one out. Two military-looking Mexican guys, identical black Broncos, AK's, no ID's with lots of cash in their pockets. Then there's the whole, 'Did you kill the Texas Ranger' message.

"I can also tell by looking at this photo of you that this was taken just outside of our sheriff's department. See that light pole right there and the corner of a building? Well, that's our building and this is you in our parking lot. That means that they were doing surveillance on us, and they managed to get a photo of you in the process. You're officially a marked man and on the Tres Paises' hit list, my brother. Congratulations," said Matt with a concerned look.

"Well, any thoughts or ideas right now?" asked Wade.

"None that either of us are going to like. For starters, you're staying right here and not going anywhere for the time being. You're certainly not going back to the sheriff's office. Guaranteed that when Tres Paises finds out you killed their guys who tried to whack you, they're gonna be gunning for you. Probably continued surveillance on my office with a sniper team in case you return there. So, you're staying here and under the radar screen for the time being. Your pick-up truck with Texas plates stays here as well. If they have photos of you, you know they have photos of your truck too.

"Next, the Hispanic gal. I didn't tell you this when you first sent the photos you took, but I know her. She's none other than our local Congresswoman. She's not only a real firebrand, but an open borders social justice warrior. Her name is Octavia Cabral. She's a rising star in Congress, always pushing an open borders, abolish ICE, and defund the police agenda.

"By the way, your Congressman Chico Silvers from El Paso, is also an open borders advocate. I'm sure there is a connection here between them. The question is are these two Congress people somehow connected to Tres Paises.

"So, just preliminarily connecting the dots, I'm speculating that both Chico Silvers and Octavia Cabral are batting on the same team. They're most likely in the pocket of Tres Paises and doing their bidding. Unfortunately, you most likely witnessed a cartel pay-off. Hence, the attempted hit on you. What else could it have been? The cell phone shows repeated calls to the dead cartel soldier from a Washington DC 202 area code, right?

"You told me that you saw two duffels under the table at that booth in the Mexican restaurant. But neither hitman had those duffels with them when you searched after the shooting, right? Well, who do you think has those duffels no doubt filled with U.S. greenbacks now?" asked Matt.

"Yeah, no duffels on either of 'em,. Makes sense, amigo. So, what do we do, call the feds?" asked Wade.

"Well, based on what you're told me so far, I think we have to report this on a couple of levels. First, in the morning, I'm going to call the State Police. Then I'm going to call my contact over at the DEA, SSA Cecil McKenry. I'll fill him in on the QT and ask who he trusts over at the local FBI office. Once I get a name, I'll call that FBI agent to report an incident of suspected Congressional corruption.

"If Congress people from both Texas and New Mexico are involved with the Tres Paises cartel, a lot of people including you, me and my deputies could also be in serious trouble. Maybe even agents over at DEA and CBP. We just can't afford not sounding the alarm. We're definitely in the shit, now partner.

"I'll vouch for you as much as I can. It's gonna make sense that you came back here and didn't stick around at the scene or go to the locals after the shooting. You can explain to them about the two Congress people you saw with probable cartel members. It would be logical for you not to trust local law enforcement who might be compromised or remain in that town. You had no idea how many more Tres Paises soldiers were lying in wait for you," explained Matt.

"Your reputation as a retired Texas Ranger will carry some weight. I'll tell the feds that you were cleared in our shooting in Las Brisas. I'm confident that they will understand. Then you'll cooperate with the feds and the State Police to get the shooting resolved as an incident of self-defense.

"It's already after 1:00 am. Get some shuteye and we'll call the State Police and DEA Supervising Agent McKenry first thing in the morning. Given the unique circumstances and the scope of these incidents, not reporting for a few hours isn't really going to matter. So, get some sleep and we'll call them at 0700 hours," said Matt.

"That all makes sense. Sounds like a plan," replied Wade as he shook Matt's hand and entered the guest house. In ten minutes, he was fast asleep.

CHAPTER 25

Special Arraignment

CONGRESSWOMAN OCTAVIA CABRAL awoke early in her home in Las Cruces. She fixed herself a cup of coffee before updating her lover Congressman Chico Silvers on what Uberto Urias had said the previous evening.

Octavia turned and looked over at the reclining chair next to her bed. The black sports duffel stuffed with cash that Sancho Villegas had given to her and Chico the previous evening in Deming was still there. She pondered their assignment as directed by Adolfo Guzman. *"What did Guzman need this time?"* she thought.

Octavia got out of bed and walked over to the recliner and unzipped the duffel oozing with money. She reached inside of the bag and pulled out several thick stacks of U.S. $100 bills and placed them on the bed. Then she dumped the remaining contents of the ballistic nylon bag onto her bed and stared in amazement.

"So, this is what two million dollars looks like!" she smiled.

Octavia took a sip of coffee, grabbed the television remote and turned on the TV to catch the local news. Las Cruces News 12 was displaying a live feed from what appeared to be a crime scene in Deming.

An attractive Hispanic female reporter was standing just outside yellow crime scene tape in an alley with Deming and New Mexico State Police marked units as her background.

"And just updating you again on this morning's breaking news story. A horrific, active crime scene here in Deming. Police are reporting that last night just after 8 pm, neighbors in this normally quiet

neighborhood called 9-1-1 to report the sounds of a car accident that was immediately followed by gunfire. "

Pointing to an alley littered with tall weeds and trash behind her, the reporter continued,

"Upon the arrival of Deming police, officers discovered these two black Ford Broncos with Mexican plates down this alley. As you can see, one of the Broncos has been involved in an accident.

"The bullet-riddled bodies of two Hispanic males in their early thirties were found at the scene. One was found still strapped into the driver's seat inside one of the Broncos. The other man was found on the ground outside of the second Bronco. Both men had been shot repeatedly and were pronounced dead at the scene. Two pistols and a fully automatic AK-47 assault rifle were recovered near the dead men.

"New Mexico State Police homicide detectives speculate that this shooting appears to have been drug cartel related. No suspects were observed leaving the scene and the investigation is on-going. We will keep you updated with any new developments.

"This is Monica Villanueva, News 12 reporting from Deming. Back to you, Phil…"

Octavia stared intensely at the TV screen, her mouth open for a moment, trying to take in what she had just heard and seen. She then used her remote to pause, replay and then freeze the story where the two black Ford Broncos were shown.

"No wonder Sancho never returned my text message or calls! Urias must certainly know his men are dead by now. The Texas Ranger had killed both of them," she thought. Not thinking, she immediately called Chico on her personal cell phone.

Congressman Chico Silvers had been up early for some exercise. He was at Top Golf in west El Paso teeing some golf balls off of the third deck when his cell phone rang. He put his driver down and picked up.

"They are dead, Sancho and his man are fucking dead!" Said Octavia loudly in an exasperated voice.

For a second, Chico thought that he had misunderstood what Octavia had just said. "Whoa, slow down Octavia. Run that past me again. What did you just say?" he asked.

Tearing up, Octavia repeated her first sentence, "I said that Sancho and his partner are both dead."

As Octavia slowly began to panic, she began yelling, "They were shot and killed last night in Deming. No doubt by that fucking Texas Ranger who saw us at Rosa's. You told them to follow and kill the guy, but that's apparently not how it worked out. He killed them both. It's all over the fucking news here!"

Octavia's voice was so loud, Chico had to pull his cell phone away from his ear. "Okay, Okay, I heard you. Calm down, just calm down for a minute. Let's try to think this thing out. Does Urias or Guzman know about this?" Chico replied.

"I have no idea. I'm not sure. Maybe, maybe not. At least not when I spoke to Urias last night after Sancho hadn't returned any of my texts of calls. Urias said that Sancho was supposed to check in with him. He said he'd call me, but I haven't heard anything from him so far. What should we do? Do I call Urias and tell him?" Octavia asked.

"Give me a minute to process this," said Chico, his mind now spinning like a chaotic centrifuge.

Octavia spoke, interrupting his thought process, "Chico, look. When I spoke to Urias last night, he was all about us influencing the Vice President to get Adolfo Guzman's nephew Chuy arraigned in Silver City this week. They must have some sort of plan concocted. He won't say, which is just fine with me.

"Just why the hell do you think they gave us all this fucking money for Christ's sake? I say we don't say shit to Urias. Let him figure it out. I seriously doubt that he'd tell us that the ranger killed his people.

"I say that we concentrate on doing what Guzman is paying us to do. We talk together to the VP and convince her to get the US Attorney in New Mexico to have Chuy arraigned in Silver City for a photo op to bolster the administration's sagging pole numbers. If the VP pushes back, Urias told me to proffer an offer of five million dollars to her and three million for the DHS Secretary. That's absolutely crazy money to turn down. This will work," she explained.

Chico was silent, thinking about what Octavia had explained. He was worried. If the ranger talked, he could ruin everything. No one could prove any connection between him and the Tres Paises drug cartel right now. However, any hint of impropriety during his campaign would torpedo any chance he had of being re-elected to Congress.

After a minute, Chico responded, "This thing is really messed up. The money has always been good, but the risks have really increased. I'm not the guy who goes back to Urias and tells him we're out. You don't fuck around with drug cartels and guys like Guzman and Urias. We'd find ourselves with bullet holes in the back of our heads and buried out in the desert somewhere.

"I agree. Let's keep quiet about his guys getting whacked and just do our jobs. Then we can slowly disengage from Guzman. Once he's got his nephew back, he'll be fat, dumb and happy again. He can find someone else to do his bidding."

It was Octavia's turn to finalize their agreement.

"Alright, we're in sync on this. We keep our mouths shut about Urias' hitmen and just do the job. I'll call the VP's Chief of Staff and set up a three-way phone meeting with all of us together for this afternoon. I'll tell them it's urgent. I'll fill them in on Chuy Guzman's arrest and the big drug seizure. Then we propose an idea on how we can all get the administration's and our own poll numbers up.

"The administration is very vulnerable right now that the elections are quickly approaching. The President has doubled down against lifting almost all restrictions on Immigration. This is causing the greatest surge of UDA's coming our southern border ever. Border Patrol just reported that nearly three million UDA's crossed over the southern border in the past eight months and if this trend continues, we'll see four million before the end of the year. New voters to expand our political power base. We will own Washington once they get the vote.

"Even though we want open borders, a lot of non-forward thinking people don't. The President is fighting a dismal economy, soaring inflation and out of control crime. Immigration is now the number three issue affecting his low polling numbers right now. The VP is in even worse shape than he is poll-wise.

"The way I see it, we can take advantage of the administration's low approval rating and exploit it towards our end game. If need be, I can also request a quick, private sidebar with the VP just in case to sweeten the deal with Guzman's offer," she explained.

Chico was on board, but he had one important condition that he wanted Octavia to mention to Uberto Urias.

"Okay, I'm with you, but I've got one condition I need you to discuss with Urias. They have to kill that Wade Justus guy. He can really hurt me in this election. I want that SOB dead and fertilizing a cactus in the desert. They've got to promise me that they'll take care of him. No loose ends. I need their promise," Chico repeated.

"I'm pretty sure that Adolfo Guzman and Uberto Urias want Justus dead even more than you do. I'll pass your request on to Urias the next time I talk with him," said Octavia reassuringly.

Right after hanging up with Chico, Octavia called Lennox Frazier, who was the Vice President's Chief of Staff and a personal supporter. She asked Frazier to arrange an expedited phone conference between herself, Chico Silvers and the Vice President.

That afternoon, Octavia presented their proposal about staging a photo-op "perp-walk" and arraignment of Chuy Guzman in Silver City, New Mexico. She offered that the administration could refer to the Guzman incident as the arrest of a "major cartel drug distributor." At the same time, the VP could highlight the seizure of a large quantity of illegal drugs in the President's on-going war on drugs. Chief of Staff Frazier was all over the idea.

"This is exactly what the President and VP need right now to get their poll numbers back up. How would this work?" he asked.

"Well, this Mexican drug smuggler named Chuy Guzman was arrested by the Gila County, New Mexico Sheriff's Department a couple of weeks ago after a shootout with authorities. He and his band were caught smuggling a large quantity of fentanyl, methamphetamine and coke into the U.S. The fentanyl recovered by the authorities was enough to kill ten million Americans. That doesn't even count all of the meth and coke they captured. That's huge news.

"Guzman is currently in federal custody by the DEA in

a secure lockdown. He is at the La Tuna Federal Correctional Institution in Anthony, just outside of El Paso, Texas. We were thinking that the VP could talk to USDOJ and get the U.S. Attorney in New Mexico and DEA on board. We could arrange for Guzman to be transported from the federal lock-up to the 6th District Federal Courthouse in Silver Springs, New Mexico for a high-profile arraignment. "

"Why Silver Springs and not in El Paso?" asked Frazier.

"Well, Silver Springs is in the 6th District which is my congressional district. Additionally, it's relatively near where the drug bust occurred. Having the arraignment in Silver Springs gives the public the appearance that the administration is right on top of things," explained Octavia.

"Makes sense. I'll communicate that to the Vice President. Let me get back to you," replied the Chief of Staff.

Two hours later, Congresswoman Octavia Cabral received a text message from the Vice President that simply said, "Call me." Five minutes after that Octavia called the VP's private cell.

"Lennox Frazier ran your idea past me this morning. What's the relationship between Adolfo Guzman and this guy Chuy Guzman. What's the rush about doing this arraignment in New Mexico?" asked the Vice President.

"Well, the guy in custody is Adolfo Guzman's favorite nephew. I'm thinking that maybe the old man wants to get the kid arraigned to work out a deal with the U.S. Attorney and DEA to get the kid back home early. I'm not really sure," replied Octavia.

"Are you out of your mind? Being busted with that much dope, that kid is going away forever. I'm not sure it's a wise move," replied the Vice President hesitantly.

Cabral realized that she was going to have to sell the idea of holding a special arraignment for Chuy Guzman to the Vice president. She began.

"Madam Vice President, with all due respect and consideration, our border policy isn't really resonating with most Americans. Yes, we have our base for support, but to be honest, the administration's poll numbers have been tanking. Mine are not so hot either.

"During subcommittee hearings, the DEA and the Center for Disease Control are telling us that last year, drug overdose deaths in the U.S. topped 110,000. Over seventy-five percent of those deaths were from synthetic opioids like fentanyl. Currently, the leading cause of death for people eighteen to forty-five years of age is from opioid overdoses. This year so far, we have twice the number of teen opioid deaths as we did only two years ago. Our opposition is making ground directly linking our open borders policies to the drug epidemic.

"Your administration and supporters like me and Congressman Silvers can only distract the people to a point. The President made you the Border Czar. I'm suggesting that what you really need is a better distraction. You need to send a clear message that the administration's war on drugs is succeeding. By highlighting Chuy Guzman's arrest and arraignment, you do just that. You show the public through our supportive news media, real-time, tangible results; a success on your watch," explained Cabral.

"Well, now that you explain it that way, maybe a special arraignment of a drug smuggler like this Guzman fellow might elevate us a few points in voters eyes," replied the VP pensively.

Adolfo Guzman's directions were clear. Time was of the essence. Octavia Cabral now needed something substantial to push the VP into agreeing to ordering Chuy Guzman's special arraignment. She now played her ace.

"Madam Vice President, I have been assured by our friends that a sizable charitable donation to your foundation through back channels is guaranteed if this special arraignment can be arranged within the next couple of days. It is a very generous offer I am told. Please call me once you have decided either way," said the Congresswoman.

Two days later, Congresswoman Cabral and Congressman Silvers received phone calls from Chief of Staff Frazier happily informing them that the Vice President had signed-off on holding a special, high-profile arraignment of Chuy Guzman in Silver City.

Frazier suggested that Octavia and Chico work out the details of Guzman's appearance at the Silver City federal

Courthouse with DEA Special Agent In-Charge Dick Vermillion and Patrick Sullivan, the U.S. Attorney in New Mexico.

It was past noon once Octavia had completed her calls to U.S. Attorney Sullivan and DEA SAC Vermillion. Vermillion said that the U.S. Marshal's Office would provide for Chuy Guzman's transportation and security roundtrip from the La Tuna FCI to the federal district courthouse in Silver City. The DEA would provide security support. Vermillion told the Congresswoman that he would update her when the Marshals and DEA had formalized their plan. He also reminded her that for obvious security reasons, such information would be strictly confidential.

After speaking with SAC Vermillion, Octavia picked up her burner phone, texted Uberto Urias in Spanish, *"55263 – Call me,"* and waited. Ten minutes later, Urias called back.

"What have you been able to accomplish?" Urias asked.

"Well, I have very good news. Chico and I have been able get our Vice President to agree to have a special arraignment in Silver City for Chuy. This was not an easy task, however. She will be taking the five million dollar campaign contribution Senor Guzman has offered. The DHS Secretary is also on board with the contribution you have offered him as well.

Urias immediately caught the meaning of the word, "contribution."

"Please tell your Vice President that I will make arrangements through the usual channels to immediately transfer the money. Your DHS Secretary will be compensated as well. What more can you tell me?" Urias asked.

"Well right now, only that the details for the special arraignment, Chuy's transportation and security are being worked out by the U.S. Marshals Office, the U.S. Attorney's Office and the DEA in Las Cruces. For the time being it is all strictly confidential, but I have been told that I will be kept in the loop. As soon as I know something more, I will call you," explained Octavia.

"Well, this is indeed good news that I will report to Senor Guzman. You and Chico keep me appraised. I need to know whatever you know, whenever you are updated, Comprende?" said Urias.

"Certainly. I should know more within another twenty-four hours so expect my call," replied Octavia before hanging up.

Cabral next called Chico Silvers and told him that the Vice President had approved for Chuy Guzman to be transported to Silver City, new Mexico for a special arraignment.

"That's awesome, so what did it take?" the Congressman asked.

"It was sort of half-and-half; first me convincing her that they needed to do something immediate to bolster their sagging pole numbers. Second, Guzman's sizeable charitable donations to her foundation and the DHS's offshore account in the Caymans," replied Octavia.

"Have you informed Guzman that we did as instructed. I just want to make sure he knows that his money is being well spent," Chico chuckled.

"Of course I did. Urias wants to make sure that I keep them informed of the transportation plans. I'm just not sure on the reason for that," Octavia replied.

"Look lover, we're not being paid to consider hypotheticals. Too much independent thinking can get us killed. We're just here to do our jobs and be rid of this guy as soon as we possibly can," Chico replied.

"I believe you're right. The VP now has the lead on this. I'm more than happy to let her office handle the rest of the details for now. Let's talk again later once we know more," said Octavia before hanging up.

Supervising Agent Cecil McKenry walked past SAC Dick Vermillion's secretary and stood in the open door.

The Special Agent In Charge was reading over some paperwork on his desk detailing his new marching orders from the DEA Director.

"Boss, we need to talk. What's all this about DEA working with the U.S. Marshals Office and the U.S. Attorney's Office in las Cruces to arrange for a special arraignment for Chuy Guzman? When were you going to tell me about this? I had to hear if from the Marshals. The Marshal in charge of the security detail just called me to work on the details," said McKenry.

"Well, don't bother knocking, just barge right in" Vermillion said sarcastically to McKenry. "For your information, I just found out about this less than two hours ago from the Director who dumped the entire mess on my lap. This is coming from the top, and I mean the very top – the offices of the Vice President and the DHS Secretary are pushing this special arraignment," Vermillion replied.

"Look sir, we can't just hold special arraignments off the cuff like this. Why the hell Silver City?" asked McKenry.

"Well for one thing, as you know, there is a federal district courthouse in Silver City. The rest is above both of our paygrades. The Director has advised me that the VP's Office wants us all to improvise and roll with it. It appears that the President's and VP's poll numbers are way down and even his friendly media talking heads are dumping on him.

POTUS, the VP and the DHS Secretary want some air time to highlight the arrest of Chuy Guzman as a major drug trafficker. Something about the administration's success in their war on drugs. Guzman's bust was in Gila County which is in the 6th District," explained Vermillion. "That's Congresswoman Octavia Cabral's territory. No doubt she's pushing this thing as well."

"I get all of that, but we already have Guzman in secure lockdown. Hell, why not simply Zoom his arraignment? This guy Guzman is the favorite nephew of Tres Paises' Godfather Adolfo Guzman. Remember Guzman? He's the character who had Gila County Sheriff Matt Fremont's son Jessie kidnapped and tortured. We haven't done shit to help that poor deputy".

"You don't see any risk in moving Chuy Guzman out of secure lockdown and then transporting him to Silver City?" asked McKenry in an obviously frustrated tone.

"Look Cecil, you can bitch and moan all you want, but this is clearly out of our hands. Our director is calling the shots here. You and I are just cogs in the federal wheel. POTUS, the VP and the DHS Secretary want to hold a public spectacle and parade Chuy Guzman around to claim some sort of victory in the drug war for political points. They own anything bad that happens. That's on them, not us. We are going to do what we're told. As a matter of fact, I'm making you DEA's point man on this. I'm going to share with you the director's memo of instructions. This special arraignment is going to happen, so you get your head on straight and work on making it happen.

You're going to work with the U.S. Attorney in Las Cruces and the Marshals in El Paso to arrange for Chuy's security and transportation back and forth from the La Tuna FCI. As you know, the Marshals handle all transportation of prisoners in federal custody. They are going to arraign Guzman at 1300 hours the day after tomorrow, so you have a lot of work to do. Clear your desk, this is Priority Numero Uno, got it?" directed SAC Vermillion.

"Sir, if that's an order, then I'll comply. But I wanted it to be clear for the record that I'm doing this under protest. This is a huge mistake. The Tres Paises are very clever and rough characters. This special arraignment horseshit is going to do is piss them off," said McKenry.

"Well, that's where you're wrong. We're ahead of you there. The U.S. Attorney was required to advise Chuy's criminal defense attorney of his special arraignment. That's already happened. We're just not telling him where the arraignment is going to be held until the last minute for security reasons. Since this is a federal matter, Tres Paises will no doubt figure on either the federal courthouse in either Albuquerque or El Paso. They'll never guess we're going to do this at the 6th District Federal Courthouse in Silver City. Just get the job done so we can move on. Your protest is noted," replied Vermillion dismissively as he motioned to McKenry to show himself out.

After SSA Cecil McKenry left SAC Dick Vermillion's office, he picked up the phone and called Congresspeople Octavia Cabral and Chico Silvers. He reluctantly informed them of the logistical plans for transporting and arraigning Chuy Guzman in Silver City in two days. He also reminded them that for obvious security reasons, the information was not to be shared. Ten minutes after receiving the call from Vermillion, Octavia Cabral used her burner phone to inform Uberto Urias of the plans.

Urias had his hands full now. He had to plan how to

intercept, rescue and spirit Chuy Guzman out of Deming and back to Mexico. Next, he had to finish off Gila County Sheriff Matt Fremont and the sheriff's mercenary, former Texas Ranger Wade Justus. Both of these men had caused an inordinate amount of trouble for Tres Paises. They had obstructed Senor Guzman's plans for taking over Gila County and establishing a power and distribution base for illegal drugs and human trafficking. But first priority was his rescue operation. He would need to equip and train a group of his best soldiers to free Chuy.

Cecil McKenry was hard at work planning how the Marshals and DEA were going to transport a high value target like Chuy Guzman the 106 miles from the La Tuna FCI to Silver City. His request for the use of a DEA helicopter had been denied. A major multi-agency operation was going down in El Paso that required air support. They took the chopper and the Marshals helicopter was down for repairs. The only other way to move Guzman was going to be via convoy using an armored vehicle. The U.S. Marshals would handle those transportation details.

The security arrangements were that DEA agents would ride in the armored Suburban driven by U.S. Marshals. The Suburban would be accompanied by two additional identical Marshals Suburban's positioned at the front and rear of the convoy.

DEA, U.S. Marshals and Grant County Sheriff Deputies would provide inner perimeter security for Chuy at the federal courthouse. The New Mexico State Police and the Silver City Police would provide outer perimeter security. The New Mexico U.S. Attorney and a federal judge would arrive at the courthouse separately in Marshals vehicles, each with a security detail.

Since the whole purpose of this exercise was to showcase Chuy Guzman, pre-selected and vetted members of the press representing national and cable news outlets would be advised by the White House of the special arraignment. Reporters would be directed to be on standby with only a four hour notice. To avoid any breaches of security, the press were told the date and time of the arraignment, but not its location.

SSA McKenry and his U.S. Marshals counterpart Justin Stepps worked out a plan to stage the press to the rear of the courthouse for a filmed public "perp walk." After members of the press were thoroughly searched by Grant County sheriff's deputies, they could film the arraignment inside the courtroom. After the quick fifteen minute arraignment, Guzman would be rapidly ushered out of the courtroom by Marshals to the awaiting vehicles. Perimeter security would then compress, and the convoy would extract and travel back to La Tuna, FCI.

Uberto Urias selected a twelve-man ground team, plus a two pilot air team to rescue Chuy. After careful consideration and weighing the odds of success, the enforcer decided to rescue Chuy at the Border Patrol's check station referred to by the CBP as "Checkpoint Delta." The station was located on the I-10, three miles east of the Highway 180 Silver City exit.

The enforcer was familiar with how U.S. law enforcement agencies like the Secret Service and the U.S. Marshals Office conducted high-value target convoys. He had seen a number of U.S. security convoys in Mexico City moving the U.S. Ambassador and other high-profile American dignitaries around the city.

Normally security convoys consisted of three Chevy Suburban's traveling tightly together at high speed. Urias had chosen the border patrol station because it was the only place where the U.S. Marshals and DEA convoy would be actually forced to slowdown or stop. This was the perfect time to strike.

Urias' daring plan called for creating a separate convoy disguised as the Marshals - DEA convoy, complete with unmarked black U.S. Marshals Chevy Suburban's. He would select English-speaking cartel soldiers dressed as uniformed U.S. Marshals with assault vests with U.S. weapons. His team would approach the checkpoint, ambush and take out all of the Border Patrol agents at the station. Then they would simply assume the agents' positions at the checkpoint and wait for the arrival of Chuy's security convoy.

When the convoy arrived, the disguised soldiers would surprise, overwhelm and neutralize the U.S. Marshals and DEA and agents. The team would then free Chuy. A radio signal would then be transmitted to a waiting helicopter matching a current Customs and Border Patrol model. The disguised CBP helicopter would quickly land, pick up Chuy and spirit him away to Adolfo Guzman's compound in the mountains just outside of Ciudad Madera in Chihuahua, Mexico.

After Chuy had been removed from the scene, vehicles driven by cartel associates would arrive at the station to provide transportation for the team. Urias and his soldiers would then shed their uniforms, don civilian clothes and simply blend into the New Mexico landscape. The plan was brilliant in its simplicity. Urias picked up his cell phone and called Adolfo Guzman. The leader of the Tres Paises drug cartel picked up on the first ring.

"Tell me that you have good news for me, Toro," said Guzman.

"Si, Jefe. There is much good news today," replied Urias who then proceeded to run down everything that Octavia Cabral had told him, as well as his plan to free his boss' favorite nephew.

"Jefe, I have all of my men selected. I have armed them, and we are currently involved in intensive training. However, my plan requires some additional resources such as vehicles we already have. I also need a special type of helicopter that we don't have. I will need your assistance. I believe that the helicopter pilots we already employ will be able to fly this aircraft. However, I know we do not have such a helicopter in our inventory. May I send you the specifications for this helicopter?" Urias asked.

"Of course. Send me the information and whatever you ask for you will receive. You are confirming that this arraignment for Chuy will take place the afternoon of the day after tomorrow?" asked Guzman.

"Si, mi Jefe. And when we are successful, your Chuy will be back home with you in two days' time," replied Urias.

"Call our pilots and have them speak with me. I will entrust them to find this certain helicopter and we will buy it. Then they will call you and you can provide them with their orders. So far, you have done well, Toro. Keep me informed," said Guzman before hanging up.

By the following morning, Uberto Urias had obtained three identical Chevy Suburban's and two Ford Explorers which had been stolen from El Paso and Las Cruces. He had the vehicles stored in a large hanger at the west end of Runway 8 at the Las Cruces International Airport.

A pilot in the employ of the cartel had called Urias advising that Senor Guzman had now obtained an Airbus AS350 B3 helicopter. This aircraft was the exact same model and configuration as used by Customs and Border Patrol. He advised that two pilots would be flying the bird to Las Cruces that afternoon.

Urias directed the pilots to fly directly to the hanger just off Runway-8. There, the helicopter would be concealed and painted to match the markings of a CBP helicopter. The enforcer was also supervising the painting of the three identical Chevy Suburban's to match the security transport vehicles used by the Marshals.

Urias had directed a surveillance team to visit and take photos, video and laser measurements of the Checkpoint Delta Border patrol station. He also had video showing how the CBP agents were checking drivers through the checkpoint. He would use this video to teach his men how to mimic the behaviors of the agents.

After the surveillance team had completed their photographic and measurement survey of Checkpoint Delta, Urias then paced the measurements inside the large hanger at the Las Cruces Airport and mapped out the CBP station. An experienced former special operations team leader, Urias used blue painter's tape to plan out the raid, marking on the cement floor the positions of the agent's four kiosks that were used to check drivers through the checkpoint.

Now it was time to practice the operation. Timing was going to be critical in the event any of the Checkpoint Delta agents managed to radio that they were under attack. In that case, law enforcement officers would be rushing to assist their brother officers. That was not an engagement Urias could afford to have since it would place their "package" Chuy Guzman at serious risk.

Urias stood outside the disguised convoy and spoke loudly in English so all could hear him.

"Amigos, from this moment on, we all will speak only in English. It is important that you all understand that this entire operation must go down in under five minutes. Five minutes and no more! That means from the moment our convoy arrives at Checkpoint Delta to the moment our helicopter lifts off with the package. Do you all understand me?!" Urias yelled.

"Yes, sir!" the men responded in English.

Urias began his briefing, "We know that Chuy is being held in a high-security lock-down at the La Tuna Federal Correctional Institution just outside of El Paso. We have that facility under surveillance. When the U.S. Marshals – DEA convoy leaves the prison, our surveillance team will send word and follow and monitor the convoy at a very discreet distance."

These three Suburban's will constitute our disguised convoy. Five miles in front of you will be the scout car with two men with silenced weapons. Their job will be to enter the station's parking lot and wait for you. Two miles behind you and concealed off the highway will be the "rear guard" vehicle with two more of our men. They will provide you with rear security.

"You men in the rear vehicle will enter the highway as the disguised convoy passes and then set up a temporary roadblock to prevent any other travelers from suddenly driving up on our operation. Traffic this time of the day should be light, but one never knows.

"The way I have planned this operation, the U.S. Marshals – DEA convoy carrying Chuy Guzman should be coming up the highway very shortly. When you get the signal that we have taken the checkpoint, quickly drive there to offer additional assistance if needed. Then secure a landing zone and wait until our ambush and rescue of Chuy has been completed. When we have secured Chuy, you will ignite a blue smoke canister to identify the landing zone for the helicopter pilot. When the helicopter lands, we will provide perimeter security for Chuy until lift-off.

"I will be driving the lead Suburban. You drivers of the other two Suburban's will tighten up your formation when we are three miles from the station. In this way, we will all arrive together in a tight formation, one behind the other. Your primary weapons will be silenced pistols. There are three kiosks but only the two to the left side will be open due to short staffing.

"As we arrive at the checkpoint, we will break formation with one vehicle entering the three separate lanes with kiosks to the left. Each driver will distract the Border Patrol agent manning the kiosk and waving you through. When the agent is distracted, the left rear passenger will use his silenced pistol to take out the agent, with the driver acting as back-up. I will take the kiosk to the far left side of the station.

"Once you men in the scout car see the convoy enter the check point, you will exit your vehicle with your silenced weapons and kill any agents in the parking lot. You will then immediately enter the building and kill everyone inside. After that, your job will be to provide inner perimeter security and immediately remove the bodies of those agents killed at the kiosks.

"The right front and left rear passengers in each Suburban will assume the dead agents' positions and await the arrival of the Marshals and DEA convoy carrying Chuy Guzman. Our sniper will climb up into the rafters above each traffic lane. When the convoy arrives at the checkpoint, understand that the person being protected is always in the middle vehicle. Classically, there is an armed driver and an armed passenger with the prisoner in a locked rear prisoner compartment by themselves.

"The middle Suburban will be armored, but not its roof. The sniper in the rafters will be armed with a .308 assault rifle with armor piercing rounds. He will direct his fire down through the roof killing the driver and front passenger of the prisoner transport vehicle.

"At this point, all of the federal agents should be dead, and the team can secure Chuy. I will be providing command and control of the operation, so radio me immediately with any issues. Once you ignite the blue smoke canister to direct our helicopter to the landing zone, we will then move Chuy under cover of any unseen threats to the landing zone. The helicopter will then land, and we will place Chuy on board and the helicopter will depart.

"Once the helicopter has left, we will drive the Suburban's into the parking lot and park. Then we will strip out of our assault vests and uniforms and put on the civilian clothes we brought with us. We will have vehicles there to pick us up and take us to safe houses for a couple of days until the heat dies down. Then we can all return to Mexico where we'll have a great celebration with big bonuses for all of you, courtesy of our Jefe, Senor Adolfo Guzman!" explained Urias to the cheers of his men.

"Now let's run through this plan several times to make sure you get it right. We need to be in and out of the check point in under five minutes. There can be no mistakes," said Urias.

The enforcer and his team spent all afternoon first practicing the operation without their equipment until the execution was flawless and under his five minute time window.

Inside the hanger, cartel men had spray painted the three Suburban's and two Ford Explorers black with subdued red and blue emergency lights. Urias used the taped-up model of the station to position his men. He then repeatedly walked them through the plan of attack and rescue.

Urias placed his men, four in each of the Suburban's and a pair in each Explorer. He then had them drive up to the station model several times, running through the ambush, and rescue drills for familiarization. Everything went smoothly.

On large tables to one side of the hanger were placed sixteen separate sets of U.S. Marshals BDU's, assault vests with integrated body armor, Sig Sauer .40 caliber pistols and M-4 assault rifles were; one for each member of the assault and rescue team.

Once Urias was satisfied that the men knew their roles, he had them dress and equip themselves as U.S. Marshals and DEA agents. Then he repeated the drill twice. Again, the execution was flawless.

At dusk, a white Airbus AS350 B3 helicopter circled the hanger and landed in front of it. Per the direction of the pilot, several men rolled out a mobile helicopter platform. The pilot re-landed the aircraft on top of the platform and the men slowly pushed the helicopter inside the hanger. Inside, the helicopter was quickly transformed into a white Customs and Border Patrol helicopter complete with insignia and its identifying CBP green stripe.

It was now time to execute the mission.

CHAPTER 26

Checkpoint "Delta"

DAWN BROKE IN beautiful hues of purple and crimson over the Organ Mountain range looking down over Las Cruces. DEA SSA Cecil McKenry was already up and working through his first cup of black coffee. The agent was focused on going over the logistics of transporting Chuy Guzman from the La Tuna FCI to the federal courthouse in Silver City.

In the past two days, McKenry had gone over the plan in his mind at least a hundred times, repeatedly asking himself if he was missing anything. He and Deputy U.S. Marshal Stepps had already amended the plan at least a dozen times, adjusting for things they thought they had missed, but then repaired.

Outside of not having a helicopter or a battalion of Marines surrounding the transportation convoy, the DEA and the Marshals had done their best given the very limited resources they had been allowed.

McKenry had one more card up his sleeve. He had become a successful DEA agent by thinking outside the box. He picked up his cell phone and called the CBP Regional Commander, Assistant Chief Katie Blackwater.

Katie's company cellphone rang, and she saw it was DEA Supervising Agent McKenry.

"Cecil, you're sure up early, what a surprise. What can I do you for?" Katie asked.

"Katie, I'm calling for a favor on a case our agencies are involved in, the Chuy Guzman dope smuggling arrest, know it?"

said Cecil.

"Sure, one of the Tres Paises' cartel's dirtbags who got popped over in Gila County by Sheriff Matt Fremont's guys. My people helped with the officer-involved shooting investigation. The deputies dumped a couple of the smugglers in the river. Our dive team recovered their weapons and other evidence. What's up?" Katie asked.

"Well, not sure if you were told but Guzman's having a special arraignment at the 6th District federal courthouse. Not my idea for sure. It's political with pressure coming from the VP and DHS Secretary. Anyway, Guzman's being held at La Tuna FCI. The U.S. Marshals and the DEA have been tasked with transportation to and back from the courthouse in Silver City.

"I gotta be straight with you, I'm concerned. We've developed a transport and security plan. We're also using State Police along with the Grant County SO and Silver City PD in support," McKenry explained.

"OK, sounds like you got it covered. What can we do to help?" asked Katie.

"Well, I'd like some additional overwatch. None of our agencies' helicopters are available for transport so we're doing a security convoy. I know DHS and CBP have a couple of drones you use for surveillance. What are the chances of getting one of those drones tasked to fly overhead for a few hours to monitor the convoy, courthouse and back while we have Chuy?" McKenry asked.

Katie smiled to herself. *"Politics raises its ugly head again,"* she mused. "Is your boss Dick Vermillion on board with this request?" she inquired.

"Well, I thought I'd check first with you for your assistance and the availability of a drone. If you can help, then I'd tell Vermillion. Just trying to stay ahead of the game. I know that will be his first question. Since this special arraignment is the administration's idea, I can just about guarantee you that Vermillion will approve. He's a fast climber," replied Cecil.

"Tell you what. If Vermillion signs off on using our drone, I'll authorize its use for your op. When would you need the bird?" asked Katie.

"Sorry for such short notice, but today from 1145 to about 1500 hours," replied McKenry.

"Give me 30 minutes to make a couple of calls and then have Vermillion call me personally to make the official request. Then I need an email from his office formalizing the request for my brass. We should be good. Always willing to help DEA out," said Katie.

"Thanks, Katie. I owe you. I'll call Vermillion right now," replied the DEA Supervising Agent.

"At least I've done everything I can think of to ensure the mission's safety. I hope we don't get fucked over on this asinine, so-called special arraignment," McKenry said to himself after hanging up.

One hour later CBP Assistant Chief Katie Blackwater was calling her Air Force cohort Major Miranda Prescott to arrange for the use of a Predator drone.

At 0800 hours, Adolfo Guzman was enjoying a sumptuous breakfast on the balcony of his palatial estate outside of Ciudad Madera, Mexico when his cell phone rang. He looked at the display that read "Toro," and picked up.

"Digame, Toro. What news have you for me today?" asked Guzman.

"We are ready to go, Jefe. Thank you so much for arranging for the helicopter. The vehicles and aircraft have been converted into U.S. Marshals and Border Patrol assets. You can't tell the difference. My men have been training hard and they look good. In no time, our Chuy will be back home," said Uberto Urias confidently.

"Our family is praying for his safe return. We hope you can pull this off. Call me when Chuy is on his way home. The family is preparing a feast and a party in celebration of his return," said Guzman.

"Si, mi Jefe," replied Urias before hanging up.

All the preparations for holding the special arraignment in Silver City for Chuy Guzman had been completed and scheduled for 1:00 pm at the federal courthouse. The Vice President's Chief of Staff Lennox Frazier now began calling the VP's favorite reporters to advise them of the time and location for the arraignment. All the reporters were told that the information was strictly confidential. Due to security concerns, there could be no teaser public broadcasts of the arraignment.

Arrangements had been made for the press to film Chuy Guzman being escorted into the courthouse and while being arraigned. A short press conference would follow. The U.S. Attorney in New Mexico would make a brief statement about the President's and VP's recent victory against transnational drug cartels. He would highlight the seizure of a "massive amount" of illegal drugs including deadly fentanyl. However, due to security concerns, there would be no questions.

Reporters were informed that instead, the VP would be holding a separate press briefing later at the White House to further discuss the administration's fight against transnational drug cartels. The various news outlets now scrambled. They needed to assign reporters and film crews to get out to Silver City, New Mexico to catch the arraignment of a major drug trafficker.

Cecil McKenry drove from Las Cruces to Anthony, Texas to meet with the U.S. Marshals and DEA agents who were already at the La Tuna FCI. A ten-man team consisting of four of McKenry's best DEA agents along with six Marshals were milling around the three Chevy Suburban's. All ten men were dressed in assault vests, BDU's and were heavily armed. This was a no-nonsense crew of hardened professionals.

McKenry was not accompanying his men on this transport. Instead, he would stay in communication with them from DEA's HIDTA Intelligence Center. The center was chosen as a command center due to the high-tech monitoring equipment that could monitor the drone and communications on large screen monitors. Cecil took a moment to address the men.

"Guys, I've worked with most of you. This is a U.S. Marshals transport operation, so we will take our directions from them. This is their lane, and they know the drill. Now I want to introduce you to my U.S. Marshals counterpart, Marshal Justin Stepps who will be in command of the security transport operation," said McKenry, handing the briefing over to Stepps.

"Men, my Marshals will be going high speed all the way to Checkpoint Delta. I'll be in the lead Suburban. Tight formation and zero stops until we all get to Delta. From there it's straight into Silver City. Once there, we'll be met by State Police and Grant County Sheriff deputies who have the exterior and interior perimeter security.

"We will arrive at the rear of the courthouse. We've been advised to expect a flock of reporters and camera crews filming the perp walk. Fuck them. We will get Guzman into the courthouse as fast as we can. Once inside, we'll also assume a tight inner perimeter security inside the courtroom. The reporters and crews will have all been vetted and searched by deputies. The arraignment will be quick, maybe fifteen minutes max. After that, let's get Guzman the hell out of there and extract back here, pronto. Any questions?" There were none.

Cecil McKenry told his men that he would not be accompanying them on this op, but that he would be monitoring their progress from HIDTA. He would see them all when they returned.

Inside the hanger at the end of Runway-8 at the Las Cruces Airport, Uberto Urias anxiously looked at his watch. The enforcer stood in front of the large doors dressed in a set of BDU's, his ceramic armor assault vest emblazoned with a U.S. Marshals badge on the front and a "U.S. Marshals" patch on the rear.

Urias looked behind him to see the transformed Customs and Border Patrol helicopter. Its two uniformed pilots poised in front of three identical black Chevy Suburban's and two black Ford Explorers. His cartel soldier team members were standing in place next to their assigned vehicles. Every man dressed in U.S. Marshals and DEA BDU's with assault vests. It was truly an inspirational sight. Urias pulled out his cell phone to take some photos to capture the historical moment.

"Activate emergency lights!" Urias yelled out in English to the drivers of the vehicles. Each driver entered their assigned black vehicle and turned on the wig-wag subdued emergency lights to show their leader that all the lights functioned correctly. Beaming with pride, Urias snapped a couple more photos.

"Good. Advance for final inspection," Urias ordered. His men all stepped forward and stood in a straight line in front of Urias. The enforcer moved down the line, carefully inspecting all of the men's uniforms, equipment and weapons. There could be no room for error today.

Once Urias' men were all in formation, he made eye contact with them and spoke.

"Compadres, you are the best and most elite of my men. All of you were chosen for this most important of missions because of your prior military backgrounds, your loyalty and dedication to Tres Paises. In the brief time we have been training, you have impressed me with your professionalism. I stand before you this morning filled with pride in seeing you all now. Shortly, we will leave not only to free our Jefe's nephew and our brother Chuy, but also to strike a blow against the American placas. I want you to leave no doubt at Checkpoint Delta as to who will control the region in the future. It will be Tres Paises!

"Senor Guzman has promised that each of you will be handsomely compensated for your participation today with both money and promotions. I say to you all, onward to victory. Adelante!"

"Adelante!" (Forward!), all of Urias' men shouted in unison.

Urias directed his men to push the helicopter out of the hanger and mount their vehicles. Once outside of the building, he stood in front of the CBP marked helicopter. He held up his left arm and began have a circular whirling motion indicating to the pilot to commence the lift-off procedure.

The enforcer then entered the lead black Suburban as the helicopter's rotors began to whirl. As the AS350 B3 Airbus lifted off the platform, the convoy of disguised black U.S. Marshals vehicles drove out of the hanger enroute to Checkpoint Delta. The operation had begun.

Cecil McKenry and his U.S. Marshal's Office counterpart Deputy U.S. Marshal Justin Stepps wanted the timing of their transport of Chuy Guzman to be tight. Travel, arrival and delivery times into the courtroom with their package were critical for security reasons.

The special arraignment was scheduled for 1:00 pm. The distance from La Tuna FCI to Silver City was exactly 135 miles. Once the convoy reached Interstate 10, their speed to the Highway

180 Silver City was going to be 100 mph. Their only slow down or stop would beat the Customs and Border Patrol station Checkpoint Delta. Three miles west, the convoy would take the Highway 180 turnoff and head south all the way to Silver City and the 6th District federal Courthouse. Upon entering Silver City, their route would be additionally protected by officers from the New Mexico State Police and the Silver City PD. These officers would block off side streets leading to the courthouse.

Marshal Stepps figured that once they reached the rear of the courthouse building, it would take them another five minutes tops to clear their vehicles. They would then surround Guzman and usher him past the gaggle of press. The security team would then enter the rear of the single-story white stucco with red brick, columned colonial style courthouse and get Guzman into the courtroom. It was a straightforward transport operation.

At the appointed time, a team of four U.S. Marshals led by Stepps and accompanied by DEA SSA Cecil McKenry gathered at the FCI sally port entrance. A Federal Bureau of Corrections SERT team sergeant appeared at the door with Chuy Guzman. Guzman was attired in a bright red high-risk prisoner jumpsuit. His hands were cuffed in the front affixed to a waist chain and leg shackles. The SERT team supervisor had Stepps sign for Guzman before releasing him into their custody.

Inside the facility's sally port, Stepps placed a Threat Level III ceramic body armor bullet resistant vest on Guzman. The drug smuggler was then placed into the rear prisoner compartment of the black U.S. Marshals armored Chevy Suburban with dark tinted windows. Stepps personally secured Guzman's leg shackles to an "O-Ring" affixed to the floor. The Marshal then secured the armored door which was then electronically locked by the driver.

Inside the sally port were two additional, identical black Chevy Suburban's. Their compliments of heavily armed U.S. Marshals and DEA agents were attired in their respective agency BDU's and tactical armored vests.

Before getting into the right front passenger seat of the lead U.S. Marshals Suburban, Stepps walked over to Cecil McKenry.

"Well Cecil, here we go. Don't worry, we'll get this piece of shit to the courthouse and back before you know it. This is what we do," said Stepps.

"Thanks Pat. Haul ass all the way, brother. I'll be over at HIDTA watching you from the Predator drone feed in real time. The armored van carrying Guzman has a GPS tracker, so I'll be following you via monitor. I'll be glued to my radio and cell phone. Call me if you need anything. Get our child home on time. The beers are on me for you and your team," joked McKenry.

"Yes, dad. Will do," replied Stepps, who then motioned to his team to start engines. Stepps got into the lead Suburban and keyed his throat mic comm system, "Emergency lights all the way and sirens whenever you need em. Tight formation, fellas. Next stop is Delta and then the courthouse. Lock and load all weapons. Move out!"

The large electronic metal doors to the facility's sally port opened. The three identical subdued black Chevy Suburban's emerged onto the roadway, their red and blue wig-wag lights flashing.

On cue, Tres Paises operatives surveilling La Tuna FCI notified Urias that the U.S. Marshals – DEA security transport convoy had cleared the corrections facility. Urias' disguised convoy then left Las Cruces with its black Chevy Suburban's and Ford Explorers spaced one mile apart from each other so not as to arouse any suspicions. All vehicles were driving at the I-10 posted freeway speed of 75 mph. No time for speeding tickets today. Urias had directed the helicopter pilot to fly in wide circles no closer than three miles out from the I-10 so he could surveil for the U.S. Marshal – DEA convoy without arousing suspicion.

Urias had directed his duplicate cartel convoy to remain approximately twenty miles ahead to avoid being overtaken by the U.S. Marshals – DEA convoy which was traveling at 100 mph. His team needed five minutes to neutralize the Border Patrol agents, remove their bodies and assume their positions. This was going to be very tight. Every minute was precious to the success of the operation.

As Urias' disguised convoy was five miles away from Checkpoint Delta, the three identical black Ford Explorers with emergency lights pulled in behind them. Two of the Explorers immediately blocked the I-10 so no other traffic could pass, while the third vehicle sped ahead of the convoy. The Predator drone pilot Major Miranda Prescott had chosen was following the path of the security transport convoy twenty miles east. He was not yet covering Checkpoint Delta.

The third blacked-out Explorer approached Checkpoint Delta. Instead of going through its checkpoint station, the SUV took the lane that led directly into the checkpoint's parking lot and parked. It's two heavily armed men dressed in CBP BDU's and baseball caps with tactical vests and silenced pistols waited inside the vehicle until the arrival of the disguised convoy.

The disguised convoy of Chevy Suburban's approached Checkpoint Delta with their red and blue emergency lights flashing. As the convoy reached a point one quarter mile out, it slowed down and separated. Urias' lead vehicle took the left station with the remaining two vehicles approaching the center and right-side stations. Seeing the convoy arrive, the two soldiers in the parking lot exited their vehicle and rapidly approached the station's office building with their pistols out and ready.

The CBP agent manning the kiosk motioned the emergency vehicle forward. Urias who was driving, rolled down his tinted window and smiled at the agent. The agent saw the U.S. Marshal behind the wheel and returned the smile. Urias smiled again, then quickly raised his silenced .40 Sig Saur pistol and cleanly shot the agent in the forehead, dropping him in place.

Urias' soldiers in the respective vehicles dispatched the startled agents at their kiosks just as swiftly. Simultaneously, the soldiers who had entered the Border Patrol office moved as a well-trained team. They quickly dispatched two CBP agents who were manning a bank of electronic monitoring cameras. As another agent emerged from the coffee room, he was also shot down. The office, restrooms and storage rooms were searched and was now clear of agents who might have reported their presence. The two soldiers quickly emerged from the building. They then assisted their colleagues in removing the dead CBP agents from the lanes and stashed their bodies inside the three kiosks.

On cue, the cartel sniper armed with a silenced .308 rifle loaded with armor piercing ammunition exited from one of the Suburban's. The man quickly climbed up and onto the upper deck scaffolding above the left and center lanes. The sniper dropped the bipod feet on the front of his rifle. He removed the range finder from his pack and verified the ranges to target which would be directly beneath him. The sniper quickly reached up and removed one click down on his turret adjusting his zero. He was at an elevated position and due to the proximity, his scope would have no dramatic effect shooting down into the SUV holding Chuy.

Urias and his soldiers now ripped off the Velcro'd U.S. Marshals and DEA insignia from their BDU's and assault vests and replaced them with CBP insignia and CBP baseball caps. The men took their positions at the kiosks and waited for the real U.S. Marshals – DEA security convoy to arrive.

The two cartel soldiers who had breached the CBP building, along with another soldier jumped into the three black Suburban's and quickly drove them to the back side of the building and out of sight. Urias radioed for the two blocking Ford Explorers to get off the roadway to allow the real convoy to pass by. The first component of the assault plan had been completed in less than five minutes. Now the assault and rescue teams waited.

Five miles out from Checkpoint Delta, the Predator drone aloft at 20,000 feet continued to follow the security transport convoy carrying Chuy Guzman. The highway was clear for westbound traffic and traffic was sparce for traffic heading east towards Las Cruces.

Two miles east of the Border Patrol station, Marshal Stepps radioed for the convoy to reduce speed. He advised that he would take the kiosk on the far left while directing the armored vehicle carrying Guzman to take the center kiosk and the third Suburban to pull into the kiosk on the right.

As the convoy approached the station and the Suburban's simultaneously separated into the three lanes. The CBP agents stepped out from their kiosks and calmly motioned them forward. All three vehicles slowed to a stop. The Marshal drivers rolled their dark tinted windows down to converse with the disguised CBP agents.

Stepps leaned forward to greet the smiling Urias who was the agent at the left kiosk. Just as Stepps was about to identify himself, Urias quickly drew his .40 caliber Sig Sauer pistol and cleanly shot both Stepps and his driver in the head. The cartel soldiers masquerading as CBP agents followed suit, quickly dispatched the drivers and front and rear passengers in the Suburban in the left and right lanes as well.

The sniper up in the rafters fired his suppressed .308 rifle with armor piercing rounds directly downwards into the armored Suburban carry Chuy. The armor piercing rounds immediately took out the driver and right front passenger Deputy Marshals.

The Marshals and DEA agents in the rear passenger seats of the Suburban's not transporting Chuy Guzman managed to draw their weapons. They began to return fire but were outgunned. They all went down quickly in a hail of bullets where they sat.

Urias' assault team assigned to breach and free Chuy from the armored Suburban approached the vehicle. One member quickly placed a small, shaped charge against the driver's side door lock. He motioned for his teammates to stand back and yelled *"Fuego!"* before depressing an electronic igniter. The muffled explosion blew the door open. The breacher then reapproached the vehicle. He yanked the dead Marshal who was still seat belted into his seat out of the vehicle.

Another soldier reached inside the driver's side door and depressed the door locks button unlocking the prisoner compartment door.

A teammate carrying bolt cutters threw open the door and cut Chuy's leg shackle chains away from the "O" ring bolt on the floor and his legs. He then cut the handcuffs chain away from the prisoner's waist chain. This released Chuy's hands so he could move freely. "Vamos Chuy!" the soldier with the bolt cutters yelled out to the prisoner as he pulled him out of the vehicle.

At Holloman AFB, the pilot flying the Predator drone had descended to 10,000 feet, monitoring the approach of the U.S. Marshals – DEA security convoy to Checkpoint Delta. Traffic remained light in both directions. So far it looked like a milk run.

The pilot observed the convoy approach and enter the covered area where vehicles were checked and waived through by CBP agents. He had been through similar stations including Delta hundreds of times. He noted that with virtually no traffic in westbound lanes, the convoy should have easily and quickly passed through the station. However, on this occasion, the convoy was still under the covered area. *"What's up with that?"* he pondered.

The Vice President and her Chief of Staff had made a strategic decision to hold two press conferences instead of one to maximize the news buzz on the administration's new victory on the war on drugs. They just didn't inform the President or anyone on Chuy Guzman's transport security team of this.

While the President was meeting with the U.S. Ambassadors to several Eastern European nations at Camp David, the Washington Press Corps received a "Breaking News Flash" of the special arraignment in New Mexico. This was what the VP's Press Secretary referred to as a "Forward Press Briefing." Field reporters and several high-profile talking heads from the national and cable news networks scrambled to the White House Press Room.

"This must be a big deal for the VP to hold a forward press briefing one hour before they had previously been told us to be present for live coverage," one prominent news anchor said to another.

The Vice President's aids ushered the news reporters into the briefing room like a herd of cattle. VP's personal press secretary took to the podium. Overhead and side lighting snapped on as she addressed the crowded room.

"Ladies and gentlemen of the Washington Press Corps, as you are all aware, during the first week of this administration, the President appointed the Vice President to oversee all operations and policies pertaining to our southern border. The Vice President appears before you today to share some positive news highlighting one of our administration's recent successes in the war on drugs. I now give you, the Vice President," exclaimed the press secretary as she pointed stage right.

A bright spotlight illuminated the raised stage, covering the Vice President as she strode purposefully to the podium in her customary black pants suit. Upon reaching her mark behind the podium, the VP smiled to those assembled. She looked directly into her teleprompter, smiled and began.

"Ladies and gentlemen, welcome. It is no secret that our

border has been besieged by immigrants seeking asylum from the ravages of war, political oppression, poverty and the upheavals of climate change.

"Our administration supports all immigration into the U.S. by the oppressed masses. As the land of the free, we are in solidarity with and fully support those whose native countries have been torn apart by unjust wars, political oppression, abject poverty and climate change.

"However, along with the struggles and challenges of immigration has been a historical war against transnational criminal cartels who have inundated our country. These criminal cabals smuggle large quantities of illegal and deadly drugs like fentanyl, methamphetamine and cocaine, just to name a few across our southern border. As a result, thousands of Americans have needlessly and tragically died from drug overdose deaths.

Our administration and our nation's federal, state and municipal law enforcement agencies wage war against the drug smuggling cartels every day to keep Americans safe.

Today, I am proud to share with you some exciting news of our administration's most recent victory on the war on drugs. As I speak right now, a major drug smuggler from one of our most aggressive transnational cartels is enroute under heavy armed security to the 6th District Federal Courthouse in Silver City, New Mexico. This criminal identified as Alfredo "Chuy" Montoya Guzman, is scheduled to be arraigned there shortly.

"This criminal was the leader of a band of drug smugglers who were interdicted by local and federal law enforcement officers as they attempted to traffic hundreds of pounds of deadly drugs like fentanyl across our southern border of New Mexico," she explained.

The Vice President's Chief of Staff Lennox Frazier had arranged through DEA SAC Dick Vermillion to also have a real time feed from the DHS/CBP Predator drone which was monitoring the U.S. Marshals – DEA security transport convoy.

"Isn't technology amazing? This is going to be great coverage for the President and VP. Real time video of a major drug smuggler being brought to justice right in front of the American people. We can probably

milk this positive coverage for half the week," thought Frazier.

As the drone pilot maintained the Predator drone on station, he suddenly observed what appeared to be the heavily armed U.S. Marshals and DEA agents moving a prisoner dressed in a bright red jumpsuit away from the covered area. That had to be Chuy Guzman. *"What's this all about? I'm sure that's not part of the security plan,"* he thought.

As Urias' rescue team moved out from under the roof of the Border patrol station, a DEA agent who was thought to be dead emerged from the rear of the Suburban in the right lane.

The seriously wounded agent was armed with an M-4 rifle. He moved towards the group from behind, raising his rifle and targeting the two rear guards who were looking forward. The agent's sudden and unexpected movement from the vehicle caught the sniper in the rafters totally off-guard. However, due to his position up inside the rafters, he had no shot because the DEA agent had disappeared from view.

The drone pilot saw the agent suddenly appear and move towards the group escorting Guzman from the station with his weapon raised. *"I know this is definitely not in the plan,"* he said to himself as he quickly enhanced the drone's video camera image to observe.

DEA SSA McKenry was at the HIDTA office monitoring the Predator's video feed and saw everything that the drone pilot was seeing.

"Holy shit! What the fuck?! What the hell is going on here?!" he yelled at the TV monitor.

McKenry and Major Prescott watched the Predator's live feed in amazement. The DEA agent engaged the group escorting Guzman, knocking two of the disguised agents to the pavement. Two more in the group pivot-turned with military precision and returned fire upon the agent, cutting him down. None of the downed men moved. They were all dead.

Cecil McKenry's cell phone rang, and he immediately picked up.

"Cecil, Major Prescott here. Your agents are under attack.

I repeat, agents under attack, officers down!" the Major yelled over the phone line.

"Major Prescott, I copy your transmission. Agents down. I'm watching the feed. I'm contacting all agencies for a mutual response to the scene to assist. Keep your drone overhead and provide emerging details so I can advise the responders. I need your eyes," replied McKenry.

"Copy that. Will do," replied Prescott.

McKenry immediately dialed 9-1-1, reaching the New Mexico State Police. He reported numerous officers down at Checkpoint Delta with a high-value federal prisoner being freed. In response, the dispatcher hit the emergency tone, called for emergency traffic only and reported numerous officers down with suspects still at the scene. She then declared an "11-99 – officers down" calling for all officers from all agencies to immediately respond to Checkpoint Delta.

Four cartel assault team members immediately surrounded Chuy for protection. The team leader yelled out to Urias that they had Chuy and that he had not been struck by the gunfire.

Urias yelled back to the leader to get Chuy to the LZ. He then radioed the helicopter pilot that was now doing aerials around the station at 1,000 feet, "We have Chuy, clear to land!"

The pilot responded, "Copy, pop smoke."

The team leader directed his team with Chuy over to the pre-arranged landing zone. The soldier removed a blue smoke canister attached to the mole webbing of his U.S. Marshals assault vest. He pulled the pin and tossed the canister onto the pavement. The device ignited, spinning around and dispensing a large, billowing cloud of bright blue smoke into the air. Chuy's protection team formed a circle around him with their M-4 assault rifles out, scanning in all directions for additional threats.

The pilot saw the cloud of blue smoke and keyed his radio, "I got blue."

Urias replied, "Affirmative, blue."

The pilot immediately landed at the LZ. Two members

of Chuy's protection team directed him to the rear door of the helicopter. A team member inside of the aircraft slid open the rear door. He reached out for Chuy's right hand, quickly pulled him into the helicopter and slammed the door shut. As soon as the door closed, the pilot pulled in pitch and pushed in full left pedal. Nosing the aircraft forward, the pilot climbed to an initial altitude of five hundred feet before racing the aircraft due south towards the Mexican border and freedom.

Major Prescott radioed to Cecil McKenry, "Agent McKenry, are you catching this? I've got a CBP helicopter that just landed at Delta. The chopper picked up your prisoner and has now departed south at high speed. What the hell is going on? CBP has no birds in the air in this area. I'd know that beforehand."

"I've got no idea what that chopper's doing there. It just can't be a CBP chopper. Are you sure?" the DEA agent replied.

"Affirm, it's got CBP insignias with the green agency identifying stripe. I'm on it and pursuing said the major who had now assumed control of the Predator. I've already notified our people. The bird is probably heading for Mexico," said Prescott.

Lennox Frazier watched the slaughter of federal agents at Checkpoint Delta in horror. He could not allow the press briefing to continue under these circumstances. The VP's Chief of Staff entered the room stage right. He whispered into the VP's ear to leave the stage immediately and follow him. The surprised Vice President thought at first it was a security breach, so she followed her Chief of Staff without hesitation.

Frazier led the VP to a nearby alcove where a flat screen carrying the real time video of the incident was being carried by the Predator drone. Frazier hit the play back button and allowed the VP to watch the footage. She saw the wounded federal agent engaging what appeared to be a small group of agents escorting Chuy Guzman away from the covered portion of Checkpoint Delta.

The Vice President suddenly turned pale and yelled at Frazier, "Those fucking back-stabbers. Stop this! Do whatever you can right now to stop this!"

Lennox in turn looked panicked and confused. *"What did the 'fucking back-stabbers' comment mean?"* he thought briefly.

Frazier pulled his cell phone out of his pocket, scrolled through his contacts and selected, "NM NG Air Force" and speed dialed the number.

At Luke Air Force Base seven miles west of Glendale, New Mexico, 56th Fighter Wing Commander Lt. Col. David "Dusty" Sheppard, looked at the display on his cell phone that read "White House" and picked up on the second ring.

"56th Fighter Wing Commander Lt. Col. Sheppard here," the officer said into his cell phone.

"Commander Sheppard, this is the Vice President's Chief of Staff Lennox Frazier calling from the White House. We have a security breach emergency just outside of Deming, New Mexico. A Customs & Border Protection drone is giving us a live feed of an unidentified and heavily armed force that has just attacked federal agents at the Customs and Border Patrol station Checkpoint Delta just outside of town. We have multiple federal agents down!

"The drone feed shows that a helicopter most probably disguised as a CBP chopper, landed at the scene, picked up a high-value federal prisoner and has just left. The drone is pursuing and tracking the helicopter which is fleeing south towards the Mexican border.

"The Vice President believes that the aircraft with the high-value federal prisoner intends to cross into Mexican airspace. What assets do you have available right now to give pursuit? The Vice President herself is authorizing immediate pursuit of this foreign aircraft. Your orders are to either force the helicopter to land, or if they refuse, to bring it down forcibly," explained Frazier.

Lt. Col. Sheppard could hardly believe what he was hearing on his end of the line. This was potentially an act of war. He needed clarification.

"Mr. Frazier, say again? Are you telling me that an unidentified armed force has attacked the CBP station at Deming? That they have killed federal agents and a helicopter disguised as a CBP chopper picked up a federal prisoner and is spiriting him to Mexico right now?" asked the Air Wing Commander incredulously.

"Yes, Colonel. The VP needs to know what armed aircraft you can scramble right now to pursue and engage the threat. I say again, this is a security breach emergency," repeated Frazier.

"Sir, let me check and I'll get right back to you. This is above my paygrade, sir. I've got to clear this with our base commander, General Millet. To be clear sir, you're saying that the Vice President herself is authorizing pursuit of this aircraft. Further, and if necessary the use deadly force to shoot it down over Mexican airspace is authorized? Has the Mexican government been advised of this?" asked Lt. Col. Sheppard.

"Our State Department and DOD will be doing that directly, Colonel. The priority is to locate our closest air assets to pursue this helicopter and attempt to force them to land. As ordered, if the hostiles refuse to land, you will destroy it with prejudice. Is that understood?" replied Frazier.

"Copy that, sir. I'll call my boss, check for available air assets and get right back to you," said the colonel before hanging up.

Lt. Col. Sheppard still couldn't believe what he had just heard. However, other than the President himself, a direction from the Vice President or Congress of the United States was the highest level of an order that could be given during peace time.

Sheppard, picked up the phone on his desk while simultaneously pushing the illuminated red button that read "SCRAMBLE."

The phone was only half-way through its first ring when it was immediately picked up, "Air Wing Control, Major Craig, here. State your emergency," said the Flight Officer of the Watch.

"George, Dusty here. Listen close and hard. We just got a bucket of shit tossed on us just now. I just got a call from the Chief of Staff of the Vice President who advised me that an unidentified armed force have just attacked CBP and other federal agents at Checkpoint Delta in Deming."

"What?!" replied Major Craig.

"Confirmed. Apparently numerous KIA federal agents. A helicopter disguised as a CBP chopped landed, picked a high-value federal prisoner and extracted. The bird is heading to Mexico as we speak. The VP is authorizing pursuit into Mexican airspace. They want us to either force the chopper to land or shoot it down. What air assets do we have immediately available that we can scramble?

"What the fuck did you just say, Dusty? We are authorized to chase some helicopter into Mexico? Then try to force it to land or blow it out of the fucking sky – in Mexico?! Does the general know about this? Is this some type of new drill to test our ability to scramble aircraft? Level with me, no bullshit, Dusty," the Major asked.

"This is no drill. I repeat, no drill, honest. Look George, the VP is declaring this to be a security emergency. A possible breach of our southern border by an unknown armed element who's slaughtered a bunch of feds. Then they've extracted with a high-value federal prisoner. Smells like drug cartel or terrorist shit. I needed to call you first to see what assets we can scramble. My next call is to the boss, so when he asks me what we have, I can tell him. So, what have you got?" Lt. Col. Sheppard repeated.

Major Craig checked the white board in his office while Lt. Colonel Sheppard anxiously held the phone.

"I've got two fully armed F-35B Lightning's doing air to air maneuvers with drones on the range right now. If the general gives authorization, I can have the assets vectored to locate the helicopter. I know Deming, it's about 340 miles from here and another 35 miles from the U.S.-Mexican border. That makes it 375 miles out," replied the major.

"Copy that. If our Lightning's travel at Mach .92 they could be in Mexican airspace in less than 20 minutes. At that speed, they can avoid sonic boom signatures that would alert the Mexican military of their presence. What type of armaments are they carrying today?" asked Lt. Col. Sheppard.

"Well, they took off about ten minutes ago and haven't engaged anything yet. They are authorized to each have two AIM-120 AMRRAM's and two AIM-9X Sidewinder missiles," replied Major Craig.

"Who are the pilots, George?" asked the Colonel.

"Captains "Outlaw" McGraw and "Tex" O'Deen," replied the Major.

"Great, they're both experienced pilots. That will give them a range of 10 miles for the Sidewinders and over 80 miles for the AIM-120(D)'s. Our birds can easily make up the difference on that chopper depending upon where it's headed.

"Make it happen, George. I'll get the OK from the general, but I want those Lightning's on afterburners to FL180 now. Also, advise and they will need separation from civilian traffic. We can always call them back if it's a 'No-Go' from the general, but you know he's going to tell us to splash 'em," said Lt. Col. Sheppard.

"Done!" replied the major before hanging up.

Four minutes later Major Craig's desk phone rang.

"George, Dusty here. The general says, 'Go get 'em!' Advise both pilots shut their ADS-B's off at the border and communicate only on the scrambled 24-Echo channel.'"

"Copy that. Lightning's are already enroute and have been cleared to climb to FL200 (20,000 feet).

Keep you posted," replied the major.

Streaking across the Arizona desert at Angel's 20 (20,000 feet), the helmet comms for Captains Virginia "Outlaw" McGraw and her wingman Captain Billy "Tex" O'Deen piloting a pair of F-35B Lightning's suddenly squawked on the 24-Echo channel.

"Luke AFB tower to Foxtrots 3-3 and 3-6, come in."

Captain McGraw was the lead F-35B, so she acknowledged the radio call.

"Foxtrots 3-3 and 3-6 copy. What's your traffic, control?"

"Priority traffic authorized by Pentagon through General Millet. You are to break off your training maneuvers immediately. You are to deactivate your ADS-B's, locate, pursue and attempt to interdict and force down unknown believed enemy aircraft. Suspected enemy helicopter currently under surveillance by DHS Predator drone involved in armed attack on CBP agents. We have numerous federal agents KIA. Helicopter believed to contain high-value federal drug cartel prisoner and is heading for Mexico. Confirm, this is not, I repeat not a drill. Confirm receipt of traffic and comm only on 24-Echo. Acknowledge, over."

Captains McGraw and O'Deen had flown closer together as they were copying the tower's traffic. They could now see each other in their respective cockpits as they turned to look at each other.

Virginia "Outlaw" McGraw keyed her mic. "Foxtrot 3-3 to Luke tower. What are our ROE's if the chopper pilot refuses to land?"

The officer in the control tower at Luke AFB responded without hesitation.

"Per General Millet, you are authorized to engage and destroy with prejudice. I say again, in that event, you are both cleared to engage and destroy suspected enemy target. Acknowledge ROE's."

Both F-35B Lightning pilots responded in kind. "Foxtrot 3-3, acknowledges ROE's," radioed Outlaw.

"Foxtrot 3-6 acknowledges ROE's," radioed Tex.

"Foxtrots 3-3 and 3-6, your enemy authentication and engagement sign is "Buster, I say again, your authentication and engagement sign is Buster, copy?"

"Foxtrots 3-3 and 3-6 copy. Our sign is Buster," replied Outlaw.

"Good hunting and God speed," replied the tower.

Outlaw looked over at Tex and keyed her mic.

"Well partner, we're in the shit, now."

"Man, don't you feel like you're in a Top Gun movie?" laughed Tex.

"Race you to Mexico!" replied Outlaw as she made a pumping up and down motion with her right hand and then pointed forward indicating to her wingman to separate, descend to Angels 18 and pursue the enemy helicopter.

Both pilots then immediately descended to 18,000 feet and at Mach .92, shot across the Arizona landscape in hot pursuit of the Tres Paises helicopter carrying Chuy Guzman.

Adolfo Guzman had received Uberto Urias' cell phone call

advising him that his sister's son and his favorite nephew Chuy had been successfully rescued. The beaming Urias gleefully informed his boss that Chuy was being flown to Guzman's mountain retreat just outside of Ciudad Madera in the Mexican State of Chihuahua.

Adolfo was overjoyed. He had been telling his sister and the Guzman family to expect a big surprise; one fit for a feast and party. When Adolfo received Urias' welcome news, he had let the cat out of the bag. The cartel boss informed his family that Chuy was coming home that afternoon. He just didn't tell the family how he had arranged for Chuy to be with them again.

Servants at the palatial compound had been hastily pressed into service. The large refrigerators and freezers always stocked with lobsters, shrimps, seafood and the finest meats had been opened. Seasonal fruit and vegetables had been prepared, bar-b-que grills ignited, and tables were beautifully arranged surrounding the enormous swimming pool for the large Guzman family.

Excitement was in the air as family members donned their most colorful and festive clothes and jewelry in growing anticipation of the arrival of their Chuy.

Inside the air-conditioned module marked UAS NM/M-1 at Holloman AFB, New Mexico, Major Miranda Prescott was aware that the Predator was now the only asset that could track the Airbus 350. Experience told the Air Force veteran that there was a very good possibility that the U.S. would immediately respond to the murder of its federal agents. She just didn't know right now what that response would be. Better to keep tracking the helicopter even if it crossed into Mexican air space and stay with it no matter what.

"No way I'm losing sight of a hostile element that was responsible for killing federal agents," she thought.

The pilot hired by the Tres Paises to fly the Airbus 350 was also a seasoned professional. He was a former Mexican military special operations veteran who was experienced in "E&E" escape and evasion tactics.

After picking up Chuy Guzman and gaining some altitude, the pilot sprinted south to the Mexican border at 170 mph. This was just below the aircraft's top speed. Five miles from the U.S. –

Mexican border, the pilot dropped down to nap of the earth only 25 feet above the landscape to avoid noise and visual detection.

"Fuck the DHS/CBP radar systems, I just don't want to get shot at. Then I'll be in Mexico and home free," he thought.

The pilot cleared the 33 mile distance between the Deming Checkpoint Delta station and the Mexican border in eleven minutes. Two miles from the border, the pilot dropped down further, skimming over the Rio Brisas with his skids literally shredding the cypress tree branches below.

"Estamos en Mexico, estas libre, Senor Guzman!" (We are in Mexico, you are free!) the pilot exclaimed as they crossed the border.

Due to the heightened stressors caused by the American President's open border policies which had driven millions of UDA's from all over the world straight through Mexico the relationship between the two nations governments was tenuous at best. Hundreds of thousands of UDA's forming human caravans were marching through Mexican villages and cities. The result was havoc and chaos compromising the fragile economic, social service, health and safety and law enforcement systems in the second world country. This had become Mexico's new reality. Presently, the Mexican President wasn't even returning calls from the U.S. President.

The cartel pilot doubted that the U.S. would respond with any of its air assets. Any Mexican air assets would never find them in time to intervene. They were home free!

What the cartel pilot didn't realize is that Major Miranda Prescott wasn't at all interested in geopolitical bullshit. American LEO's had been senselessly slaughtered on our side of the border. Miranda now knew why and who was responsible. *"Better to beg for forgiveness later than ask for permission,"* she figured.

Miranda climbed the Predator to its maximum altitude of 50,000 feet. *"Fuck this shit,"* she thought as she increased the drone's speed to its maximum 135 mph and pursued the chopper across the U.S. – Mexican border.

The red phone buzzed next to Miranda, and she immediately picked up.

"Major Miranda Prescott, what's your emergency traffic?" she inquired.

"Major Prescott, this is Lt. Col. Dusty Sheppard, Luke AFB. We have a DOD Priority One task for your Predator, stat. Drop whatever you're doing. We have an incursion into U.S. soil by an unknown enemy element. We have numerous CBP assets down at Checkpoint Delta Deming. We believe that a component of that element is presently escaping into Mexican airspace in a helicopter disguised as a CBP chopper. We need your Predator tasked to surveil and track that chopper until our air assets from Luke can intercept, do you copy?"

"Sir, I am already aware of the incident and circumstances. We were asked to task our drone to surveil the U.S. Marshals – DEA security convoy transporting the high-value cartel prison to and from the federal courthouse in Silver City, New Mexico.

FYI, I am now personally in command of the Predator and have the target in sight on the Mexican side of the border at compass heading 210 degrees southwest. The chopper's speed is 170 mph at nap of the earth. Its destination is unknown at this time. I can vector your birds to the target. Do I have permission to cross the border?" Miranda lied.

"Affirmative. Permission granted, Major. Thanks for the brief," replied Lt. Col. Sheppard.

"What do you have up?" asked Miranda.

"Two F-35B Lightning's fully armed with air-to-air missiles. Our pilots are now descending from Angels 18 to 500 feet and entering Mexican airspace in pursuit now," said Sheppard.

"Copy that. Patch me in to your pilots. Be advised, just before I crossed over into Mexican airspace, I turned off the drone's transponder. Make sure your pilots know that my bird is at Angel's 50, speed 135 mph on the same compass heading as the Airbus 350. I'll remain above the fray to advise. The airbus is going faster than my Predator. I have to stay high so I can look down on the chopper from behind as it increases distance from me. Also advise your pilots that I can transmit the chopper's location via datalink directly to their HUD's until they get visual on the target," explained Miranda.

"Copy Major. Switch to scrambled channel 24-Echo to contact my Lightning's, designations Foxtrot 3-3 and 3-6. They're stealth aircraft so we are flying black on this mission. Confirm," directed Sheppard.

"Copy switching to channel 24-Echo, Lightning's designations Foxtrot 3-3 and 3-6, confirmed," repeated Miranda who immediately switched to 24-Echo and contacted the Lightnings.

"Foxtrot 3-3, Foxtrot 3-6, this is Eagle, a Predator drone, do you copy?" radioed Miranda to the F-35B's now streaking across the Mexican state of Chihuahua.

"Ah, roger Eagle, we are Foxtrots 3-3 and 3-6. Where are you and what do you see?" radioed Captain Virginia "Outlaw" McGraw.

"Foxtrots, this is Eagle. You should see my bird at Angel's 50 at 135 mph in pursuit of Airbus 350B disguised as a CBP chopper. Your target is white with a green stripe. Eagle is following the Airbus on a compass heading of 210 southwest. Your target is steady and straight with no deviations at 500 feet, speed 170 mph. Destination is unknown at this time," radioed Miranda.

"Foxtrot 3-3, copy Eagle, repeating target is on course heading 210 southwest at 500 feet, speed 170, straight flight path. Airbus 350, white with green stripe. We are behind you at 500 feet doing Mach .92. We will pass you in less than 5. Keep an eye out for us," replied "Outlaw."

The co-pilot of the Airbus 350 helicopter used his cell phone to call Adolfo Guzman with an update on their location, He advised the cartel leader that they were thirty miles out and would be soon landing at the compound.

Adolfo gathered the large family together near the swimming pool overlooking the concrete helicopter landing pad to make a short speech welcoming their Chuy home. The servants began to put meat on the grills in preparation of the feast.

Eight minutes later, Captain McGraw radioed Major Miranda Prescott.

"Eagle, Foxtrots 3-3 and 3-6 coming up your position, slowing to Mach .25. We have the target on HUD and visually in front of us at 5 miles. Confirm target to be 5 miles southwest of you with speed now reduced to 100 mph? Confirm," said Outlaw.

"Foxtrots 3-3 and 3-6, I've got you. Affirm, looks like your target is heading to Ciudad Madera or somewhere nearby. He has now dropped down to 100 feet, no doubt to avoid Mexican radar," replied Miranda.

"Foxtrot 3-3 and 3-6 copy. We are now 5 miles behind target. Luke tower, we have target in sight. Advising "Buster, Buster," Copy, Luke?" radioed Outlaw.

"Foxtrots, this is Luke tower. We confirm Buster. Attempt to force pilot to land immediately and advise on response, copy?" radioed Lt. Col. Sheppard.

"Copy Luke tower. Stand-by a couple, will advise," replied Outlaw. She then motioned to Tex to overtake the helicopter as both F-35B's streaked forward towards the unsuspecting chopper pilots.

The cartel pilot glanced nonchalantly down at his mid-air collision avoidance system or ADS-B Out as a matter of custom during the flight and as usual, saw nothing. They were almost at Guzman's compound and home free.

The F-35B's stealthfully approached the Airbus 350. The pilots slowed their speed to 100 mph to match the helicopter's and suddenly appeared to the port and starboard sides of the aircraft. This of course completely freaked out the flight crew.

"Dios, Mio!" exclaimed the startled pilot. Chuy saw the F-35B's suddenly appear on each side of the helicopter.

"American Air Force? How can this be?" yelled Chuy to his pilots.

Captains McGraw and O'Deen were twenty yards to each side of the helicopter. Capt. Outlaw McGraw motioned to the pilot to land and then drew her left hand across her throat in the universal language that said, "If you don't, you're all dead men."

The cartel pilot spoke first. "Senor, the Americans are telling us that if we don't land immediately, they will shoot us down. What should we do? What are your orders?"

Chuy had also seen the pilot's threat, but he was more obstinate. He looked directly back at Captain McGraw and flipped her the bird, a gesture that is understood in all languages.

"Pinche American putos. This is a bluff. They are bluffing. They would never violate Mexican air space and shoot us down over our own country. I can see the fucking compound. We can make it. Get me to the compound immediately. I order it!" screamed the angry and concerned Chuy.

"Si, senor," replied the pilot who now increased the helicopter's speed to its maximum of 178 mph while remaining at 100 feet to make a run for the compound.

The jet pilots increased their speed to again match the helicopter. When the pilots were 100 feet abreast of the fleeing helicopter, Outlaw radioed to Tex.

"I was actually hoping that they would try this bonehead move. Hover here, let them get no more than five miles in front of us and let's smoke em."

Just before the F-35B's commenced their hover maneuver, Outlaw looked at Chuy Guzman. She waved goodbye and moved her left index finger across her throat. The die was cast.

Adolfo Guzman and his entire family could now see the counterfeit CBP helicopter racing towards them at top speed. Adolfo now addressed the gathering.

"To my family and especially to my dearest sister Augustina and her family. We are blessed to have our wonderful Chuy returning to us from his captivity in the U.S. We are victorious! Look outwards as we see our beautiful boy approaching us to be reunited with his family. Viva Chuy! Viva Tres Paises!" shouted the jubilant Adolfo Guzman. The Guzman family joined in on the cheering and clapping as the Airbus 350 approached quickly from two miles out.

As the cartel helicopter raced towards the safety of the compound, McGraw switched back to military scrambled radio channel 24-Echo and keyed her mic.

"Foxtrots 3-3 and 3-6 to Luke tower, the pilot is refusing to comply. He has now increased speed to evade. We only have time for one shot on target. Confirm authorization to engage?"

Lt. Col. Dusty Sheppard had already anticipated the pilot's resistance to capture. He keyed his mic and turned off the tower's air control recording device.

"Copy last transmission, deadly force is authorized. Shred those motherfuckers!"

Outlaw McGraw and Tex O'Deen immediately pulled up to 5,000 feet in unison. The Airbus 350 carrying Chuy Guzman was now five miles in front of them and nearly at the compound. McGraw flipped up the red protective flap on the missile fire button on her joystick. She looked at the holographic HUD on her front canopy windshield and selected an AIM-120 Advanced Medium Range Missile. She then radioed to her wingman.

"Tex, selecting AIM-120-B, one missile each, that's all we have time for, copy?"

The AIM-120-B's had an air-to-air range of at least 40 miles, and now the F-35B's were now only five miles behind the Airbus 350. This was easy pickings. The AIM-120's flew at Mach 4, or 3,000 mph. At five miles it would take the missile just three seconds to reach the chopper.

Outlaw McGraw keyed her mic, "Tally-ho, Fox -1!" she radioed.

Tex O'Deen saw the AIM-120 fall away from Outlaw's F-35B and ignite, screaming towards the helicopter with a white plume. He depressed his missile fire button and keyed his mic. "Fox-2!" watching as his own AIM-120 ignited and sprinted in pursuit of Outlaw's missile and the chopper.

The pilot of the Airbus had begun to slow down and feathered his tail back in preparation of landing on the helipad inside the compound.

Chuy Guzman removed his seat belt as he peered forward through the front windshield between the pilot and co-pilot. He watched the family clapping their hands and waving joyously at the incoming helicopter. The smiling Chuy patted the pilot and co-pilot on their backs. He was returning back to his family the triumphant hero. *Oh, the story he would tell!*

Foxtrots 3-3, 3-6 with Major Miranda Prescott piloting the Predator drone all watched intensely on their enhanced video screens as the AIM-120 air-to-air missiles closed on the Airbus 350.

Three seconds, two seconds, one second....

One quarter mile from the Guzman compound, the first missile struck Airbus 350. The supersonic projectile completely obliterated the aircraft and its occupants in a violent orange, red and white cloud burst.

Two tenths of a second later, the second AIM-120 penetrated the orange and red cloud of debris. The supersonic projectile exploded into the bright fiery ball completely shredding what was left of the fuselage. Flaming metal and body parts tumbled out of the sky to earth, igniting the mountain side in front of the horrified Guzman family.

Adolfo Guzman bit his clenched fist as he watched his favorite nephew literally disintegrated. His sister fainted into the arms of his wife. Those in the crowd of family members who weren't screaming in panic were frozen in place and speechless.

Major Miranda Prescott had the best seat in the house with the Predator drone's enhanced camera and video capabilities. She keyed her mic on the 24-Echo channel.

"Foxtrots and Luke AFB, be advised, target destroyed, I say again, I can confirm target destroyed."

Lt. Col. Dusty Sheppard keyed his mic. "Copy target destroyed. Foxtrots 3-3 and 3-6, beat feet outta there, return to base. Congrats!"

Captains Virginia "Outlaw" McGraw and Billy "Tex" O'Deen keyed their mics, "Copy Luke, returning to base." Both Lightnings immediately climbed rapidly in unison to Angels 45, did a victory barrel role and screamed back to Luke AFB, Arizona at Mach .90. As soon as they crossed over and into U.S. airspace, they met up with a KC-767 refueler waiting to gas them up for their return back to Luke AFB.

USA-1, Tres Paises-0.

And just like that, Alfredo "Chuy" Montoya Guzman was no more.

CHAPTER 27

"I want them dead, all of them dead!"

THE STRESS FOR even a cold-blooded killer like Adolfo Guzman watching his beloved Chuy disintegrating before his eyes was too much. The drug lord became unsteady on his feet and sought a nearby chair for relief. He sat down, took some deep breaths and looked around. He saw his sister on the ground barely conscious in the arms of his wife. Family members were in tears. His bodyguards and servants were milling around with the look of shock and utter surprise on their faces.

A balmy Spring breeze blew the sickening smells of burning aviation fuel and human flesh into the compound. Several family members vomited. For the moment, Adolfo was getting a taste of his own medicine.

Major Prescott maintained the Predator aloft over the compound, climbing the UAS to its maximum altitude of 50,000 feet.

Cecil McKenry called Major Prescott on her cell phone.

"Stay on the compound and enhance the video. Give me shots of everyone there. That looks like Adolfo Guzman in the chair. I want to be able to positively identify that son of a bitch with HIDTA. I also need any good photos you can get me on the debris from that phony CBP chopper," he said.

"Copy that, but not much left to show you, Agent McKenry," replied the major as she zoomed in on the compound, capturing some great video footage and still frames of Guzman.

Lt. Col. Sheppard radioed to Major Prescott over the 24-

Echo frequency. "Time to clear Mexican airspace and return to base, Major. We've got what we came for. Thanks for the eyes," he said.

"Copy that, Colonel, Predator returning to base," replied the Major. The officer tapped the "Home" icon on her screen, tasking the Predator on a pre-programmed course back to Holloman AFB.

The Vice President was nearly apoplectic after watching the shootout at Checkpoint Delta and the apparent rescue of her self-described high-value federal drug smuggling prisoner Chuy Guzman.

The Air Force was pursuing the helicopter carrying Guzman into Mexican airspace. Major Prescott knew this was a deliberate violation of international law, as well as U.S. – Mexican accords. Therefore, Miranda had deliberately blocked the White House from the Predator video feed. This provided the VP and her Chief of Staff with plausible deniability. Instead, Lt. Colonel Dusty Sheppard called Lennox Frazier and reported that the suspected cartel helicopter and all on board had been "terminated with prejudice on direct orders of the Vice President."

Frazier took the call from Lt. Col. Sheppard and acknowledged the information that the cartel helicopter had been shot down and all aboard including Guzman had perished. He then walked over to his VP and whispered into her ear.

Frazier observed that the Vice President's facial expressions and demeanor appeared to those of anger and relief. However, he interpreted his boss' strange behavior to be the result of the normal panic and confusion from being suddenly surprised by the horrific murder of numerous federal agents and the escape of Chuy Guzman. Actually, most of that was not true.

The Vice President had realized that she had been played for a sucker. She had been bribed to direct federal agents and a U.S. Attorney to place Chuy Guzman into a position where the Tres Paises cartel could rescue Chuy and spirit him away to Mexico. That was infuriating, hence the anger. The fact that federal agents had been ambushed and slaughtered in the process justified the attack on the cartel helicopter and the summary execution of Chuy Guzman was inexplicable and treasonous on her part.

The Vice President's expression of relief was that Chuy Guzman and all abord the disguised CBP helicopter had been terminated. That was a loose end she didn't need to worry about.

"You just don't fuck with the Vice President of the United States, assholes," she said to herself, think that the loose end had been addressed.

However, what she and her press team did need to worry about was how to wipe the egg of their combined faces with the press. This would also no doubt negatively affect the President's approval rating. Their bogus victory on their war on drugs had instantaneously evaporated, leaving in its wake fifteen brutally murdered CBP officers, DEA agents and U.S. Marshals.

The United States had just experienced its single greatest loss of law enforcement lives since 9-11. There would be some serious explaining to do and right now she had no good answers. There would be hell to pay when the President found out and she would have to be the one to make that call. The southern border and all the baggage that went with it was her baby. Right now, she looked like the manager of a Samsonite factory.

Once the more fragile members of the Guzman family had retreated to their various quarters on the estate and Adolfo had time to collect his thoughts, he called Urias. The chief enforcer and author of Chuy's now doomed rescue plan immediately picked up, anticipating joyous news and a pat on the back from his patron.

"Si Jefe. I trust all is well," Urias said into his cell phone.

"Where the fuck are you?!" demanded Guzman angrily into the phone.

This was certainly not the response Urias had expected.

"As planned, my men and I are evacuating. We have crossed the border and are back in Mexico on our way to you, senor. What is wrong?" the enforcer asked.

"Your plan failed, and our Chuy is dead. I don't know how they did it, but the Americans shot the helicopter carrying Chuy out of the sky right in front of us at the compound," Guzman yelled into the phone.

"But senor, how could this be? The Americans would never enter Mexican airspace without contacting our Air Force and the Mexican government. There are rules, there are diplomatic protocols. There are international laws. Our contacts would have warned us," replied Urias.

"Look, all I know is what we saw. Chuy's helicopter was approaching the compound. It was preparing to land and it... It just got fucking blown out of the sky right in front of us. Me, my wife, his mother who is my sister, the entire family watched it!" yelled Guzman again.

"Did you hear or see any American Air Force jets? There must have been jets," exclaimed the confused and frustrated Urias.

"No, nada, you pendejo! Your fucking plan was a total failure. The Americans killed my nephew. How am I now to explain this tragedy to my family, to my sister, to my own wife? I look like shit in front of my own family. I was supposed to be a hero, but now I am the villain," said Guzman in a depressed voice.

Urias had no good response for his boss. It was better just to incur his rath. Just let him vent. Perhaps he could still be of service so that Guzman would not react emotionally and kill him. Urias was definitely worried. Guzman was emotionally captured. He was on a rant. Just keep quiet, be patient and his boss' thoughts would reveal themselves soon enough.

"My Jefe. My deepest and most sincere condolences to you and your family. You know I would give my life to protect Chuy and all of you," replied Urias sympathetically. He could hear Adolfo breathing heavily on the other end of the phone. Then there was a very uncomfortable minute of absolute silence which raised the hairs on the back of Urias' neck. His own life stood in forfeit right now... Then Guzman spoke in a clear and very deliberate manner.

"I want them dead. I want all of them dead. Dead, do you hear me, Toro? Sheriff Fremont, his deputies and especially that mercenary former Texas Ranger Wade Justus. All of them, dead. Comprende?" Said Guzman.

"Si Jefe. Entiendo. All of them dead, senor," replied Urias obediently, knowing now that his life would be spared.

"And that's not all. They hurt my family, so we are going to hurt the sheriff's family as well. We will make a new plan, a plan to first kill the sheriff, his men and Wade Justus. After that is done, I want Sheriff Fremont's family eliminated as well. All of them, not one of them is to be spared," directed Guzman.

"Si senor, you have my word," replied Urias.

"When you arrive, we will develop this plan. How did your operation go at the Border Patrol station in Deming?" asked Guzman.

Urias realized that this was a good time for him to explain to his boss that his plan had actually succeeded and that they had rescued Chuy. The rest of the unfortunate matter had been out of his control.

"Senor, all had gone exactly as planned. We arrived on time and managed to deceive all of the Border Patrol agents. We eliminated all of them at the station. We assumed their positions and when Chuy's security convoy arrived, we quickly took out almost all of the federal agents. One agent survived and was in a gunfight with my men. We lost only two men, but the agent was killed.

"The helicopter team did their job and we managed to extract Chuy. All of my men and I evacuated the area as planned and dispersed before any law enforcement arrived at the station. We never saw any American law enforcement or military air assets," explained Urias.

"Toro, there can be absolutely no mistakes in this new plan. My objective is to eradicate the entire Gila County Sheriff's Office and the Texas Ranger. Once they are gone, we move to take over the county once and for all. Gila will become the Tres Paises' center for all of our American smuggling operations. Drugs, illegals, women and child trafficking, stolen vehicles; everything.

"Although the sheriff's administration will change, the new sheriff will not be as uncooperative as Matt Fremont. We will own him, all of his deputies and the county commissioners. Gila County will become Tres Paises territory, I assure you of this," declared Guzman.

"Of course, Jefe. I should be at the compound by tomorrow morning. We will make this plan work," replied the enforcer.

"Hasta manana, Toro," replied Guzman before hanging up.

CHAPTER 28

An Audacious Plan

MATT FREMONT CALLED Wade's cell phone from the Sheriff's Office. Wade had been lying low at Matt's ranch per his instruction. He was waiting for an opportunity to tell his story to the New Mexico State Police about his shootout in Deming two days previous.

"Wade, I hope you're sitting down because you won't believe this," Matt began.

"What, I'm getting arrested for the shooting in Deming?" asked Wade.

"Nope, my NMSP commander got back to me briefly and told me that your case is on the back burner and not to worry about it right now. They have far more important things on their plates right now," replied Matt.

"Well, that's good to hear, so Okay, I give. What's up?" asked Wade.

"It's been all over the law enforcement traffic. Seems that the feds decided to do a special arraignment for our old buddy Chuy Guzman at the 6th District Federal Courthouse in Silver City, over in Grant County. The U.S. Attorney in Las Cruces approved it. Word is that the pressure came from the Vice President. Press briefing, photo-op war on drugs BS. The U.S. Marshals and DEA arranged for a security convoy to transport Guzman round trip to court.

"Well, this is only preliminary intel, but it appears that Tres Paises put together a strike team of cartel soldiers dressed and equipped as U.S. Marshals, DEA and CBP. They even had an identical disguised convoy. They rode up to Checkpoint Delta just east of Deming and took out all of the CBP agents there. They assumed their positions and ambushed the real convoy when they arrived there.

"The bad guys managed to free Chuy from the armored transport vehicle. A helicopter disguised as a CBP chopper landed at the station, picked up Guzman and sped off with him across the border to Mexico. The feds had agents down," explained Matt.

"Holy shit. How many down?" asked Wade.

"All of them," replied Matt in a low voice.

"What do you mean, all of them? How many survived? That's a lot of agents," replied Wade incredulously.

"I mean they lost them all, Wade. Fifteen CBP, DEA and U.S. Marshals. No survivors. They're all gone, partner. It was a well-planned ambush, they were massacred. They never knew what him 'em," replied Matt.

There was a long silence over the phone as Wade tried to wrap his arms around what Matt Fremont had just told him.

"So where's Guzman now?" asked Wade.

"I don't know at this point. Your guess is as good as mine. I've got a call out to Cecil McKenry, my contact over at DEA. I heard that Cecil was the co-coordinator for the security convoy. Half of the security team were DEA agents, and he was their supervisor. I'm sure he's plenty busy right now since there's no doubt DEA lost agents at Delta. Maybe his whole squad," said Matt.

"Tough shoes to be in right now. So, what's the response plan right now?" asked Wade.

"Well, all the agents killed were feds from three different agencies. I suspect that the involved agencies will develop their intel, use their CI's to the max and try to shake something out of the trees. This is very high-level stuff with the Vice President allegedly approving of the special arraignment of Chuy Guzman. I suspect that NSA will be covertly listening in on all the chatter between the U.S. and Mexico right now.

"DEA knows most all the cartel players. They'll feed all their HIDTA intel to NSA to follow-up on. It won't make a bit of difference if the cartels are communicating via regular or burner phones, or via the Internet. NSA and DEA will find out who's responsible. No doubt the players will either be bragging about it or calling each other to cover their tracks.

"It's not gonna be too hard to figure out. Who's to gain from freeing Chuy Guzman from federal custody? My money is on Adolfo Guzman and his henchman Uberto Urias. The feds will widen the net to see if the Juarez, Sinaloa, or any of the other cartels provided any support.

"Believe you me, the shit is gonna hit the fan on this one and some Mexican cartel assholes are gonna pay for this big time. If the feds establish that the ambush and lynching of Chuy emanated from Mexico, that makes it international, and the CIA can enter the game. The use of CIA wet boys to hit those responsible is certainly in play. We've never lost this many LEO's in one operation in the history of this country. I'd expect that we could certainly retaliate using black ops assets," explained Matt.

"No Doubt about that. See you when you get home and keep watching your six. They may still have you under surveillance," replied Wade before hanging up.

Uberto Urias reached Adolfo Guzman's mountain retreat outside the rural town of Ciudad Madera mid-morning. He noted that the grounds were heavily guarded with armed guards. Two narcotanques, armored vehicles also known as "Rhino Trucks" were blocking the sole roadway leading up to the compound. Guards on four corners of the compound carried Russian RPG's. Two guards on the roof of the three-story mansion had anti-aircraft Stinger missiles. Senor Guzman was taking no chances of a repeat air attack by U.S. or Mexican military forces.

Urias was immediately ushered to Guzman's expansive study on the third floor of the mansion, overlooking the mountain city. He found his employer seated behind a large, ornately carved desk made of beautiful multi-colored tropical woods. The cartel boss was smoking one of his favorite Cuban Cohiba Behike cigars.

Guzman bade his enforcer to sit down and offered him a cigar. Urias gladly accepted the cigar which allowed the two to break the ice. Guzman began the discussion.

"Now that the initial shock of losing our precious Chuy has subsided, I have been carefully thinking of how we can set the trap for Sheriff Fremont, his deputies and this Wade Justus. However, it's not only setting the trap, but getting them to come to the bait without the assistance of other law enforcement agencies. The American federales will no doubt want revenge for the loss of so many of their agents," said Guzman.

"Agreed Jefe. We must beguile them with a prize they could not possibly refuse to take. Yet, provide them with the information at the latest possible time in the game. Then Fremont will have no time to request the assistance of other agencies or the federales," replied Urias.

"Si, Toro. Our informants tell me that the entire region and all of the federales in Tejas, Nuevo Mexico and Arizona are engaged in re-grouping. They are trying to find out who is responsible for killing their agents. Of course, we are at the top of the suspect list. To our benefit, we killed so many of their field agents, that the federales will need time to move new agents into the region.

"With so many agents now tasked with the investigation and intelligence gathering, they won't have the manpower to offer assistance in any narcotics operation a small, pinche agency like the Gila County Sheriff's Department would put together. Our dealers in Las Cruces, El Paso and Tucson are already telling us that the HIDTA task forces and strike teams are being bled to work the shooting investigation. No one is bothering our people. They could sell drugs in front of the DEA offices and not be arrested," Guzman laughed.

"What do you propose, Jefe?" asked Urias.

"Something that will whet the appetites of Sheriff Fremont and the ranger. Actually, two things; lots of drugs and you, Toro," replied Guzman as he looked directly into his enforcer's eyes.

"Me, senor? Tell me about your plan," asked Urias.

"Well, first of all, it will be *our* plan, not just mine. This will take all of our combined skills, logistics and resources of Tres Paises to pull off this coupe.

"We will arrange a way for Sheriff Fremont to learn about a huge shipment of drugs that Tres Paises will be smuggling across the border in Gila County. The sheriff must also learn that you will be personally leading the smuggling team.

"The sheriff already knows that it was you who tortured and was going to execute his only son. The combination of capturing both a big shipment of illegal drugs, coupled with arresting or killing the man responsible for maiming his son will be too much for Sheriff Fremont to ignore. I guarantee you that he will take the bait. Of course, the sheriff will depend upon his mercenary Wade Justus to help him. We will trap and kill two birds with one stone.

"Now that I have provided you with the basic idea. I am depending upon you to make all of the arrangements to set the trap. As before when we murdered the federales and freed our Chuy, you will train and equip the men. I will provide the finances and resources. I promise you that you will have everything you need. All you must do is ask. Money is no object.

"We will avenge our Chuy. Once we have completely eliminated our adversaries, we will take over Gila County. No one will be able to stop us. No one will dare to oppose us. The American politicians are weak and easily bought like their Congress people, the Vice President and the Secretary of Homeland Security," explained Guzman.

"Si, Jefe. I will immediately begin work on this plan. We must now act swiftly while the American federales are distracted with investigating the murder of their agents. The longer it takes to develop and implement, the more time the Americans have to recover and possibly thwart it," said Urias.

"Agreed. Get to work, Toro. I need your very best effort on this. Speak to me once you have an outline with a list of what you will need. Now stay here for the remainder of the day. Get some rest. Reach out to me when you are ready for our next discussion," directed Guzman. "Si, mi Jefe. Gracias," replied Urias as he excused himself and left Guzman's study to begin work on a plan of revenge.

Although Chuy Guzman's death had been out of his control, Urias none the less felt bad that he had let his boss down. He would work tirelessly to develop a spectacular plan. A plot far beyond anything the Americano placas could ever imagine. And as his Jefe had directed, Sheriff Matt Fremont, his deputies and the troublesome Texas Ranger would all die.

The next morning bright and early Adolfo Guzman was quietly enjoying his first cup of coffee in his study. Urias knocked on the door and requested permission to enter. The enforcer had not slept the previous day or night working on his plan.

"Buenos Dias, Jefe, I think I have the outline of a plan and a list of things I will need for you to review," said the enforcer.

"Good. Café, Toro?" asked Guzman, offering his henchman a cup of dark Mexican coffee.

"Si, gracias, Jefe. Here is what I have so far," Replied Urias, placing an outline in front of his boss.

"First, is the method of making sure the information about Tres Paises smuggling in a very large quantity of drugs into Gila County reaches Sheriff Fremont.

"Our soldier who was wounded in the shootout at the cantina in Las Brisas has provided us with the identities of three people who were with Wade Justus the night when the man was wounded, and our two soldiers were killed by the ranger. One is the local Catholic priest; one is a man with metal legs and the third is a local helicopter pilot.

"*Go on*," said Guzman.

"Well, I have made some calls with our new point man in Las Brisas. He made some inquiries of his locals and has told me that all three of these men frequent this cantina called the Roadrunner. The place is run by an ex-puta. It seems that one of our men tried to extort the woman into selling her cantina. This Justus character apparently objected to the manner in which the offer was made and this is what led to the confrontation and gunfight," explained Urias.

"And so, the importance of these men in your plan is what exactly?" asked Guzman.

"Jefe, my thought is that we send in a couple of our men on a night when any of these three men were inside the cantina. Our men could sit next to the priest or these other men. Then they could speak among themselves about a major drug shipment coming across the border in Gila County with me being with the drugs. If any of those three men were to overhear the conversation about the drugs, they would no doubt tell Sheriff Fremont," Urias.

"This is an interesting idea that might work. How do you propose to arrange this surreptitious exchange of information about the drugs?" asked Guzman.

"I don't believe it will be difficult, but timing is everything, senor. I will simply have our men surveil the Roadrunner cantina. When they observe any of these men to enter, they will follow directly and commence the ruse," replied Urias.

"So once the sheriff has this information about the drug smuggling and you being present, our trap is set. What is your plan to eliminate our enemies?" asked Guzman.

"This is where your influence, resources and finances come in, Jefe. I plan to use all of the men I already trained who were involved in the operation to rescue Chuy. They are all well-equipped. I will be adding a few more men as well with expertise in the use of heavy machine guns.

"I have planned our engagement with the sheriff, his men and this Wade Justus as a military operation. For this we will need military-grade vehicles and what are referred to as "mechanicals," explained the enforcer as he now handed a list of required equipment to his boss.

"Explain," replied the intrigued drug lord, now reviewing Urias' list.

"Mechanicals are four-wheeled pick-up trucks with heavy machine guns mounted in their truck beds. They are not armored, but the benefit in using them is in their speed, maneuverability and lethality. They can carry four heavily armed soldiers plus the machine gunner in the bed. I will want four of them. They are not hard to build. We currently have two military heavy machine guns in our arsenal that are Soviet, and Chinese made. However, we will need to buy four more from our Mexican military contacts.

"Next, I will want two narcotanques. These are the moderately armored vehicles you have parked on the roadway. These vehicles have turrets for mounted heavy machine guns, bullet proof windshields and can carry heavily armed soldiers. There will be one of these for each of us, should you decide to join me, mi Jefe," said Urias.

"I see, Toro. This is something that I may be interested in. I would enjoy seeing you and your men slaughter the sheriff, his deputies and their Texas Ranger mercenary. In this way, I could recover some of my dignity and respect from my family in avenging our Chuy," replied the now smiling Guzman.

"I thought you might like to be involved, mi Jefe," replied Urias.

"Tell me, Toro, how long would it take for you to put together your army," asked Guzman.

"Well, senor, we already have the narcotanques here. In addition, I will need two or three RPG's in the event that we need to take out any police vehicles the sheriff and his men bring with them. They would come in handy against other agencies who try to assist them," explained the enforcer.

"How do you plan to move these special vehicles and men into position. How would they cross the border without being detected by the Mexican Army or the Americans?" Asked Guzman.

"I have anticipated your question, Jefe. First of all, the mechanicals will be easy to obtain. Like I said, they are just heavy-duty off-road capable pick-up trucks with mounts for heavy machine guns.

In America, there are associations for recreation vehicles referred to as "off-road vehicle clubs." The Americans use them to compete in climbing over rough terrain and racing in the desert. It is mostly young men who do this. Our soldiers are all military-aged young men. We will simply disguise the mechanicals as an off-road vehicle club. These trucks can be stolen in the region, built up and disguised as off-road competition vehicles. We can mount the heavy machine guns in their beds in our hanger at the Las Cruces Airport," explained Urias.

"And the narcotanques, Toro. How do you propose to get these monsters across the U.S. border?" asked Adolfo.

"Well, this will also not be as challenging as it seems. We

will simply disguise them as Mexican Army armored command vehicles. Of course, I will need your influence with our military contacts to make sure that Mexican military patrols stay clear of the border in the Gila County sector.

"We will keep the armored vehicles concealed on the Mexican side of the border until four hours before our drug smuggling operation ruse goes down. Then we will cross at the shallowest section of the river and meet up with the mechanicals and the bulk of our men at a location I am having surveyed right now. I will make sure that our men and equipment are all in position long before the sheriff and his men begin their surveillance for our smugglers," explained Urias.

"And how will you spring the trap, Toro?" Guzman asked.

"I am going to use three off-road trucks with snorkels with six men as our decoy smuggling team. They will cross the river again at the shallowest position. When the sheriff and his men move in to arrest the decoys, that will be our cue to attack. The sheriff, his men and this Wade Justus will be caught in the middle with no place to retreat to. Then our trap is sprung, and victory will be yours, Jefe. We will cut them to pieces," explained Urias quite confidently.

Adolfo Guzman studied his enforcer's plan and list of needed equipment carefully for a couple more minutes. He took a long puff on his Cohiba Behike, staring out the large window of his study for another moment, pondering the risk versus reward before he responded.

"Si Toro, we will proceed with this plan. I will immediately arrange for everything. I will also put you in touch with our contacts in the Mexican Army to ensure that our trip to the U.S. southern border in Gila County is not impeded. You will have everything you need shortly," replied Guzman, satisfied that he was making the right decision.

"This will be an amazing victory, Jefe. We will be unstoppable, I promise," replied Urias.

"I'm counting on it, Toro. We must avenge our Chuy. I need to restore my family's trust in me. Now go and make things ready. What is the date you have planned for our battle with the Gringo placas?" asked the drug lord.

"Seventy-two hours from now, Jefe, if our men are able to tell their story and it gets back to the Sheriff. We must strike quickly before the federales have time to regroup and assist Sheriff Fremont. We need the Sheriff to be under-manned and outgunned," replied Urias.

"Three days from today, bueno, Toro. Make it happen and keep me informed," said Guzman before waving his enforcer out the door of his study.

Uberto Urias left Guzman's study with a new spring in his step. Adolfo Guzman gazed out the window of his study overlooking the burnt hillside where his favorite nephew had been incinerated. He drew long, pensive breaths.

"You will be avenged, my Chuy. We will kill them all. I promise you we will slaughter them all," whispered Adolfo through the open window.

CHAPTER 29

Setting the Trap

LOCAL INTERNET PODCAST and private radio sensation Johnny Wake was in his thirty-five foot Class-A motorhome "production studio." He was preparing his equipment for the evening's *"Wake-Up America!"* radio broadcast. Johnny was going to lead with a couple of breaking news southern border stories he needed to get out pronto.

Johnny began prepping for his show. He set and tested his Yeti mic, adjusted the sound level on his sound board and donned his Bose 350 acoustic head set. Next, he programmed the digital timer for his first five minute segment before he would go to a two minute commercial break. Johnny next cued his twenty seconds of beat thumping, heart pounding intro music, came out of the musical bridge and began.

"Wake-Up America! Breaking news out of San Antonio, Texas. San Antonio PD and Texas DPS officers responded out to a report of a suspicious tractor trailer truck abandoned off of Highway 35 and the 1604 in the more rural northeast section of the city. Upon reaching the vehicle the officers heard banging and the cries of people in distress emanating from the interior of the attached trailer. Opening the rear doors they were horrified to find piles of dead bodies inside with only sixteen survivors.

"Turns out the trailer was filled to the brim with UDA's who had been trafficked over from Mexico. The death toll is now confirmed at fifty-three including eight women and children. The sixteen survivors included twelve women and four children, all of whom have been hospitalized.

"Law enforcement investigators including the DHS have

determined that the truck passed through the Laredo, Texas checkpoint and then traveled 150 miles to San Antonio. Police have now arrested two suspected human traffickers from San Antonio. Both suspects are UDA's out of Mexico. This is going down as the worst human trafficking death toll in our nation's history. I'll keep you up to date on any new developments. Keep it tuned to "Wake-Up America" on FM 103.5. I'm your host, Johnny Wake.

"In more southern border news, the Department of Homeland Security's Customs and Border Patrol reports today that last month saw our highest UDA interdiction numbers to date. The agency reports that they detained 239,534 UDA's attempting to illegally cross into the U.S. This astonishing number actually surpasses last month's previous highest number of UDA's which was 235,500.

"If you add up the UDA's who have been apprehended by the CBP over the past four months of this year, they exceed by almost 10,000 the total population of the state of Alaska at 720,000. Scary numbers when you understand that we haven't even hit our peak summer season when illegal aliens from over 150 nations make the dangerous trek through Central America, Mexico and across our perilous southern border.

"I'll be back with this month's drug interdiction stats from CBP and the DEA, right after this commercial break. I'm Johnny Wake and this is "Wake-Up America" on FM 103.5."

At the end of his three-hour news and opinion program, Johnny followed his normal security protocol. To avoid detection, he packed up his radio equipment and moved his RV five miles to another location.

Johnny wasn't afraid of FCC agents storming his RV. He had a valid FCC radio communications license and station identifier. What he was concerned about was being discovered by the Juarez, Sinaloa or Tres Paises drug cartels.

Years earlier, one of the cartels had firebombed his Las Brisas radio station in the middle of the night as a warning. *Stop reporting on cartel activities in New Mexico, Arizona and Texas* was the message spray painted in red on the sidewalk in front of the burned out office. The message was not lost on Johnny. However, the arson did not deter him from continuing to produce his daily program. Johnny continued to relentlessly slam the drug cartels as well as inept, corrupt politicians on both sides of the border.

Johnny reached his pre-arranged destination and uncoupled his Jeep Wrangler Sport from the RV's rear tow bar. It was time to drive into town for a beer or two and get some chow. It was Wednesday hump-day evening. That meant that his old friend and fellow vet Black Jack Stryker would be at the Roadrunner Saloon. Johnny and Black Jack had a standing weekly hump day get together for dinner and drinks at the saloon.

Johnny pulled up in front of the Roadrunner just after 6:30 pm. He spotted Stryker's military surplus Humvee with its Valkyrie Helicopters logo on the driver's side door parked across the street. Johnny sauntered into the saloon and greeted the owner Sally DuBois. The matron was positioned behind the bar attired in one of her many sensual and revealing, low cut numbers.

"Yo, Sally! You look absolutely stunning in that blouse. Muy caliente, girl," said Johnny placing his hand under his t-shirt, making a thumping heart gesture.

"Well, thank you sir. I wore it just for you," Sally laughed. "Stryker beat you here, he's in the far corner," gestured Sally. "Can I bring you your usual?" she asked.

"By all means and one for my compadre as well. How's the brisket tonight?" inquired Johnny as he walked over to the far corner to greet Stryker.

"Never better, sweet pea," said Sally.

"Well then fix me up a plate. I'm feeling like a big spender tonight," laughed Johnny.

"That will be the day. Two PBR's and a brisket dinner coming right up," said Sally.

Stryker acknowledged Johnny with a salutation, "Caught your late afternoon program as I was leaving work and driving over. You'd better keep moving that RV of yours after each time you hammer those cartel shits with your breaking news stories. One of these days, amigo… One of these days," remarked the helicopter pilot.

"Already moved it. Fuck those assholes. It's my private war. I ain't losing any sleep over it," replied Johnny.

"Well, we all have our own private wars with those pendejos," said Stryker in return.

Sally DuBois sashayed over to Stryker's and Johnny's table with a platter in one hand and two PBR beers in the other. She leaned in close to Johnny, intentionally brushing her large breasts up against the side of his cheek as she placed his brisket dinner in front of him.

"Caught your show on the radio this afternoon. Good stuff. Keep it up. You're the man," said Sally, flirtatiously winking at Johnny.

It was hard not to stare at Sally's cleavage. Sally noticed the stare, smiled and looked over at Black Jack and asked, "And whatta you have tonight, lover?"

"Me, I'll have the breasts, of course... You still got those bar-b-que'd chicken breasts on the menu?" Stryker replied, smiling directly at Sally.

"Well, hope you came hungry because there's more than enough to enjoy. You're gonna need both hands," Sally chuckled.

"Well, then the breasts it is. Plump 'em up and bring 'em to me," laughed Stryker.

"On the way," said Sally as she swished away slowly, making sure both men got a good look at her nicely curved rump.

The Roadrunner began to fill up with patrons. Sally's Wednesday Humpday $3 PBR beers special was always a hit during hard economic times. Sally was getting overwhelmed at the bar, so she yelled over to Stryker that his order was up. Black Jack ambled over to the bar, grabbed his order and another round of beers and returned to his table.

Stryker and Johnny immersed themselves in small talk about their days in various combat theaters. Distracted by Sally, the men didn't notice the two military-aged Mexican males with short-cropped hair walk in and take a table next to them.

Over the background noise of people conversing and country music playing on the jukebox, Stryker's keen ear caught portions of the conversation in the adjacent booth in Spanish mixed with

English. The Mexicans appeared to be discussing drugs. In fact their topic of subdued conversation was a sizable drug shipment that was to be coming across the border in three days.

Stryker tapped Johnny Wake's forearm and motioned with the slight turn of his head towards the adjacent booth. Then he tapped his ear, indicating that he wanted Johnny to listen in.

"I hear it's going to be the biggest shipment of drugs yet," the first man said to his partner.

"Yes, in three days everyone is going to get high. Five hundred thousand fentanyl pills, 250 kilos of meth and 10 kilos of the new drug ISO. We are going to flood Nuevo Mexico y Arizona with our drugs, and we are going to be rich," whispered the second man.

Johnny looked back at Stryker with a perplexed look. He had captured the words *"drugs, fentanyl, meth, ISO"* and *"three days,"* but the rest of the conversation was lost on him. Stryker was now intently following most of the conversation between the two men.

The first man leaned forward towards his partner across the small table in the booth, whispering just loud enough to be heard in Stryker's and Johnny's booth.

"I hear Toro is going to be personally accompanying this drug shipment. It's too important for anyone else to be trusted," he said.

"That makes perfect sense. Where will they cross the border?" asked the partner.

"I was asked to find a crossing spot. It will be at the Rio Brisas, one kilometer west of the place where Chuy was captured. It is shallow enough there for trucks," replied the first man.

Stryker was deep in concentration. He took a pen out of his shirt pocket and began writing some brief notes on his paper napkin. *"Huge drug shipment, Rio Brisas, one click west. Where Chuy was busted. Shallow place. Trucks, meth, fentanyl, Iso. Toro. Three days from now."*

Both of the Mexicans finished their beers, got up from their table and walked out of the saloon without looking at Stryker or

Johnny.

"Jesus, what the hell was that all about?" Johnny asked Black Jack.

"Young man, what we just overhead were plans for a major drug shipment coming across the border into Gila County. I gotta tell Sheriff Fremont about this right now. You head back to your place. I'm gonna call Fremont and fill him in," replied Stryker.

Sheriff Matt Fremont and Wade Justus were enjoying a cold beer out on the back porch after a pleasant dinner when Matt's cell phone rang. He looked down at the display, saw "Stryker," and picked up and put the call on speaker.

"Jack, what can I do you for?" Matt said into the phone.

"No, Sheriff, it's actually what I might be able to do for you," said Stryker.

"Pray tell. What would that be?" asked Matt.

"Well, Johnny and I usually have dinner together at the Roadrunner on Wednesday evenings. We're tucked into a corner booth and telling war stories. All of a sudden, I catch a conversation over in the booth next to us between these two Mexican fellas that raised my antennae. As the conversation became more interesting, I started taking some notes on a napkin. I still have it if you need it," replied Stryker.

"Go on, what were these fellas saying that caught your attention?" asked Matt.

"Well the essence of the discussion was that there is going to be a large shipment of drugs coming into Gila County three days from now. It's apparently being brought in with trucks. I definitely caught the types of drugs and weights. It's heavy duty, man," said Stryker.

"What kinda dope are we talking about?" asked Matt.

"I wrote it all down, one guy said five hundred thousand pills of fentanyl, 250 kilos of meth and 10 kilos of that new drug called ISO. That's some major weight, Sheriff," replied Black Jack.

Overhearing the conversation, Wade spoke up.

"Stryker, Wade here. I'm with Sheriff Fremont. Can you tell me what these two guys looked like?"

"Hi Wade, sure can. I know the type. Military-aged males in their mid-thirties, short cropped dark hair, and looked like they were pretty fit. I made em for ex-military, probably cartel soldiers, but very low-key," replied Stryker.

"What else did you hear?" asked Matt.

"Well again, like I said. These guys said that the shipment was coming over in three days. They mentioned a shallow crossing at the Rio Brisas about one click west of where your guys popped those Tres Paises smugglers. One of the guys said he had been given the job of scouting out a crossing point. He found this shallow place where the trucks could cross.

I also caught a name of the guy who's going to be in charge of accompanying the drugs this time. Let me check my notes. I heard the name "Toro" mentioned," explained Black Jack.

Upon hearing the name "Toro," Matt Fremont and Wade looked at each other at the same time.

"Jack, run that name past me again," said Matt.

"I'm pretty sure the one guy said the name "Toro," it means bull in Spanish. At least that's what I wrote down, Toro. The other guy said that the shipment was too important for anyone else to be bringing it across," replied Stryker.

"Did they talk about anything else you can remember?" asked Matt.

"Nope, that was pretty much it," replied Stryker.

"Now you guys hang pretty frequently at the Roadrunner. You guys ever seen those two Mexicans in there before?" asked Wade.

"Nope, never seen either one of 'em before," replied Stryker.

"Do you think they knew you or Johnny?" asked Matt.

"Hard to tell, but they really didn't pay us no mind. Tell you the truth, we never even seen 'em come in and sit down. We were eating and drinking at the time. We wasn't paying no attention.

Afterwards, they just finished their beers, got up and left. They never even looked at us and I was not gonna give anything away by staring at them," explained Stryker.

"I think you played it well, Jack. Thanks very much for the tip. I'll call you if I need anything else," said Matt.

"Got ya, Sheriff. Me and Johnny are always available if you need us. All you have to do is call. Have a good evening," said Black Jack before hanging up.

After hanging up, Matt looked at Wade. "So what do you make of all of that?" he asked.

"Sort of hard to tell. A couple of military looking Mexicans who obviously aren't from around here walk into the Roadrunner and just start discussing a major drug smuggling operation? In a crowded room of other people including other Mexicans they obviously don't even know?

"Even an idiot has gotta figure that the gringos in these parts can grasp some of what they're talking about. I'm not so sure about this, Matt. Sounds a bit hinky to me. But it definitely has got to be followed up," said Wade.

"I'm with you. The problem is that just who do I go to for confirmation. I guess I could call Cecil McKenry over at DEA to find out if he's heard anything," replied Matt.

"Pretty sure McKenry has got his hands full with nearly his entire squad slaughtered at Checkpoint Delta this week. Running down rumors of dope smuggling operations in Gila County is going to be pretty low on his list of priorities.

"This information sounds pretty fresh and time sensitive to me. I think you ought to prepare for any eventuality and sounds like you only have two days to do it in," said Wade.

"I'm with you there, partner. I've got a couple of cards I might be able to play here to at least BOL for any narcotics smuggling activity out of Mexico. At least that might be able to give us some advance warning in the event that the operation actually goes down. If Tres Paises is going to be humping major weights of fentanyl, ISO and meth across the Rio Brisas into Gila County, it's got to be all hands on deck.

"You and I both know that if the powers that be wanted to, they could mobilize sufficient agents to help us. But, it's doubtful that they are going to do that in this case. Both Cecil and Katie are indicating that there's pushback from above. The administration is probably gun shy after losing so many agents. Maybe they think the optics are bad for them right now. Who the hell knows?"

"There's another thing that both intrigues and concerns me. Sounds like our nemesis Toro Urias, Adolfo Guzman's chief enforcer is going to be personally involved in the smuggling operation. I haven't forgotten about what he did to Jessie. I've got a score to settle with that piece of shit," said Matt.

"Doesn't it strike you as odd that this new intel is just a bit too convenient? I mean, a couple of Mexicans, Jack Stryker makes for ex-military just suddenly show up at the Roadrunner. Two guys that Jack and Johnny Wake have never seen before? Those guys hang there all the time. The place is crowded, and these two hombres just strike up a conversation about what should be a very covert op while they're having a couple of beers, surrounded by people who could easily burn them?

"If you believe Stryker and I do, the stuff these two guys were discussing could easily get them both killed by the cartel if the operation was compromised. I got a strange feeling about this, Matt," said Wade.

"Again, I'm tracking with you, Wade. Everything you're saying pops up red flags. But as the Sheriff here, I gotta consider every bit of intel we get as possibly the real deal.

"Tomorrow, I'm gonna make some calls. Cecil McKenry will be my first one. We'll find out if Cecil has the 4-1-1 on this. If he doesn't, I'm gonna make a couple more calls to make sure we stay ahead of Tres Paises just in case this is some sort of set up.

"We have to keep in mind that Adolfo Guzman has got a hard-on for you, me and everyone who had anything to do with barbecuing his favorite nephew Chuy," explained Matt.

"You'll get no argument from me on that plan. I'll talk with you tomorrow morning. I'm going back to the guest house and crash," said Wade.

"Manana, compadre," replied Matt and both men turned in for the night.

CHAPTER 30

Aces Up Our Sleeves

THE NEXT DAY bright and early, Matt phoned Cecil McKenry to find out if he had heard anything about any drug smuggling operations scheduled for Gila County.

"Hi Sheriff. What's up?" the agent asked.

"Sorry to bug you at this time. I'm sure you have a lot on your plate, but I've got an important question to ask," replied Matt.

"So ask ahead," said McKenry.

"We got a recent tip from a reliable source who says they overheard a couple of military-aged Mexicans talking about a major drug smuggling operation going down in my county the day after tomorrow. Uberto Urias's name was mentioned, and my source says he's never seen these guys before in town," explained Matt.

"Urias, as in Uberto "Toro" Urias, Adolfo Guzman's top killer?" McKenry asked.

"One in the same. Heard anything that we might need to know about?" asked Matt.

"Not so far. I think that is something our CI's would have told us about. What have you heard?" asked McKenry.

"Our source says that Tres Paises is set to move some major weights of fentanyl, meth and that new synthetic opioid ISO into my county day after tomorrow. It's said that Urias is personally accompanying the shipment. For sure, nothing on your end?" Matt asked again.

"Negative, my friend. Look, information like this would mean a high dollar pay-off for any of our CI's. They know that. I guarantee you that they would want to tell us about this and cash in," replied McKenry.

"Makes sense, Cecil. Look, you know I only have a half-dozen deputies here, If this happens to go down, can you lend me any support?" asked Matt.

"Unfortunately, no can do, Matt. As much as DEA would want to jump into this with both feet because that murdering asshole Urias might be involved, it's not gonna happen. I just lost six of my best agents at Checkpoint Delta. Our agency's administration is reeling. It's gonna take weeks for us to get new agents over here. If we do get new agents, they will more than likely be rookies. Who would voluntarily want to come to Las Cruces or El Paso after this?

We've been ordered to just stay on top of cases we are already adjudicating. Why don't you try CBP. Maybe they can lend you a few of their agents," suggested McKenry.

"Hey, I understand. I get it. I'm sorry for your loss. I had to ask though and thanks for the suggestion. I'll call my contacts at CBP to see if they've heard anything and can help if we need it. Prayers out for your people. Talk soon and be safe out there," said Matt.

"You too, my brother. And you and yours be safe as well," said McKenry before hanging up.

In Matt Fremont's mind, there was absolutely zero doubt who his next call would be to. He brought up his speed dial and touched "KB," and on the second ring CBP Assistant Chief Katie Blackwater picked up.

"Katie, it's Matt Fremont. Got a minute?" the Sheriff asked.

"For you, all the time in the world. What's up?" she asked.

"Well, I'd like to run a couple of things by you. First, is that we just received some intel from a reliable source you know who called me last night. He said that he was in the Roadrunner Saloon over here in Las Brisas. Says he overheard a conversation between a couple of Mexicans about a major drug shipment coming across the border from Mexico here in Gila County day after tomorrow. Have you guys heard anything about this?" Matt asked.

"Well, I just had my morning briefing. No one brought this up including our intelligence agents from the field. What have you heard and who's your source if I may ask?" Katie asked.

"Jack Stryker. Says he was with Johnny Wake at the Roadrunner Saloon here in Las Brisas last night when a couple of Mexicans he made for ex-military came into the place. They had some beers and were talking about a heavy weight shipment of fentanyl, ISO and meth coming in over the border near where we snagged Chuy Guzman almost two weeks ago. Stryker told me that the men mentioned the name "Toro" as the lead guy bringing over the dope.

The only guy we know who has the street name of "Toro," is Uberto Urias, the chief enforcer for Adolfo Guzman. As you already know, Guzman heads the Tres Paises drug cartel," Matt explained.

"You're telling me for sure that Stryker told you the Mexicans said "Toro" or Urias was bringing in the dope?" Katie asked with her voice elevated.

"Yup. I thought the same thing, so I asked Stryker to confirm. He did. He even had the name "Toro" written down on a bar napkin so he wouldn't forget the name," replied Matt.

"Well, I know Stryker from our off the books op with your son. Our intel is that Urias led the assault team who murdered our people along with the U.S. Marshals and DEA agents at Checkpoint Delta. If this 4-1-1 isn't bullshit or a set-up, I want in. Only there's a problem on our end," said Katie.

"What's the problem?" asked Matt.

"Well, for one, after the slaughter of our agents at Checkpoint Delta, our chickenshit DHS Secretary has reigned us all in. We've been directed to lay low and regroup. DHS/HSI and ICE are depleted working the Delta incident. We're also dealing with that high casualty UDA tractor-trailer death case out of San Antonio. We just don't have the agent's to spare for what might or might not be a drug smuggling operation in your county.

"With this newest border surge going on, most all of our field assets are playing 'Just herd the UDA's and process them' game. It's total administrative, social service bullshit that our agents are neither trained nor equipped to deal with. Our field force has now been spilt up supporting migrant captures in the Del Rio, Eagle Pass and Tucson ports of entry. I'm doing all I can right now just to maintain minimum staffing in my region of New Mexico. This whole thing's a cluster fuck. Even if I wanted to give you some agents, I just don't have 'em," said Katie.

"Katie, I get it. I just heard the same thing from Cecil McKenry over at DEA. Both of your agencies have taken major hits, so I completely understand you not being able to lend us some people to interdict these drugs," said Matt in a somewhat dejected voice.

There was silence on Katie's end of the phone for a long minute while the CBP Assistant Chief mulled things over. This was Uberto "Toro" Urias, no doubt the mastermind behind the massacre of CBP agents. Agents she knew and had worked with. Men with families and futures. All gone now.

Katie pondered her predicament and her future with DHS and CBP. This had to stop. Brave men, tens of thousands of American citizens and hapless UDA's including innocent women and children. All being indiscriminately murdered, maimed, raped and sold into sex trafficking rings because of men like Urias and Adolfo Guzman. No one in the current administration including DHS was lifting a finger to stop this war on America and its people. It was time to push back, to go rogue.

Matt Fremont spoke into the phone. "Katie, you still there?"

"Yeah, I'm here. I've just been thinking. Look, just because CBP is presently not in a position to help you doesn't mean that I can't be of some assistance," said Katie.

"Where are you going here, Katie? You're a Chief, you're CBP administration. You're leadership. You can't get any more involved than before. That was different. This is different. The two are not the same things. They are different levels of involvement. Helping us on your own could get you canned. You'd lose everything you've worked for your entire career; your job, you're pension, benefits, the whole enchilada. Hell, with this administration, they would probably prosecute you," replied Matt.

"Matt, look, you didn't have any compunctions about pulling out all of the stops when it came to rescuing your son Jessie. At least your son's alive and well. I lost six men under my command at Delta; six men for God's sake!" said Katie as she raised her voice over the phone.

"So far, this administration hasn't done squat to hit back at Guzman except to incinerate his nephew Chuy. Yeah, Miranda Prescott told me. One fucking cartel piece of shit, when I've got six men who are never returning to their families again. Six fucking funerals and six fucking American flags draping their coffins I'm gonna see when I attend them.

"I'm the CO who will have to hand those flags to each of their wives and families. I'd be sick to my stomach looking everyone one of those family members in the eye, knowing I didn't do a damn thing to avenge their deaths. The way I figure it, I'm no leader to my people if I'm not fully engaged in going after the people responsible for butchering my men.

"So here's the deal, I'm all-in. I've got a couple of ideas that as you like to say are "off the books." According to Stryker, I've got two days to do it. That actually means that I have only 24 hours to make some arrangements to provide you with some proactive and reactive support," said Katie assuredly.

"Like what kind of support? What are you thinking, Katie?" Matt asked.

"Well, this could be the real deal, a major drug smuggling op. Or it could be just BS like many of our tips are. Or, it could be a set up. Any way this pans out, I'm gonna make some calls and see if we can get you and your people ahead of Urias, Guzman and Tres Paises. The less you know right now, the better.

"Just do your thing with your people and keep me posted. Let me take care of things on my end. If I can pull in a couple of favors and line up some resources, I'll call you and we can more forward from there.

"I will promise you one thing, Matt. You and your men are not going into this thing without some aces up your sleeves. My men never had a chance. Not this time, my friend. You and your men are going to have a fighting chance. I'll call you if and when I'm set," replied Katie.

"Well, this was unexpected. Thanks in advance for the help, Katie. I'll work things on my end, and I promise to keep you posted," said Matt before hanging up.

After speaking with Katie Blackwater, Matt called Wade and advised him he was returning back to the ranch for a meeting. After Wade had shown him the bloody photo taken from the dead cartel soldier's pocket, there was no way he was having Wade meet him at the Sheriff's Department. He just assumed that the office was under constant surveillance by Tres Paises.

When Matt arrived, the men had coffee in the breakfast room. Matt began filling Wade in on his morning's activities.

"Well, I called Cecil McKenry at DEA and Katie Blackwater over at CBP. Neither one has heard anything about a heavy weight drug smuggling op going down day after tomorrow in Gila County," said Matt.

"You know these people. What's your sense having worked with both of them on their agency's intelligence capabilities? I know the Texas law enforcement landscape, but not New Mexico or the feds," said Wade.

"Both Cecil and Katie are solid people. Both agencies have pretty good intelligence assets in the field. DEA works their buy cases almost exclusively through CI's, introducing them to dealers and suppliers. They start low and work their way up the chain to the big dealers and suppliers.

"DHS has their Homeland Security Investigations division. The division has a Strike Force headquartered in Las Cruces. They work the same way. CBP gets their intel from UDA's and feeds that information to the HSI Strike Force. The Strike Force in turn shares that information with DEA. It's a symbiotic relationship.

"I just think it's pretty strange that with a supposed major dope smuggling op going down in my county, none of the federal agencies who do this for a living haven't heard zip," said Matt.

"That's what gets me too. How did Stryker and Wake get so lucky as to overhear such critical information? Like I said before,

Stryker makes those guys for ex-military like the two guys who tried to take me out in Deming the other day.

"I mean, anyone could have overheard that conversation, and someone did. You gotta ask yourself, what are the odds of that happening? You know what we used to say in the Rangers; cops hate coincidences, right? So what do you call that?" asked Wade.

"I'm there partner. I'm working on plans to cover both contingencies. The first one is that the intel is legit, Tres Paises and Urias are bringing in a huge shipment of dope. The second one is that it's a set-up. That gives Tres Paises a pretty good opportunity to try to take us out if we try to interdict the shipment. As the Sheriff here, I gotta anticipate and address both options," explained Matt.

"So here's my dilemma and part of my plan. But I'm gonna need your help if you're so inclined," said Matt.

"My problem is that in calling Cecil and Katie, I found that we just can't expect any help from the feds on this one. After Checkpoint Delta, both agencies just don't have the manpower. They've both been directed to stand down until they can regroup with more field agents. Unfortunately, that's not happening any time soon.

"Katie told me that CBP is in even worse shape than DEA. Apparently, their chickenshit Secretary has their agents playing housemaids to a couple hundred thousand UDA's sneaking across the border each month. So, both agencies are definitely out.

"Just between you and me, Katie Blackwater has offered some covert assistance. She just hasn't specifically told me what that might be as yet. I hope to hear from her soon," explained Matt.

"Well, you know I'm staying here with you. I'll help you every way I can. You just tell me what you need and I'm your Huckleberry," said Wade.

"Well, first of all, with a shipment this big and Urias possibly being involved, it's gonna be all hands on deck. That means I've got to involve the entire patrol division. That's six deputies and at least a start," said Matt.

"What about Stryker? That's an air asset. It would be

beneficial to have a bird up as an elevated intelligence platform providing real time intel," offered Wade.

"You read my mind. I'm going to call Jack when we're done. He's already got a score to settle with Tres Paises, so I'm pretty sure I won't have to twist his arm. This is going to be some tricky shit. No doubt Urias and Tres Paises will come armed to the hilt. He might even use some of the same guys he had at Delta. That's a pretty bad ass group of pistoleros," said Matt.

"Well, don't sell your people short. You also have some pretty damn good warriors working for you too. No doubt that Urias and Guzman suspect us in the rescue of Jessie and taking out his men," replied Wade.

"No doubt. So what's Guzman's play here, Wade?" asked Matt.

"My thinking is that either way you look at it, Guzman figures he can turn Gila County into a major distribution center for all things Tres Paises. That means drugs, smuggling in UDA's and trafficking women and kids. To accomplish that, he's got to either bribe or kill his way in.

"Guzman already knows you can't be bribed, so for me the alternative is logical. He's got to kill you and your men. Once you're gone, he can try to bribe whoever takes your place. Toro Urias is the stick if the carrot doesn't work," said Wade.

"Well, we're two days out from Tres Paises coming across our border and I've got a ton of work to do. I'm also gonna change tactics a bit where you're concerned. I'm going on offense a bit. I'm calling everyone in for a special briefing for 1500 hours today. I want you there. I'll have my patrol guys sweep the immediate area around the station for any suspicious people who might comprise a Tres Paises surveillance team. I'll have one of my guys pick you up. Tres Paises already know your truck. See you at 1500," said Matt as he walked out the front door.

As he drove off his property, Matt Fremont picked up his cell phone and made two calls. The first one was to his administrative secretary Lisa Owens. He told her to personally call each of his patrol deputies into the station at 1500 hours for a special briefing, no exceptions and no radio traffic. His next call was to Black Jack

Stryker to tell him to expect a visit.

Fifteen minutes later Matt pulled up in front of Valkyrie Helicopters. He found Stryker and Johnny Wake working on Stryker's Hughes 500-D "Little Bird" in the hanger.

"So what brings the Gila County Sheriff to my door. I swear to God that I paid those parking tickets," grinned Stryker as he stepped forward to shake Matt's hand.

Johnny Wake walked over to Matt wearing a set of matching green camouflage titanium prosthetic legs, "I saw nothing, said nothing and heard nothing. If you're here because some woman of questionable character has made accusations, I'm denying everything and making counter accusations," said Johnny grinning as he also shook the Sheriff's hand.

"Well, glad to see that I found you both together. It saves me the trouble of getting a posse to round both of you up," joked Matt.

"Actually, I'm here to ask another favor from both of you. Truth is that I'm in desperate need of your unique skill sets and the use of your Little Bird here, Jack," said the Sheriff.

"Pray tell. So what am I, I mean *we* volunteering for?" asked Stryker.

Matt went over what had transpired since Jack had told him about the two Mexicans discussing a possible major drug smuggling operation going down in Gila County two days hence.

"I have had conversations with DEA and Katie Blackwater. The way Wade and I figure it, Adolfo Guzman is either really going to run some major weight dope across the border here, or it's some sort of set up designed to draw us in and take us all out. I need to plan for both scenarios, fellas. That's where you guys come in, if you want a piece of this," said Matt.

"Tell us more, we're all ears," replied Stryker.

"Well, no matter which situation presents itself, me and my guys are gonna need some eyes in the sky. We'll need some advanced warning on how Tres Paises will be positioning themselves as they cross the border. I'll need to know in advance where exactly they are crossing, how they are setting up and their strength. I figure that you flying the Little Bird can do that for me," explained Matt.

"And what about me; observer in the chopper?" asked Johnny.

"Not exactly. Scenario number two is that Urias and his cartel soldiers will try to ambush us and take us out. Wade and I are pretty sure that these are the same guys that took out the U.S. Marshals, DEA and CBP agents at Checkpoint Delta a couple of days ago. If that's the case, then it's war and I'll need some heavy duty knock down power.

"Your MOS in the Corps was EOD, right? I want you to think of ways that we can disable vehicles and/or blow bad guys up if it comes to that. I'm not even going to ask you if you guys have any explosives laying around here," said Matt.

"Okay, that could happen in a strictly hypothetical kinda way," chuckled Johnny as he and Stryker shared grins.

"The problem is that we only got one day to get things ready. All indications are that this thing is going to go down the day after tomorrow. On the previous occasion, Tres Paises crossed the Rio Brisas after midnight. That means that all of your preparations need to be completed, tested and ready to go no later than tomorrow afternoon. Can you do it?" asked Matt.

"That's sort of a tall order, Sheriff. Not much time for R&D. I'll will get cracking and will give you an update as soon as I have a few things put together," replied Johnny.

"Same thing for me. I've gotta make a few alterations to the bird. It's an improvise, adapt and overcome sort of thing. I've done this a few times before in a prior life, so I'll be ready when you need me. Me and Johnny will need a couple of hours of advanced warning before lift-off if you can arrange that," said Stryker.

Matt looked at both men intensely before he spoke.

"Look fellas, right up front, this is my war, not yours. There's absolutely nothing in it for you. You'll be risking your lives doing this. This is the second time for you, Jack. You could both get yourselves killed. These are tough characters; stone cold killers. Any second thoughts?" asked Matt.

Stryker spoke first, "The way I see it is these cartel a-holes are invaders as much as any belligerent nation coming in to take over our country. Gila County is our beachhead. If we don't stop 'em here, who's gonna do it? Certainly not this administration. Hell, they might as well be working with them the way they've handled this entire fiasco.

"Americans are dying by the tens of thousands from the poison they sneak in here. Millions more families are affected by the loss of their loved ones. The illegals they smuggle in are just an additional, expendable revenue source. Once they've got their money, they could give a shit less about them. Those illegals are dying too. I've got a personal score to settle with these people. I'm down. Whatever you need, I'm here for you," said Stryker.

"Black Jack said it all. Nothing more to add. Let me see what I can dig up. I'll probably have to jury-rig some things, but the testing may be an issue. The stuff I build makes noise. Might have to test it way out in the boonies. I'll let you know what I come up with. If I need any help, I give you a shout," said Johnny.

Matt thanked both men and headed back to the Sheriff's department. He and Wade had plans to make and resources to organize. This was going to be a long day and night.

By the time Sheriff Matt Fremont made it back to his office it was noon. His administrative secretary Lisa Owens was waiting for him.

"All of your deputies have been contacted and advised via landline to attend your mandatory special briefing, boss. You want to let me in on the secret?" asked Lisa.

"Since you're the hub of our wheel here, yes I will. Now don't get alarmed but where do you keep you piece and when was the last time you qualified on the range?" asked Matt.

The fifty year old seasoned secretary raised one eyebrow. "So, where are we going with this line of questioning, Matt? My gun is in my desk, like always. I qualified last month and did fine, ask Blake," she replied.

"This is strictly between you, me, the deputies and Wade. I think we are shortly going to be in the shit with the Tres Paises drug cartel. These are the same thugs who kidnapped Jessie. I'm trying to cover all my bases here. I want you armed from here on until this thing gets resolved. After briefing this afternoon, I'm assigning Blake to take you back out to the range and re-qualify you. I want your handgun and reloading skills up to speed. We're adding shotgun training as well. I want you strapped at all times from here on in," said Matt.

"Are you expecting Tres Paises to assault the station?" Lisa asked.

"No, but I'm covering all options. it's gonna be all hands on deck with me and our patrol deputies in less than two days. That puts you here alone with the corrections deputies when this goes down. We are going to lock down. For security reasons, I'm not sharing this with the jail staff or dispatch until zero hour.

"Tres Paises is smart. They've got us under surveillance. I want no radio traffic because they no doubt have scanners too. I also don't want any big mouths in the jail blabbing about our plans because it's sure to be overheard by the inmates. Once they know, Tres Paises knows, copy?" said Matt.

"Sure Matt. So what gives with the special briefing?" Lisa asked again.

"Short version? We recently got some intel that Tres Paises might be trying to smuggle a sizeable quantity of dope across the border in Gila. I plan to interdict that shipment and bust those assholes.

"Second scenario, this might just be an elaborate trap where Tres Paises tries to draw us in and knock us off. I tried arranging some back-up from the feds, but after their losses at Checkpoint Delta, I've pretty much been told that we're on our own on this one. This is why I want you armed and ready for anything.

"I'm calling in every deputy. Every man is going to count, no matter which situation plays out. The word is that the cartel will try to sneak across our border the day after tomorrow after midnight. We don't have a lot of time to plan and set up," explained Matt.

"Got it. Don't worry about me. I'll be fine here, but I want you to tell Blake to teach me how to use one of our patrol rifles too just in case. I also want the combination to our armory in case we need the jail staff defending the place," said Lisa.

"You got it, Lisa. Now I got work to do. Let Wade in when he gets here," said the Sheriff as he walked down to his office.

Matt had just sat down when his cell phone rang. He looked at the display which read, "KB," Katie Blackwater.

"How you doing, Katie? How did you make out?" asked the Sheriff.

"Actually, not bad. What I've arranged has got to be completely black, if you know what I mean," replied Katie.

"Agreed, can you help us?" asked Matt.

"Affirmative. I got hold of my Air Force contact with the drone. I've already arranged for our MQ-1 Predator to be up for long-range reconnaissance. That's the same CBP drone we used when Chuy Guzman got shot down. I'm also using the same pilot as before because they already know the circumstances and the players.

"I've arranged to have the Predator fly high altitude over the Mexican border. It will go black, transponder off. My contact has placed the drone off-line for maintenance and testing. It's been tasked to run patterns from seventy-five miles south of the border to the U.S. border looking for a small convoy or, trucks; anything irregular. That far out from our border should give you a few hours of lead time to set up to interdict or defend.

"Once any hostile elements cross our border, the drone will come back over to our side and remain on station. The pilot will provide you with real time intel of their strength, resources and movements," explained Katie.

"Wonderful, when is the drone going up?" asked Matt.

"It took off two hours ago," replied Katie.

"That's great, Katie. How will we communicate?" asked Matt.

"Well, we're black so all the normal comm options are out. We're going low-tech and just using burner cell phones. However, If you give me access to one of your guys who might be tech savvy,

I can have my contact network with your person. With the right adjustments, my pilot can transmit video data directly to you on the ground. Like I said, the data link will be real-time video, so all they really have to do is watch and tell you and your people what's up in the field," said Katie.

"Excellent, will do. Anything else?" asked Matt.

"Nothing that I can discuss with you right now. I'm still working on another ace to put up your sleeve. This option is more complicated, so no promises. But you know me; I play to win. Keep me posted," said Katie.

"Will do and you do the same," said Matt before hanging up and making one more call. He scrolled through his contacts and dialed, "Tom Black Arrows."

Thomas 'Fights with a Knife' Black Arrows picked up on the first ring. Matt asked him if he was available for a special meeting at the Sheriff's Department at 1500 hours. He said that his son Jacob was going to be there. Before hanging up, Matt asked Tom to keep the meeting confidential.

Wade got the all-clear that a protective sweep of the area around the Sheriff's Department was negative for explosives, listening devices and suspicious persons. Wade arrived for the briefing at 1430 hours. He was directed straight back to Matt Fremont's office by an armed Lisa Owens. This new addition did not escape Wade, who noted the Glock 17 in a Kydex holster on Lisa's right hip.

"Strapped, Ms. Owens?" asked Wade with a smile.

"Order of the day Ranger Justus. The Sheriff told me to send you right in," replied the secretary, returning the smile.

"By the way, nice piece of iron you got there. I'm suggesting a double mag holster on your left side to match. It's much faster accessing your mags from a holster than trying to pull them out of your pockets," Wade said as he walked past Lisa into Matt's office.

"Afternoon Sheriff. I see you got the hired help packing now," said Wade in his salutation.

"Damn straight. Like I said, all hands on deck, ranger,"

replied Matt continuing.

"So we're doing a special, mandatory briefing at 1500. I want you and Blake Sheridan to help me with the planning and logistics. In the event this is combat, I want my two best battle tested LEO's to help me in plotting strategy, Okay?" asked Matt.

"Sure thing, Matt. What's our manpower and resources so far?" asked Wade.

"The same team as we had for Jessie's rescue, plus Deputies Marcus Carter and Pete Vasquez. So patrol-wise including me, that's seven uniforms since Jessie is now back to full duty status.

"Next, there's you, Jack Stryker and his helicopter. Johnny Wake is handling explosives, plus Jacob Black Arrows dad Tom, who you already know.

"I reached out to Assistant Chief Katie Blackwater over at CBP. She's arranged to get us the same Predator drone and pilot that was used in the black op that shot Chuy Guzman's helicopter down. So that makes a total of ten bodies, one helicopter and one high-altitude drone for advanced observation, and intelligence gathering.

"Katie's promised me that we'll also have real-time communications on enemy strength and movements. I just hooked Tristin up with Katie's drone pilot. Tristin will be our Team's eyes and ears on this one," explained Matt.

"Well, in consideration of all of the shitty things happening with the feds right now, that's not bad for just 24 hours. But you know that if Guzman's out to get us, he'll bring at least twice that many soldiers to try to overwhelm us. By the way, did you say *explosives*?" asked Wade.

"That I did. As you know, Johnny was in EOD in the Corps. If this has the potential of, pun intended, exploding into an all-out war, I want someone on our team who knows how to blow shit up," said Matt.

"Makes sense. So where are the explosives coming from?" asked Wade. "Don't even ask cause I'm sure not gonna.

"So, now that you know what our manpower and resources

look like, what are your preliminary thoughts with respect to engagement and ROE's?" asked Matt.

"Well, as always, we plan for the worst and hope for the best. I suggest we plan and stage for both of the scenarios we've discussed. First, interdicting a drug shipment brought in on trucks. Katie's drone pilot will be of immense help there. We should know well in advance how many vehicles will be coming our way. The drone might even tell us numbers of men with the shipment.

"We set up our interdiction force not far from the river. We let them cross over to establish the elements of illegal international drug trafficking. We use a double flanking maneuver and trap them on our side. When we spring the trap, the truck drivers will have a hard time turning around and re-crossing the river.

"My concern is that we don't know what type of firepower the convoy will have with them. Hell, with cartels, it could be anything from AK's to heavy machine guns, to even RPG's. We gotta plan for the worse there. The most they would have to respond to would be our sniper and patrol rifles," explained Wade.

"Okay, and for the second scenario?" asked Matt.

"Well, the second scenario could actually be part of the first. Soldiers could be hiding in those trucks with heavy weaponry to take out our patrol vehicles and then us. They know that if they can destroy our patrol units, the only way we can escape is on foot. They could easily catch up to us and take us out one by one at their leisure.

"With the Predator drone and Stryker's chopper, we would have elevated platforms providing us with advanced notice of the cartel's strength, types of vehicles and their locations. No one is going to be sneaking up on us for an ambush, or a pincer maneuver with a crossfire.

"So what do you suggest for the second scenario?" asked Matt.

"Well, the worst thing that they might try to do is use their drug convoy as a distraction while we're busy trying to deal with an arrest. They could pincer us either by attacking both of our flanks, or by attacking us from our front and rear simultaneously. The drug trucks would be in front of us, and a second attacking element would hit us from behind.

"If we had advanced warning, we could covertly insert a sniper-observer team, say Blake and Tristin a hundred or more yards away from our main element on our right flank. We then put Black Arrows and Johnny Wake the same distance away on our left flank. Sheridan and his sniper rifle would not have much difficulty taking out soldiers and vehicles attacking from our rear.

"Blake could also hit and possibly disable the trucks in front of us. We'll need another force projection weapon system on our left flank for Jacob to shoot. I'm thinking a grenade launcher. I'll ask Blake about that. If Wake could rig up a larger IED or two, our fellas could wreak some havoc and give us a fighting chance.

Of course, then there's you, me and your two additional patrol deputies doing double duty defending against front and/or rear attacks. We would probably have to divide up at that point in the attack and pick our targets based upon priorities," explained Wade.

"IED's? How the hell would Wake be able to make IED's for Christ's sake?" asked Matt.

"Isn't this a mining region? Should be able to find some explosives somewhere. But like you said, don't ask," replied Wade smiling.

"Oh, and one more thing. This is your county, your department and you're the Sheriff. I don't set the ROE's, you do. So if it's scenario number two and all-out war, then for me it's kill or be killed. In that case, I know what I'm gonna do. I'm just a civilian these days. I don't have to worry about department use of force policies. You just got to tell the men what to do. They work for you," said Wade.

"Well, then it's gonna be reasonable belief of imminent life threats, disengaging and lower force levels not required. Deadly force justified and approved in advance depending upon the unique and exigent circumstances," said Matt.

"I can live with that. Right out of the Texas Ranger duty manual," replied Wade.

"Where do you think I got my policies from?" laughed Matt.

Okay, your preliminary plan sounds solid. Is this what you intend to present at the briefing?" asked Matt.

"Yup, but I want to run it by Blake. His war experience and tactics are more recent than mine. As our sniper, he's gonna be our point man out there," replied Wade.

Shortly before 1500 hours, Jessie Fremont accompanied by Tom Black Arrows, Black Jack Stryker and Johnny Wake began entering the briefing room. When all were present and accounted for, Matt and Wade provided the men with some background on the intelligence that Stryker had shared with them on the possible Tres Paises' plan to smuggle a large quantity of illegal drugs across the Rio Brisas into Gila County the following day.

Wade had a diagram on the white board detailing a plan of engagement. He began going over the two possible scenarios. The first, a classic drug interdiction and arrest op. The second, a set-up and ambush by the cartel. The men were keenly listening. Everyone was aware of the recent ambush and massacre of federal agents at Checkpoint Delta just outside of Deming.

Wade discussed his plan to divide the men into teams once they arrived and dismounted from their patrol units. Jacob and Tom Black Arrows would ride with Deputies Marcus Carter and Pete Vasquez and would come in from the left flank. Once their vehicle had stopped, Jacob and Tom would quickly assume a forward position on the left flank to guard against any rear attack by any surprise cartel element.

Matt explained that the team would also have covert Predator drone capability for long-range observation and intel in real time, with air to ground communication.

"Did you make contact with the Predator drone pilot, Tristin?" Wade asked.

"Affirmative, Ranger Justus. I'll have a data link for video with positions, ranges and directions in real-time and directions via cell phone from the pilot," replied Tristin. The men were duly impressed at the mention of a military grade Predator drone supporting them.

Wade continued his briefing, "If the drone video indicates there are no hostile elements to their rear, Jacob and Tom can move up to the main enforcement element. They will assist in taking people into custody or providing cover for arresting officers."

Wade outlined that Jessie Fremont, Blake Sheridan and Tristin Peters would drive together. Jessie would drop the sniper/scout team of Blake and Tristin off much earlier before covertly moving into a right flank position. Blake and Tristin would be dressed in camouflaged Ghillie suits to blend in with the natural terrain and brush. Tristin would also have his backpack portable observation drone for scouting the horizon for cartel members and vehicles.

Blake, armed with his sniper rifle, would provide overwatch for the drug interdiction op, or any surprise ambush. The team would remain in place throughout the operation unless the enforcement element was overwhelmed. In that case, the men would move forward and engage enemy targets at will.

Wade explained that he and Sheriff Fremont would ride together and take the middle vehicle position. Stryker would pilot the Little Bird chopper and Johnny Wake would act as his observer. This way, the team would have real-time observation intel of their immediate environment.

Blake Sheridan chimed in and stressed the value of having interlocking fields of fire. He also discussed the importance of flexibility of movement to engage simultaneous threats from their front and rear positions. So far the battle plan looked well thought out.

Matt asked Stryker how he was coming with the Little Bird.

"Nearly done, boss. Me and Johnny have got a few surprises for Tres Paises if they try anything sneaky," replied Stryker.

"Like what?" asked Matt.

Stryker showed Matt and Wade a photo on his cell phone of his Little Bird with its side doors gone and a heavy machine gun mounted on the starboard side of the aircraft.

"So, what's this?" Matt asked with surprise.

"It's our insurance policy, a Soviet NSV 12.7 mm heavy machine gun. Weighs fifty-five pounds, fires 700 – 800 rounds a minute with an effective range out to 2,200 yards. It'll cut a truck in half if we need to, and mow men down like tall grass," explained Stryker, smiling.

Blake Sheridan came over to look at Stryker's cell phone.

"Oh, yeah. I remember those well from Afghanistan. Nice work Stryker. That'll do the job. I like your style, brother," he said.

"I'm pretty sure that's illegal," said Matt as Wade laughed.

"I only borrowed it. I'm gonna give it back afterwards," replied Stryker chuckling.

"To whom?" Matt asked.

"Well, if you must ask, the Military Museum in Albuquerque. I've got Nam friends over there who are tour guides. I promised I would bring it back in one piece afterwards, so I gotta keep my promise" replied Stryker as the room full of men laughed.

"However, if we ever have to use it from the air, the ground will be littered with empty Soviet 12.7 mm cartridges. Know who is known to use this type of weapon? Drug cartels, Sheriff. We'll be clean and gone. It will be a messy and complicated crime scene for sure," explained the pilot.

"Nice thinking, Jack," said Wade who then turned to Johnny Wake.

"Johnny, you got anything for us yet in the explosives department," Wade asked.

"Yup, I got a couple of things to give us an edge," said Johnny as he picked up a large black Pelican case off the floor. He opened it and removed an intimidating weapon. "For a force projection weapon, I brought this Milkor M240 MGL Multiple Grenade Launcher. Six round capacity with a rotating cylinder. It fires 40 mm explosive grenades with a range out to 400 meters. Very good at blowing up vehicles and people," explained Johnny.

"Great weapon to have. I've used it a few times myself on deployments. Looks and works a lot like our own 40 mm less-lethal munitions launcher. Exact same principle, only extremely lethal," Blake said.

Johnny handed the weapon over to Blake Sheridan. "This is for you, Blake. Think you can handle it?" asked Johnny.

Blake handled the weapon, cleared it for safety and rotated the cylinder. "Yup, almost like our system. Can do," he replied handing the weapon back to Johnny.

"Anything else, Johnny?" asked Matt.

"Well, two things. First, I've concocted a flyable IED for Tristin to attach to his drone. The device made with a couple of two-pound blocks of C-4 has an impact detonator. All Tristin has to do is flip a switch to arm the device and let her fly. Then he simply flies the drone Kamikaze-style into whatever target he has selected and *whammo!* Target destroyed. But unfortunately, so is his drone. Sorry, kid. Just the cost of doing business," Johnny smiled as he looked at Tristin.

"Now, the piece de resistance," said the explosives expert as he walked over to the white board and drew a diagram of a strange-looking device.

"Know what this is?" he asked the assembled.

"Oh yeah, I do, but I don't want to spoil your surprise," said Blake. When no one else spoke up, Johnny continued.

"Well, this is what referred to in my former trade as an "EFP" or an explosively formed penetrator," said Johnny pointing to his crude diagram.

"Sort of looks like an oxygen tank with a concave lid. How does it work?" asked Tristin.

"Well, just to keep this simple for everyone," EFP's were originally developed during World War II as an effective way to destroy tanks and armored vehicles. During the war in the Middle East, the Iranians perfected them, sold them to our terrorists adversaries and also taught the terrorists how to make and use them against our troops.

EFP's are not real difficult to make. You basically take a strong metal cylinder, fill it with high explosive powder, C-4 or Semtex and place a concave shaped piece of strong metal like steel or iron at the business end. When the boosted explosive is triggered, a wave fed by the main explosive is created at the plane of ignition. In turn, the metal plate which is curved inwards becomes deformed into the shape of a slug or rod and accelerates towards the target.

"At short distances, the kinetic energy and velocity are so great that the newly formed projectile is able to penetrate through rolled metal plate. A relatively small EFP like this could easily disable a moderately armored vehicle. We're not talking tanks here," explained Johnny.

"How is the device detonated?" asked Tristin.

"Simple. They can be detonated electronically by using a cell phone which was the terrorist's detonator of choice when I was in EOD. In fact, I lost my legs to one in Afghanistan," replied Johnny, while tapping his titanium legs.

"The second item is a present for Tristin. I'll show you when we get over to Stryker's compound. I want to let the excitement build," said Johnny.

Tristin's cell phone sudden rang. He looked at the display and he immediately picked up holding up his hand to ask for silence. The deputy listened for a moment, zipped open his back pack, removed his iPad and turned it on.

"Copy that. Affirmative. Logging on now, stand by," Tristin said into the phone while the men waited silently.

"I'm up … got it … zoom me in … I see them. Affirmative, north by northwest at 330°, copy your GPS coordinates. I'll advise Sheriff Fremont immediately. Keep us posted. Thanks Eagle, out," replied the deputy into the phone before hanging up. Tristin then addressed Sheriff Fremont.

"Sheriff, our Predator, code named "Eagle" reports a convoy of three light trucks moving in a tight formation sixty miles south of the U.S. – Mexican border. They are traveling at 330° in a northwesterly direction towards Gila County. Eagle advises that the tight formation of the vehicles is consistent with a drug convoy, using an established smuggling route to the U.S. Looks like these might be our people," said Tristin.

"Well, that's good news and validation of the information Stryker and Wake heard at the roadrunner. Looks like this is going to go down as a drug smuggling operation," said the Sheriff.

Wade spoke up. "Agreed Matt, but it's still early in the game. I suggest that we continue to plan for both contingencies just to be safe."

"I second that suggestion," said Blake.

"Agreed, fellas. We're not taking any chances here. We continue with our plans for both scenarios," said Matt.

"Okay, listen up, I need everyone completely geared up with vehicles ready to go no later than 1700 hours. Blake, issue everyone Threat Level III ceramic body armor, helmets, NVG's and plenty of ammo. How many M240 grenades do we have, Johnny?" asked Matt.

"I could only get my hands on four grenades, so Blake will have to make them count," he replied.

"Fine. You will all leave separately and staggered after you get your equipment, weaponry and ammo. I don't want anyone surveilling us getting suspicious. They know we are going to try to interdict the drug shipment, so they already figure we'll come out in a group. What they won't know is how many of us will be out there and what additional resources we'll have to support us.

"We rendezvous at Valkyrie Helicopters at 2000 hours. Make sure that you are not followed. Final weapons and equipment checks there. Once we hear from Eagle on the most probable river crossing point, we'll stagger leaving Valkyrie in five minute intervals and deploy out to the site to wait for them.

"One more thing. We are not using our radios for this mission. It will be radio silence unless I advise you are clear to communicate on the radio. These guys are experienced, and they may have scanners to monitor our radio traffic. We will all use our department issued cell phones with the pre-programmed Uni-channel so we can use them like radios. The bad guys won't be able to hear us, but we can all communicate on the party line. Copy?"

The men nodded affirmatively. "See you there. Now get moving," said Matt.

Wade stayed behind as the men exited the briefing room for

the armory.

"So what do you think, old friend?" Matt asked Wade.

"Well, all things considered, we've done the best with the manpower and tools we got. Let's see how things pan out. We'll deal the hand we're dealt and that's the best anyone can do or expect," said Wade.

As the two former Texas Rangers and partners were walking out the back door, Matt shook Wade's hand.

"Any way this goes down Wade, I just wanna say thanks for being here for me and my men, especially Jessie. It means a lot, partner."

"Hell Matt, you'd a done it for me. You know what we say, "One riot, one Ranger. But in this case, it looks like it's gonna take two rangers," joked Wade, returning Matt Fremont's hand shake.

The two men went out into the parking lot to ready their tactical equipment and make sure that Matt's patrol unit was prepped to go.

Wade went to his truck, grabbed a Pelican hard case, a three-day pack and his Texas Ranger assault vest with the Ranger badge and patch removed over to Matt's patrol unit.

"What's in that case, partner?" asked Matt.

Wade placed the Pelican case in the back of Matt's unit, opened it and removed a cut down AR-15 .223 rifle with a pistol grip green laser light and 800 lumens light with OEG sighting device combo on a Picatinny rail.

"This is my insurance policy. Had it custom made to fit my own specs. It's called a Nichols Custom Commando. AR platform with a shortened ten inch barrel. Light, very maneuverable with low recoil. A real tac driver. A retired gunny sergeant and small arms expert buddy of mine in New Braunfels built it for me. I can made solid hits off handed at 200 yards every time," replied Wade.

"I see you kept your old Ranger vest too," said Matt.

"Yeah, a retirement present. Since it was custom made for me, it wasn't gonna fit anyone else, so the boss said I could keep it. I've got my ceramic plate inserts too. Should stop .308 and AK rounds, hopefully," replied Wade.

"Well, I hope so tonight," said Matt laughing.

Matt stowed his tactical gear in the back. "Let's head over to Stryker's place. It's getting close to spin up time," said Matt. Both men got into the patrol SUV and drove off to Valkyrie Helicopters.

CHAPTER 31

Into the Valley of the Shadow of Death

MATT AND WADE arrived at Valkyrie Helicopters an hour ahead of the deputies and parked near the hanger. Stryker had already pulled out his Hughes 500-D "Little Bird" which remained on his rolling platform. As before, Stryker had blacked out the tail numbers and taped over its navigation lights.

Next to the Little Bird was a duplicate Hughes 500-D helicopter that was also blacked out. However, no heavy machine gun on this bird.

Matt and Wade found Stryker inside the cockpit. Johnny Wake was in the back loading belts of 12.7 mm ammo for the Soviet NSV heavy machine gun. The formidable weapon was bolted down to the floor on the starboard side door area of the aircraft.

Matt walked over to Stryker, "Two choppers, Jack?" he asked.

"Always gotta have a back-up plan when you're flying into a potentially hot zone," Black Jack replied.

Wade walked over to visit with Johnny. "That's the NSV, right?" he asked.

"Sure is. The weaponry of our enemies. Fight fire with fire I say," replied Johnny.

"So, how did you do with the explosives?" Wade asked.

"Not bad. I'll bring them out when everyone arrives. I'll need to spend some time with Deputy Peters and Blake Sheridan, the point man. I gotta fit one IED on the kid's drone and teach Sheridan how and when to set off the EFP," Johnny replied.

"Well, glad you guys are on our side," said Wade.

"Fortune favors the prepared mind. Better to have them and not need them, then need them and not have them," replied Johnny.

"No disagreement with you there, brother," said Wade.

Wade and Matt left Stryker and Johnny Wake to finish up the aircraft. He returned to Matt's patrol unit to re-check and put their own gear on. They would put on their heavy Threat Level III ceramic armor assault vests last. By the time they had readied their weapons and tactical gear, the deputies began arriving. Next came Tom Fights with a Knife who rode in with his son Jacob Black Arrows.

When everyone was present, Matt directed them into the hanger. Once inside, he took Stryker, Johnny Wake and Tom aside.

"Look fellas, I don't know how this thing is going down tonight but I want you all covered liability-wise. Raise your right hands, I'm swearing you all in as reserve deputies for tonight," said the Sheriff.

"You realize that this is going to destroy my well-cultivated outlaw image," said Stryker chuckling.

"I wouldn't worry much about that Jack. Like I said, it's just for tonight. I'm sure that your outlaw image will remain intact," said Matt wryly as everyone laughed.

After Matt had sworn in the civilians, Tristin Peter's cell phone rang. The deputy looked at the display and immediately picked up saying, "Gila up. Talk to me Eagle."

The conversations appeared to be involved. The men gathered around Tristin as he hurriedly pulled out his iPad from his backpack and turned it on.

"Copy, Eagle, opening the link now," said Tristin.

The electronic link sent to him from Major Miranda Prescott aka "Eagle" opened, displaying a large area that encompassed from the Mexican side of the Rio Brisas tributary into Gila County on the U.S. side.

The Predator drone's FLIR was showing real-time images at night in shades of black, grey, and white. The major then expanded the area to show three vehicles moving in convoy formation on the Mexican side of the border. Tristin put Major Prescott on speaker.

"Gila, Gila, this is Eagle. Do you copy? Do you have the link up?" Major Prescott asked.

"Affirmative, Eagle. We see them. What do you think?" asked Tristin.

"These are the same three vehicles I've been tracking since my last report. I put them about ten miles from the river. They match the smuggling profile. As you can see, one is a converted military four by four. The other two are high-rise 4x4's. All three vehicles have snorkel attachments to their engine compartments for river crossings. I didn't see the snorkels before but that's a strong indicator that they intend to cross. Strongly suggest you move into the area to interdict. I can advise when they are ready to cross and give you the GPS coordinates so you can position tactically," replied Eagle.

"Copy that. Will give you a heads up when we are moving out," replied Tristin.

Matt spoke up, "Looks like our smugglers are early. Let's stay with our original plan. Johnny, take Tristin and Blake over to the side and go over the IED's you have with them. Everyone else, it's weapons and equipment checks. Wade will check you out. Once we're done it's saddle up time. Remember who you're driving with and what your assignments are. Questions?" There were none.

While the deputies busied themselves with their weapons and equipment checks, Black Jack Stryker returned to his Little Bird to pre-flight the aircraft.

Johnny Wake went over the technical aspects of the Milkor M240 Multiple Grenade Launcher again with Blake Sheridan and then handed him four 40 mm explosive grenades.

"Keep in mind that four grenades are all you've got. Make 'em count," said Johnny who then showed Blake the Explosively Formed Penetrator IED.

"Remember that you set this charge with the concave steel end facing towards the enemy. Think of it like a cylindrical shaped Claymore mine. Here's the cell phone detonator and it's already programmed to blow. All you do is wait until your target's driver side door is perpendicular to the IED. Then you press the "call" button and wham! Just remember that you don't want to be anywhere near this thing when it blows. Think of it as a Civil War era mortar with a cell phone fuse. Effective but unstable. It could also blow backwards, but hopefully not," the EOD expert explained.

"What's my safety distance?" asked Blake.

"To be safe, I suggest at least 80 yards," replied Johnny.

"Okay kid, you're up next. Where's this drone I'm hearing about?" asked Johnny as he looked at Tristin.

Tristin reached down and opened a large, square, black Pelican case. With two hands, he carefully extracted a carbon fiber heavy lift hexacopter drone and placed it on its landing gear on the ground. With press of a button, he unfolded each of the six arms and unfolded the propellers one by one.

Johnny reached into his own plastic case and retrieved a square shaped device about half the size of a shoe box that was packaged in black, waterproof duct tape. The device had a couple of wires attached to some type of detonation device that was about the size of a carton of cigarettes. There was a small switch and two tiny LED lights, one green and one red adjacent to the switch.

"This is the IED package. It's made of molded C-4 explosive and weighs just under five pounds. How much weight can that drone carry safely?" Johnny asked.

"It's milspecs are a carry weight of five kilograms or eleven pounds. I brought a demo six-pound weight for test purposes," replied Tristin.

"Great, this ought to work. Set your drone up with your weight and let's see how it flies for stability. We don't want this IED blowing up prematurely," said Johnny.

Tristin had built a strong plastic square basket which he had affixed to the bottom of the drone. He placed his six pound weight inside the basket and powered up the drone. Then he grabbed the dual-joystick controller, powered it up and paired it to the drone. In just a few seconds, he had initiated the rotors and throttled up the drone and then hovered it at eye level while checking for any issues or abnormalities.

Satisfied that all components were working properly, Tristin took the drone up to thirty feet AGL and flew in a wide circle pattern to see how the test payload affected the maneuverability and stability of the drone.

With a self-approving nod, Tristin abruptly stopped and hovered the drone thirty yards from the front of Black Jack Stryker's Humvee, which immediately drew the pilot's attention.

Johnny Wake looked at Stryker and grinned, "Okay kid, put the drone into attack mode. Go!"

Before Stryker could say much more than "Hey, wait… Tristin flew the drone at full speed directly towards the front windshield of the Humvee. The drone stopped and hovered less than four feet away from the glass thanks to the LIDAR obstacle avoidance sensors.

"Kaboom! Bye, bye assholes!" yelled Johnny.

"The drone is sometimes mightier than the sword," remarked Tristin.

"Well, I'm sold. Nice flying, kid," said Stryker.

"I'm sold too," said Matt Fremont.

"So how do you make and detonate an IED like this?" asked the curious techy deputy.

"Well C-4 is made from a chemical slurry known as RDX or Research Developed Explosive. It is a very stable compound. You can even burn it and shoot a hole straight through it and it won't blow. Back in 2000, terrorists used C-4 to attack the U.S.S. Cole in the Gulf. They also used it to blow up the Khobar Towers U.S. military housing complex in Saudi Arabia. C-4 is also the favorite explosive used by Palestinian suicide bombers in Israeli occupied territories. Detonating C-4 is a relatively simple affair. You classically use some det-cord or an electronic detonator that provides what is referred to as shock energy to set it off.

"For this occasion, I've rigged a simple pressure switch attached to a blasting cap. See that switch there? Well, when you switch it on in the field, you will see that LED light turn green. It's on, but on "safe." Just before you launch your drone, you are going to flip the switch in the opposite direction, and you will see the other LED light turn red. That means that the device is armed and ready to go.

"All you have to do next is simply fly the drone into the windshield of any armed vehicle they throw at us. Four and a half pounds of military grade M112 C-4 should be enough to disable a vehicle and kill anyone sitting in the front. Of course, your fancy drone here is history too, but that's the cost of doing business," explained Johnny.

It was coming up on 10:00 pm and time to go. Matt Fremont called all of the men together for remarks and a prayer. The men gathered together in front of the Little Bird and Matt asked them to remove covers.

"Men, if you will bear witness with me and Ranger Justus, I'd like to recite from the Good Book, Psalm 23 to bless this mission and all who are about to go on it."

The men bowed their heads with hands clasped together in front of them. Some of the men placed their hands on each other's shoulders for support.

"The Lord is my shepherd; I shall not want. He makes me to lie down in green pastures. He leads me beside the still waters. He restores my soul. He leads me in the paths of righteousness for His name's sake. Yea, though I walk through the valley of the shadow of death, I will fear no evil; for You are with me. Your rod and Your staff comfort me. You prepare a table before me in the presence of my enemies. You anoint my head with oil. My cup runnith over. Surely goodness and mercy shall follow me all the days of my life; and I will dwell in the house of the Lord, forever. Amen."

"Amen," replied the men in unison. Matt continued.

"We are all here as patriotic Americans, law enforcement officers and supporters to vanquish an enemy who has invaded our land and is killing our people. In personal terms, they have tried to kill Jessie and Ranger Justus. They are here to spread their poisonous drugs to kill and enslave our sons, daughters, family, and friends. They are here to take over Gila County and it is my belief that they will stop at nothing to do so. This past week they have killed fifteen of our law enforcement brothers at checkpoint Delta.

"Even though we all wear badges, do you know the history of the law enforcement shield?" Matt asked. None said they knew.

"The history of our badges actually comes from a warrior's shield. In the olden days the Greeks, Romans, Spartans, and Carthaginians carried shields into battle to protect themselves from harm. Knights of the various royal houses carried shields with a coat of arms representing their kingdoms. The shield was carried in the left hand to protect their hearts while weapons were yielded in their right hands. The knights swore a holy oath to defend their people, uphold justice and be loyal to their faith and the royal kingdoms.

"The Spartans had a saying that a warrior came home either holding their shield or being carried home on top of it in death by their surviving brothers. This is why law enforcement officers today wear either a shield or a badge over their hearts. Our oath to protect and defend the United States of America against all enemies both foreign and domestic is sacred.

"I am confident that each of you will do your duty. Obviously, I hope that this will be a drug interdiction and arrest mission. However, if it turns into a fight with armed men, never hesitate for one second to defend yourselves, your brothers, Gila County and the USA.

"These soulless, cartel barbarians intend to kill any and all of us who stand in their way. It must stop. We are the vanguard of safety and security for our county, our state and our nation. As your Sheriff I will do all in my power, and if need be with my last dying breath to end this reign of terror tonight.

"Remember that once we leave this compound, we will all switch to the Unicom app, so we are all communicating on a party line via our department cell phones. That includes our air support.

"May God bless and protect us all tonight. Now let's mount up, take our positions and execute this mission," concluded Matt.

The assembled men shook hands and broke from the circle

in pairs, heading for their assigned patrol units with their tactical gear and weapons.

Matt, Wade and Black Jack Stryker stood together for a moment, watching the deputy sheriffs and newly appointed reserves readying themselves. Stryker was in his glory in his classic shoulder-length pigtails, attired in a well-worn, faded Navy blue Air Cav troopers campaign hat. His uniform for the evening was a faded olive green Viet Nam era military M65 zip-up jacket with Warrant Officer wings and First Air Cav shoulder insignia.

"Nice speech, Sheriff. I was truly touched. I have recited Psalm 23 many times before going out on a mission. It was very appropriate and appreciated," remarked Stryker.

"Thanks, Jack. Good luck to you and Johnny. See you downrange," replied the Sheriff as Matt and Wade took turns shaking his hand.

Stryker turned around towards his Little Bird and looked at his door gunner Johnny Wake. The pilot raised his left hand in the air and twirled his index finger. "Let's spin her up, Johnny," he yelled out to his door gunner who was already strapped in, helmet and comm gear on and ready to go.

Johnny was seated directly behind the NSV Soviet 12.7 mm heavy machine gun with his camouflage titanium metal legs extended outwards under the gun. Acknowledging Stryker, he raised up his left arm, repeating the twirling gesture with his index finger and then gave a thumbs up signal indicating that he was ready.

Stryker entered the cockpit, removed his blue Air Cav trooper hat and replaced it with his own helmet. He reached down for his ancient boom box and flipped the "play" switch. Out boomed Jimmy Hendrix's classic "Voodoo Child" vocal and electric guitar.

> *"Well, I stand up next to a mountain,*
>
> *And I chop it down with the edge of my hand.*
>
> *Yeah. Well, I stand up next to a mountain...."*

Stryker pushed the starter, rolled in the throttle until his gauge showed 15% of fuel, and the engine began to whine. After a few moments he heard the turbine engine roar to life. When engine and rotor gauges were all in the green, Stryker applied left pedal and brought the Little Bird up to a three-foot hover. Stryker then relaxed the pressure he had on the left pedal, and the Little Bird began a slow, right-hand pivot, allow Stryker to ensure all was clear 360 degrees around him. He then added more pressure to the left pedal and pulled in the pitch. The pilot pushed the collective forward and the Little Bird started flying, gaining altitude as he flew over the convoy of patrol units.

While heading for the border, Deputy Tristin Peter's cell phone buzzed. It was Eagle.

"Go Eagle, ready to copy," said Tristin into the phone.

"Gila ground element, be advised your convoy of three light trucks are staged on the Mexican side of the Rio Brisas under a canopy of Cypress trees at GPS coordinates 31°47'00.59 North by 107°56'28.37 West. It looks like they are getting ready to cross. Suggest you position yourselves accordingly and advise once in position. If they move, I'll call you. Eagle, out," said Major Prescott.

"Gila copies, Eagle. We'll get into position and advise. Ground element, out," replied Tristin.

Tristin immediately called Sheriff Fremont's cell and repeated the information that Major Prescott had told him. In turn, Matt asked the units if they were up on Unicom and copied the transmissions. Each unit, including Stryker advised that they were up and copied.

"Guys, when we are two miles out from the Rio Brisas, I want Jessie to drop off our point men, Deputies Sheridan and Peters and proceed to the interdiction rally point. Blake and Tristin will hold our left flank as we face the Tres Paises convoy. Deputies Carter and Vasquez will drop off Jacob and Tom Black Arrows on our right flank and proceed to the rally point.

"Ranger Justus and I will drive directly to the center of the formation. We'll take 'em right after they cross our border. Remain blacked out and use your brake kill switches, copy?" directed the Sheriff. The units responded that they understood.

Jessie spoke up, "I know this property, it's the old Landry

family cotton farm. Nothing but an abandoned house and a large cotton barn about a half mile from the river. Pretty much flat terrain except for some knolls."

Sheriff Fremont got back on the line, "Copy, Jessie. Stryker and Johnny, you guys stay back for a bit until we've got 'em in our sights. We'll use Eagle for overwatch, until then watch our sixes for tail gunners, copy?"

"You got it, boss," said Stryker.

Tristin had his iPad open and was watching the cartel convoy.

"They're still under the canopy, Sheriff. I'm not sure what they're waiting for," said the deputy over the phone.

"Fine with me. Let's get into position," said Matt who turned to Wade and asked, "What do you think they're waiting for?"

"Maybe they know something we don't," Wade replied. He then asked Tristin, "Check with Eagle to see if she sees anything suspicious. Make sure she knows that we have Stryker in the Little Bird just over the horizon. That Hughes 500-D is our bird," said Wade.

"Copy that," replied the deputy, who immediately asked Major Prescott for a status check.

"Eagle to Gila, negative on any other suspicious movements or threats," was the response.

Jessie Fremont dropped off Blake Sheridan and Tristin Peters with their equipment. Sheridan removed the large metal cylinder from the trunk and checked Tristin to ensure he had all of his needed equipment. Blake had checked his gear several times before he left Stryker's compound, so he was confident he had everything he needed.

Blake used his Garmin AB Foretrex to confirm their position and the direction they needed to move. Then he and Tristin began moving towards the position Blake had selected earlier where he could best establish their sniper's hide.

Blake and Tristin maneuvered stealthily for about thirty minutes before Blake signaled that they were at the position to select their hide. He was pleased that his new partner had adapted well and was moving quietly.

The first area that Blake examined was disappointing because there was too much brush. The brush "blinded" them from the terrain surrounding them. They moved to an alternate location that Blake decided was better suited for their hide. Blake directed Tristin to drop his pack while Blake removed his. He then assisted Tristin in removing the IED explosive pack.

Setting a sniper's hide is challenging because it needed to provide them with cover and concealment to protect them, while allowing them to clearly observe the target area. The challenge was making sure that they could see their targets and engage without those targets spotting them. Beyond that, Blake had to make sure that he could position the improvised gas cylinder that contained the Explosively Formed Penetrator towards an enemy armored vehicle. However, he also had to be able to observe the device and the targeted area from their hide.

Blake pointed to the GPS on his wrist, indicating that they would set up at those coordinates. They then returned to their packs. Blake reached into his pack, retrieved his Cobra hood, and told Tristin to remove his as well. After laying their hoods out in front of them, Blake used his pruning shears to trim vegetation from the area. Then he showed Tristin how to stuff his hood to help them blend into the environment.

Once they were both properly concealed, Blake started to set up the rest of the hide. He removed his AllTerra Arms sniper rifle chambered in the 338 Lapua. It was a larger caliber than he normally preferred but this evening he expected to be busy. The larger caliber bullets tended to remove the argument as to who was going to prevail in any engagement. Blake fully intended to win every argument tonight.

Blake attached the bipods to the rifle and set it up facing the area he expected the cartel would approach them. He began cutting the silver sage from behind them and built it up in front of them in order to conceal their silhouettes. He intended to cover everything except for the crown of his barrel and rifle optics. The sniper needed to see what he needed to shoot, while ensuring that his bullets wouldn't strike anything that would push them off course. Once Blake had properly concealed the hide, he reached into his pack and retrieved the finishing touch his rifle needed, his AN/PVS 30 night vision scope.

After Blake had readied his rifle, he removed the hair bands from his wrist and snapped them around the barrel. He then attached just enough bits of vegetation from the area to the bands to conceal the barrel without obstructing the barrel or the scope.

Once Blake was confident he had properly concealed the hide, the sniper performed the finishing touches for operational efficiency. He placed his ruck to his left with the top cover towards him so he could easily reach inside and quickly grab whatever additional gear he needed during any fierce engagement. The sniper placed his M4 carbine and his M203 to his right. To prep the grenade launcher, Blake chambered a 40 mm grenade in the tube, closed it and engaged the safety next to the trigger. *Done!*

While Tristin unpacked his drone with its IED explosive pack, Jessie helped Blake carry and set up the Explosively Formed Penetrator (EFP) about 80 yards from their position.

The two men walked back to the patrol unit and the three deputies shook hands and wished each other luck. Jessie then drove off to the interdiction rally point.

Blake showed Tristin how to put on his Cobra hood and then checked the young deputy's M-4 rifle to make sure all was in order. Tristin unpacked his drone and went through the usual pre-flight checklist. Once that was done, he took a deep breath, reached under the drone and flipped the switch. As he did, the status LED on the IED turned from green "safe" to red "armed."

"Good to go," replied Tristin.

On the right flank of the cartel convoy's estimated river crossing point, Deputies Marcus Carter and Pete Vasquez dropped off Jacob and Tom Black Arrows. Both the deputy and his father were attired in standard desert BDU's with assault vests, side arms and M-4 rifles with EoTec holographic sights. However, being Apache's, Jacob also had his subdued black Hoyt Carbon RX-7 bow and a quiver with 20 black broad-tipped carbon fiber arrows. His father Tom Fights with a Knife also carried an eight-inch warrior's hunting knife which he had personally fashioned as a young Apache brave.

After they had been dropped off, Jacob and his father sat on the dusty desert floor facing each other and applied war paint to each other's faces.

Tom reached down into a beaded leather bag he had around his waist and removed some brown powder that had the scent of sage and smoke. He gave his son half a handful and kept the remaining powder. Jacob knew this Chiricahua tribe warriors ritual well.

"We cannot have a fire tonight my son or we would use smoke. Our white brothers have led us in prayer to our Father in Heaven to keep us safe if we should enter into battle tonight. But now, I want us to share our own personal time together and pray to our Father Ussen to protect us." Tom placed the light powder in both palms and sprinkled it into his face with his eyes closed as he silently prayed. Jacob repeated the ritual.

"Although it is a Lakota Sioux phrase, it is appropriate for us to say tonight. Yutta-hey. It is a good day to die," said Tom as he placed both of his hands on his son's shoulders. "Yutta-hey, father," said Jacob who repeated the gesture, laying hands on his father's shoulders. Both men were now mentally and spiritually ready for battle.

Matt Fremont and Wade Justus had arrived at the interdiction rally point. They parked their patrol SUV in the middle of the field just beneath a rise. From this covert position, they could not be seen by the cartel members who undoubtedly would have NVG's. The men were soon joined by Jessie Fremont and Deputies Carter and Vasquez.

Matt and Wade got out on foot and crouch-walked over to the rise with their own NVG's to look across the Rio Brisas. At the same time they began to see movement in the Cypress grove, they heard Tristin over the Unicom phone line whisper, "Eagle advises here they come." It was finally time.

Matt Fremont got on the Unicom and told his men, "Here they come. Make ready." Simultaneous to Matt's direction, he heard a series of M4 bolts being pulled back and released forward to charge weapons. Matt ran back to his unit, grabbed a portable PA bullhorn and returned to Wade.

"I'll try to do this by the book once they get to our side of the river. I'm praying they just give up or try to high tail it back over to their side of the river," said the Sheriff.

"Aren't you the optimist," Wade chuckled.

"I'm the Sheriff. I gotta say that at least I tried to take them peacefully into custody. It's their choice how they want to play this out," replied Matt.

"Well, being that I'm retired, I must admit that I don't share your optimism, but I'm game," said Wade

The men watched the three trucks with snorkels enter the water and slowly make their way across the Rio Brisas in the dark.

Matt looked over at Wade and said, "As soon as the first truck hits land, we'll run back to our vehicles. Then drive them on top of the ridge so they can see us. We'll turn on our emergency lights and then hit 'em with our high lights and take down lights so they know we're the law. I'll do the announcements over the PA, advising them that they are under arrest.

"If they fire on us, I want Wade and Marcus to remain on top prone and cover us. Me, Jessie and Pete will back our units down the ridge and park 'em about 80 yards back, so they're protected, and we have a defensible position. Then we'll join you guys back on the top of the ridge and return fire. The goal will be to disable their vehicles and engage anyone who poses a lethal threat."

The Sheriff repeated his direction to his men over the Unicom line and told Tristin to advise Eagle that they were engaging the convoy in an attempt to affect an arrest.

The three Gila County Sheriff's Department SUV's cleared the top of the rise and in unison turned on all their lights. Matt got out of this unit with his bull horn in his hand and made the announcement.

"This is the Gila County Sheriff's Department. You have trespassed onto U.S. soil and are under arrest! Get out of your vehicles unarmed, throw up your hands and get down on the ground on your stomachs!" Matt was good enough with his Spanish to repeat his orders in their native language as well.

"Este es el Departmiento del Sheriff del Condado de Gila. Ha invadido suelo estadounidense y esta bajo arresto! Salgan de sus vehiculos desarmados, arrojen sus manos y acuestense en el suelo boca abajo!"

In response to Matt's announcements, the canvas sides on the four-by-four military truck raised up and a cartel soldier inside the bed opened up on the deputies with a mounted heavy machine gun. Fortunately for them, the gunner appeared to be either aiming for their emergency lights or was blinded by their lights, miscalculating their distance and elevation. Most of the rounds went over their heads, with a few obliterating the light bars on two of the units.

"Pull back! Pull back!" Matt yelled out. Jessie and Deputy Pete Vasquez jumped back into their units and backed up to a position 80 yards beneath the rise. The deputies quickly rejoined Wade and Deputy Marcus Carter who engaged the soldier firing the heavy machine gun which was their prime threat.

"We gotta take that heavy gun out, Wade. Got any ideas?" Matt yelled out over the ferocious gun fire that the belt fed weapon was spewing.

"Yeah, as a matter of fact I do. Take over for me while I work on something quick," replied Wade.

Wade pulled back from the rise a couple of yards and pulled out his cell phone. He tapped his "compass" app and pointed the phone in the direction of the four-by-four truck to get a compass reading.

"Matt, what do you make the distance from the ridge and that 4 x 4 truck with the machine gun?" Wade yelled over the barrage of gun fire.

"One fifty yards, max," Matt yelled back and then fired another three-round burst at the gunner.

"Copy!" Wade replied as he dialed the Unicom line.

"Archangel, Archangel, we need fire support, do you copy?"

"Archangel copies, sounds like you got your hands full.

Watta you need? the sniper asked.

"I need a grenade on a military 4 x 4 bearing 150 yards and 210° South of our position. I know you can't see 'em, but I fixed the compass heading and am pretty sure on the range," yelled Wade over the incessant gun fire of the heavy machine gun.

"Copy Wade; can do. Give me a minute," replied Sheridan.

Blake settled on his gun, looked through his scope and saw the familiar greenish blue screen to which he was accustomed. He pointed it in the direction he heard the loud rattle of the machine gun. He was looking around and was glad there was a grove of trees between him, and the flashing emergency lights. The strobing lights were washing out his view in some areas. He scanned around until he saw the repeated muzzle flashes of the machine gun on the other side of the ridge.

"I think you've said enough tonight, princess and it's time for you to go to sleep," Blake said under his breath.

Blake Sheridan picked up his range finder and fixed the range between himself and the top of the ridge where Wade and the other deputies were at 110 yards. He then added the 150 yards Wade had given him and picked up his M240 grenade launcher with three 40 mm grenade rounds. Blake found the 210° South bearing on his compass watch and got back on the Unicom.

"Archangel copies, I make the range 260 yards at 210° South heading. One on the way. Keeps your heads down and advise on impact," he said to Wade over the phone

"Copy Archangel, one on the way," replied Wade.

"Incoming from Archangel, keep your heads down, fellas," Wade yelled out to Matt and his deputies.

Blake Sheridan estimated the apogee of the 40 mm grenade and depressed the trigger. A dull *"thunk"* reported from the barrel of the M240 Multiple Grenade Launcher. There was a couple of seconds of hang time while the grenade traversed the distance, followed up a huge explosion culminating in a red and white fireball.

"Direct hit! Son of a bitch. I say again, direct hit, target eliminated!" Wade yelled over the phone to the cheers of Matt and the deputies.

"Jesus, you did it and you couldn't even see the target," said Tristin in amazement.

"Fucking-A, kid. Watch and learn. Watch and learn," Blake replied with a wink to his young partner.

The fireball briefly illuminated the night sky, allowing Wade, Matt, and the deputies to concentrate on selectively picking off the cartel soldiers in the remaining two trucks with three more probable kills. The last two Tres Paises soldiers dropped their AK-47's, removed their heavy ammo vests and ran for the Rio Brisas to swim back to Mexico.

"Cease fire, cease fire!" Matt yelled. He didn't want to explain why cartel soldiers, even those who just tried to kill them had bullet holes in their backs.

Matt, Wade and the others heard Black Jack Stryker over the Unicom, "What the fuck was that explosion? You guys okay down there?" said Stryker.

"Little Bird, Little Bird, affirmative. We are Okay. Scratch one military grade 4 x 4," replied Matt.

Just then, Tristin's cell phone buzzed, and he immediately picked up.

"Gila ground element. Eagle here, come in. You've got company and you've got trouble and I mean real trouble," said a startled Major Prescott.

"Say again, Eagle. That wasn't us who exploded. We're Okay," replied Tristin.

"No, you're not, Gila. You got a war coming in your direction and I mean at full speed. While we were all looking at the river, a formation of six, I say again, six vehicles came out of a large barn to your north and are heading directly towards you. They are all blacked out. That's a lot of whoop-ass! Get ready cause here they come!" yelled the Major over the phone.

"Gila copies. What more can you tell me, Eagle?" asked Tristin.

"Gila, I make two moderately armored military grade vehicles and four 4x4 off-road mechanicals rapidly closing distance on you. Unknown weaponry on the armored vehicles. Two of the mechs are mounted with heavy machine guns and the other two have cartel guys armed with AK-47s in the beds. Speed estimated at 30 mph and distance closing at 1,000 yards in a staggered, horizontal formation, copy?" said Major Prescott.

Blake Sheridan heard Eagle's transmission over Tristin's speaker.

"Let 'em know what's coming, kid. Get ready because this shit is going to get real in a couple of minutes. And listen, we are both going to get very busy so remember what I taught you. It's 'Remember the Alamo' time and we fight to the end, together, agreed?" asked Blake.

"Yes, sir. To the end," replied Tristin with a surprisingly calm demeanor.

Tristin immediately got on the Unicom and advised every one of the coming threat.

Matt got on the Unicom. "Stryker, looks like we got a war coming our way. You are authorized to engage targets of opportunity with deadly force, copy?"

"We already heard. We are locked and loaded. We are going to drop down and come in from behind them and attack their right flank facing you guys. Then we'll strafe right to left. Hopefully, we can hit a mech or two; maybe take out one of the armored vehicles. Keep your heads down when we pop up," said Stryker.

"Copy, remember that we have our point elements on both of our flanks ahead of us. Don't hit them," cautioned Matt.

"Copy, we're on NVG's. Point elements turn on your IR identifiers so we can ID you," Stryker directed over the Unicom.

Blake, Tristin on the right flank and Jacob and Tom on the left flank replied that they copied and switched on their IR strobes attached to the shoulders of their assault vests that were invisible to their enemy.

"We're going in hot, Johnny. Rack that fucker!" Stryker

radioed Johnny Wake over the Little Bird's comm system. The double amputee veteran racked back the charging lever on the NSV Soviet era 12.7 mm belt-fed heavy machine gun.

"Copy that, skipper. I got a Woodie. Let's tear 'em up!" replied Johnny.

Inside the two converted military armored vehicles, Uberto Urias was communicating to his Padron Adolfo Guzman. Guzman had demanded to be in on the final slaughter of the Gila County Sheriffs, Matt Fremont, and their former Texas Ranger mercenary Wade Justus.

"Jefe, the Gringos blew up the decoy truck with the heavy machine gun. Our men report some killed. I can't reach them now. However, we have the element of surprise, our narcotanques and over twenty men. This is over three times what the placas have. We will overrun and kill them all!"

"This is our time, Toro. After tonight, Tres Paises will rule Gila County. We will entrench ourselves on this land and no one will dare to defy us. I am going to personally put a bullet into the head of Sheriff Matt Fremont," replied Guzman.

"And I will do the same to this pendejo Ranger Wade Justus, Senor," replied Urias.

"Adelante mis hermanos!" yelled Guzman to his men over the comm system.

The staggered formation of cartel vehicles were approximately 700 yards away. They appeared as steadily moving large, black objects in front of a large, billowing cloud of desert dust.

Using his sighting system, Blake Sheridan was able to follow the custom, high-rise 4x4 off-road truck on the farthest right flank of the formation with armed soldiers in its bed. The truck was traveling in a straight line, its driver oblivious to any sniper engagement.

Blake steadied his sight on the bouncing vehicle. He decided that he would let the truck get to within 500 yards before he took out the driver. Blake reviewed his range card and found a small mound with three trees silhouetted on top of it. The range he had written in was 508 yards. It was a difficult, but not an impossible shot. He began the distance count in his head.

"650….600….550…500… Blake slowly depressed the trigger of his .338 Lapua with 230 grain armor piercing bullets. Blake normally only used AP ammunition if the shot required it. However, tonight he was breaking his rule because he knew that he would have multiple targets. He didn't want to change ammunition once the ruckus started.

Slow…compression…break. Blake felt the recoil of the rifle in his shoulder and the hiss of the round leaving the silenced muzzle. The round impacted between the driver and his front passenger, traveling through the cab's rear window, and taking out one of the armed men in the bed. The surprise impact caused the driver to hit his brakes, abruptly stopping the truck.

The soldier in the bed who was facing outward was struck with such force that the terminal wound cavity cleanly severed his body at the midsection. Seeing their comrade in the back blown in half, the remaining men in the back of the truck ducked down.

The stopped truck gave Blake a second opportunity to chamber a new round and fire a clean shot at the driver. The second round struck the driver in the head. The power of the round's impact immediately exploded the driver's skull like an over-pressurized balloon, filling the cab and the front passenger with brain, bone, and blood spatter. The passenger screamed and jumped out of the now driverless truck.

At that moment, Black Jack Stryker and his door gunner Johnny Wake popped up from 100 yards behind the truck. Stryker jammed left pedal, bringing the Little Bird into a sideways skid in the air, with the starboard side of the aircraft now facing the line of trucks and armored vehicles. Johnny had the first and second mechanicals in his gunsight and let loose a barrage of belt-fed 12.7 mm AP rounds at 700 rounds a minute. The rounds shredded both mechanicals on the right flank, immediately killing their occupants and effectively taking the vehicles and cartel soldiers out of the action.

As the Little Bird traversed the front of the formation, a lone survivor from the second to the right mechanical raised up from the truck bed and began shooting at the aircraft. Blake settled his reticle on him and shot the soldier straight through the back, knocking him completely out of the truck bed.

Flying the Little Bird as if was an extension of his body, Stryker brought the chopper back around to make another gun run.

The formation continued forward, absent the two destroyed mechanicals. A cartel soldier in the farthest mechanical on the left flank closest to Jacob and Tom Black Arrows fired an RPG from its bed. The winged grenade struck just in front of Matt Fremont's patrol unit sending metal fragments into the engine compartment and front windshield. The white-hot shards of metal narrowly missed Matt and Wade. Unfortunately, both men were unable to accurately return fire due to the distances at this point.

However, the mechanical was only 75 yards away from Jacob and his father who were concealed on the left flank point. Jacob wanted to keep their position a secret, especially once he knew that the Tres Paises soldier had a rocket propelled grenade.

As the soldier reloaded his RPG with a fresh grenade, Jacob loaded a carbon fiber broad tip into his bow. The Apache deputy took quick aim and fired just as the soldier was again taking aim at Matt and Wade. The arrow struck the soldier under his right armpit, entering his chest cavity and penetrating his heart. The sudden impact of the arrow, locked up their soldier's right arm. The kinesthetic response caused the man to lean forward and depress the trigger of his RPG. This in turn caused the weapon to discharge directly into the bed of the truck, blowing the vehicle and its occupants to bits.

"Holy shit! Did we give those guys grenades?" exclaimed Matt to Wade.

"Nope, I have no idea what happened over there, but they're still coming so get ready to engage. They're now in range for us to return fire," replied Wade.

The cartel's formation was now down by half of its vehicles but was now approaching the deputies from a distance of less than 150 yards. The mechanical to the left of Uberto Urias' armored vehicle had a heavy machine gun which began to engage all three patrol units, raking them with armor piercing gun fire.

Matt, Wade, Marcus Carter, Pete Vasquez, and Jessie fired

back with three-round bursts in an effort to hit the rear gunner. However, the fusillade of heavy machine gun fire was just too much to overcome. This forced the men to retreat to the far rear of their patrol units under intense fire. Matt and Wade remained together behind Matt's unit but behind the engine compartment of the right front side of the vehicle. They were hoping that the engine could stop the rounds. The AP rounds continued, penetrating the rest of the vehicle, turning it into Swiss cheese.

Black Jack Stryker and Johnny Wade began their second attack on the formation with another right to left flank pass.

"Hit that fucker!" Stryker yelled out to Johnny over the comm. As brazen as a former Viet Nam helicopter pilot could be, Stryker hovered 200 feet to the right of the mechanical, directly exposing his door gunner to the machine gunner in the bed of the truck. The cartel machine gunner looked up at the helicopter and elevated the barrel of his machinegun towards the Little Bird. In the blink of an eye, both he and Johnny simultaneously screamed out and fired upon each other.

Johnny depressed the trigger of the NVS, raining lead down onto the machine gunner in the truck bed. Johnny's fire was more accurate, turning his adversary into a pink mist of blood and bone. Unfortunately, the deceased soldier's return fire had struck the Little Bird's tail rotor. Two rounds had also struck Johnny's right titanium leg, shattering his metal foot.

Sounding like rocks striking the side of the aircraft, Stryker heard the rounds impact the Hughes 500-D. As he increased collective to gain speed, the Little Bird yawed to the right, yet applying left pedal was useless.

"Shit!" Stryker thought, I've lost tail rotor control. The pilot increased speed up to 60 knots as gently as he could. The airspeed "wind-vaned" the Little Bird causing it to yaw farther to the right. Stryker was forced to make a critical decision to try to head back to base or risk crashing and killing them both.

Black Jack immediately got on the comm to Johnny, "Are you Okay? Shit, we're hit. I've lost tail rotor control. We can't stay here. I gotta get this bird back to the compound. Hang on, brother. This might be rough."

"I'm good, skipper. Just took one in my right leg and foot. Thank God for VA titanium legs. I'm strapped in and good to go," Johnny yelled back.

Stryker got on the Unicom to reach Sheriff Fremont. "Gila, we're hit, we're hit! Lost some controls. We're gonna to try to make it back to base. Hang in there fellas. We're coming back in the other chopper,"

"Copy that, Jack. Good luck and safe landing. We'll manage. Will call you if we need a dust off," replied Matt.

The Little Bird was now in a crab, flying almost sideways. Stryker knew he had a difficult balance to maintain. He had to keep the aircraft from yawing past the 90 degree point, yet not descend into a forced landing. If he continued to increase power, the Little Bird would begin spinning and they would crash, burn and die.

As Stryker headed back to base, he struggled to keep the Little Bird at altitude without increasing power. A sense of relief swept over him as the Valkyrie Helicopters hanger came into sight.

Stryker lined up for a straight-in approach and prepared for a running landing, as if he was flying a fixed wing. The Little Bird was now flying almost sideways. As Stryker reduced power, the nose of the aircraft began to pivot to the left. Perfect, Stryker thought, as the Little Bird descended over the runway, still flying like a crab.

When the Little Bird was at 40 knots and still flying like a crab, Stryker rolled off the throttle enough to bring the nose of the aircraft in line with the runway. He then lowered the collective, and the Little Bird settled onto the runway. Sparks were flying as the skids scrapped to a stop over the asphalt.

"Right out of the training manual," Stryker thought, although he knew from experience that this was a situation pilots rarely survived.

The occupants of the sole mechanical left weren't done. With their machine gunner dead, the driver careened towards the left flank. This way, he could get a better angle of the deputies who were crouched behind their patrol units. The driver and his three passengers dismounted and began concentrating their fire on all three patrol units. The driver's problem was that he was not aware of the presence of Jacob and Tom Black Arrows. The concealed, war painted Apache warriors remained positioned at the left flank's point, now only fifty yards away and behind the soldiers.

Matt, Wade and Jessie had a good angle of fire on the driver and his left rear passenger and quickly took them out. Tom looked at his son and removed his heavy ceramic assault vest.

"Son, I can't move with this thing on. We're behind them. Use your bow so we don't give away our position. You take the man furthest away and I'm going to jump the closest man from behind," Jacob's father directed.

Jacob removed a carbon-tipped arrow from his quiver, notched it into his bow string. He placed the farthest man with an AK-47 in his sight. Jacob pulled back and released. The arrow flew silently and struck the man square between his shoulder blades with a sickening thump. The cartel soldier collapsed forward, dead in his tracks.

As soon as Tom Black Arrows saw the impact of the arrow, he was off and low crouch sprinting towards the closest man who was distracted in watching his comrade suddenly pitch forward. As the Apache chief got within ten yards of the Tres Paises soldier, Tom let out a blood curdling Apache war cry. The soldier suddenly turned around, raising his automatic rifle.

Tom quickly ducked underneath the barrel of the AK and sliced the inside of the soldier's right leg, severing the femoral artery. The severely wounded man dropped his rifle and drew a military combat knife that was attached upside down to the front of his assault vest.

It was now a knife fight. As the man lunged towards Tom, the Apache moved to the soldier's inside right and stabbed into his kidney. He quickly pulled out the knife, reversed its cutting angle, pivoted behind the man and back slashed him behind his right leg, severing the ligaments behind his knee. This deep laceration dropped the man to his knees.

In response, the soldier dropped his knife and accessed a semiautomatic pistol he had holstered across his chest. The soldier drew and raised the weapon upwards towards Tom who was now only an arm's length away. The Apache grabbed the muzzle and slide of the pistol which prevented the soldier from firing a round.

With his right hand Tom thrust his warrior's knife straight into the center of the man's throat, penetrating out through the back of his neck. The soldier's arms collapsed downwards as blood spurted out of the severed neck. Tom Black then delivered a front kick to the soldier's chest to clear his knife from the man's neck, knocking the man onto his back. It had been a fight to the death.

Jacob had been well trained by his father, but he had never seen his father in an actual fight before. It was a gruesome struggle, but his father had prevailed. Jacob and his father looked at each other, raised their hands to the sky and yelled out an Apache war cry in victory over their adversaries.

All the occupants of the last mech were down and out of the fight. This left only the two converted military armored vehicles that continued their approach from a distance of 80 yards. It was time for Tristin to launch his drone.

With his controller in hand, Tristin initiated the drone's rotors by pushing both sticks forward and down. Then he quickly rose the drone up to thirty feet AGL by pushing the throttle stick all the way forward. Tristin quickly scanned the area using the drone's IR camera feed on his iPad and located the AV's. Zooming in on the AV to the left, he spotted Urias. The adept drone pilot tapped the screen in the center of the AV's windshield, locking in and transmitting the AV's GPS coordinates to the drone.

"Target Lock" flashed on Tristin's iPad screen. "I've got a lock on target," radioed Tristin.

"Take 'em out!" exclaimed Blake.

"Copy that, on the way!" replied Tristin who then tapped the "Launch Mission" icon on his screen, which began flashing red.

The autonomous drone took a direct path straight into the center of the armored vehicle's windshield, exploding and completely obliterating the driver's and front passenger's compartment. The AV immediately came to an abrupt stop.

Blake Sheridan had the armored vehicle on the right. When Tristin's drone disabled Urias' armored vehicle, the driver of Guzman's armored vehicle stopped to assess. Unfortunately for the driver and passengers, the AV had stopped perpendicular to Blake's EFP charge.

"Bye, bye, assholes," said the sniper as he hit the pre-programmed phone number on the cell phone Johnny Wake had given him. The EPF went off in a thunderous explosion causing its newly shaped projectile to penetrate completely through the driver's side door, both driver and right front passenger and out the right front passenger door.

With both armored vehicles now disabled, their drivers and front passengers dead. Urias, Guzman and their six bodyguards quickly exited through the rears of each vehicle. Each man was armed with short barreled AK-47 fully automatic assault rifles.

At that instant, out of nowhere a blacked-out Eurocopter EC-120 screamed across the battlefield less than 100 feet off the deck.

Apparently Matt Fremont and his men weren't the only people that Major Miranda Prescott had been communicating with. The aircraft was piloted by CBP Lt. Bert Medina with Assistant Chief Katie Blackwater as door gunner on the port side. Katie's favorite pilot had removed the port side door of the chopper and had bolted down a belt-fed Chinese QJC-88 12.7 mm gas operated heavy machine gun confiscated from the Juarez Cartel in a previous arrest. Bert had apparently liberated the heavy weapon from the CBP evidence locker.

"Bert, we gotta give those guys a fighting chance. We only have time to make one pass. Get me a shot at those assholes next to those two AV's," Katie told her pilot over the comm.

"Copy, can do boss. Hold on, I'm gonna spin her around," replied the former 160th SOAR Nightstalker's pilot.

The blades of the helicopter slapped the air as Lt. Medina made a gun run from left to right in front of the two armored vehicles, Katie unleashed the full devastating power of the 850 rounds per minute killing machine upon Guzman, Urias and their men. Four of the soldiers immediately went down, literally shredded by the lethal 12.7 AP rounds.

As two of the surviving soldiers began firing back at the chopper, Bert Medina made a sweeping turn to the left to return for a second volley.

"What the…. Holy Jesus! That's Katie Blackwater on that gun!" Matt yelled out to Wade over the gunfire.

Matt and Wade took the unexpected distraction to briefly leave cover to engage the remaining men, Matt with his M-4 and Wade with his chopped Nichols AR Commando. Urias saw them now in front of Matt's patrol unit.

"Estos son el Sheriff y el guardabosques. Matalos!" (That's the Sheriff and the ranger. Kill them!"), screamed Urias.

Guzman's enforcer and a soldier immediately to his left fired upon Matt and Wade with their AK's, striking both men and knocking them down.

Tristin who saw his Sheriff and Wade go down, responded with unbridled anger. The deputy got up from his position of cover, threw off the top portion of his Ghillie suit and grabbed his M-4 rifle. Tristin shouldered his M-4 rifle and began moving forward towards the Tres Paises soldiers in a "Groucho walk." The young deputy was screaming angrily and repeatedly firing three-round bursts at his adversaries.

Men on both sides of the battle could not believe their eyes. Tristin's fire immediately knocked down and killed one soldier to Guzman's left. A stunned Blake Sheridan immediately got up on his sniper rifle and traversed towards Guzman and his men. He then stopped on the first person he crossed and took out the man to Guzman's right.

Seeing two of his best men go down next to Guzman, Urias physically grabbed Guzman by the back of his vest, dragging his boss behind one of the armored vehicles. The enforcer ordered his remaining two men to retreat and regroup behind the AV's.

As the enraged Tristin continued to move towards the AV's, Urias peeked around the left rear of his armored vehicle and fired an accurate burst which struck Tristin hard. The deputy spun around from the impacts of the rounds and collapsed to the desert floor.

Urias, Guzman and their remaining two men retreated behind their AV's. This allowed Deputies Carter and Jessie to run up and grab onto Matt Fremont who had been wounded in the left arm and leg. The deputies were able to move their Sheriff to cover.

In turn, Jacob Black Arrows and Deputy Vasquez sprinted over to rescue Wade who was shot up pretty bad. They dragged the unconscious Texas Ranger to a safe position behind the shot-up patrol units.

It was now down to Urias, Guzman and two of their soldiers. Sporadic gunfire between the Tres Paises and the Gila County deputies continued. From Blake Sheridan's position, he could not get an accurate shot with his sniper rifle. The patient sniper continued observing through his scope, scanning the area he knew they were cowering behind with his gun up, waiting for an opportunity.

Urias told his men to cover him while he briefly entered the rear of the AV he had been riding in. He soon emerged with an RPG. The enforcer slowly and carefully took aim at the patrol unit that Deputies Carter and Vasquez had taken cover behind.

Archangel saw a portion of Urias holding the unmistakable Chinese grenade launcher from behind the AV. He fired just as Urias was depressing the trigger. Blake's round struck the right rear corner of the armored vehicle just above Urias' head. The .338 caliber round's loud impact caused the enforcer to flinch and duck as his RPG fired.

Urias' sudden downward movement caused the trajectory of the grenade to explode just in front of the deputies' patrol unit. The shrapnel from the Soviet grenade shredded the entire side of the vehicle. It's blast and resultant concussion catapulted both deputies into the air. Carter and Vasquez struck the ground hard, rendering both unconscious and out of the fight.

Blake saw the RPG's grenade explode, throwing Carter and Vasquez into the air. How could anyone survive that? He figured them as dead. If he couldn't take an accurate shot, he was going to take out the AV's.

"Two can play this game. Go big or go home," Blake said to himself as he put down his sniper rifle and grabbed his M-240 grenade launcher. He had two rounds left and had to make them count. Blake rotated the six-shot cylinder, cycling the next 40

mm grenade into the chamber. He took aim at the closest AV and depressed the trigger. *"Click."*

"What the hell?!" Blake thought. It must have been a dud. But if it was a "slow-burn-round," he was about to be a gonner if it exploded in the chamber of the M-240. He had to act fast if he was going to live. Blake quickly popped the cylinder open, found the unexpended round with the primer mark. He immediately extracted and tossed the grenade away from him and proned out. A half-second later the grenade exploded less than fifteen yards away.

"Shit!" Blake screamed out. There was no time to waste. He cycled the final grenade into the chamber, took aim again and fired. The 40 mm grenade struck the left rear corner of the closest AV, cutting one of the Tres Paises soldiers to shreds.

The surprise of the sudden explosion behind caused the remaining soldier to bolt from cover. That soldier was easily picked off by Jessie Fremont yielding his M-4 rifle. It was now down to Urias and Guzman.

Jacob Black Arrows had dragged the severely wounded Wade Justus to safety. In the heat of the battle, the deputy only had time to shove a battlefield compress under the Ranger's assault vest where at least two AP rounds had penetrated his left upper chest just above his ceramic armor plate. Luckily, the pressure of the vest against the compress had prevented from Wade from bleeding out, but he had lost a lot of blood. Wade also had a through and through bullet wound just under his left clavicle. Jacob quickly covered Wade with a plastic tarp out of one of the SUV's in an attempt to hide him.

Wade felt as if his mind was drifting. He was somehow transported to the bank of the river at his ranch. He gazed up to a blue sky with white puffy Texas clouds, his horse grazing in tall grass next to him. All was peaceful and calm.

As Wade gazed skywards, his wife Helen appeared over him. She was in her police uniform, looking down at him with a concerned face. She was absolutely beautiful. *"I love a woman in uniform,"* he mused.

"Wade, wake up! You must wake up now and get back into the fight!" Helen pleaded.

"What are you talking about, honey? Let's enjoy the river together," Wade replied, smiling.

"No Wade. This isn't real. You must wake up. You must live! You must live for both of us, sweetheart. Please wake up. They are going to kill you and your men. You must get back into the fight!" repeated Helen.

Wade stirred. He realized that his eyes weren't really open, they were closed. He opened them to darkness, not a blue sky. The acrid smells of smoke, cordite, silver sage and his own blood filled his nostrils. Pain immediately shot through his upper body.

Wade found himself covered by some type of cover. He tried to use his left arm to pull back the tarp and rise but collapsed backwards into the dirt. His left arm was useless. Wade transitioned to his right arm and forced himself to stand. He was unstable and felt nauseous and woozy from the loss of blood. In the background, he could hear Jessie Fremont yelling.

"Gila County Sheriff's. It's over. Drop your weapons, throw up your hands and surrender! All of your men are dead, we have you surrounded, and more officers are coming. Give yourselves up, now!"

Wade forced himself to concentrate. He checked himself and what equipment he had left. He realized that he had been hit multiple times in his left side chest and shoulder. He was weak and his breathing was labored. No way he could hold or fire a rifle. The former ranger reached down for his side arm and found that he still had his 1911A pistol secured in its holster. At least he was still armed and could fight.

Wade concentrated on his situational awareness as he looked all around him. To his immediate left he saw that Deputies Carter and Vasquez were down and unresponsive. He saw their shredded patrol unit and figured that they were dead.

To his right, behind the left front engine compartment was Jessie Fremont yelling out commands, but he couldn't yet see to whom. Immediately in front of him he saw Matt Fremont propped up behind the rear of his patrol unit. Bloody battle compresses were taped to his right upper leg, right forearm, and the right side of his head. Matt was conscious, alive, but definitely non-ambulatory.

As Jessie continued to yell out commands, Wade crouched down and approached his old Texas Ranger partner.

"How you doing, partner? Did I miss the party?" Wade croaked in a half-hearted attempt to perk Matt up.

"They winged me, pard. My gun hand is useless and just in case you haven't noticed, we're still at the party, so keep your damn head down," replied Matt.

Wade bent down, unholstered Matt's .45 pistol and placed it into his left hand with an extra magazine. "Remember how to drop and exchange mags with one hand?" Wade asked.

"Screw you. I'm the guy who taught you that shit, rookie," replied Matt weakly with an attempt at humor.

"Where's the rest of us?" Wade asked.

"I don't know where Sheridan, Tristin, Jacob or Tom are, but from here it looks like we *are* the rest of us," replied Matt.

"Stay in the fight, Matt. I'm going up front to see what's up. I'll back Jessie. He's yelling commands at someone," said Wade. Wade patted Matt's good shoulder to reassure him and moved over to where Jessie was.

Matt's son was still yelling for people to surrender, but no one was responding. For the time being, what had turned into a battle field was deathly quiet and still. It was eerie. Wade came up on Jessie from behind and startled him.

"So, what's the score and who are you yelling at?" Wade asked.

"Jesus, Wade, I thought you bought the farm. Good to see you're still with the living," said the surprised deputy who now took a quick glance at Wade. Jessie saw that his Godfather's entire upper left chest, shoulder, arm, and side were drenched in blood.

Wade saw Jessie's obvious look of concern and tried to assuage him. "Don't worry, kid. I'm a little banged up but still good to go. I just checked on your dad and he's still up for a fight. Where are the bad guys?" asked Wade.

"Well, the good news is that it looks like we got most all of them except for Urias and an older guy he seems to be protecting. They're both behind the AV on the left," explained Jessie.

"An older guy Urias is protecting? Shit, that has got to be Adolfo Guzman, the big dog himself. What the hell is Guzman doing here?" Wade replied in amazement.

"Where's Archangel, Tristin, Jacob and Tom?" Asked Wade.

"Blake's still out there somewhere on the right flank. If he had a shot, he would have taken it by now. Tristin's down about fifty yards to the right of the AV's. When Matt and you went down, the fucking kid charged them, guns a blazing. He got one before Urias took him out, poor kid. I don't know if he's alive or dead and we sure can't get to him right now.

"I think Jacob and Tom are still on our left flank just in case there's more of them than this. Right now, it's just you and me in the middle," explained Jessie.

"So right now, it's two against two unless some other Tres Paises ahole pops up," replied Wade affirmatively.

"Correct," replied Jessie.

On the other side of the two military armored vehicles a very angry Uberto Urias was trying to rally his boss. Urias did not have a full understanding of what had already transpired during the battle. He believed they had more Tres Paises soldiers at their disposal.

"Jefe, we have killed both the Sheriff and his Texas Ranger. Our men are regrouping as we speak. This is the last of them. The Gringo deputy who we kidnapped and tortured is giving commands because his padre is dead. This is all false bravado. We can take these placas. We are both well-armed. I will make the challenge," said Urias.

Adolfo Guzman had been surprised by the amount of firepower the American placas had managed to bring to the battle. The helicopter attack had stunned he and Urias. The only thing psychologically holding the drug lord together was his massive ego. Guzman thought they could still achieve victory.

As Urias loaded fresh forty round magazines into both of

their AK-47's, Guzman asked his enforcer what his plan was.

"We challenge the gringos to show themselves to prove that there are more of them than us. When the sheriff's son comes out from cover, I will personally cut him down. All you need to do is watch my back. The sheriff's son makes an empty bluff. Let's finish this, Jefe. Gila County is ours to take," encouraged Urias.

Guzman's greed and ego overwhelmed his common sense.

"Yes, Toro. Let's do this thing. Let's make sure that they are all dead," the drug lord replied.

Urias took his cue and yelled out from behind the AV. He needed to push the deputy's buttons.

"Deputy Fremont, remember me from the mine in Mexico? How's that ring finger of yours? Not so good for the marriage, eh?" the henchman laughed loudly.

"Urias, it's over. See any of your men coming to your aid? They're all dead, Toro. We're giving you and your boss a chance to surrender peacefully. You can get yourselves a high-priced lawyer and try to beat the wrap. What do you say?" asked Jessie.

Wade knew that Urias was just trying to get Jessie jacked up so the deputy would make a mistake. He knew that no son of Matt Fremont was going to fall for a rookie trick like that. Wade was a behaviorist and had a good feeling of what made criminals like Urias and Guzman tick.

"Two can play the button pushing game," thought Wade who then turned to Jessie.

"You ready for a fight, kid? Let me see whose buttons are easier to push. Let me take a shot at this piece of shit," said Wade who suddenly stepped out from behind the cover of the patrol unit.

"Well, Senor's Urias y Guzman. Looks like you got delt a bad hand of cards, que no? Allow me to introduce myself, Wade Justus, formerly of the Texas Rangers. I'm the guy who set up the mission that killed all your soldiers at the mine, remember?

"Oh, and those two pendejos in the black Broncos in Deming? Mi Tambien. By the way, Senor Guzman, seen your nephew Chuy lately? I heard we lit him up like a Tejas barbeque.

"If you were real men instead of a couple of putos, we would go mano y mano, que no? So, amigos, are you up for it? Quien es mas macho?" said Wade in his best calo street Spanish.

Adolfo Guzman was fuming to learn that the former Texas Ranger was still alive. Wade had struck a nerve. Guzman pressed forward towards Wade and had to be pulled back by Urias.

"Calmate, Jefe, tranquillo. I can handle this. Just back me up," said the enforcer. Urias couldn't help but notice that the retired Texas Ranger was covered in blood, droplets slowly falling from the side panel of his tactical vest.

"So, Ranger Justus, it looks like I hit you pretty good, eh? That must hurt quite a bit, que no? Sabes que, I hear that the loss of so much blood makes one feel, how do you say, a bit light-headed, Si?" Urias yelled out.

Wade was indeed feeling light-headed. He had to blink from time to time to maintain focus on Urias and Guzman. Wade was focusing on his breathing to lower his heart rate and blood pressure. He apparently couldn't sense it, but he was slightly gait ataxic, causing him to sway slightly forward and backward like a drunkard.

Jessie saw his Godfather unsteady and offered, "Hey Wade, I got this."

"Not on your life, Jessie. Just keep a close eye on Guzman. Urias is mine," replied Wade assertively.

Urias saw Wade wobbly and blinking to stay focused. *"He must be bleeding out pretty good by now. It won't be long. Here's my chance to kill this ranger in front of my boss,"* thought the enforcer.

"Tell you what, Ranger. I'll put my AK down and let's go pistols. Like you say, mano y mano. Tienes las pelotas? (Do you have the balls?)" asked Urias.

"Well, you put your AK down and I'll raise my hands away from my pistol as a show of good faith. Then it's pistols when you're ready. Say when," Wade yelled out.

The egotistical Urias wouldn't let it go. "Well, that's fine with me but I feel like I'd be taking advantage of a Viejo and a wounded one at that," said the smiling henchman.

Wade knew how to jack Urias up. "Well, we're doing this in front of your boss. You want to impress Senor Guzman, right?" said Wade, formally throwing down the gauntlet.

"Okay ranger, I'm putting down my weapon so don't shoot me," said Urias as he bent down with his left hand to deposit his AK on the ground. Wade's right hand as promised were out in front of him chest high. His useless left arm was down at his side. Wade's 1911-A .45 pistol was cocked, locked and secured in a Threat Level I friction release holster.

As Wade's eyes followed Urias bending down to deposit the AK on the ground, the enforcer quickly reached behind his back. In the blink of an eye Urias withdrew a concealed Glock 23 .40 caliber pistol from behind his back.

It is well known that action is faster than reaction. An aggressor drawing a concealed weapon from behind his back can access and fire the weapon in only twenty-five hundreds of a second. Psycho-physiologically, an officer facing the armed suspect must transition through what is referred to as the "OODA Loop" of observing, orienting, deciding what defensive option to take, and then acting upon that decision. Therefore, officers are always behind the curve and often lose those gunfights.

As a former firearms instructor, Wade had taught law enforcement officers that the average time it takes a trained officer to transition through the OODA loop and draw from a holstered position was just under two seconds under the best of conditions.

In Wade's compromised physical state, his responses would be way off. Wade realized that in his condition, there was only one way he could possibly defeat his experienced and much faster adversary.

As the enforcer raised the weapon up from his hips, Wade quickly stepped off the line of attack. With a one-handed draw, he double tapped two .45 caliber rounds center mass into Urias' chest. Both of Wade's rounds struck Urias mid-sternum, one just below the other, four inches apart.

Although Wade's rounds simultaneously impacted Urias' upper torso, they were stopped by the ceramic body armor of the henchman's assault vest. However, the bullet strikes distracted Urias' aiming focus just enough for Wade to again move off his adversary's line of attack a second time just as Urias returned fired.

Urias' round was directed at where Wade was initially standing – but the former Texas Ranger was no longer there. Wade immediately fired two more rounds in rapid succession at Urias' head. The first round grazed his enemy's skull, but the second found its mark, penetrating through the center of Urias' forehead and exploded out of the back of his head.

Uberto "Toro" Urias stopped dead in his tracks, his eyes focused upon Wade Justus in a blank, "thousand yard stare." The murderer and torturer of countless victims dropped to his knees and then collapsed, his face planting into the desert floor in a puff of dust.

Well trained in mortal combat, Wade followed Urias to the ground, his .45 now quivering in his right hand. The survival chemical cocktail of adrenalin, pain suppressing dopamine and endorphins now exhausted. Shock and the loss of so much blood had taken its toll. The ground seemed to quickly rise up as if to hit Wade in the face as the former Texas Ranger began to slump to the ground.

Adolfo Guzman saw that Wade was going down and took this cowardly opportunity to strike back. The leader of the vicious and violent Tres Paises cartel stepped out from behind the armored vehicle. Guzman raised up his chopped AK-47 towards the falling ranger and screamed, *"Tres Paises!"*

Jessie saw the imminent life threat and immediately shouldered his M-4 rifle. The deputy illuminated the drug lord with his Sure-Fire light. Jessie instinctively placed the holographic green circle and dot of his EoTec sight square in the center of Guzman's head. He depressed the trigger and fired a three-round burst from thirty yards away, both men now firing simultaneously.

Jessie's rounds found Guzman first, striking and cleaving the cartel leader's head in half. The force of the impact of multiple .223 caliber rounds threw Adolfo Guzman backwards. Guzman's finger remained on the trigger causing his AK to spray rounds in a brilliant golden arch into the black night's sky. It was over.

Jessie ran up to Wade, took the pistol out of his right hand, decocked it and laid it to the side for safety. He turned Wade over onto his back and checked his breathing and circulation. Respirations were short and shallow, and Wade's pulse was weak. Neither presentations were encouraging.

Jessie next removed Wade's heavy ceramic armor assault vest and saw that the Ranger was bleeding again. He grabbed a couple of battle wound compresses from a lower BDU pocket and applied them with pressure to staunch the flow of blood.

Jacob and Tom Black Arrows ran up to Jessie. Jacob had been cross trained as the department's medic.

"Get my medic bag from my unit, Jacob. Wade's bleeding pretty bad. I found three bullet wounds, all in his left upper chest and shoulder. Looks like he's already lost a lot of blood. Respirations are short and shallow; his pulse is weak. My dad's hit too, but Wade is worse," said Jessie.

Jacob sprinted to retrieve his medic bag. Jessie directed Tom to call Black Jack Stryker, advising they had multiple wounded and in need of immediate evacuation to a hospital.

Jacob returned to tend to Wade while Jessie ran to his unit and radioed Gila County dispatch, declaring an 11-99 and providing their location. *"Officers down, officers need immediate assistance!"* The call for emergency assistance for an officer down would bring everyone coming hell bent for leather now to assist.

Jessie saw that Blake Sheridan had left his position and was sprinting over to where Tristin Peters had fallen. Jessie yelled out to him. "Check Tristin and let me know if you need Jacob!"

Blake had also been trained in emergency triage in the Marine Corps. The sniper checked Tristin and found that the young deputy was breathing but also had a weak pulse. He discovered that Tristin had been wounded in the left side just outside of his protective ceramic armor and in his upper left leg.

The sniper removed Tristin's assault vest and saw that Tristin's left side wound was still bleeding. The leg wound was thankfully through and through and didn't appear to be bleeding much. Luckily, no contact with the femoral artery which would have been fatal under these circumstances. Blake just couldn't tell how bad the side wound was. He applied battle compresses to the wounds on Tristin's left leg left side, pressing forcefully to staunch the flow of blood.

Blake turned Tristin over to see if there was an exit wound on his left side. There was, so he applied a second battle compress to the gapping exit wound caused by the tumbling projectile. This was not good. Blake removed a third battlefield compress, rolled it up into a narrow cylinder and literally shoved it painfully inside of the exit wound.

Feeling the pain, Tristin moaned weakly, opened his eyes and saw Blake.

"Blake…. Is it over? I don't feel so hot…. My back feels like it's on fire."

"Shut up, knucklehead. You've been hit. I got you. You're gonna be okay, but you gotta stay awake for me, okay? Just stay awake. I know it hurts. We're getting you to a hospital just as quick as we can. You done good kid, real good tonight," said Blake, trying to assure his scout observer.

Blake then yelled over to Jessie.

"I'm gonna need Jacob over here! Tristin's been hit in the left side and leg. I got the leg wound covered, but I can't tell how bad his side wound is. The kid is conscious, breathing, and responsive," Blake yelled out to Jessie.

"Stryker is in-bound, he'll be here in five," Tom Black Arrows yelled out to Jessie who certainly had his hands full now.

"Check on my dad, Marcus and Pete," he yelled back to Tom.

Tom jogged over to Matt Fremont who was still sitting, propped up against the left rear tire of his patrol unit.

"How do you feel, Sheriff?" Tom asked.

"Like I got hit by a Mack truck. How's Wade?" asked the Sheriff.

"Ranger Justus took a couple of hits, Jacob's working on him now. Stryker is flying back out here to pick up you guys. It won't be long. Can you hang on a bit?" asked Tom.

"I've had worse. I'll be okay. Please check on Marcus and Pete over there. They went down after the RPG hit near their unit and I haven't seen 'em since. I hope they're okay," said the Sheriff.

"Will do, Sheriff. Just hang tight. Yell out if you need anything," said Tom as he left to check on Deputies Carter and Vasquez.

Tom Black Arrows found Marcus Carter conscious, on his knees, and tending to his partner Pete Vasquez.

"You Okay, deputy?" Tom asked.

"You gotta speak up. I can hardly hear you. My bell got rung pretty good. I checked myself and I'm not bleeding much except for my head somewhere. I can't get this ringing out of my ears and my arms feel weak. Got one hell of a headache too," replied Marcus.

Tom removed a pen light flashlight from his pants pocket and shined it into the deputy's eyes briefly. Marcus' pupils were in opposing degrees of dilation. The ringing in his ears and weakness in his arms were sure signs of concussion.

Tom examined Marcus' head and found blood inside both ear canals. The deputy's face was also bloodied, and pock marked from particles of safety glass most probably from the windows of his patrol unit exploding from the force of the blast of the RPG into his face.

"Okay, deputy. Don't rub your face or ears. You've got glass in your face, and you've suffered a pretty good concussion. Do you feel nauseous?" asked Tom.

"Yes, a bit," replied Marcus.

"Best to just lay here on your back and I'll tend to your partner," suggested Tom.

Tom checked on Deputy Vasquez who looked like he was also coming around. Tom couldn't find any obvious wounds on the deputy but noted that his ears and face were also bloody and pocked marked with safety glass.

Pete Vasquez opened his eyes and appeared to be breathing okay. Tom gave the deputy the same instructions as his partner and reminded both deputies not to move.

In the distance, the men heard the sound of helicopter blades beating the air. The fires from the blown-up mechanicals and armored vehicles illuminating the area provided an excellent point of reference for Black Jack Stryker to set down.

Stryker and Johnny Wake surveyed the area of the fight between the deputies and Tres Paises as they dropped down.

"Holy Jesus, it looks like a fucking battlefield. There are bodies everywhere!" exclaimed Johnny.

"I've seen worse, I hope we won, or our LZ is gonna be very hot in a second. Get ready, here we come!" yelled Stryker. The pilot flared as he quickly set the Little Bird down 30 yards behind the devastated patrol units. Dust, tumble weeds, and smoke swirled in the air around the craft until Stryker had fully lowered the collective and the rotor blades were no longer biting the air.

Jacob, Jessie and Tom jogged towards the helicopter, ducking low to avoid the twirling blades, covering their eyes from the swirling debris in the air. Stryker opened his door and Johnny came to the port side of the aircraft as the men approached.

"We've got three wounded, two seriously and two concussive injuries that can wait if they have to. How many can you carry with you in this thing?" yelled out Jacob over the noise of the rotating blades.

"I can take all three including you. We'll definitely need a medic. No one dies on my watch. Load 'em up. Where am I going to?" asked Stryker.

"The best ER in the region is University Medical Center in El Paso. I did my medic training there. They're great with gunshot wounds. That's about 125 miles from here and they've got a chopper pad on the roof," replied Jacob.

"Copy that, I'll have 'em there in forty-five minutes. Unfortunately, everyone's gotta lay on the floor. I got no cots in here," said Stryker.

"It is what it is. I'll take speed over comfort every time in a case like this," said Jacob who then yelled out to Jessie, Blake and

Tom,

"Let's get these guys loaded up and strapped in. The order's gonna be Tristin, Wade and then Sheriff Fremont. Marcus and Pete are stable and can wait until EMS arrives. We're already got EMS and the posse coming. They should be here in a couple of minutes," directed Jacob.

The deputies and Tom Black Arrows paired up, retrieved the seriously wounded and brought them to the chopper. Johnny and Jacob assisted with placing the men into the chopper and securing harnesses for each wounded man. When Matt Fremont got to the door, he handed his son Jessie his cell phone.

"Son, grab Katie Blackwater's cell number and tell her we need a dust-off for two of our wounded. This will give Katie some cover to return out here in a different bird. She can make it to the hospital before any ambulance or patrol unit can. Our units are all shot to shit. Advise her that Wade and I got hit, but we'll make it. Tell her where we're being taken to. I'll see you soon, Jessie. Take care of the men and the scene. You're in charge now.

("And listen carefully; be easy on your mother. Tell her I'm a bit banged up, but I'm gonna be okay. I don't want her worrying about me; promise?" said Matt.

Jessie took down Katie Blackwater's cell number and handed his father's phone back to him.

Stryker yelled back into the aircraft, "Everybody in? We gotta go! Stand back, keep your heads down moving away from the chopper and…..Clear!"

His actions slower now, Stryker started pulling pitch. With the extra weight, he needed to ensure they weren't overloaded for a safe departure. At a three-foot hover, Stryker was almost at full collective. He had little more to pull as he gently started hovering forward. The Little Bird shuddered through the transitional lift, and Stryker and the aircraft were now safely flying back.

As the Little Bird rose from the battlefield, Jacob got on his cell and dialed up University Medical Center ER in El Paso.

"We're inbound with multiple gunshot wound casualties, two are serious. ETA 45 by chopper. Code Blue times three. Get your teams ready. These are wounded deputies," he advised along with a descriptions of their injuries.

Ten minutes after the helicopter left, the remaining men heard and saw what appeared to be at least a score of emergency vehicles approaching. As they began to arrive, a Blackhawk helicopter with CBP markings piloted by Lt. Burt Medina and carrying Assistant Chief Katie Blackwater landed to transport Deputies Carter and Vasquez to the hospital in El Paso.

The Gila County deputies played it perfectly, never once giving away their CBP comrades in arms' participation in the fray.

Black Jack Stryker slowed for his approach to land on the University Medical Center's helipad. Johnny and Jacob saw thee complete medical teams waiting for them with gurneys and medical equipment. Upon landing, Jacob filled in the triage teams with his assessment of their wounds. He remained with his wounded teammates as they were rushed off the helipad to their separate ER's.

Stryker got on the comm to Johnny Wake, "Let's get the hell out of here before someone figures out who we are and starts to ask questions."

"I'm with you, skipper. Let's roll," replied Johnny

Free of his wounded comrades, Stryker returned to his aggressive flying. He yanked in pitch, applied plenty of left pedal, and the Little Bird sprung off the helipad. As they gained altitude over the illuminated city of El Paso and the I-10 highway, the first crimson tinge on the eastern horizon announced the coming dawn.

Stryker and Johnny were less than a mile from the Mexican border. As they sped southwest back to Las Brisas, the men couldn't help but gaze down at Juarez, Mexico. From their vantage point, it was hard to separate the two disparate cities; one full of promise and growth, the other a Third World cesspool awash with cartel violence and exploitation.

Stryker looked back at Wake and remarked, "Well, at least we beat 'em this time, my friend. Revenge is mine saith the Lord. We paid back a couple of debts tonight. At least I can look my deceased wife and daughter in the eye and tell them that they can finally find peace," said the now weary Viet Nam helicopter pilot.

"I'm pretty sure your family has been at peace for some time, Jack. I just hope you're finally at peace," his good friend replied.

"Maybe you're right, Johnny. Maybe you're right," said Stryker.

Epilogue

WHILE SHERIFF MATT Fremont, Wade and Deputy Tristin Peters were in surgery, Jacob was left with the responsibility of helping to make notifications. He called Jessie to update him on the status of the men and his dad.

"Jessie, I know that you're updating your mom and family about your dad. The ER physician doing his triage says he's gonna be fine. Nothing major hit, but he's gonna be in recovery here for at least a week before they release him to return home. Then probably a month taking things easy at home.

Tristin is a bit more serious, but stable. After surgery, he's gonna be in ICU for two weeks. He lost a lot of blood, and they want to guard against infection. The doc said that the exit wound in his back was bad, and they are guarding against sepsis. He'll be on heavy antibiotics for a while. After that, at least a month or so for recovery. If you get me his mom's contact information, I'll call her and let her know her son's gonna make it," said Jacob.

"How's Wade? He looked pretty bad out there tonight. He's my Godfather you know," asked Jessie.

"Well, Wade took three solid AK rounds to his upper left torso. Two rounds in his upper pectoralis and a third penetrated and busted his clavicle. All just above his body armor. Two were through and through and the surgical team removed a third from his back. No spinal or cardiovascular issues thank God. The doc said he's one tough SOB and he's gonna be okay but will probably be laid up for a while here. After that, he's gonna need several months of physical therapy to get full use of his left arm due to that shoulder injury. They basically had to bolt his shoulder back together.

Wade's in quite a bit of pain. The docs are keeping him sedated for the time being. They don't want him moving around and tearing the delicate work they did on his shoulder and chest," explained Jacob. He then asked, "I see he's wearing a wedding ring. Do you want me to call his wife and fill her in?"

"Actually, Wade's a widower. He lost his wife several years ago in an OIS. She was a cop in Texas. He still wears his ring to honor her memory.

"Wade's got a son named Hunter who's a Special Agent for the Tennessee Bureau of Investigations in Nashville. I'll make the call. I'll text you with Tristin's mom's contact information. How are Marcus and Pete doing?" Jessie asked.

"Both of them are doing fine. Concussive injuries as I figured. Got the glass fragments all removed from their faces and got 'em both cleaned up. The doctors told me that they are going to have some hearing loss for some time. They just don't know if it's gonna be long term right now. They want to wait a week or so before they test their hearing. The boys will probably be released in a couple of days," explained Jacob.

"Well, all in all that's better news than we expected, right? One hell of a firefight. I'll tell the guys. Nice job tonight with everything. You and your dad were amazing. Keep me in the loop." said Jessie.

"Sure thing," replied Jacob before hanging up.

Two days later, Wade stirred out of his dilaudid haze and opened his eyes. He found his son Hunter with forensic pathologist and now friend Dr. Dakota Shannon next to his bedside looking down at him. Both were smiling and Dakota was holding Wade's right hand.

"Well, well, the White Knight awakens. How are you feeling, Texas Ranger Justus?" asked Dakota who was wearing a white doctor's jacket.

"Hunter …. Dakota …. I'll be …. Dakota, what are you doing here?" asked Wade with glassy eyes and a slight smile, woozy from the drip sedatives and analgesics he had been on.

"As one of your official physicians of record, I'm asking a medical question ranger. How are you feeling was the question," said Dr. Shannon, still smiling and squeezing Wade's hand.

"Dad, as soon as Jessie called to tell me that you were here, I called Dr. Shannon and asked her if she could fly out from Nashville with me. When I heard your prognosis from your surgeon, I told Dakota. She called the hospital, spoke with the chief surgeon and asked to be added to your medical staff. I think there might have been a little white lie about her being your GP," explained Hunter, chuckling.

"Yup, Ranger Justus, I've taken a whole month off and I'm going to be one of your attending physicians, assisting you with your recovery. Before I became an ME, my specialty was orthopedics," said Dakota.

"Wow, imagine that," replied Wade groggily, still under the influence.

"How long have I been under?" asked Wade.

"Two and a half days. The sedative – analgesic regimen was temporarily ceased so we could evaluate you for pain and cognition," explained Dakota. So once again, how are you really feeling?" asked Dakota.

"Well, since you put it like that doc, I feel like one of my bulls threw me and did a tap dance on my left chest and arm," replied Wade smiling up at Dakota.

"Pain level one to ten and don't lie. It's important for your pain management regimen," asked Wade's newest physician.

"Honest, I'd say about eight, but I want to keep my wits about me. Don't dope me up too much. I got a couple of things I need to do from bed as soon as I can," said Wade.

"Like what?" asked Dakota.

"Like giving a couple of statements about our encounter and OIS's with Tres Paises. I also have to give a separate statement to the U.S. Marshals, DEA and Customs and Border Patrol in another matter I was involved in in Deming, New Mexico," explained Wade.

"Damn right he does. We both have statements to make," said a voice behind Wade's curtains in the same room.

Hunter pulled back the privacy curtains to find Sheriff Matt Fremont sitting up in bed wrapped up in bandages like Wade

"Ranger Justus in the living flesh. What a surprise to see you here. Heard you was dead," joked Matt Fremont.

"Yeah? I get that a lot, but as you can see, just a false rumor. I could say the same about you, Sheriff. So who's watching the store while you're laid up here in …. In …?" replied Wade, stumbling for a bit with a location.

"You're in a hospital in El Paso, Wade," prompted Dakota.

"Well, partner, now that you're up and off the dope for a little bit," I'm calling over to Cecil McKenry at DEA and Katie Blackwater at CBP in Las Cruces. I'm pretty sure they will want to hear your story. How long before they dope him up again, doc?" Matt asked Dakota.

"Four hours tops, and that's pushing it. Ranger Justus here has got a few holes in him, and we'll need to stay ahead of the pain. This is just a brief assessment period to see how he is adapting. I advise against it, but I'm familiar with the procedure, so I'm sure it's work that needs to get done," replied Dakota.

Wade did the introductions. "Sheriff Matt Fremont, meet forensic pathologist Dr. Dakota Shannon, from Nashville. A dear friend, confidant and apparently now one of my physicians."

"Pleasure to meet you doctor Shannon, but isn't a pathologist a little premature? He looks fine to me," joked Matt.

"It's a long story Sheriff. So my suggestion is that you make your calls and get your interviews out of the way as quickly as possible," because by 5:00 pm, Ranger Justus here is going back on the buzz cocktail," said Dakota.

Within two hours, McKenry, Blackwater and newly transferred U.S. Marshal Glen Wright were in Wade's and Matt's hospital room with the door closed. U.S. Marshals were guarding the door and the investigators had their recorders on.

Over the course of three hours, Matt and Wade provided a chronology of events leading up to Gila County Sheriff's Department's intense battle with the Tres Paises drug cartel. The details of Jessie Fremont's rescue from the abandoned silver mine in Mexico were conveniently omitted, even though McKenry and Blackwater were well aware of them. Some things were better left unsaid.

Wade went over his chance encounter with Congressional members Octavia Cabral and Charles "Chico" Silvers in the Mexican café in Deming. He discussed observing the two politicians receiving duffle bags of payola from two Tres Paises goons. Wade explained his self-defense shooting of the two Tres Paises soldiers. He also explained why he was forced to leave the town and not report his shootings to police.

Matt outlined the drug intelligence information his department had received. He explained why he had made the decision to keep the interdiction of the supposed drug smugglers "in house." For obvious reasons, Matt and Wade were careful not to implicate any other supportive actors in the firefight.

Since the battle with Tres Paises had occurred in Gila County's jurisdiction, Sheriff Fremont was in charge of the investigation. His trusted son Jessie was the OIC of the massive crime scene. It would be Jessie who would be calling the shots in directing mutual aid agencies on evidence identification, collection, preservation and scene reconstruction.

Since there was an incursion into the United States by Tres Paises, Matt made sure that CBP Assistant Chief Katie Blackwater was going to be the sole DHS observer at the scene. No other DHS people would be involved. A full report of the incident sans confidential details privy to Matt and Katie would be provided to the feds. Katie would see to it that DHS only played an "observation and assistance by request only" role in the investigation.

With the current administration still humiliated by the brutal murder of fifteen federal agents at Checkpoint Delta in Deming, the U.S. Department of Justice and their FBI would want to keep their heads low on this one. It would be difficult to explain why they would finally be investigating anything having to do with drug cartels. Now there was evidence that the Vice President and two Congresspersons had essentially brokered a deal with Tres Paises and had profited by it. This was treason.

Matt, Jessie and Katie had conveniently "reconstructed" the crime scene and manufactured a solid story. The Gila County Sheriff's Department had actually found themselves in the middle of a drug war between two warring cartels. How else to explain twenty-four dead, unidentified cartel soldiers, and the deceased drug king pin Adolfo Guzman?

After all, the scene was literally littered with bodies, weapons, destroyed mechanicals and armored vehicles, and thousands of empty Soviet and Chinese AK and machine gun cartridges. It had been one hell of a battle over new drug territory.

As to the evidence of explosives at the scene? Well, the rival cartels obviously blew each other up with RPG's found at the scene. How else to explain it?

Of course when threatened, Sheriff Fremont, his deputies and the department's law enforcement consultant former Texas Ranger Wade Justus were forced to defend themselves. Yes, the attending pathologists would indeed find .223 and .45 caliber rounds inside a few of the bodies including Uberto Urias and Guzman. This was objective evidence that deputies had been forced to defend themselves when attacked.

And yes, one or two cartel soldiers would have carbon fiber, broad tipped hunting arrows projecting through their bodies. While unusual to a layperson, one of their deputies was in fact qualified with a bow as a lethal force projection weapon. He had provided a statement that when threatened, he was forced to defend himself.

Sheriff Fremont had noted that "unfortunately" due to time of night and the very rural location of the incident, there were no independent witnesses. No, there were no dashcams or Body Worn Camera videos to review. Gila County was an underfunded law enforcement agency and could not afford them.

As anyone reviewing the incident would clearly see, the Gila County deputies and retired Texas Ranger Justus had only been doing their jobs, protecting the citizens of Gila County. Sheriff Fremont's call to the county's District Attorney would ensure this legal determination. As the DHS's federal government's representative, Assistant Chief Katherine "Katie" Blackwater would rubberstamp that finding as well. End of story.

One week later, Congresspersons Octavia Cabral and Charles "Chico" Silvers each received personal office visits from investigators from the United States Marshal's Office. Both politicians were advised that they were now subjects in an on-going criminal investigation involving contacts of an unknown nature with a transnational drug cartel.

Octavia and Chico were handed search warrants for their offices, vehicles and residences to include all cell phones, PC's tablets and laptops. The Marshals confiscated their work, as well as their personal and "drop" cellphones for digital downloads and tracking information. The Marshals next advised each Congressperson to appear at the U.S. Marshal's office in downtown Washington D.C. with their attorneys for interviews within seventy-two hours, no excuses allowed.

Back in Mexico, the news of the violent deaths of Adolfo Guzman, his henchman Uberto Urias and over twenty of the organization's most experienced soldiers sent shock waves through the Tres Paises and Juarez drug cartels. The next person in the line of succession as chosen by the Juarez cartel was a ruthless cartel captain named Benito Chacon. Chacon was someone with whom you just didn't mess.

Following the debacle and embarrassment caused by Guzman and Urias, Juarez wanted one of their own to take over and rebuild Tres Paises. Chacon arrived at the Tres Paises compound three days after the bloody battle. The new drug lord immediately decided that now that the American federales were investigating the incident, Tres Paises and Juarez who funded the sibling organization were exposed. Chacon called a meeting of the remaining Tres Paises assassins.

"We have loose ends that must be cleaned up immediately. Here are the target packages for each of them containing names, photos, work and residence addresses, and known vehicles with licenses. You have forty-eight hours to take them out and report back with evidence of their deaths," ordered the new Tres Paises Padron.

Back in Washington DC, Octavia Cabral and Chico Silvers were frantic after their visit from U.S. Marshal's investigators. Using new cell phones, they called each other's offices and arranged for a noon meeting. The location was the walkway near the Japanese Lantern next to the Tidal Basin across from the Jefferson Memorial. The two corrupt lovers found each other at the lantern and embraced.

"They got all my phones at the office. My drop phone with all of the text messages to Urias and Guzman too. My messages to you and the VP were on that fucking phone including discussions about money! We are fucking toast!" the frenzied Cabral told her lover.

"They hit my office and got my phones, laptop and iPad; everything. I never saw 'em coming. You're right, it won't take them long to dump our phones and then they'll have everything," replied Chico.

"Well, we've got to get out. We have to leave DC… leave the U.S. immediately. At least they didn't snag my passport. Did they get yours?" Chico asked.

"No, but that's probably next. Look, I've got my share of the money in a storage locker. They rest is in that account we set up in the Caymans. We can have that money electronically wired from wherever we are in the world. Do you have an exit plan?" Octavia asked.

"Yes, Montenegro. They don't extradite to the U.S. and are straight across the Adriatic from Italy. Small country with a population about the size of Las Vegas. Italy almost next door, think of it!

"Anytime we want, we can jet to Venice, Florence or Rome in an hour. Hell, before the feds or Interpol can track us, we'd be back and safe. In Montenegro we can buy forged passports, change our identities and live La Dolce Vita. I already booked us one-way tickets out of Reagan National Airport for tomorrow morning at 5:00 am. Pick me up at my place and we'll dump your car at the airport. Who cares if they find it later.

Pack lightly and bring your money. TSA is not going to be checking for money, only weapons and dope. They won't dare search a Congressperson's luggage. This will work!" explained Chico as he kissed Octavia solidly on the mouth.

"All right, all right, Chico. I'll pick you up at 2:00 am just to be safe. Montenegro, Italy. We could be going to worse places I suppose. Remember, 2:00 am, don't be late," said Octavia as she returned the embrace and kissed Chico good bye.

As per their escape plan, Octavia Cabral picked up Chico Silvers in front of his posh condominium building on time at 2:00 am. The lovers embraced and got into her shiny black and politically correct four-door Tesla Model S. The couple's luggage was light on clothes and heavy with a combined four million dollars in drug money from their Deming meeting with the Tres Paises operatives.

Octavia and Chico were westbound on Malcolm X Avenue SE to get to Highway 295 which was the fastest way to get to Reagan National Airport. They were passing through a somewhat seedy area of the city. Tents and cardboard box residences of their capitol's homeless population adorned the sides of the roadway. It was undoubtedly the closest either politician had been to the unwashed masses since taking office. At this time of the very early morning, traffic was nil except for a pair of single headlights that suddenly appeared fifty yards behind them.

The couple conversed about how their lives were suddenly going to change and what their constituents would think of them. The vibe between the two corrupt, traitorous lovers in the car was a combination of anxiety and uncertainty.

Octavia pulled the Tesla up to the intersection of Martin Luther King, Jr. Avenue SE to stop for the red traffic light. At that moment, the pair of lights separated. The couple observed two black Ninja motorcycles with a pair of black helmeted riders and passengers on each side of them. As the light for west to east traffic on MLK Avenue SE turned yellow, the drivers of each motorcycle looked directly at the couple which made them both feel uneasy.

Octavia was thinking that when the light turned green, she was going to speed away from the motorcyclists. They were creepy. As she gauged the light, the passengers on the bikes on either side of the Tesla suddenly reached towards the left driver's side and right front passenger doors and the couple heard a pair of thuds. Chico exclaimed, "Those fucks just kicked your doors!"

As the light turned green, Octavia sped forward to get away from the motorcyclists. She looked back into her rear view mirror and saw that curiously, the pair of motorcyclists remained at the limit line back at the intersection.

The speeding Tesla Model S carrying fleeing Congresspersons reached a distance of one hundred yards away from the intersection. At that instant, each of the motorcycle passengers dialed a pre-programmed number on the cell phones they had retrieved from their pockets.

The electronic detonators in the mini magnetic mines

containing compressed C-4 in shaped charges detonated the mines. The small, shaped charges exploded inwards into the vehicle and upwards through the roof. In a nano-second the Tesla, OC, Chico and all of the contents of their luggage were consumed in a yellow, red and white fireball extending fifty feet into the air with a fifty yard blast radius.

The force of the blast blew out the windows of businesses on both sides of Malcolm X SE Avenue. Nylon tents and cardboard refrigerator box homeless condos caved in, and cars alarms sounded throughout the neighborhood. What was left of four million dollars in cartel cash rained down from the sky.

The homeless denizens were immediately awakened and rushed into the street. Screams of joy and good fortune filled the air as the street residents in a scene of sheer chaos plucked falling fifty and one hundred dollar bills from the air and off the roadway.

Crime scene evidence was rapidly vanishing as the crowd swelled, kicking bloody body parts out of their way. First responding officers to the crime scene had to threaten to tase people to keep them away from the blast area. It was truly a sight to behold.

The only tangible evidence that could be recovered sufficient to identify the owner of the vehicle was the chassis of the Tesla S buried three feet beneath the pavement containing the vehicle identification number which would eventually provide registration information. Officers also recovered a pair of hands, one belonging to a woman which had penetrated halfway through a store window, and man's hand found in the gutter eighty yards up the street. Viable leads towards identifying the occupants at least.

By the afternoon of the day of the blast, the FBI issued a press release. The notice detailed the assassination of the two prominent and rising star Congresspersons, Octavia "OC" Cabral and Charles "Chico" Silvers. The mainstream media were stunned.

The White House press briefing that night was a maelstrom of reporters and celebrity talking heads. Everyone yelling questions at the beleaguered Press Secretary who was understandably unable at that time to provide more information.

Two days later, an unofficial, rogue "task force" of U.S. Marshals, DEA and DHS-HIS agents with skin in the game after the Deming massacre of their friends and colleagues had time to forensically download the burner phones, cell phones, iPads and PC's of Octavia Cabral and Chico Silvers.

The agents recovered a treasure trove of information, evidence and tracking data. The data revealed a conspiracy of the largest order between Tres Paises drug cartel and Congresspersons Octavia Cabral, Charles "Chico" Silvers, the DHS Secretary and the Vice President of the United States. Specific correspondence tied Cabral and Silvers directly to drug lord Adolfo Guzman, his enforcer Uberto Urias and Tres Paises intermediaries.

As the saying goes, the investigators "followed the money" which in the end, directly tied the VP and DHS secretary to payments from the Tres Paises and Juarez transnational drug cartels.

The motive of the co-conspirators of course was gaining increased political power through the eventual legalization of millions of UDA's. This along with the corrupt politicians' own personal enrichment by accepting millions of dollars of cartel blood money.

The task force's mutual agreement was that both the FBI and the Secret Service were to be kept in the blind until arrests were to be made. Honest and ethical agents had made that mistake before and it wasn't happening this time. Let the cards lie open for all to see, they agreed. They would deal with any disciplinary repercussions later. They were pissed. It was time for a reckoning.

Three days after the assassination of Congresspersons Cabral and Silvers, two separate teams of U.S. Marshals simultaneously breached the outer offices of the Vice President and the Secretary of Homeland Security, startling the office staff and in the VP's case, her Secret Service detail.

The head of the Vice President's Secret Service detail stood in front of the lead U.S. Marshal, attempting to block the path of the agents.

"What's this all about? You can't just barge into the Vice President's offices," said the Secret Service agent holding up his hand.

"We're here on official business. If you guys know what's

good for you, you'll stand down and let us do what we came here to do," the U.S. Marshal said, handing the Secret Service agent copies of arrest and search warrants for the VP.

I suggest you carefully read the accompanying Probable Cause Affidavit before you say one more word," the Marshal said assertively. He and his men were not taking no for an answer.

The lead Secret Service agent did just that. Three minutes later you could see the blood draining from his face as he read the document.

"Holy shit. My God….."

The lead Secret Service agent slowly handed the documents back to the U.S. Marshal. "We're not getting in the way of this. We'll stand aside but we will have to observe for security reasons. It's our job. You guys do what you need to do. You won't have problems with us," he said in a low voice.

The agent then told the Secret Service detail to allow the U.S. Marshals through to the see the Vice President.

The Vice President was in the process of signing some papers when the double ornately carved oak doors to her office and chambers suddenly opened. The contingent of U.S. Marshals followed by members of her Secret Service detail approached the VP's desk. The VP appeared genuinely startled.

"Can I help you gentlemen?" she asked.

"Madam Vice President, we are from the United States Marshal's Office. We are here to place you under arrest for conspiring with a known transnational drug cartel and terrorist organization. You are charged with treason and violating several U.S. Immigration laws in accepting bribes from the Tres Paises cartel.

I must also advise you that you are under investigation for providing assistance and support to the cartel which indirectly led to the murder of fifteen federal agents in Deming, New Mexico two weeks ago.

Please stand away from your desk and place your hands behind your back. I am required to advise you that you have the right to remain silent and if you give up the right to remain silent, anything you say can and will used against you in a court of law. You have the right to counsel ...."

The Vice President's world had just imploded. The U.S. Marshal's Miranda admonition was now merely a dull buzz as she felt the cold steel of the handcuffs securing her hands behind her back. Her political career was over, and her legal nightmare had just begun.

Two weeks after the arrest of the Vice President, the stories continued to fill the nightly news broadcasts. It was almost unimaginable that a sitting Vice President, a high level cabinet member and two members of Congress could be involved in a traitorous act to conspire with a transnational cartel and terrorist organization to subvert the sovereignty of the United States. But it was true, all of it.

Wade had been released early from the hospital under the care of Dr. Dakota Shannon who had attached herself to a surgical and recovery hospital in Boerne, Texas near where Wade's Shady Creek Ranch was located. As promised, Dakota was staying at the ranch so she could care for Wade through his first phase of recovery. Hunter had finally used up all of his vacation and special leave time from the Tennessee Bureau of Investigations in Nashville and was back at work.

Dawn was breaking and Wade was sleeping soundly. He suddenly heard his wife Helen's soothing voice. In Wade's mind he had opened his eyes to find Helen standing at the end of his bed and gazing lovingly at him.

"You made it sweetheart, just like I knew you would. It's wonderful to see you again," said Helen.

"Helen ... Thank you for waking me up and getting me back into the fight. Yes, I made it. It's over and Jessie and Matt are fine. I did what I went there to do. I kept my promise, thanks to you," replied Wade.

Helen walked over to Wade and took his right hand, squeezing it as she looked deeply into his eyes. She smiled, noting that Wade still wore his wedding ring on his left hand.

"Forever the romantic and loyal as a dog," she laughed.

"Always, Helen. Always," replied Wade.

"Wade, I see that there maybe someone new in your life. I came to tell you that it's time, honey. It's time to let go and live your life again. A man like you needs a good woman. I see that's what your Dr. Dakota Shannon is, a good woman. I'm fine with it. I'm happy for you.

"We'll have our time again together my love. I'll wait for you. But for now, you need to live again. I've been watching over you. You are alive, but you haven't been living life. It's time to live again. I will always be with you. I'll always be watching over you and Hunter. I'll always love you," said Helen softly as she bent down and kissed Wade's lips.

Wade watched Helen walk back to the end of his bed. Helen blew a kiss, waved and slowly faded away.

Wade awoke to the first rays of light and walked out onto his back porch for a view of the Guadalupe River flowing past. Spring mornings were the best at this time of year in Texas. The birds were up and chirping. Squirrels were jumping from tree to tree chasing each other. Everything was alive. His red nose Pit, Desi came out onto the porch, greeted Wade with a couple of licks to his hand and laid down quietly next to him. Desi was an empath.

Wade was thinking about grabbing a cup of black coffee from the kitchen when Dakota walked out onto the porch in a robe with two cups of black coffee.

"How's my patient doing this morning. You look well rested. I brought you some coffee," said Dakota smiling down at Wade.

"You read my mind. Thanks," said Wade as Dakota sat down in a chair next to him.

"So it's been a few weeks since your incident. I don't mean to pry, but how are you doing up here?" said Dakota pointing to Wade's head. He knew what she was referring to.

"I appreciate your checking in with me. I guess that's what good doctors do, right? In answer to your question, I'm doing fine upstairs. I'm not going to dwell on it, that's not me, except for one incident in my past. Maybe someday when I feel comfortable, we'll talk about that one.

"Tres Paises messed with family. It was a different paradigm. We Texans are particular about people not messing with our family members. I made a promise to Matt and his family regarding his son Jessie, and I kept it. I'm Jessie's Godfather. Matt and I were partners back in our rangering days.

"After we got Jessie back to his family, Tres Paises came after me and tried to kill me. That was their biggest mistake. I don't take threats like that lightly. In short, the gloves came off and I did what I needed to do to end it. Luckily, that's exactly what happened, and it all worked out for the good guys.

We won't need to talk about Tres Paises again, Dakota. I've made peace with it. I will tell you this though. This world lately has become upside down and crazy. Justice today is fleeting. Most often it's absent entirely. What Tres Paises received that night was exactly what they deserved; justice – border justice."

Wade and Dakota quietly sipped their coffee as they watched the Guadalupe River flow past on its way to the Gulf of Mexico. Wade looked over at the lovely and caring Dakota Shannon, remembering what Helen had told him.

It was a special time, maybe a new beginning for both of them he thought. Time would tell.

Key Terms Used

952 – Check Status Of

10-7 – Police radio code for out of service

10-8 – Police radio code for back in service

10-20 or '20' – Location as in "What's your 10-20?"

10-87 or '87 – Police radio code for "Meet with me."

MQ-1 – The military's drone designation for the first series "Predator"

AD – Accidental Discharge

ADS-B – Automatic Dependent Surveillance Broadcast

AKA – Alias

Angels – Flying designation for 1,000 feet. *"Angels 25"* = 25,000 feet flying altitude.

AP – Armor piercing ammunition

BDU – Battle Dress Uniform (military/law enforcement fatigues)

BOL or BOLO – Be on the look-out for

BP – Border Patrol

CBP – Customs & Border Protection

CAD – Computer-Aided Dispatch

CI – Confidential Informant

Code-3 – Law enforcement term for driving with lights and siren on

Code-7 – Out of service to eat

CO – Commanding Officer

DEA – Drug Enforcement Administration

DHS – Department of Homeland Security

DHS S&T - Department of Homeland Security Science & Technology Directorate

DOPE – Sniper acronym for "Data On Previous Engagements"

EFP – Explosively Formed Penetrator

EOD – Explosives Ordinance Division

EoTec – A holographic sighting device for firearms/rifles

FCI – Federal Correctional Institution

FLIR – Forward Looking Infrared Radar

HIDTA – High Impact Drug Trafficking Area

HQ – Headquarters

HSI – Homeland Security Investigations Unit

HUD – Heads Up Display

IAFV – Improvised Armored Fighting Vehicle

ICE – Immigration and Customs Enforcement

IR – Infrared

LED – Light Emitting Diode

LEO – Law Enforcement Officer(s)

LRRP – long Range Reconnaissance Patrols

LZ – Refers to Landing Zone

Mag or mags – magazines of ammunition

MITRE – Multi-Static Radar Project (DHS & CBP Radar Program)

MOS – Military Operations Specialty

NOD – Night Optical Devices

NSV – Soviet era 12.7 mm heavy machine gun

NVG's – Night vision goggles

OEG – Occluded eye gunsight, a holographic aiming system for a firearm

OIC – Officer In Charge

OIS – Officer-Involved Shooting

PC – Probable Cause to arrest

PD – Police department

Placas – Mexican gang slang for badges or law enforcement officers

POTUS – President of the United States

PRC – People's Republic of China

QJC-88 – People's Republic of China 12.7 mm heavy machine gun

ROE's – Rules of Engagement with deadly force

RPG – Rocket-Propelled Grenade

SA – Supervising Agent or Special Agent,

SAC – Special Agent in Charge

SERT – Special Emergency Response Team

SO – Sheriff's Office

SOAR – Special Operations Aviation Regiment

TDY – Temporary Duty

UAV – Unmanned Aerial Vehicle

UDA's – Undocumented aliens

Ussen – The name members of the Apache Nation refer to as God

VP – Vice President

Wade Justus Book Series – Book 4 "Force of Justus"

On the anniversary of the heroic battle between Wade and Syrian terrorist Jamal the Jackal in Florence, Italy, the Italian Carabinieri national police invite Wade and his son, Tennessee Bureau of Investigations Special Agent Hunter back to Florence to lecture at an anti-terrorism conference in the beautiful Tuscan city of art and romance.

Little do the former Texas Ranger and his son know that Jamal's twin brother Khaled, an international narco-trafficking terrorist has learned of their appearance at the conference. Khaled has sworn a blood oath to avenge his brother Jamal. The terrorist has concocted a diabolical scheme of revenge against Wade, Hunter, the Carabinieri and the Italian people.

Will Wade, Hunter and the Carabinieri be able to intervene in time to thwart the terrorists' impending carnage? Or will the duo and thousands of Italians become victims of the devious and deadly plan. Join Wade, Hunter and the brave Carabinieri in another thrilling Wade Justus adventure in – *Force of Justus.*

About the Author

Dr. Ron Martinelli, Ph.D., is a retired San Jose Police Department (CA) police detective and a nationally renowned forensic criminologist and medical investigator who leads the nation's only multidisciplinary Forensic Death Investigations Team.

Ron enjoyed an exciting law enforcement career and remains active as a much sought-after expert in forensic investigations within the legal and law enforcement communities. He is frequently seen on national and international television networks including FOX NEWS, Once America News, BBC, SkyNews and others as an expert in crime and forensic investigations.

Ron and his wife Linda live on a ranch in the beautiful Texas Hill Country. The pair who are also stock contractors who compete in the Professional Bull Riders (PBR) circuit. They travel the world for work and pleasure as Ron gets background for his popular book series.

Ron is a prolific writer within the law enforcement and forensic communities and has now become an Amazon Best-Selling Author. Wade Justus Texas Ranger is his first fiction series.